THE SENTINEL:

A Wildfire Story

THE SENTINEL:

A Wildfire Story

Written by Jim Moran

Edited by George Tompkins

Trafford
PUBLISHING®

Printed in Victoria, BC, Canada.

ISBN: 978-1-4269-2337-1 (sc)
ISBN: 978-1-4269-2338-8 (dj)

Library of Congress Control Number: 2010900226

*Our mission is to efficiently provide the world's finest, most comprehensive book publishing
service, enabling every author to experience success. To find out how to publish your book,
your way, and have it available worldwide, visit us online at www.trafford.com*

Trafford rev. 3/16/2010

www.trafford.com

North America & international
toll-free: 1 888 232 4444 (USA & Canada)
phone: 250 383 6864 ♦ fax: 812 355 4082

To W.S. McNeice

Acknowledgements

THE ONTARIO MINISTRY OF NATURAL RESOURCES was instrumental in providing information so that I could remain true to the way their Aviation and Forest Fire Management Branch does business. I would like to especially acknowledge Ed Ducharme and Barry Sigmann at the Falcon Response Centre in Sudbury, two ex co-workers who probably thought that I was dreaming in Technicolor when I said I was writing this book.

A big thank you goes to Gerry Page, a brother in retirement who works during the fire season for a contractor, Hawkeye Fire Services out of Beardmore, Ontario, which in turn provides infra-red services to Ontario's fire program. Thanks, Gerry. You took my requests seriously. You should have known better. And thanks, Brenda Caroll, owner and manager of Hawkeye, who doesn't know me at all but let me use her company's name and gave Gerry the go ahead to provide information.

I'd also like to thank my editor, George Tompkins from Lively, Ontario. I'm sure he would have had an easier job with "War and Peace" or the "Hobbit Trilogy."

Thanks Gerry Spray, for taking the time to review my book for technical authenticity. Between the two of us, we may have got it right.

I would like to extend a warm thanks to my first Ministry of Natural Resources' boss and mentor, Wally McNeice. Wally was never judgmental and gave me the opportunity to make mistakes, and to correct them. To this day, I believe my confidence, and consequently my career within the Ontario Ministry of Natural Resources was a result of Wally's patience and guidance.

And finally, I would like to thank my wife Joan for believing in me. Actually, she never really said that; I just assumed it after thirty-nine years of marriage and friendship.

Introduction

WITHIN A RELATIVELY SHORT SNAPSHOT IN TIME, thirty-four days, on a significant piece of forest land, eighty thousand one hundred and fifty hectares, or close to two hundred thousand acres, a drama unfolded. It was the drama associated with the very real story of wildfire. Antagonists impacted by wildfire included not only the higher species, or so we'd like to see ourselves, but also our co-dependants we categorize as flora and fauna. The protagonist in this story is not benign; it is a very animate, living, breathing dragon in the form of an escaped wildfire.

Forest fire management programs throughout the world battle with the same protagonist every year, and in some cases, the dragon wins. This is one such story, for as fire people will confirm, every wildfire that is contained can be their own personal dragon slain, and every fire that escapes is a dragon victorious.

Although this book and all of the characters and their relationships portrayed within are fictional, I have made an effort to ensure that organizational, technical, statistical and geographical information is accurate. My intention is to provide a balance between accuracy and entertainment. Please keep in mind that the story line associated with fire fighting begins in 2005. The Ontario fire program will have advanced their planning and improved some of their systems and technology since then. They may also have changed some of their organizational structure. But by and large, the business of managing wildfire will always be the same.

Just a few facts to put things into perspective:

Forests cover 85% of Ontario's land base much of which is "boreal" (coniferous) and "mixed wood" (coniferous/deciduous) forests. Ontario's fire program responds to an average of thirteen hundred fires annually. They don't respond indiscriminately. Their fire management planning is eco-region based—not geographic or political-based. Consequently, the province is comprised of six fire management zones from south to north—Southern Ontario, Ontario Parks (throughout Ontario), Great Lakes/St. Lawrence, Boreal, Northern Boreal and Hudson Bay. Each zone has specific fire management strategy. Fire *response* in these zones is balanced between risk (to people and property) and fire's ecological benefits. To provide that response Ontario has twenty-nine strategically located fire attack bases, two hundred and twenty-five permanent staff and seven hundred and sixty seasonal staff.

I hope the reader not only enjoys the reading but also learns something in the process. It is also my wish that the reader develops an appreciation of the complexity of response to wildfire and the dedication of those involved in the undertaking.

What I share with you in this book happens every day, in every part of the world that has the ability to generate and regenerate the forest growth required to support and sustain wildfire. Although media may tend to sensationalize wildfire (it is in their best interest to do so), those associated with managing it tend to "take it in stride" and "deliver with pride".

There is, however, a gap or window of opportunity between planning for a battle and executing effective tactics. Within that window, glitches will happen. The processes associated with wildfire fighting are fairly similar to war. So, too, is the propensity to generate "glitches". There will be some in this story line, most patterned after actual occurrences.

Until recently, Ontario had its own distinctive fire management hierarchy with positions and titles different from those of the United States and some of Canada's other provinces. Ontario has now adopted the U.S. Incident Command System (ICS), as have many of the other provinces. The reason is simple. The United States and provinces in Canada have limited fire-fighting resources. This is by design as a part of risk management philosophies. It is simply too costly for each jurisdiction to maintain fire response resources based on "worst year" scenarios. Consequently, they routinely share resources (people, information and equipment) when there is a need.

Where there are bordering states and provinces, actual resource sharing agreements have been in place for years. The Great Lakes Forest Fire Compact (GLFFC)[1] with its membership from Michigan, Wisconsin, Minnesota, Ontario and Manitoba, has a resource sharing agreement. The Northeastern Forest Fire Protection Commission (NFFPC)[2] is the oldest such association. The United States Congress passed the original 16 Articles of the "Agreement" that provided legislation enabling it on June 25, 1949. Membership includes Maine, New Hampshire, Vermont, New York, Massachusetts, Connecticut, Rhode Island, New England National Forests, Quebec, New Brunswick and Nova Scotia.

It simply became necessary for each fire agency to have the same organizational command and control structure with the same identifying titles in order to reduce confusion and become more effective in wildfire response. That is why the ICS system is becoming standard in North America.

The following page in this introduction is a conceptual map of Ontario, pinpointing locations of actual fire headquarters, aircraft bases and crew and air attack resources. It also pinpoints the mythical project wildfire, Wawa 43, described in this novel. It is followed by simplified graphics of Ontario's Aviation and Forest Fire Management Branch *Management* structure and *Response* structure.

Strategy and tactics used to combat a project wildfire would be similar to those used in battle. It is a fire so large and complex that it requires an "incident management team" to manage and direct the resources required to battle it. In war, the commander's objective would be to attack, surround, contain and eventually destroy the enemy. The incident commander's goal in fighting a project fire is the same.

In this story, the *project* fire is Wawa 43 (the 43rd wildfire in the Ontario Ministry of Natural Resources' Wawa administrative district in the 2005 fire season). It is a mythical fire, but its beginning, escape, "project" designation and eventual containment are patterned after real occurrences.

Enjoy the novel.

---

1   Their web site is www.glffc.com
2   Their web site is www.nffpc.com

ONTARIO FIRE HEADQUARTERS

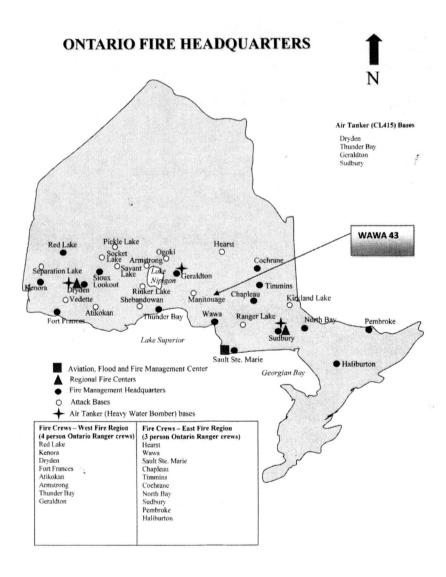

N

Air Tanker (CL415) Bases

Dryden
Thunder Bay
Geraldton
Sudbury

WAWA 43

Red Lake
Pickle Lake
Socket Lake
Armstrong
Ogoki
Hearst
Cochrane
Separation Lake
Savant Lake
Sioux Lookout
Lake Nipigon
Geraldton
Kenora
Dryden
Rinker Lake
Shebandowan
Manitouage
Chapleau
Timmins
Kirkland Lake
Vedette
Atikokan
Thunder Bay
Wawa
Ranger Lake
North Bay
Pembroke
Fort Frances
Lake Superior
Sudbury
Sault Ste. Marie
Georgian Bay
Haliburton

■ Aviation, Flood and Fire Management Center
▲ Regional Fire Centers
● Fire Management Headquarters
○ Attack Bases
✦ Air Tanker (Heavy Water Bomber) bases

Fire Crews – West Fire Region (4 person Ontario Ranger crews)	Fire Crews – East Fire Region (3 person Ontario Ranger crews)
Red Lake	Hearst
Kenora	Wawa
Dryden	Sault Ste. Marie
Fort Frances	Chapleau
Atikokan	Timmins
Armstrong	Cochrane
Thunder Bay	North Bay
Geraldton	Sudbury
	Pembroke
	Haliburton

ONTARIO'S AVIATION and FOREST FIRE MANAGEMENT BRANCH

'MANAGEMENT' STRUCTURE

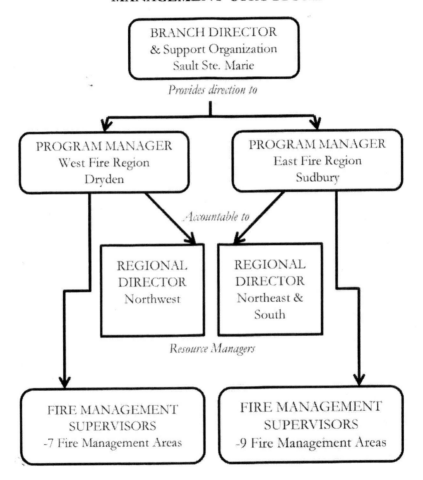

BRANCH DIRECTOR
& Support Organization
Sault Ste. Marie

Provides direction to

PROGRAM MANAGER
West Fire Region
Dryden

PROGRAM MANAGER
East Fire Region
Sudbury

Accountable to

REGIONAL DIRECTOR
Northwest

REGIONAL DIRECTOR
Northeast & South

Resource Managers

FIRE MANAGEMENT SUPERVISORS
-7 Fire Management Areas

FIRE MANAGEMENT SUPERVISORS
-9 Fire Management Areas

ONTARIO'S AVIATION and FOREST FIRE MANAGEMENT BRANCH

'RESPONSE' STRUCTURE
(Contactable 24/7 during the fire season)

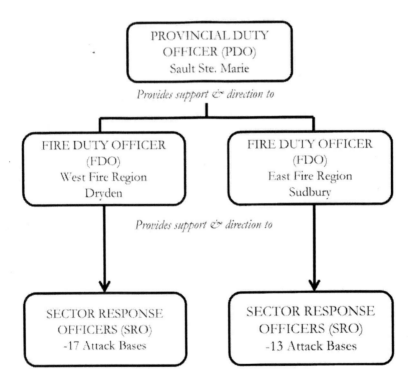

PROVINCIAL DUTY
OFFICER (PDO)
Sault Ste. Marie

Provides support & direction to

FIRE DUTY OFFICER
(FDO)
West Fire Region
Dryden

FIRE DUTY OFFICER
(FDO)
East Fire Region
Sudbury

Provides support & direction to

SECTOR RESPONSE
OFFICERS (SRO)
-17 Attack Bases

SECTOR RESPONSE
OFFICERS (SRO)
-13 Attack Bases

We look upon this world as ours alone, indiscriminate in our choices for sanctuary. We puff up our collective chests and thrust out stubborn jaws, declaring our superiority over God's kingdom and all it harbours. Invariably, nature will stretch and yawn and pique her restlessness with wind, flood and fire. Our bridges and bastions are no match. We stagger, shocked and beaten. Although we have chosen to be in harm's way, we are angered at our inability to respond, pointing fists of rage at those charged with our protection. In truth, we are but ants with egos, reluctant to accept that we are a part of His plan and not the architects of our own.

Author's opinion

The Sudbury Star, Saturday, January 28, 2006

Old pine tree gets a little older

Ontario forest researchers say giant white pine is actually 355 years old

BY MICHAEL PURVIS

Osprey News Network

A centuries-old white pine that once towered above all others in Ontario is a little older than once thought, say Ministry of Natural Resources researchers.

The giant tree, located in the Kirkwood Forest north of Thessalon, was considered the largest of its kind in the province until it fell during a harsh wind storm in June 1997.

At the time, it was believed to be between 260 and 300 years old. However, scientists at the Ontario Forest Research Institute have measured samples and have now determined the famous Thessalon pine had stood in that spot for a positively ancient 355 years.

"We were surprised that it had a relatively slow growth rate," said Bill Cole, a research scientist at the Ontario Forest Research Institute.

The tree, which contained enough lumber to build a three-bedroom house, grew to a height of 49.4 metres and expanded in diameter at an average of less than half a centimetre a year to be about 1.4 metres wide at chest height.

It was 1642 when the tree first started growing and was 27 years old by the time the settlement of Sault Ste. Marie received its current name.

The tree was 253 years old when the Canadian lock opened on the St. Mary's River in 1895.

That the Kirkwood Forest tree remained standing so long was likely a testament to its inaccessible location nestled at the bottom of a deep, narrow valley.

Prologue

NORTH OF LAKE SUPERIOR, 1705

THE ALGONKIAN SPEAKER WALKED AHEAD OF HIS WOMAN, following a narrow path that wound its way upward, through a dense forest of pine, spruce and balsam fir. The path had been broken by animals such as deer and moose following the way of least effort. It was taken by predators following their prey, especially in the spring when the does and cows were dropping their newborn. It was soon used by people because it was easy and therefore natural.

He was of the Ojibwa people that called themselves *Anishinaabe* or *original men*. The French in the Sault Ste. Marie area, called his clan the *Saulteur*. At almost two arms' length, he was considered tall. He wore his long, black hair in two braids that dropped gently to his shoulders and fell to his back. He proudly wore the buck-skin jacket provided by his woman along with his breech-cloth and leggings. His moccasins were the mark of the Ojibwa. Their distinctive puckered seams gave them their name, *Ojibwa*. It came from the word *otchipwa* (to pucker). He bore no skins or packs, only his tools and weapons, for he needed to be able to move quickly to defend himself and his woman. His weapon of choice was the bow; his pouch of arrows was slung over his shoulder and rested on his back. The hatchet at his waist had been a gift from a French fur trader.

He carried no fat and moved with grace and purpose through the underbrush that crowded the trail. He knew he had no choice but to move westward and find a place to hunt and trap for he was three, not one. She was heavy with child, but she would not complain. This was the man who had chosen her. She was of the *Nehiyawok*, speakers of the Cree language, and their joining was not well accepted by his clan. She was much shorter than he was, her face broad. He had, however, been taken by her large, dark eyes, like the forest owl, a wide smile and tinkling laughter—like a soft wind in a fall aspen thicket. Although their clans were con-nected by custom and years of trade, language was still a barrier. They struggled to make each other aware of needs and feelings, but they had grown together with the swelling in her belly.

As a child he had survived the smallpox that had purged his clan. It had taken his parents. As a man, he had survived the bea-ver wars that pitted the *Nadouessioux* or rattlesnake people (also called the "Sioux" by the French) against Algonki. It was part of a long-standing war between the English and the French. His taste for fighting had now faded like the thin veil of mountain fog as it rose to the heavens. Although the Algonki and Sioux had "touched the pen" in an agreement of peace four years past, his head was still weary from battle.

Shunned by his people, he chose the difficult path of solitude. He had been a part of small family group that followed its food and clothing in the winter and joined the much larger Saulteur clan in the summer season. He secretly hoped to meet other Ojibwa who would accept his decision to choose a Nehiyawok woman. He longed for the company of other Anishinaabe so he could share stories of his journeys. He missed the quiet humour and patient lessons from his grandfather and gentle scolding of his grandmother. He missed, more than anything, her stories around the campfire. Huddled together on a cool night, the stars hidden by the light of a warming fire, her wrinkled eyes wide with embellishment, she would whisper of the seven great *miigis*—the radiant people, who taught the clans the way of life. He was particularly taken by the story of the vision. A radiant one had appeared and warned the Anishinaabe that strangers from the east would take away their traditional ways. They must move west to protect their beliefs.

Although it was the early fall season, "she of the round face" wore her long deerskin dress without its removable sleeves for it was warm this day. She carried a roll of birch-bark and a rabbit-skin pack on her back. The bark would be used as the bottom layer for their next *wikowin* (house). She would find the willow or birch for the frame and the bull-rush for the upper layer at their new place of rest. Her pack carried food used to supplement their travel, the furs they used to bed down and a net made of willow cord for fishing. Her limited supply of food was well preserved. The berries were dried and shrivelled. The venison had been hung for days and was brittle but nourishing. She had spent many days smoking fish caught by her man. It was now firm and easy to pack. Separated within the skin wrapped larder was the prize she coveted the most, the sweet maple sugar they had prepared the previous spring.

She paused to take air, turned and looked back down to the lake they had called their place for the summer. It was late in the day and she could no longer see the interwoven young birch that provided the framework for their house or the birch-bark canoe he had made in the spring. He had decided that traveling the water would take far too long to reach the flat lands that other travelers had talked about as they passed by their wikowin. Their word barrier was getting better, but she still had difficulty referring to him as *inini* as he instructed, rather than napew as she preferred. "Niin inini [I man]" he would say solemnly as if instructing a child. "Giin ikwe [you woman]." When she understood, he would smile and she would blush with pride. Their dependency on each other grew with their ability to communicate. Their bonding grew from the joy of daily companionship and understanding.

The sun had moved down three hands in the sky and gently sat on the ridge before their eyes. It was time to rest for the night. He signed her to stop and with a look of understanding and concern bade her to rest while he searched for a place of protection. He returned, gave her a warm smile and motioned for her to follow. An opening in the forest on the ridge top provided a place to put down balsam fir bows for sleep. Smooth fingers of bedrock supporting large stones, some three arms high, surrounded the pocket of soft earth. The stones would act as shields in their battle against night breezes. They would also provide a place for him to protect his back if he needed to defend his family from dangerous intruders.

She studied the site, slowly taking in what it had to offer. Then with a smile and nod of approval, she promptly dropped her pouch and roll. As she pulled out the furs that would provide them with warmth, her pouch fell open. She laughed with the merriment of a child as a lone pine cone rolled out of the pouch and sat like a tiny porcupine on the patch of fertile earth. It must have been a traveler with them one summer's past from the Saulteaur land to choice of home on the lake below.

She mused. *The little cone traveler had rested in the bottom of her pouch all this time, waiting for release. He is looking for a home as we are.* It was slightly curved, almost two fingers long and one finger wide, the colour of earth and hard like an acorn. It was open, and she imagined each separation as a little child stretching to the sun. *Perhaps we shall call our child "little pine cone".* The tall Ojibwa warrior gave her a frown of disapproval at her hesitation, so she quickly kicked the cone away and prepared for the night.

The next morning, the two lone travelers broke camp quietly and disappeared down the ridge enveloped in morning fog. Their subsequent story was that of many—hardship, joy, sorrow—never to be told, only to be lived. The legacy of the Ojibwa man and the Cree woman may have been the single pine cone, wedged in a rock, sitting on a patch of moist earth. The cone sheltered a tiny, winged seed that had become dislodged from its cone protector. Who knows what happened to the seed's seventy siblings, lying in the bottom of the pouch. Perhaps they were destined to travel to far away places and produce hardy seedlings that would grow into mighty trees, offering nourishment and shelter to the forest dwellers.

THROUGH FIVE EARTH ROTATIONS around the sun, the little seed struggled to take root and battled to grow past the decaying cone and through the shade of its secondary protector, the stone. Once its shoots crept above the stone, it flourished with full sunlight, stretching out its probing tap-root and five large lateral roots as anchors to battle prevailing winds. To survive was not easy. It would be challenged by a variety of insects and diseases common to its species. The white pine weevil fed voraciously on the pine's new growth in the early stages of its life, causing an off-shoot leader and a bend in its growth. White pine blister rust had attacked twice, causing constrictions and then sunken areas in some of its lower branches. They would "weep" with white pitch like tears of pain.

Perhaps its efforts and environment made it strong of will, for it grew and grew over many years, perched precariously on a ridge. It would become a watcher, witness to birth, tragedy and natural death, fire and wind. It would become both a father and mother to thousands of pine seedlings in the valley below, for it carried both male and female flowers within its foliage. Their pollination produced cones and, invariably, seed every three to five years. The white pine would also become a provider, for the seeds produced from its cones were nourishment for a community of birds such as the colourful yellow-bellied sapsucker, pine grosbeak and red crossbill. It would welcome the nervous activity of the white-breasted nuthatch and platoons of black capped chickadees and witness the song of the pine warbler.

Many of the pine's offspring were providers as well, but in their provision, they would not survive. Their bark was food for snowshoe hare, porcupine, red squirrel, deer mouse and white-tailed deer. **This** pine would survive to become not only a provider but a protector as well. It would serve as shelter to red squirrels and invariably attract their nemesis, the relentless fisher. Later in life, because of its location, size and bearing, the pine's stature in nature seemed to be confirmed by the arrival of a visitor—the American bald eagle. This magnificent bird would frequently use the pine as a resting place and look-out. Neither would acknowledge the other, but they appeared always vigilant, as comrades and "sentinels-in-arms."

The old pine would also bare witness to onslaught from the mightiest predator—man. Prior to man's arrival, half of the forest cover was comprised of stately white pine. Thirst for the pine to make booms and masts for the British Royal Navy, buildings and furniture, reduced pine to a mere quarter of the forest cover, limiting its ability to produce and disperse cones and seeds. The population of white pine would be but a shadow of its former self. The ability for a single pine to reach matriarch status in the future would be next to impossible.

This pine, however, would survive the forces of nature and man and grow into a magnificent tree. Oh, the stories it might tell—if it could.

PART 1

THE STORM

It uncurled its scaly body
And stretched translucent wings
Fierce yellow eyes, twin mirrors of evil
Gazed over ridge and forest.
The dragon awakens.

Chapter 1

NORTH OF LAKE SUPERIOR, 2005 (300 YEARS LATER)

T HE WHITE PINE STOOD ALONE ON THE RIDGE, towering over the forest cover like a sentinel, never resting, ever vigilant. The ridge itself was the most prominent geographic feature on the landscape, making the pine even more formidable. This had been its posting for three centuries. Its frame arched to the southeast, branches sparse, some skeletal-like without foliage, others like tattered coat sleeves with fingers pointing aimlessly in every direction. At close inspection, the dull armour of thick, impenetrable bark had been torn open in a descending spiral pattern, its wound appearing in various stages of whites and greys, in stark contrast to the rest of its vestment. The wound, the result of a thunderbolt of lightning, had healed as a prominent scar—a testament to its ability to survive. It had not only survived an assault from the sky, but had also persevered through three hundred frigid winters, well north of its optimum growing range. However, nothing was immune to the forces of nature.

If the old guard could see, to its far north lay a uniform blanket of olive green that stretched to the horizon. The blanket was, in reality, a stand of eighty-year-old jack pine, spawned by the last great fire to visit the area. The old pine had been witness to this phenomenon and watched countless numbers of jack pine stretch, twist and struggle from birth to adulthood.

Closer north and south of the old pine stretched the ridge that was its home. It was sliced at angles with hollows and valleys and

3

supported rock outcrops in various hues of grey. Overall, the ridge took on a narrow quilt-like appearance with a patchwork of greens, each signifying a different tree species or groups of species. Teal green was dominant and represented balsam fir and white spruce, both species struggling to combat a relentless infestation of the voracious spruce budworm. Throughout this sea of teal, splashes of khaki and dark reds signified a struggle by individual trees to stay alive—while spears of grays and blacks poked through the patch as pointed monuments of mortality. Other large patches of poplar and white birch stood out as pale green and spring-green. The pale green patches of poplar tended to sit atop smaller ridges while narrow spring-green patches of birch hugged side slopes. The ridge was a ragged "man-of war" and the pine was its worn and tattered main mast.

It was just to the north-east that the old pine seemed to point its largest bows, as if reaching out, beckoning for comfort and compassion. For it was here that a few other white pines appeared among the spruce, poplar and other tree species. This was no patchwork, but an eclectic array, like a poorly fitted puzzle with no apparent picture yet surfacing. The puzzle pieces were three dimensional and popped up, some bent, some separating, all in various shades of greens, the darkest of which were other white pine, offspring of the patriarch on the ridge. Their proof of life gave comfort to the old pine. It stood as tall as it could, despite the ravages of weather and time, like an old man steeling himself against weather to some purpose. The pine's purpose was singular, yet daunting—watch over and protect its children and their children.

An incongruity to this pristine forest setting stretched westward. Man had left his unrelenting mark. In stark contrast to a solid mosaic of rich and subtle greens, splashes of ochre and sienna browns dominated the western vista, broken by muddy shades of grey where soil gave way to bedrock. If it weren't for the occasional dirty white, wart-shaped rock outcrops and sand coloured, worm-trail roads crisscrossing this unremarkable blanket of dull, an observer could be forgiven for losing focus and slipping into thoughtless, slack-jawed depression. At intervals, along the roads, piles of harvested tree-length pine appeared like neatly stacked tooth picks. They lay as rows of long, narrow caskets, a testament to man's avarice. There was, however, a light peppering of standing pine and neglected or undeveloped spruce and balsam shot-gunned across the landscape. They were conspicuous by their limited numbers and appeared like tiny, folded cocktail umbrellas. The remaining pine were the trees left to provide a seed source for the next generation, but they appeared tenuous in their footing, embarrassed by their nakedness without the cover and protection of their siblings. If the pine could rationalize, it would re-call seeing this intrusion in the past and revel at the ability of the forest to struggle back into form over time. Perhaps it would live to see yet another re-birth to the west.

As if providing relief from despair, in all directions from the ridge, various shapes of silver appeared as countless shards of broken glass thrust down in no apparent pattern upon the landscape. These were the lakes and ponds that served as reservoirs, holding the key of life and survival for all forms of flora and fauna in the area. Many were connected by silver threads of rivers and creeks that undulated in all directions, forming countless loops as they faded into the distance. The largest body of water was to the east. Daily as the sun rose and if the sky chose to be clear of cloud cover and if the wind was gentle, the lake shimmered with countless points of sapphire-spawned light, each sparkling with its own unique size and intensity, as if reaching out and twinkling for a viewer's attention.

If the old pine could rationalize or had the ability to comprehend, at close inspection it would puzzle over the shorelines of the lakes and rivers. It would see signs of low water—darker grey below lighter grey on the shoreline rocks, signalling a drop from the high water mark. Shoreline ferns and bracken had prematurely turned to gold and rust-brown. Smaller streams and ponds hung slack with brackish water. Elsewhere, beaver houses appeared abandoned, showing as pick-up sticks and lacking the presence of the tell-tale pantry of last winter's remaining poplar and birch cuttings placed just beyond their entrances.

If the old pine could really look in any direction, it would worry that in the seventh month of this year, in the three-hundredth's year of its life, some of the traditional shades of green showed fringes of yellow and gold. And if the old pine could remember, it would recall the year when a similar change had last occurred—the year of the heat, smoke and flame, the year when it was struck, no, shaken to its very core by the awesome, searing flash from the sky.

But the old pine could not see, nor feel, nor rationalize. It could just be, and continue to appear as a sentinel on the ridge, on the horizon, never resting, ever vigilant, and ever weary.

Chapter 2

THE SOW WAS IN HER 10TH YEAR, her prime, and had given birth three times in her lifetime. She was average for a female. Walking flat-footed on all four paws (each with an impressive array of five curved, 1¼ inch claws), she was over three feet from ground to shoulder and weighed in excess of one hundred and eighty pounds. At this time of year, had she been well fed, she would normally carry another twenty-five to thirty pounds. There was nothing out of the ordinary about her. Her close-set eyes were not particularly effective in supporting her role as teacher, provider and protector of her cub. Her relatively short, oval-tipped ears worked somewhat well as tools for picking up and separating sounds, sounds that might signal food or foe. It was, however, her tapered, white-tan nose with its long nostrils that were her greatest asset. It channelled an amazing sense of smell, sometimes picking up scents over long distances, depending on winds and air currents. This was the primary tool used to support a never-ending search for food supply.

In her quest to store body fat for the annual quasi-hibernation, the sow was omnivorous. She would eat almost anything. She was predisposed to vegetation such as grass, berries (blueberries, strawberries, raspberries, elderberries, pin cherries, choke cherries) and nuts (beech nuts, acorns, hazelnuts), but, as a supplement, she would turn to almost anything that crawled—ants, grubs, worms, grasshoppers and other insects. She had been known to take a moose calf or fawn in the spring, following the pregnant cow or doe, then waiting patiently for it to drop its offspring during the birthing. She would not turn her nose up at carrion; it was easy to locate with her sense of smell and easier yet to obtain. There was no hunting or chasing carrion. It was a fair return on a limited effort. Small mammals were quick, and more difficult to catch. Ants served only as snacks, and grubs were relatively limited in number. As a predator, perhaps what set her apart from similar species (carnivores such as wolf or lynx) were her lips and tongue. The lips were separated freely from the gums making them tactile and finger-like in their grasp of berries and insects. The tongue was manipulative and versatile; it could probe, prod and collect.

Almost jet-black, with an occasional "artist-brush" fringe of dark brown spattered across her fur, she walked low at the front and slightly higher at the back. One might be amused by her meandering, awkward, shuttle-like gait. However, amusement would undoubtedly give way to astonishment if she chose to run down the over-confident observer at bursts of up to fifty-five kilometres per hour. An antagonist could be sixty metres away and be set upon in less than six seconds. It would require the six seconds, to remove one's hands from one's pockets, look frantically in three different directions for a place to find shelter (no sense looking towards the sow) and finally turn towards the path of choice in order to affect an unlikely escape. This is the very same final, adrenalin-pumping, wasted six seconds prior to being struck down by a single blow powerful enough to kill.

The sow, however, was not aggressive by nature and would not likely react in such a manner even if she, her cub or her food were threatened. Her first instinct would be to warn the aggressor. Because of her long, thick hair, she was not predisposed to raise it on the back of her neck like a canine would to signal warning. Because of her short tail, she did not have the ability to "swish" it back and forth like a feline. Her body language, showing intent, would be conveyed through her head, neck and mouth. If she were agitated, she would likely approach cautiously with her head held low, below the shoulders. She might bare her teeth, snarl, open and close her mouth rapidly or actually make chomping noises.

Today, however, like most other days, was uneventful. Her sole, instinctive purpose was to search for nourishment. She was driven by the desire to "over-indulge"—store body fat for next winter's trance. The reserve of body fat was required to support herself or her suckling newborn cubs that might arrive late winter.

In her lifetime, of her seven offspring, four had survived. Now, her lone cub, trailing behind her, was the latest survivor. Born with a twin in late winter, each at ¾ of a pound and nearly hairless, the cub now followed the sow alone. In the early months, a territorial boar had cornered the sow and her offspring on the fringe of a swamp and killed the twin. Not heeding the sow's warning, a low throaty "woof, woof", the twin hesitated for a split second and died instantly from the blow. The surviving cub had, upon instinct, climbed the nearest black ash, a tree tall enough and strong enough to support the cub's weight, but not so large as to support the boar. The sow's response was too late to prevent the boar from lumbering off with its prize.

NORMALLY CONFINING HER ROUTINE to a familiar patrol within a ten kilometre square area, the sow began to extend her search into new territory. It was dry; more so than her senses had experienced in the past.

Ancient ponds and connecting black-blue ribbon creeks that had been traditionally protected by thick, black spruce swamps held little water. Fringes of waist high, emerald green saw grass had prematurely turned a wheat-yellow. The pale-green tamarack that stood as bastions between the black spruce and the grass-lands were now showing some of their early winter colours, bright yellow spikes of soft needles. Their needles, unlike those of other coniferous trees, were preparing for their annual, quiet descent to the forest floor. This was, however, mid-summer.

It was seasonally hot that day, with little air movement, the sky a light-cyan blue with high, semi-transparent, tissue-like clouds stretching from cotton balls to ribbons. The sow and her cub wandered mid-day. This was usually her time for rest but she was hungry and anxious about her off-spring. The cub tended to lag behind more often and complained with frequent grunts and bawls, likely because of the slight discomfort in its stomach. The cub was weaned and no longer required the sow as its food source. It would eat what its mother was teaching it to find. Food was scarce.

If one could view the sow's travels from high above, and took the time to scan the landscape, one would see not a homogeneous forest, but a patchwork of cutover, broken by uneven corridors of immature forest, protecting ribbon-like streams. In some cases, these narrow stands of spruce mixed with balsam fir, poplar and white birch encompassed lakes and ponds. Terrain was flat to rolling and in the lower areas the corridors and fringes were predominantly comprised of black spruce.

Had the observer taken flight over the area a few years prior, the patches on the landscape would not be brown to grey spotted occasionally with green and strewn with residual logging debris. They would not be bisected and dissected by countless threads of winter logging roads and trails. The patches would be a forest green of countless jack pine, in their immature to mature stage—all even aged and even height, growing soldier-straight and packed tightly like matchsticks in a jar. If one rose higher, still higher, to extend perspective, the brilliant patches would join seamlessly as a quilt with one colour, broken only by variations of greens, represented by narrow stretches of other species.

The quilt was the result of natural wildfire occurring over eight decades ago. It would take the intense heat associated with fire to force open the bullet-hard jack pine cones so their seeds would be exposed for germination. It was this very same jack pine that grew so tightly packed and straight at over twenty-five hundred trees per hectare that would be used to manufacture the studs for home construction. It would do no good to selectively cut this species. The shallow rooted, remaining jack pine could not support themselves in the open and would be subject to "blow-down" from heavy winds. Consequently, the harvesting prescription of choice was clear-cut. Required follow-up regeneration either took the form of aerial seeding or tree planting. In both cases, it would be several years before an observer would notice the young jack pine becoming a predominant species within the patchwork. Soon after the clear cut, a succession of other foliage would establish itself. Wild raspberry would appear on the side slopes. Tag alder and red osier dogwood would grow in the lower areas close to water. Blueberry bushes would spring up along the higher, drier sites on the cutover. Poplar and white birch seedlings would drift in from some of the fringe areas and establish themselves in a "shotgun" pattern. Hidden among all of this new growth were count-less numbers of rock-hard, slightly curved jack pine cones. Had man not taken the effort to artificially regenerate the area with new jack pine, the cycle would still take place over time. New jack pine seedlings would reappear, but only with the arrival of the next great wildfire.

THE SOW WAS IN UNFAMILIAR TERRITORY. She would nor-mally avoid the more open areas associated with the cutover, but she sensed that the new growth raspberries and blueberries would provide the nourishment her cub required. As they wandered aimlessly from shrub to shrub, they found some sustenance, but most of the crop was either sparse or shrivelled from many days of drought. There had not been enough precipitation to encourage an adequate supply of berries, a staple in a bear's diet this time of year.

Hours turned into days as the sow and her cub wandered far-ther from her traditional forage grounds. Progress was slow; her travels were increasingly halted by the cub's inability to keep up and its need to rest. With little to be found in the cutovers, the sow moved into the protection of a mixed wood forest with an advanced over-story of white pine. Here, shade maintained mois-ture, and moisture permeated into the first layers of the forest floor called "duff layers". Woody, decaying debris lay strewn on top or partially buried within the duff. It was here that the grubs and in-sects she coveted could be found. However, due to the lack of mois-ture over a long period of time, they had crawled deeper into the duff and worked their way further into the debris. For the sow and cub, more effort to retrieve the food source expended more energy. It was a losing cycle of "nourishment in, energy out". If it appeared the sow seemed to lose focus and resolve, she could be forgiven; she was depleting her own energy reserve.

DURING THE COURSE OF A DAY'S WANDERING, the sun came up warming her right shoulder and at the end of a day, settled softly on her left. Her travels did have a sense of direction; she was heading east and appeared to be climbing steadily, followed slowly by the whimpering, bawling cub. She sensed she needed some control over her desperate situation. Control meant protection, and protection could be found in the advantage associated with higher ground. She also needed a place for her cub to rest, a place that provided adequate cover and fair warning from her biggest threat—man. High ground collected sounds and updrafts of odour laden air from great distances.

By mid day, the sow had found her sanctuary. A group of large boulders that collected heat during the day and retained it at night also provided shade to a small, soft depression on a patch of earth. As she and her cub, both weak, fatigued and in need of sustenance, settled down in this small cathedral shelter, she was not aware that additional shade was being provided by a large white pine standing next to her temporary den. She also had no knowledge that the white pine had a large, bleached, spiral scar running down the length of its body. Nor did she have the ability to rationalize that the watcher had existed thirty times her own life span. She could not imagine that the pine appeared as a sentinel on the ridge, breaking the horizon and was weary—weary like its charges below, curled together in fitful rest in the depression at its feet.

Chapter 3

"**D**AMN, ONLY SIX MONTHS TO LIVE," Wally murmured to no one in particular. *Six months to achieve—what? Take a trip to a place with a better climate? Get laid by a pair of twenty-one year old Polynesian twins?* "Not likely, not even if I could afford to pay for it", this time spoken to a horizontal, cedar log wall. *How about the big city?* "People piss me off!" *How about the kids?* "I piss *them* off!" *I have to stop talking to myself like this!!*

Wally McNeil was a sixty-four year old, self-centred, self-proclaimed hermit whose claim to fame was two-fold. He had survived a tour in Vietnam when he was a young American and was recognized as one of the best trappers around as an old Canadian, his country of choice some thirty-eight years ago. It didn't matter to him what nationality he was; he just wanted to live and die north of Lake Superior. Besides, he strongly believed that everyone in the western hemisphere was an American. Canadians, "U.S.ers" and Mexicans were North American. Belizeans, Guatemalans, Hondurans, Costa Ricans, and Panamanians were *De America Central*. Venezuelans, Columbians, Brazilians, Bolivians on down to Argentineans were *Sudamericano*.

Before his beloved Julie had passed away from the insidious worm called Cancer—the same worm in different form he was battling daily, they had traveled as much as they could. Traveling had confirmed what Wally had already learned in Southeast Asia—people were basically good as long as they were left to their own devices. Corner or threaten them, take away what they had worked hard for and earned, there was sure to be trouble. Wally learned early to respect all races of people and their cultures. What he couldn't abide was bullying and arrogance, lying and cheating. In short, he didn't have much use for government in any form.

At only five foot, eight inches tall, he was a bow-string of a man, taut with knotted, twisted muscles that seemed to coil and uncoil like snakes whenever he was committed to labour. He was carrying ten pounds less then he should have, a sign that his body was more preoccupied fighting his disease then it was contributing to his health and well-being. His eyesight wasn't exactly 20/20, so he wore wire rim glasses, much to the dismay of his two, fashion conscious daughters. This and his traditional ensemble caused them no end of embarrassment (and afforded him much reason for satisfaction—their embarrassment, that is). A handle bar moustache bristled out, like a pair of miniature fox tails. Bushy eyebrows sat precariously on top of the glasses. The eye brows, the glasses and the moustache framed an unimpressive nose slightly bent from a punch-out in a Da Nang bar where it is said he got the better of two burly, somewhat surprised MP's. Slap on an old, misshapen fedora (overtop thick, unruly, salt and paprika hair), faded plaid shirt, bright "Mickey Mouse/Goofy/Daffy" suspenders, baggy, worn blue jeans, untied, scuffed leather work boots and Voila! Behold a masterpiece. But this masterpiece seemed to be born a hundred and fifty years too late.

Wally might have been taken for a "bush bumpkin" unless you looked beyond his attire and spent more time studying his face. You would automatically be drawn to a pair of intense, sea-green eyes that could speak volumes depending on his mood. At times, it was as if he was mute and used only his eyes to convey his message. If you ventured further scrutiny, the cognitive side of your brain would sense a hint of mischief flashing periodically like a lighthouse beacon supported by a slight upturn of his mouth. If you were really cerebral, you would surmise, no, you would know that this man holds within the knowledge of the ancients. He has been there, seen it and done it. These days, if Wally didn't think anyone was watching, you would sometimes see his eyes widen with the recognition of pain, followed by a flash of anger and frustration.

Julie was gone some five years now. He had sold the lodge and tourist business on White Lake soon after she passed away. She had talked him into buying it with the proceeds she inherited from the sale of her father's lodge in 1970, and she had managed their business with tender loving care for thirty years, while he worked as a forester for Carmichael Lumber. After she died, Wally purchased a small non-descript house outside of the White River town limits and managed to pick up a trapper's cabin complete with a government-issued, land-use permit for crown land. The cabin was situated on a small lake fifty kilometres north of town. He secretly named the lake after the pet name given to his wife, a pet name spoken only to her and only when no one else was present. He called it Lake Jewel. On the map it was called Siren. In his heart it was and always would be, Jewel.

Wally's girls were good girls. They loved their father, and he, in turn, cared for them. He and Julie had raised them to be independent. They were provided a good upbringing, a good education and knowledge that the world had a lot to offer and, as Wally had constantly reminded them, "Not so big as you can't see most of it in a lifetime." The problem was that White River, like so many Northern Ontario resource-based towns, had very little to offer a pair of young ladies, eager to follow their father's advice. Away they went as most fledglings do. An occasional visit followed by frequent, good-natured reprimands for his state of being did nothing to make Wally want to change his ways. Besides, he knew they were proud of him, and, in return, he was especially proud of the independent, single-mindedness that they both inherited and used to torment their significant others.

WALLY KNEW THAT "HOLLOW" CAME WITH A FEELING. You see, Wally missed Julie—missed her with every reminder of her being, including his two beautiful daughters who, through genetic wonder, each carried part of their mother with them. Mementos in the house, pictures, "bonhommes" (the name given to nic-nacs by his French Canadian friends), linen on the bed and Julie's clothes still in the closet after five years were all reminders that triggered memories. These were memories that Wally had little difficulty absorbing and filtering; he just had problems filing them away. That damn Mexican puppet, the colourful Costa Rican donkey cart and the cheap Portuguese seascape were cerebral snapshots that served up a plate of reminders complete with the complementary pain and emptiness he never ordered, but could not return. He avoided looking at them but couldn't convince himself to get rid of them. As he circled the house from room to room, he would first become irritated, then tense, like a caged cat looking for a way out. Try as he might to avoid it, his eyes would be drawn to her mementos. Close to hyperventilating, he would draw in a needed breath and will himself to look away, but the routine was wearing him down. He begged the girls to take what they wanted, but they didn't want their mother's things. They were polite about it. *Didn't want to hurt the old man's feelings.* Their biggest concerns were where to stick them (didn't fit the décor) and how to respond if dad showed up and they forgot to put them out. He knew he had to get out of the house. His trapper's cabin was his salvation.

The specialist had given him six months and insisted that he be provided care in a good institution in Sudbury, eight hours to the east. Besides, he would be a day closer to his daughters. His response was a predictable, "No damn way! I choose where I die, and I choose not to be in Sudbury. For that matter I choose not to be in White River! Just give me something for pain and lots of it!" Wally sold the house near White River and moved out to Lake Jewel.

NOW HERE HE WAS AT THE CABIN, two months earlier than usual, organizing his trapping gear. This year would be a little different. He would still make rounds on the thirty kilometres of trap line, but he would make them without his favoured body traps called *Conibear*. He had replaced his old leg-hold traps with the more humane Conibear using the six-inch '160' for fisher and the ten-inch '330' for beaver and otter. This trip would just be a "visit" to take it all in one last time and make peace with any of the fur bearers he might run across. He had been a good trapper, never exceeding his quota, doing his rounds frequently to prevent spoilage and ensure there was purpose in the killing, a quick, instant death due to the Conibear's double spring loaded design that targeted the animal's neck. Yes, there was always remorse, the same remorse felt by any good, respectful hunter since long ago when man had the audacity to rise up on two limbs and chase his food. This reoccurring feeling of remorse prompted the need to seek understanding, maybe even forgiveness. His mind told him to be more rational but it was his conscience, perhaps his very soul that ruled the day. Wally felt one last connection with his fur bearing co-tenants, coupled with some form of penance might help. Guilt was the one feeling he did not want to live with in his final days.

Today, however, was a day of rest and contemplation. Wally sat on the porch with a fresh cup of coffee this very morning and looked across Lake Jewel—looked up, up on the silhouetted high ridge to the west. There he was. That big white pine standing out above all others, like a bent flag mast with many flags, flung in every direction, but most pointed towards him and to the right. The flags were pointing to the northeast as if they were saying, "Head in that direction, stranger." Wally new that there *bent* was due to years of giving in to southwest prevailing winds. Wally mused. *If you ever get turned around in the bush, look for ridge-top pine; nine out of ten will point northeast.*

For the first time, Wally noticed something different about the ridge. Perhaps the morning sun had given it a different perspective. Perhaps it was Wally's need to be more observant before his last days on this good earth. The ridge was, in fact, a series of four ridges, appearing as if one was piled on top of the other, each falling back as distance increased. The shoreline ridge across the lake was the most obvious layer. It took on a black-green cloak with sweeping fans of white pine, spikes of white spruce and tear-drops of cedar, all more obvious with contrasting variations of green. An occasional smudge of grey-white, or grey-pink along the water's edge signalled rocks and boulders. Vertical slashes of white birch stood out in stark contrast to the black-green backdrop. The morning sun provided definition between each ridge. Where its rays directly blanketed a ridge, the foliage took on a pale, yellow-green hue with splatters and slashes of random black shade flecked into the hillside. Wally thought absently, *If God was the artist, then He took His paint laden brush mixed with ivory black and burnt umber and flicked it towards his earthly canvas.*

Boy, that old pine stood out—had to be three feet across. Probably impossible to get at in order to live that long. From my front porch to that pine, including a kilometre of lake, it had to be four kilometres. Wally was distracted with a sharp abdominal pain that reminded him of why he was here. When the pain subsided, his attention focused on the matter at hand. It was time for his daily discussion. Talking to the dead had its advantages. One, there would be no interruption. And two, you could be candid.

God, I wished you were here, Julie. I'm scared, more scared than I've ever been in my life. Wrestling with mortality is tiresome and somewhat confusing. The rational side of my brain contends that, once the body gives out, the mind turns off like a light bulb. No more being, no more thinking, just no more. The "flight or fight" side of my somewhat limited intellect hopes my wretched helium filled soul will rise and float gloriously upon the trade winds to Heaven before the devil has a chance to burst it with his inferno-heated pitch fork. Now, you know I've never been religious and carry more than my share of sins. We've talked about this many times, and we both know there is a "grand planner" out there. We agreed that he goes by many names. You insisted the planner was a "she" but we both agreed to disagree on that point. We talked about reincarnation. Remember, I always said I would come back as a captain aboard a stellar bound space ship, one built to transport interplanetary miners. What I forgot to mention was that I would be proud to have you as my first officer, anytime.

Wally put his mind in park for a moment then eased it back into gear. *It won't be too long before we get the opportunity. I just want to apologize to you for spending my last days here and not with the girls. I think they understand, and I promised to check in with them every three days on the SAT phone they gave me for Christmas. Speaking of Christmas, remember our last one together? I guess I have to apologize again for being a slightly inebriated Santa Claus to the girls and their boyfriends on Christmas Eve. Besides, they were as inebriated as I was. That was the last time I really saw you laugh, and boy, do I miss that throaty, ten-decibel laugh of yours—so much volume and pitch from someone so tiny. Sorry, I digress.*

Now, down to business. You probably already know this, but the girls will be well taken care of. Between the lodge and the house and my lack of spending on clothes and entertainment, there's more than enough to help them out. I hope you don't mind, but I changed the will and insisted that some funds be set aside for their kids' education and travel, when and if they have kids. As for me, there won't be a burial. This old body is going through the non-traditional short-cut (not likely to go to Heaven) practice of cremation and the ashes will be cast upon your lake. Hopefully they won't kill any fish.

I ran into father Mcginn last week on my monthly trip into town. He greeted me with a bear hug and a hellava lot of fanfare. According to him, he thought I had already died and had risen from the dead. Appears I haven't been to church since the last time he'd given up drinking. I didn't have the heart to tell him he wouldn't be overseeing (and celebrating) my permanent placement for prone rest.

There, I feel better already. What would I do after sixty-four years of existence, anyway? Play bingo? Take up square dancing or basket weaving? Find some store mall or school gymnasium to walk in slow, endless circles with my "peers" so my ancient body won't rust like the tin man? I don't think so!

The girls want me to move in with them. I told them it was too far south for my clothes. Bye the way, as we're talking, I'm now saluting that big white pine on the ridge with my coffee, you know, the one we always talked about, the one we said, "If that tree could talk, wouldn't it have some tales to tell".

Well, goodbye for now, Julie. Think about signing on as my first officer. I'm just going to sit here a few minutes more before I organize and work on my traps. I think I have a buyer and I want to make sure they're in good shape. Oh, I know I never said this often enough, but I love you.

Wally looked up again towards the ridge and the silhouetted pine. He gazed higher still and made a mental note of the wispy, veil-like clouds. They sported long, curved tails that melted into a clear blue sky. *As I recall, those are called "mares tails" stretched by strong, upper winds, usually followed in a day or two by unsettled weather. Good. Could use some rain, could use lots of rain, followed by a shit load of rain.*

His steady gaze dropped down from the ridge and followed the water's edge to the other side of the lake. Sound carried well over water, and he could occasionally hear the distinct cry of a bear cub. It seemed to role down from the ridge, gather steam and bounce off the lake. Wally felt a slight chill go up his spine in this warm, windless morning when he heard the cry again. He didn't know why or how, but Wally knew he would meet that cub. He also sensed that it wouldn't be in the best of circumstances.

Chapter 4

AN EXTENSIVE COLD FRONT MOVED RAPIDLY OVER NORTHWESTERN ONTARIO, pushing warm, moisture laden parcels of air just ahead and upwards from the earth's surface. The cold front was the result of surface spawned thunderstorms that had developed over the prairies, each fifteen to twenty kilometres in diameter.

The front was, in fact, an "outflow boundary" where the cooler air associated with the storm met warmer air as it advanced. As a result, thick, billowy clouds formed along the front, some white, some grey and some charcoal. These *cumulonimbus* clouds were rising thousands of feet in the air and appeared to fold within themselves, creating moving, roiling mountains of tri-coloured cotton balls that curled across the sky as if pushed by a giant, invisible snow plough. At thirty thousand feet, the warm, moist air had released even more latent heat and ceased to rise. Some of the great cloud formations began to flatten out, taking on the form of steel-grey anvils. The squall line of storms had now reached the mature stage, picked up momentum and galloped across the sky like horse-drawn spectres, intent on wreaking havoc and destruction in their path.

Engulfing and even dwarfing the clouds associated with the storms, ribbons of unseen, huge magnetic and electric fields arched high above the thunder clouds to the top of the atmosphere and careened downwards, like a thousand roller coasters that had breached the apex in their climb. Each took a different twisting, contorted path back to earth. Because the earth and the atmosphere were connected like two giant circuit boards, electrical currents were driven back up again, forming a constant barrage of charged particles. The electrical field was now so strong that the earth's surface and everything on it including grass, trees and mere mortals became charged.

The most obvious indicator of the super-electrical phenomenon was lightning. Searing, crackling bolts of pure power resulted from the build up of negative electrical charges within the clouds. At the same time, oppositely charged particles gathered at ground level. The air's resistance eventually succumbed to a 'fatal attraction' as negative and positive particles charged headlong towards each other like enraged bulls in a fight to the death. Once they smashed into each other, a spontaneous charge from the ground surged upwards at one-third the speed of light, ninety-nine thousand two hundred kilometres per *second*. This spawned an explosive, brilliant flash of lightning.

This day's impressive series of thunderstorms created thousands of lightning strikes. The air reeked with the pungent odour of cordite, a smell usually associated with holiday weekend fire works. Each strike between cloud and ground had the potential to produce a peak electrical current of thirty thousand amps with extreme charges reaching ten times that. In terms the average mortal could understand, the electricity flowing within an extreme lightning bolt could reach two hundred million volts.

Associated thunder rumbled and faded, cracked and tore, some reverberating for up to twelve seconds, an eternity for those huddled in fear, a welcome "percussionist's solo" for those revelling in morbid fascination with the sounds and sights of the symphony of storm. The drum roles and cymbal cracks were created by the expansion and contraction of air associated with a lightning strike. The air around each strike heated to forty-three thousand degrees Fahrenheit, then quickly cooled. Sound waves were created with air molecules rushing back and forth, and thunder was the result. The god Thor had nothing to do with it.

PEOPLE IN THE NORTH-WESTERN PART OF ONTARIO
are used to thunderstorms and tend to take them in stride.
Flashlights, oil lamps, candles and battery-powered radios are
brought out of hiding. TV's, radios and computers are turned off
and unplugged. Outside umbrellas are closed, boats are tethered
to their docks more securely, laundry is brought in off the lines,
and working people call home to make sure all is well. As a storm
approaches, some stand in fascination on porches, watching and
carrying on one or two word conversations with themselves.
Phrases like "wow", "amazing", "holy shit", and "sonofabitch" are
muttered simultaneously in thousands of households, shops and
businesses across the northwest. Others take out a book and hun-
ker down in their favourite chair or couch, looking up with each
flash or rumble, losing their place on the page and then searching for it with dutiful resignation. Others become anxious and
follow their pets down to the lower recesses of their homes, impressed with the common sense displayed by their four-legged
companions.

The day following this series of storms conversations were re-
markably similar. In family discussions around the breakfast table,
in small cafes and coffee shops where retirees met in the morning
and shop owners and business people met at lunch, discussions
centred on the same topic. Where kids hung around pool halls
and basketball courts, in gyms and clubs where desperate women
and men met in mortal self-combat to ward off the ravages of ag-
ing and over-indulgence, and outside offices where smokers huddled and looked up occasionally with furtive, guilt-ridden glances,
there was a common ribbon of thought: this just had to be the
worst series of storms anyone had seen in their life (if they were
young) or since 1988 (if they were older). Some even compared it
to July of 1976 where the ground "literally shook" with each awesome strike. One old timer told another over a second cup of coffee
in the Dragon Restaurant in Dryden (affectionately known as the
"Yurasis Dragon" Restaurant), "In the storm of '76, if I hadn't been
wearing a hat at the time, my hair woulda stood straight up, which
is quite an accomplishment since I've been bald mosta my life."

This particular cluster of storms was predominantly of the LP
(low precipitation) super cell variety. The combination of LP super

cells, significant cloud-to-ground (positive), lightning strikes and extreme drought conditions was a classic formula for wildfire.

The cold front moved eastward, creating thunderstorms in its path that provided little precipitation. The super cells rumbled across the landscape like death ships in a Star Wars battle, each laser bolt of lightning, accompanied by the cannon-like roar of thunder appeared to pick out targets at will on ridge tops and rock outcrops, hill sides and valleys. Each volley had the potential to ignite tinder-dry forest fuels and spawn wildfire. Depending on associated precipitation, wind and relative humidity, each potential wildfire could rise from the surface fuels of grasses, leaf litter, needles and dead branches and climb up to the forest canopy using *laddered* fuels such as brush, vegetation, low-hanging branches and smaller trees to reach the upper branches.

Each potential wildfire could also creep down into the sub-surface fuels of old, decomposed needles, leaves, twigs and live roots, and wait for the opportunity to rise to the surface. The sub-surface fuels normally carried enough moisture down to mineral soil to reject fire, especially in the spring. Spring wildfires did not normally burn deeply and were wind-driven, racing across the forest floor and climbing, with the aid of laddered fuels, into the forest canopy. Trees or groups of trees would either *torch* from top to bottom or the fire could *crown* racing through the forest canopy, driven by wind.

However, this was a summer storm and one with severe drought conditions. The sub-surface fuels carried little or no moisture. Fires would burn deeply and require back breaking digging and grubbing with hand tools mixed with abnormal amounts of water in order to extinguish them. Under drought conditions, if the task at hand was not done thoroughly, a burning ember or coal of fire buried up to three feet down could smoulder for days, creep to the surface and re-burn anything left that was combustible. The fire cycle would begin all over again.

The cold front continued to sweep eastward, skirting the top of Lake Superior, looking for new targets while the wildfire organization in the West Fire Region of Ontario scrambled daily to keep up to a rash of new fires. They were desperately trying to prevent even one of the new fires from escaping and becoming a dreaded "project fire", a wildfire so large and complex that even a single project fire could tax the resources of the region. The front had now entered the East Fire Region and was west and north of the town of Wawa, Ontario, home of the Wawa Fire Management Headquarters. They were organized and ready—or so they thought.

Chapter 5

T HE NEXT MORNING, WALLY SENSED THE IMPENDING STORM before he could see it. It smugly announced its arrival to him with the onset of a migraine headache as he sat down in the old chair on the front porch. The chair was actually the front seat out of a 1956 Chevy Impala, probably a mate to the first new car he ever owned and the only automobile he ever fell in love with. Actually, he was only sixteen at the time, and his parents owned the car, but he liked to think it was his. Its green and beige leather was worn, cracked and faded. A few of the springs had sagged, creating shallow pockets in the padding, but the old bench seat served its purpose—a place to reminisce and stretch the boundaries of his imagination. Wally was doing just that. *If I sit in just the right place, my scrawny ass cheeks fit snugly in two sagging pockets. It's the adjustment for the middle spring that I have a little trouble with.*

Let's see. Migraine, low pressure system, bad weather's coming. I'll have to keep an eye open and pop one of those expensive pills the doctor prescribed. Besides, who wants to die feeling poorly? There I am, feeling sorry for myself again. I probably deserve the long, overdue silence that's sure to come my way.

Wally sipped his coffee (which was a no, no. Migraines and coffee *did not* go well together) and thought once more about the '56 Chevy. The thought lead to a quick flashback—his first attempt to get lucky with "whatshername". Hormones and a '56 *Chevy* did go well together. He got the most out of that thought and looked westward for more signs of impending weather. At the same time, in his peripheral vision he took in the pine, a miniature spike on the distant ridge, and subconsciously tuned his senses to pick up the sound he had heard the previous day. There was no wind and all was quiet—too quiet, in fact. This time of day, it was usually like downtown Manhattan or Toronto, only with wildlife, not people.

He could usually count on those damn red squirrels to chase each other across the roof, down the red pine hanging over the camp and across his deck. What did he call them? Ah yes, 'Motor Mouth!' He didn't know which one was which but he did know they reminded him of his twin cousins, the notoriously loquacious Balinda and Calinda. Once they had an audience, they were both like red squirrels around a campfire; they could not, not even if their lives depended on it, not for one minute, shut up.

Where was that family of mergansers? One female and nine ducklings—she must have picked up another family of orphans. They were a joy to watch. When spooked, the little, awkward balls of down propelled themselves across the water like miniature paddleboats.

Even the magnificent osprey missed her morning pass over the lake near his camp. Wally never ceased to be amazed at her ability to spot a fish from over fifty metres aloft, fold her wings and dive-bomb her prey. He would catch himself holding his breath as she stopped forward flight motion, paused and maintained altitude, then began her decent. Only when she ascended with a fish in her talons, would he take a breath and mutter an appreciative "Wow!" His fascination led to a little research on this member of the hawk and falcon family. It was the perfect fisher. It had the feet of an owl and the eyesight of an eagle and could carry fish equal to its size with the average osprey weighing 2 to 4½ pounds. Its four-toed feet not only had prickly spicules on their undersides to assist in holding slippery fish, they also had a reversible toe, capable of pointing forward or backward, much like the owl. Its legs were heavily scaled to allow it to assist the feet with grip on its prey. In flight, it could reach speeds of fifty kilometres per hour, while in a steep dive it could reach a speed of one hundred and twenty kilometres per hour. It would then pull up feet first at the last second, enter the water with a splash, in some cases going under a metre to

reach its prey then surface and rise aloft gracefully with a squirming fish in tow. *Remarkable bird. Should be out today. Something's up.*

The lake itself seemed to give testament to impending turmoil.
Not a wave, not a ripple. No fish surfacing, no water bugs circling,
no dragonflies swooping. Wally scanned the surface with a critical
eye. *Flatter than piss on a plate.* "Too damn quiet", he said to the coffee cup. He looked again to the west and made a mental note of the
solid line of dark clouds closing in and covering the morning sky
like a slowly drawn curtain engulfing afternoon light.

THE SOW ALSO SENSED A CHANGE AS WELL. She looked
down at her cub, tucked into her belly, snuffling and snoring in
a fitful sleep. She looked around at her temporary cover and appeared to be satisfied that it would provide appropriate shelter. She
then looked skyward and sniffed the air, her nostrils flaring in
rapid succession in order to catch and sort out the various scents.
An empty feeling gnawed inside her very being, but she sensed
that this day was not a day to venture. Nourishment would have
to wait. She put her head down, gave the cub a single caress with
her tongue and closed her eyes. Just as she was about to drift off,
her short, thick ears stood straight up and flared outwards and her
soft chestnut brown eyes opened briefly in response to the sound
of distant rumbling, one thunderous drum role after another, each
tapering off into nothingness.

THE PINE ALONE SEEMED TO DISPLAY NO REACTION to
the approaching storm. No stirring of needles, no movement of
branches. If the pine could pass judgement, it would likely think
that the storm was a rank amateur in the cycle of life. The world
spins at sixteen thousand kilometres an hour. Light travels at two
hundred and ninety-eight thousand kilometres per second. If the
pine could speak, it might declare, "I was once a seed and rode
the prevailing winds. I have withstood the ravages of time and
all the earth's elements for over three hundred years. I've been

spared the axe, the cross-cut saw and the chain saw. I've survived the rapier-like slash of a bolt of lightning. What is one, insignificant storm?"

The pine stood tall, alone and determined as brilliant flashes of energy raced through darkened clouds in the distance while others struck the earth often and with impunity.

Chapter 6

OH, OH. TIME TO MOVE INSIDE. Wally tossed the last cold inch of coffee on the yellow stubble of what used to be grass. He stood up tentatively, a calculated move intended to ward off another sharp, staggering pain. "Also time to water the piss patch", he announced to his preferred target location on the poor excuse for a lawn. No matter how much rain this storm brought, the patch stood little chance of recovery. He finished his ritual with a sigh, a shake and a zip, took another furtive glance at the sky, marked a lightning flash and counted the seconds until the mandatory rumble of thunder.

Rule of thumb: every 5 seconds between flash and rumble was a good kilometre. A thousand and one, a thousand and two. Wally counted to a thousand and fifteen. *Four kilometres to the west, just about at the top of the last ridge. The next one could be pretty close. Imagine being zapped with your pecker in your palm while piddlin' in the patch (could be a country and western song. Cue the steel guitar: "I was struck with my"—never mind). Wouldn't that be a zinger! You could be zapped into a permanent, standing 'penile' position. I'd make a great statue on main street in White River. Maybe they'd put me next to the Winnie the Pooh statue.*

Wally shuffled through the screen door with the "you can't sneak up on me" hinges, looked around and shook his head slowly. The camp, he noticed with some pride, definitely had a bachelor's touch. *Where the hell was the maid? Should call into one of those TV stations and put my name on the list for "This Old House", "Extreme*

Home Makeover", "While You Were Out", "House Swap" thingy. The place was untidy, but clean. Wally knew Jewel wouldn't stand for a filthy camp. Once he had smugly declared to her, "Real men don't do dishes". Without even a glance in his direction, she shot back, "Real men don't get supper unless real men do dishes". Wally had slunk to the dinner table with a T-towel over his shoulder and a wounded look on his face. The T-towel was his muted way of saying, "You win this time".

The big room was a living area and kitchen combined. The camp was simply planned with two bedrooms on the south. To anyone who was interested, Wally would often describe the outhouse, called "facilities", as "tasteful yet contemporary" and "twenty-five metres from the camp." Jewel used to complain that by the time she made it to the facilities, it was either too late or she had forgotten why she was there. Her biggest complaint was that "the plywood toilet seat was damn cold and I don't appreciate splinters in my cheeks!" Wally had surprised her during their last Christmas together with a gift he announced "no woman could refuse", a piece of two inch solid, blue styrofoam made to fit around the hole. "Voila, madam!" he exclaimed with a hint of humour in his voice. "Simple but warm, smooth but not slippery, with colour but not garish. Would madam wish to try it?" In truth, hard styrofoam made an excellent toilet seat. It didn't retain odour, was somewhat comfortable and stayed surprisingly warm, even in cold weather.

Wally's favourite tree was red pine. He liked the way they stood on shoreline parade like palace soldiers. He admired the colour and texture of their bark. Thin, washed-white to pale-red flakes of bark cloaked each tree. From a distance they truly did look like "red" pine. He also liked the five to six inch long, firm needles, each set in clusters of two when compared to the shorter prickly white spruce or jack pine. *White* pine's two to three inch, soft clusters of five needles came in a close second to the red pine as his favourite.

Wally liked red pine so much that it was the main reason he had purchased his trap camp. Its exterior was constructed of red pine logs in the round and most of the functional furniture was made from red pine. Although it did not have the durability of white pine for construction purposes, when repairs were required, it was lighter and easier to handle. Also, it didn't have the sticky,

gum-like resin that white pine exuded. Anyone who knew anything about working in the bush avoided sitting on a freshly cut
white pine stumps.

The roof was a made of practical steel sheeting in a forest-green
colour. Propane provided the essentials for cooking and lighting.
Water was drawn from the lake poking up through a dug well in
front of the camp. Besides the camp and outhouse, there was an
out-building, large enough to provide a home for his ATV, tools,
fishing equipment, trapping room and an old wood stove. It wasn't
too efficient but it could bring the chill down a degree or two. The
camp itself was accessed by logging road, a kilometre away, and a
trail directly to the camp, wide and sound enough for the ATV.

The living area sported a couch, matching chairs with two coffee tables and two end tables in vintage red pine. This room was
bathed in natural sunlight provided by five generous windows
each with a pair of pale green, middle-tied curtains compliments
of Jewel.

The centre-piece, however, was the free-standing, air-tight wood
stove in the middle of the south wall, adjacent to the door on the
west bedroom. Its wood-loading door was of simple design with
a brass handle and a tempered glass window. The stove stood on
and was backed by a base and wall inlaid generously with red and
white quartz found in an abandoned open-pit mine exploration
site on the north side of the lake. Each piece of quartz was inlaid
with stark flakes of shiny black silica and flecks of fool's gold.

PHOTOS DOMINATED THE WALLS. Most were of immediate
family. A discussion with those photos was part of Wally's daily
ritual. He would get up, put on his slippers and make the bed. He
would then stoke the fire, put on the coffee and carefully make his
way to the facilities (there was a reason slippers were called "slippers"; just try walking anywhere outside on a wet or frosty morning). Finally, he would strut back (mission accomplished), pore a
coffee and talk to each and every photo between measured sips.

The bedrooms were Spartan but functional. The larger, master
bedroom had a single, queen-sized bed, chest of drawers and a
night table. The smaller, second bedroom had twin single beds,

a chest of drawers and two night tables. Wally spent most nights in the smaller of the two bedrooms. Sleeping in Jewel's bed only brought him unwanted memories and sleepless nights.

Wally proudly took credit for the clutter. Every flat surface had books and magazines, piled and laid out like puzzle pieces waiting for a match. To his credit, Wally's mess was associated only with reading material. Dishes were always done and food put away for pragmatic reasons. Wally didn't like finding mouse turds in his cereal bowls and plates. It tended to curb his appetite. Magazines included *Ontario Out of Doors, Field and Stream* and *The Ontario Trapper*. Current versions were in camp; old versions were relegated to the facilities.

Wally's book reading was eclectic. Authors tended towards *James Lee Burke, Sebastian Junger, Elmore Leonard* and *James W. Hall*. Next to his bed he kept a copy of A.A. Milne's *Winnie the Pooh*, a gift from Jewel in 1971. He read it in pieces, unconsciously resurrecting those wondrous, innocent feelings of childhood. His latest book selection however, deviated from his steady diet of intrigue and suspense tinged with a light frosting of tongue-in-cheek. He was reading Mitch Albom's *The Five People You Meet in Heaven*. It was one of those inspirational books that women read in order to cleanse their teat ducts. One of his daughters had left it in camp a couple of years back, perhaps to provide some comfort to a man who refused to be consoled. It was a story of death and redemption. *Perhaps my story,* he mused. *I doubt, however, if anyone's gonna meet me in heaven.*

So here he was, trapped inside with a major storm approaching. He admitted that thunder and lightning tended to increase his pulse rate and blood pressure. He could already feel a slight, drumming pressure throughout critical points in his body. It was something he could usually control through self-deprecating humour. He gazed at the cupboards and exclaimed, "Better avoid the "all-bran challenge" for breakfast—too much distance and too little time between thunder and outhouse." *Just pick up a book and wait it out.*

The storm lasted all day into the evening. It came in waves, accompanied by unrelenting lightning, deafening thunder, but very little rain. The staccato lightning reminded Wally of his tour in Viet Nam. Ten months of living (and dying) hell. He had finished university during the draft and wasn't eligible for a deferment. He was a citizen, single, no longer a student, wasn't smart enough to declare himself a conscientious objector, didn't have the balls to run to Canada, wasn't a farmer or minister and his very good health worked against him. He was classified as "1-A"—"registrant available for military service". He vividly remembered telling a buddy, "I'll fix those bastards. I'll join the marines!" Little did he know at the time that the standard twelve month tour became thirteen if you were a marine. His tour was cut short by three months. His thoughts turned to December 9, 1965, a defining moment in his life, one he had trouble forgetting.

Chapter 7

1965
QUE SON VALLEY, QUANG
NAM PROVINCE, VIETNAM

*J*ESUS! HERE I AM, *curled up like a baby in a fetal position, clutching the M-16 to my chest, pressed up against the side of an 18 inch rice paddy dyke somewhere in the Que Son, scared shitless. Old at 25. Waiting for support from AHC. Why did everything have to have an acronym—not enough time to say "assault helicopter company" before dying? Not alone, thank God. A new cherry, what was his name? Jeff? Jerry? At the same dyke, in the same position, eyes as wide as saucers. Flashes of light fifteen hundred yards out and the drum shattering thud-crash of Charlie's 120 mm mortar rounds everywhere, all around us.*

"Bohica, Jeff!"

His response is frantic. "My name's Jerry, asshole, and what does *bohica* mean?"

Both men pulled their heads down and frantically tried to make themselves smaller. *Man, I wish I could pull a plug out of my butt and deflate!* A mortar round BOOMED next to their narrow cover and threw debris and mud on top of them. Each round was in rhythm—THUNK, WHOOSH, CRACK! pause, THUNK, WHOOSH, CRACK!

"IT MEANS 'BEND OVER, HERE IT COMES AGAIN!' AND DON'T CALL ME ASSHOLE—ASSHOLE! WE'RE IN DEEP SERIOUS, HERE!"

I see that Jerry already has the thousand yard stare, a result of combat, usually reserved for those of us long gone in the tour. Gotta focus on something—think back. I went DIE (draft induced enlistment. Hope the acronym isn't prophetic) after college. Let's see if I got this right. I was going to be drafted, so I enlisted first. Not only did I enlist, but I enlisted in the marines. Dumb and dumber. Boot camp—three months in sunny San Diego, CA—going toe to toe, eyeball to eyeball, drill instructor to recruit, him and me, daily, the only two people in the world. I still get "the fear" when I think about it. My drill instructor, sergeant Mendez, was the catalyst for the five stages of boot camp: regret (worst mistake I ever made in my life), despair (will I ever get home?), rage (I will not let that son-of-a-bitch defeat me), pride (I can do this and he's getting the headache when he's shouting at me) and respect (I want him as a leader when I go in country).

I survived boot camp and was assigned as a grunt to the 3rd platoon (one of the forty-five, tough and stupid), LIMA Company (a hundred and eighty men), 3rd Battalion (eight hundred men), 3rd Regiment, 3rd Marine Division (twenty thousand strong). Strength in numbers, until you get shot at. So here we were, located in "I Corps" country, Quang Nam Province, Que Son Valley. Operation "Harvest Moon". Sounded romantic like "Shine On", but it was an order to rescue the 5th ARVN regiment (it seemed the South Vietnamese always needed rescuing). Some rescue! We were being followed by the guys in black pyjamas but we kept on moving. I'm thinking "why not stop and waste the little bastards", but orders were orders. By noon, we had been funnelled into a classic triangle ambush by Charlie. The VC that had followed us simply closed the back door. We were now facing hill 43 [their hill] and taking heavy mortar and machine gun fire.

Think of something else, music, a song! Come on! Any song! His mind couldn't handle an attempt to conjure up music at this moment.

THUNK! CRACK! "Shit!!"

I feel a punch. The air is torn from my lungs. Too close. I'm wet. Must be the mud. Shit, it's blood. "Jeff, I think I'm hit!" I look over at Jeff, no, Jerry. Half his face is gone. I think, "Maybe it's his blood. God, make it his blood". Pain, dull at first, sharp with time, radiating from my ass. I reach back and gingerly run my fingers across my left cheek and look at my hand. Nope, it's my blood.

I believe I passed out. Was I dead or was I dreaming? Ordered to take hill 43 (probably only way for some of us to survive). Everyone is up and running. So was I—damned if I was going to be left alone. Didn't feel a thing. Probably fear adrenalin—fight or flight? We were fighting. Couldn't hear a thing, like the adrenalin over-amped my receptors. It was getting dark. Oh how I hated being out here at dark! I see tracers from Charlie's RPD light machine guns. They released a hundred and fifty rounds of 7.62 mm shells per minute, but the tracers seemed to loop in slow motion, like shooting stars in a clear night sky. Beautiful, but we'd be in their range in seconds. Run, scuttle, drop, find a target (or not) and shoot. My pucker factor was twelve out of ten. Wished I'd taken an extra dose of cork, our name for a drug used to prevent the shits. Getting hard to see (open your blinking eyes, Wallace!). Thank God for the green eye. This scope gathered serious light. We could see not only Charlie but also friendlies. Hate to think I was going to get shot in the other cheek by a friendly. Well within Charlie's mortar range. The faster you moved, the more likely it was you could run under it before Charlie had time to adjust. Out of the rice paddy—heavy with soaked battle dress—thirty yard sprint and I hit the ground running. My helmet slams into the baked earth before my nose does. I lie there, hyperventilating, looking at red tinged earth. A small colony of leaf-cutter ants marches below my eyes in single file, carrying foliage three times their size, oblivious to the carnage around them. They are so tiny, yet so powerful. Wished I was a leaf-cutter ant.

Utter confusion, screams, curses, but our training keeps us moving—a hundred yards from our targets. I skid behind a mound of dried elephant grass, usually found in the highlands. Thank God for elephant grass. I love elephant grass. Think I'll plant elephant grass when I get home. If I get home. Up with the M16. Fresh thirty-round clip. Scope to eye. Search for a kill. Control breathing. Pale green light now, fine cross-hairs. A large command post from the base of the view finder to the middle of the cross-hairs. Two Charlies on a mortar. Which one do I choose? Eenie, meenie. Best target is crouching over, can't be anymore than seventeen years old, looks like seven. He raises his head and looks in my direction, fear stamped across his face. I squeeze, the rifle recoils a little, I hear nothing. It seems like minutes later a dark flower miraculously blooms on his forehead. He appears surprised before the dead look. I search for target number two. Target two stands to run, his mouth stretched in fear. Too bad for you buddy. I squeeze; he dies. Survival lesson number one: don't stay in one spot too long. Up and running. I don't think my feet touch the ground. It seems like I am all alone in spite of the chaos around me.

I begin to slow down, no more energy, little needles of pain grow sharper, adrenalin draining, pain increasing. Oh shit! Medic! Medic! A doc crawls over to me, unceremoniously flips me over and tells me that I would live but I needed to get out shortly. I think, 'how can these guys do it'. I'm prone but he's sitting up, focused on my wound with all this shit coming down. He gives me a fix and he's away to another grunt yelling behind me, "Where's my friggin leg!" When the morphine takes hold, the pain subsides and I'm in La La land. As I drift off, a Med-Evac Helo touches down. My dust-off is finely here, like a winged chariot. I'm pushed in. The pilot looks back and down upon me, the face of Gabriel himself, grins, takes a round between the eyes and is no more. I'm told to "un-ass" from the pilot-less helo, a machine without a brain, literally. I have to wait until total darkness before a next rescue attempt is made. I recall not caring. I think I said, "No dust-off? No problemo", just before I passed out.

Flash forward. I was having a final meal at Ton Son Nhut air force base. The classic "duffle bag drag and a bowl of corn flakes" prior to boarding the big bird for the flight back to the land of the "big PX [post exchange]". I leave with a flurry of irrational feelings: excitement, guilt, apprehension, guilt, relief, guilt. I had taken shrapnel in the ass, not an uncommon injury given the circumstances. I think now that I'm glad I didn't know Jerry or the pilot. A selfish thought but not uncommon given the circumstances. I hope no one is waiting for me and I can slip away like a phantom. Another selfish thought, but not uncommon given the circumstances.

SNAP OUT OF IT. Back to reality. It's forty years later and yeah, my ass still gets sore on the left cheek, but I can still sit on my right if I lean that way a little. Wally looked down. His hands were shaking. There was a fine sheen of perspiration on his forehead. He thought he was over chronic posttraumatic stress disorder. He could sleep and had no problems concentrating, but he often wondered if his trapping and semi-isolation from friends and family was a result of his tour. He also wondered if he would ever really get over it. At times it seemed like a movie. In his mind, he was watching someone else, an actor playing him. At other times, in other dreams and thoughts, there was no actor, only himself, played by himself, watched by himself. The fear and the anxiety were his alone. Another intense flash of lightning and role of thunder. *Wonder how the cub is doing on the ridge? Wonder when the next sneaky, bottom-feeding stab of pain in my gut is going to hit? Wonder how long I can hold out?*

Chapter 8

FIERCE, STABBING, UNRELENTING PAIN! Unable to cry out, unable to run, no defences: no ability, even, to give up and die; just stand and accept.

The white pine accepted the searing spiral of flash-white, intense energy. Positive charges at the base of the tree had spiralled up and raced skyward to meet negative charges from the storm. The result was a four inch wide laser incision of lightning that penetrated the 1½ inches of bark with little effort. The spiral wound ran twenty metres from the base of the tree towards the top, its terminus hidden by foliage. Where the new wound intersected the older wound, intense heat seared the unprotected layer of wood to a depth of six centimetres.

The heat had also penetrated the ground cover, a "duff" cover made up of thick, matted leaf, pine needle and twig litter and animal residue. Its thickness ranged from twenty to thirty centimetres. The cover below the litter was stratified and contained partly decomposed organic residues above highly decomposed organic matter above minerals mixed with humus. Woven through the mat was a network of roots, intertwined laterally and vertically in every direction, and of various diameters.

The duff layer had been washed by frequent rains and compaction by annual snowfalls. Oxygen in the duff layer was provided by light compaction and insect, grub and small animal activity. Oxygen was one of three components necessary to support a fire. Pure soil couldn't burn, but the duff layer and organic material stratified in the soil provided a second component of the fire triangle—fuel. In this particular summer, the duff layer and organic materials trapped in the soil were super-dry. All that was needed was heat. It was provided this day. Combustion began as a result of lightning and a fire dragon was spawned.

The storm had been followed by precipitation, a light rainfall of two to four millimetres that provided some moisture and cooling to the forest floor. It was, however, more of a nuisance than a benefit. The dragon could not surface, but it could descend and move laterally. It crept slowly downward, consuming the drought-dry litter in its wake. At times, the infant-dragon was starving for oxygen, but seemed to sense where small pockets lay and crawled towards its life support. When it hit mineral soil, it took the path of least resistance and feasted laterally and upward until it hit the moisture laden upper duff. Where smoke could break through the surface, it did so, but with little conviction. The cycle repeated itself and the dragon grew larger and took on an undefined shape as it consumed the compacted fuels. It longed to break free of its subsurface prison. All that was required was more drying of the top layer of duff. It was just a matter of time.

WALLY WAS UP, BENT OVER IN PAIN, clutching his abdomen, fearing that it would burst open and his very life would spill out. "Oh God! Work, pills, work!" It was pitch dark in the living room save for the frequent flashes of lightning. With each flash his face revealed a different expression of desperation. FLASH! Clown face grimace, mouth turned down in agony; FLASH! Beads of sweat running down his temples, dripping off his quivering chin; FLASH! Eyes looking upward in supplication, tears streaming down his cheeks. FLASH! FLASH! FLASH! Head turning in slow motion pictures, towards the shotgun in the corner that was revealed in stark clarity by another flash. It was time. FLASH! Trembling hands on the shotgun. FLASH! Barrel in Wally's mouth, clenched by grinding teeth.

FLASSSHHH! "My God!" Wally's head wrenched away from the barrel and looked through the picture window to the ridge. In the millisecond it took for him to pinpoint his distraction, Wally saw the awesome arc and spiral of blinding energy pirouetting around the big pine. "Aw shit!" His tears of pain were now mixed with tears of anguish. *We're both going down. Please God, let her stand so my girls have something to inspire them cause it sure as hell won't be me.* It was suddenly shutter-dark. Wally made himself ready for the next final picture, giving into despair but now more relaxed. *Ready, set*—FLASH! Unbelievably, the pine still stood, enveloped in a cloak of mist and translucent smoke, appearing determined, stubborn as if challenging the angry sky to deliver another blow. Wally's meds finally started to kick in and the pain eased. *So, you old prick, you live to fight another day.* Wally wasn't sure if he was referring to the pine or himself. *If my friend can take it, so can I.* The shotgun made its way gingerly back to the corner. It stood alone again, steel and wood, in rigid disappointment. *Perhaps there's a reason for both of us to carry on, at least for another day.*

Another flash. More subtle now, the pine again in silhouette, standing tall in silent agreement. The sky was intensely dark with frequent flashes that retreated into the night followed by occasional low, extended rumbles of thunder. Wally shuffled to bed, exhausted by pain and his decision to prolong his sorry life.

WALLY COULDN'T SLEEP and chose, instead to reminisce. *Could be dangerous. Where do we go tonight? How about something comforting? I'll just flip through my memory catalogue. Let's see now. College and Jewel. This could be good. Drinking, sex, love, sex, marriage, sex, children—no sex.* He struggled out of bed, put on the worn slippers and went out to the living room. He ignited the kitchen stove, put on a kettle of water, stoked the fire and sat down into his favourite chair. *I think I'll close the mind catalogue until the tea is ready. Maybe I'll even pull out an old photo album or two. Real men don't go through photo albums, at least when someone else is around. Screw it. I'm alone, which is the rule, not the exception, and I need to dredge up as many memories as I can, while I still can. It'll be like taking a mental holiday. Tea's ready. Settle back down, comforter on my lap, photo albums on the floor next to the chair. Shit! Forgot the milk and sugar. Thank heavens there's a bottle a Bailey's Irish Cream liquor just within reach on the coffee table.* He spiked his tea and took a long, slow sip. A song from the

60's was playing in his head, over and over again. He opened the first photo album.

SHE GREW RESTLESS with the incessant flashes of light and cracks of sound. Her cub slept fitfully, tucked tight up against her belly. With each flash she looked skyward, the pupils of her honey-brown eyes dilating like shutters on a camera lens, closing as darkness snapped back again. She put her head back down. She had seen this many times over her existence; it was part of her very being, like walking and smelling and eating. It was part of what she accepted with each change of the light from black to grey to bright on a daily basis. The next brilliant stream bolted out of the dark, hurled towards her like a horse-drawn ghost carriage and struck with such violence that the coarse hairs on her body crackled and stretched with a force she couldn't comprehend. Her cub sprang up and cried out. She rose quickly and looked towards the old pine, her eyes reflecting the drama of heat and energy clashing with the protection above her. The surface on which she stood trembled, and the pads on her feet tingled and grew hot. She pushed the cub roughly with her nose and sprang away, running downhill away from the source of confusion. She ran as fast as she could, the cub not far behind. Both were swallowed up in the darkness.

Chapter 9

WHO THE HELL COMES FROM BIG FORK, MINNESOTA? *Let's see—population a whopping five hundred.* Wally was looking at a high school photo. Short, skinning, narrow, pimply face—a scruffy trace of facial hair, a shock of red hair above blond, bushy eyebrows that was crying out for a trimming (the hair, not the eyebrows)—madras shirt and black jeans, way too tight (*virtually no ball room*)—a veritable collage representing teenage raging hormones. Wally suffered a fit of adult embarrassment. *What a loser!* His two buddies in the photo, Erin & Justin (the 'in' brothers), didn't fare much better. *Why was it called Big Fork (used to call it Big Dork)? Right, the town was built on the Bigfork River.*

As Wally flipped through pages of photos, he recalled his elementary and high school compressed into one campus called, with little imagination, Bigfork Elementary and High School. Twelve years (two thousand, six hundred and forty days) of his life dedicated to the quest for higher learning. When they graduated, he and the 'in' brothers knew this: the Woodsman Restaurant and Bar, south on highway 38 had beer and served minors; Grand Rapids, 20 miles to the south had strippers; and all girls had boobs of varying shapes and sizes.

Not bad after two thousand, six hundred and forty days of education.

Two years earlier, Wally's parents realized that his focus was relatively narrow and felt it was in everyone's best interest to ship him away for the summer. Wally's "best interest" was served in avoiding early fatherhood. His parent's best interest was served in avoiding premature grandparenthood. Wally's father had arranged for Wally to work in Canada for a friend who owned a fishing lodge, a lodge that his father could visit from time to time using the ruse of fishing to offer kind, fatherly direction should Wally falter in his duties. It wasn't too far, less than an hour to the Canadian border at International Falls, three hours east to Thunder Bay, Ontario. Then three hours north to Armstrong country would get you there.

Wally never wondered where his predilection for forestry evolved. He knew. Big Fork's history was rife with the stories of logging, fur trading and trapping. His father had worked as a buyer and manager for Bishop Mill, a company with ninety-five years of tenure in the area to this day. Established in 1910, it directly managed thirty-five thousand acres of timberland in the area and routinely purchased logs from other landholders.

In 1959, at the ripe old age of nineteen, Wally enrolled in the forestry program, Department of Forest Resources, University of Minnesota in St. Paul. From time to time, when Wally was back in town, he would check the university web site to see how the program was evolving. It was now called the Natural Resource Science and Management Program but he knew as time went on, things remained the same. *If it looked like a frog, hopped like a frog and croaked like a frog, then it was likely a frog.*

He recalled the many courses associated with the program. He had a hard time swallowing the Economics and Policy Management course; he spent enough time in a logging town to be part of the real world where "hi-grading" timber was the preferred logging practice. His dad called it "take the best and leave the rest". Wally's favourite course was 'Silvics and Silviculture'. Silvics described how trees grew, reproduced and responded to environmental change. Silviculture was the agriculture of trees, how to grow them, maximize growth and manipulate tree species composition to meet landowner objectives. *Boy that must have been pounded into me.* Simply put, Silviculture meant best practices of harvesting trees before nature burned them, ate them or blew them down. An ethical forester would ensure the landowner's objectives weren't solely focused on profit in the short term and would encourage return over a long period of time. The difficulty here was that human nature being what it was, most people or organizations didn't want to wait forty to eighty years for the rest of their forest products and profit. They wanted it all and they wanted it now.

Then of course there was the other side of the equation, the anti-logger groups. *Jeez, they still burn my ass. Each morning they get up from their wood frame two thousand dollar beds, take their designer watches and jewellery from their fifteen hundred dollar wood dressers, leave their five hundred thousand dollar jack pine framed house, drive their one point five children to school in their fifty thousand dollar gas guzzling SUV (silly, useless, vehicle) that consumes a non-renewable resource (wood is renewable), go to the office where they sit a their three thousand dollar oak desk and stare at their wood framed pictures or read their wood product newspapers and magazines. Then they attend a meeting where the table and chairs are made of white ash that cost the company ten thousand dollars, pass around two hundred pounds of meeting notes (made from paper) and get their secretaries to print off another two hundred pounds of paper with the obligatory changes. And finally, there was the after-meeting ritual bathroom visit where they: wiped their butts with paper products, dried there hands with paper products and drank water from a paper cup. Man, I'm on a roll and I'm close to making my point to myself. Not there yet, so I'll continue.*

Ah, the weekend cometh. Time to put the kids in the "truck" (when you live in the city and have a SUV, you proudly declared it was a truck), throw the wood framed canoe on top, pulled the wood frame camper behind, went to a state or provincial park where the "Walt Disney" forests were manicured, not managed, and then, with as much indignation as their egos could muster, tied themselves to an over-mature tree to protest logging.

Or better still:

Put the kids in the truck, go to three hundred thousand dollar timber framed, cedar-sided cottage, put on a wood fire (it's OK—they didn't cut it, they bought it), make a phone call to hire a local to cut the trees obstructing their view of the lake and make a sign out of wood and cardboard (another paper product) so they can protest logging on Crown Land (government managed) somewhere behind their cottage.

My emotions are overtaking my common sense again. What else did I like? Let's see: Timber Harvesting, Sustainable Forest Management (a myth!), Forest Disturbance (the stuff on wildfire was interesting), Forest Pathology (diseases) and Pest Control (man, did we pull some boners in the early days with pesticide application) and Timber Supply Analysis (what's out there and when can we cut it).

What didn't I like? I hated the bullshit on Policy and Planning, and Taxation Considerations (avoidance). Then there was Resource Economics and Industrial Organization (as if forest economy was tied solely to the forest industry). Now, according to their web site, the university has introduced ecology into its courses. As I recall, there are courses on Eco-Physiology (physical and chemical phenomena of the ecosystem—heavy stuff), Ecology and Economics and just plain Ecology. That has to throw in a whole new dynamic into the mix.

Let's see if I get this right. Trees are not just meant to be harvested. Here's some for the eco-tourist, who wants to see old growth forest (stuff we couldn't get at sixty years ago). And guess what, there's money to be made in eco-tourism, so don't cut trees, look at them and play on them. Problem is, too many tourists are hard on the landscape. They build platforms on the trees so they can glide through the bush like Rocky the Flying Squirrel, only in a harness. Armies of them pound trails throughout the forest, compacting the soil so root growth is inhibited and confusing wildlife that don't know which way to run. Wally pictured little miniature "animal balls" in a pin-ball machine bouncing off tree blockades and being swatted by short, stubby paddle-arms with tourist faces.

Here's some trees for the creepy-crawlies (trees got really old, died, fell, rotted, were invaded by bugs, eaten, shat out and became soil, a bed for new growth). Don't cut that tree! It has a hole in it. Probably inhabited by bats or a red squirrel. Stay half a mile away from that heronry. They're hatching eggs (when they're not squawking, fighting or shitting).

You can't cut near that lake! It's a cold water fishery. No, not that lake either, it's reserved for a fly-in fishing business. Ah, come on! I shouldn't even have to tell you that you have no business near that body of water. Look at all the cottagers on it, including the local member-of-parliament's cottage. Your skidders and heavy equipment will cause soil run-off into the lake. Gee, that would compete with the out-house and ancient field-bed run-off, spilt gasoline and oil, and empty beer and liquor containers. Hardly enough room for water, let alone soil. Bite my tongue. Oh yeah, this is just a brain seizure.

Wally felt it was tough for the forest industry, everyone competing for the same piece of pie. Ontario was a mosaic of land and lakes. There were a thousand little battles going on in every crook and cranny of the province, the NIMBY's (not in my back yard) against the forest industry.

He also acknowledged grudgingly, that most of the concerns associated with land use were valid. He did not, however, miss the public forums and open houses required as a part of forest management planning: angry people, fingers thrust like rifle barrels, rage-red faces, words of defiance and spittle broadcast before the brain had time to engage. He would have to stand there, wearing a mask of gentle concern and understanding and swallow the *Buckley's cough syrup* insults and threats. *I can feel my blood pressure rising—time to move on.* Wally continued to flip through the album. He knew he had to find something that didn't bend him out of shape, or he would never get to sleep.

MY LIFE NORTH OF THE 49TH PARALLEL IN ONTARIO—the four summers Wally spent working as a grunt in a lodge in northwestern Ontario—the summers that had shaped his appreciation for the bush. He was bitten by the "bush bug". Every curve on a bush road, every rise and fall on a forest trail, every stream crossing and every change in forest type and pattern was a new adventure for him. In his four years during university semesters, he realized early on that he enjoyed those field sessions at the Cloquet Forestry Centre the most. Classroom education was OK, but practical application was even better. He knew he was destined to be a field forester, one who practiced his craft on foot and not in an office. *Man, was I ever naive!*

As each plastic page glided in an arc to reveal new memories, Wally was taken back to his early days on his first real job with Carmichael Lumber. It was run by two brothers, Jason and Rick. They not only had a saw mill outside of town; they also had a timber license, compliments of the Ontario government, for a forest area around White River. The license area was the size of the state of Rhode Island, daunting at first blush but it paled in comparison to the amount of forest land in Ontario, seventy million hectares (one hundred and seventy-three million acres)!

Wow, a hundred and seventy-three million acres available for harvest, ladies and gentlemen! However, let's take a closer look. 90% is publicly owned, or "Crown" land. Now we're at a hundred and fifty-six million acres—still lots of forest land. But wait a minute, only 31% of this is "production" forest, or forests able to grow and sustain trees desirable for "producing" wood products. Now we're down to forty-eight million acres. Now the competition is heating up.

Wally knew that "non-production" forests could still be used for other activities such as recreation and/or protection for wildlife, soil structure and geographical features. *So why didn't the tree huggers confine their activities to non-production forests? Big reason 1: because of site and soil variation, production and non-production forests co-mingled. Usually you had to travel through one to get to the other. Big reason 2: non-production forests, which tended to grow in swamps and on bed rock, didn't have the same ethereal attraction as the "tall-tree", robust, production forests. So now, everyone was competing for 31% of the publicly owned forest-land.*

But, times they were a-changin'. The one thing, above all the rest, that the fisher and hunter wanted was fishing and hunting opportunities. There was either too much competition or not enough product left in the production forest areas. The one thing that the eco-tourist wanted was solitude (until he or she got bored or lonely or needed an urban fix) and it wasn't as crowded in areas of non-production forests. The eco-tourists were also voyeurs—they wanted the opportunity to see flora and fauna, not to kill it or eat it (until they ran out of bottled water and meals-in-a-pouch). Plants and animals were generally indiscriminate; they would live in non-productive forests as well as productive forests. In fact, animals were often pushed there because of human activity (eventually the eco-tourists will push them back to productive forests, and so on, and so forth). And the hard-core snowmobiler and ATVer rumbled so fast through the bush that they didn't see anything, anyway. Stick a trail anywhere with a lodge and beer at the end of it, and they will come. Production forest was not the prerequisite it used to be.

Boy, my opinions are wearing me down. I'm actually getting sleepy. I'll visit the Carmichael brothers some other time. Wally closed the photo album, drained the last of his coffee/Bailey concoction, rose from the chair with the customary twinges and cracks provided generously by his body, and shuffled to the bedroom. As he crawled in, he silently said goodnight to Julie, the girls, the bear cub and the white pine. He finished off with his little night-time superstitious ritual. He wasn't sure he believed in God, but knew a wise man hedged his bets. Each night took on a different theme. Tonight's *was acknowledgement. God, as much as I hate to admit it, I do think you're out there. My proof is what you've generously provided here on earth. Now, I'm no different than the rest. I'm like a kid with a new toy that gets tired of it. I have either discarded or destroyed the gifts You've provided. Jewel used to forgive me. I hope You can, too. Good night.*

Wally drifted off and seemed to be caught in that fitful world between consciousness and deep sleep, slipping into dreamscapes. His dreams were like the evening news— no one theme, each story non-connected; some were just fillers and meant nothing. The last dream he would recall later on, was one of smoke. It seemed so real that he would swear he smelled it, felt it—an insidious, drifting, searching smoke, like a thin, intoxicating veil drifting down over his body. It began as a gentle lover's touch, then an enveloping, stimulating pressure as it climbed astride him, then wispy, narrow hands sliding to his neck, gently covering his mouth and nose, unspoken reassurance as suffocation began. *This* dream felt so real.

PART 2

THE FIRE AND INITIAL ATTACK

The old knight stands bent and weary,
The sword now heavy in his hands.
He fears it will take the intensity of youth
To carry on this war with dragons.
He must search out a new champion
And steel himself to pass on the way of the sword.

Wednesday, July 20th, 2005 between 09:00 and 17:00 hours

Chapter 10

DAY 1: WEDNESDAY, JULY 20, 09:00 HOURS, EAST FIRE REGION, FALCON RESPONSE CENTRE

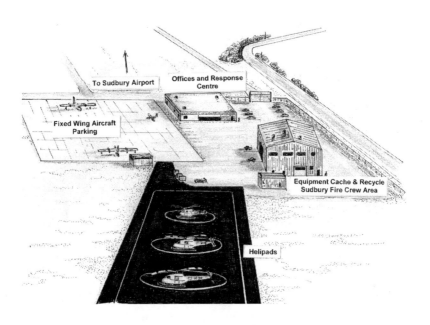

"THERE ARE PRESENTLY ONE HUNDRED AND TEN FIRES DECLARED OUT, forty-seven fires under control, twenty-two fires being held and eight fires not under control in the East Fire Region." Shiela Monahan, the regional fire intelligence officer was in the process of briefing the regional fire duty officer (FDO) and his staff in the fire centre. She would normally use the acronyms, OUT, UCO, BHE and NUC, for the stages of control, but they had a visiting entourage of high level Ministry of Natural Resources' staff attending the briefing and she wanted to keep the questions to a minimum. The information could be daunting and a lot of detail had to be covered.

Sheila was diminutive, quick and always active. Staff referred to her affectionately as *Chickadee*. Her short-cropped auburn hair perched atop her head like the cap on the little bird. Her dark eyes sparkled under long lashes and her figure belied the three children she struggled to deliver and raise. Her husband had passed away two years earlier. Contrary to any reaction her stature might suggest, she commanded attention. Sheila knew her stuff. Educated in Forestry at the University of Toronto, having worked four summers in the fire crew system during her education, and possessing a mind that consumed and filtered detail economically, the fire program snapped her up without hesitation.

Two of the dignitaries were regional directors. It was an atypical organizational reporting relationship within the fire program. There were two fire regions in the province of Ontario—east and west. Within the East Fire Region (EFR), there were two MNR administrative regions that delivered resource related management. These were the Northeast and Southern Regions, each with a regional director. The head of fire within each fire region (East and West) was called the fire program manager and he or she reported to their respective regional directors. The EFR fire program manager was therefore responsible to two regional directors. In essence the fire program manager was providing a fire prevention, protection and response service to the regional directors, who in turn provided resource management (e.g., forest management, lands and waters management, fish and wildlife management and Ontario Parks) to the province.

In order to ensure coordinated fire management delivery to the province as a whole, a central branch out of Sault Ste. Marie called the Aviation and Fire Management Branch (AFFMB) interacted directly with each fire program manager and his/her staff between fire centres during the fire season (April 1 to October 31). The two fire regions (east and west) could be competing for the same resources to respond to fires. It was the fire duty officer at the AFFMB in Sault Ste. Marie who would deal directly with the fire duty officers in the East and West Regional Fire Centres and have the last word in any conflicting requests.

Although the AFFM Branch provided daily strategic and tactical direction to the two fire regions, there was a good reason why those fire program managers reported to the regional directors responsible for resource management. A totally centralized service could have a tendency to become an entity unto itself and lose touch with the programs that required the services. In this case the service was fire protection. There was also a danger that a centralized service might inadvertently develop program strategy in isolation. It was imperative that the managers of the natural resources had a strong hand in developing fire management strategy. After all, it was their responsibility to manage Ontario's resources. It would also be through these same resource managers that Ontario's public would be privy to and influence fire management strategy.

THE ONE HUNDRED AND TEN 'OUT' fires were fires that had started in the EFR since April 1. The UCO, BHE and NUC fires had occurred in the last two weeks—seventy-seven fires, eight of which they still didn't have a handle on (NUC). Sheila continued with her briefing. "Right now, the NUC fires causing most concern are WAW (Wawa) 42, presently at twenty-two hectares, SAU (Sault Ste. Marie) 13 at forty-four hectares, and SUD (Sudbury) 22 at one hundred and two hectares. Most of the fires are burning in M-2 fuels, boreal mixed wood stands. Yesterday's fire behaviour patterns on these fires included fires that were running and torching with average rates of spread at ten metres per minute."

Of the eight staff and four visitors in the room, none was paying more attention than the regional fire duty officer, Rick Sampson. He was the "queen bee" of the fire program. He had full command and control of resources within the EFR and made the final decision on fire response tactics. Administratively, he reported to the fire response coordinator, one of four coordinators who in turn reported to the fire program manager. The other coordinators were responsible for fire equipment, fire service and fire integration and management (integrating with other agencies such as municipal fire organizations) respectively. The response coordinator, Rick's supervisor, built and managed a response organization within the fire region. Rick shared his role with one other person. Between the two of them, they were either on duty or on call 24/7 during the fire season and made the necessary fire response decisions on a daily basis. Someone always had his or her hand on the controls of fire response.

On a daily basis, however, the fire duty officer was never left 'hanging to dry'. An executive officer (EO) was always available for guidance, counsel, and, if necessary, direction. The EO's focus on a daily basis was the big picture. The FDO dealt with fire planning and response. The Executive Officer kept his or her finger on the pulse of resource management concerns across the East Fire Region. At any given time, the EO could be one of the four coordinators, the fire program manager himself or even a resource manager or coordinator brought in to assist in heavy fire situations. Today the EO was the fire program manager, the fire program's "top of the food chain" person, Doug Rainville, presently one of the visitors sitting in on the morning briefing.

Besides the FDO calling the shots in the fire centre, and the fire intelligence officer, Sheila, who gathered and analyzed information, there was a logistics officer who arranged for resources, an aerial operations manager who managed aircraft within the fire region, an aerial suppression officer who managed aircraft that were dedicated strictly to fire attack. There was also a response centre clerk, a personnel clerk and a radio operator.

Rick Sampson looked around the room. *God, I'm tired already and it's only 09:00.* Rick was at the end of his "10 days on" stretch, but he wouldn't get a break anytime soon. His counter-part was sick, and there wasn't a replacement to be had for at least another four days. It was the two and three a.m. calls from the answering service that were the killers. To top it off, at age fifty-four, Rick was less than a year away from possible retirement. Tall with a brush of salt and pepper hair kept short, Rick was pale, his skin slack and grey, eyes red-rimmed and watery. He had looked in the mirror that morning while shaving with mild shock. *You look like crap, buddy. This job is wearing you down. Not retiring is not an option.* He had always kept himself fit since his early days as a fire crew leader. He knew it wasn't the lack of daily physical activity on the job that would get him. It would be the continual stress associated with making right or wrong decisions that could have terrible consequences. To top it off, he was now on blood pressure medication—*at fifty-four!*

He looked around the fire centre, slack-jawed, eyes at half-mast and wished that the furniture, displays and monitors could give him moral support. The centre was an efficient room. Too much floor space would invite what he and his staff secretly called "JAFO's". When someone new entered, the furtive looks among staff mirrored simultaneous thoughts, *here comes another JAFO.* They even had a hat made up to hand out to a visitor they knew would receive the response with a sense of humour and not take exception to the lightly-intended insult. Of course, as soon as the hat was received, the question followed, "What's a JAFO?" The response was reserved for the fire duty officer whose authority would temper any unexpected reaction. With eyebrows raised in the "innocent" position and a smile that said "hook, line and sinker", the FDO would pause then respond, "Just Another Friggin' Observer!"

In the very centre of the room sat a six-sided table with a pedestal chair assigned to each side. It was, in fact, a desk with each of its occupants facing in, maximizing face-to-face communication. Perched on each desk was a monitor, keyboard and conference telephone. Through the monitors, each person could access the tools and data required to do his or her jobs. This was the work station for the fire centre team. Here, the fire duty officer and staff practiced their trade. The final two sides were reserved for zone duty officers when they were required. The FDO, along with the executive officer might decide that decision-making help was needed. A zone duty officer would exercise the power of the FDO over a specific geographic area or project fire(s).

Each wall had a purpose. The south wall had two ceiling to floor maps. One displayed the south half of the EFR; the other displayed the north half. The maps were laminated to metal so magnets could be set on them. Round magnets, the diameter of pen caps, represented "fires". Red magnets were NUC fires (not under control). Orange magnets were BHE (being held) and yellow were UCO (under control but not yet out). Each magnet would have a fire number written on it using a non-permanent marker. There was a complete set of small rectangular shaped magnets, each with a fire crew number on them. There was an assortment of other rectangular magnets with pictures of the various air attack resources, each one also identified with a number.

Consequently, a red, round magnet representing an active fire could have, for example three fire crew magnets next to it. As well, it might have rectangular magnets with, for example, one a picture of a CL415 water bomber with a number T-6 (or tanker 6), one with a picture of a Birddog or lead aircraft with BD-4 on it (Birddog 4) and a couple with pictures of helicopters, one a light helicopter with H-07 and a medium helicopter picture with H-39. So, the round red magnet in this example would be Sudbury fire 20 (it was in the Sudbury administrative district on the map); it was Not Under Control (red) and had three fire crews, one heavy water bomber, one Birddog aircraft and two helicopters assigned to it. A fire duty officer now had a visual fire situation to help with the decision making process. In the macro perspective, he or she could see the whole fire region and patterns of fire. In the micro, he or she could see what was dedicated to a single fire.

The east wall was dedicated to six monitors, three large and three small. Each had a purpose or a dedicated number of purposes. All provided fire or weather data to assist in making appropriated strategic and tactical decisions.

Tucked in the top left hand corner was the chart showing the "Fire Weather Index Classes." Every fire person in the province cut their teeth on the numerical data on the chart. The series of numbers was the code that would tell a fire person how easily a fire would start (called the Fine Fuel Moisture Code or FFMC), how deeply it would burn (Drought Moisture Code or DMC and Drought Code or DC), how fast it would grow (Initial Spread Index, ISI), and how much of the available fuel would likely be consumed (Build Up Index, BUI). The final numeric rating, the Fire Weather Index, FWI, was a general numeric rating of fire weather. Fire weather stations were set up across the province, and data such as temperature, relative humidity, precipitation and wind speed and direction was collected twice a day. From this source data, the indices were calculated for each station and a "fire weather picture" could be formed across the province.

Fire Weather Index Classes						
	FFMC	DMC	DC	ISI	BUI	FWI
Low	0-80	0-15	0-140	0-2.2	0-20	0-3
Moderate	81-86	16-30	141-240	2.3-5.0	21-36	4-10
High	87-90	31-50	241-340	5.1-10.0	37-60	11-22
Extreme	91+	51+	341+	10.1+	61+	23+

How easily fires will ignite

How much of the duff layer will be consumed

How deeply fires will burn

How quickly fires will spread

How much of the larger fuels will be consumed

General numeric rating

Most sectors were either in, approaching or exceeding the "extreme" ranges.

The north wall was used to display hard copy weather data and aerial detection planning. Hard copy actual weather and forecasted weather data as well as actual and forecasted fire weather indices were posted on a large panel. The daily aerial detection plan was displayed on a large map of the fire region. Beside it were two displays showing configurations of ramp parking for aircraft at the Falcon Response Centre, the name given to the office and warehouse complex for the EFR, next to the Sudbury airport. The ramp, or parking area, could accommodate two CL415 heavy water bombers, two amphibious Twin Otter aircraft used for water bombing or personnel movement and two Birddog aircraft that lead the CL415s to their targets and controlled airspace.

The west wall afforded access to the radio room and the logistics officer's room. In addition, the five phases of fire response activity were posted. They were simple guidelines used as one of the many tools to assist the fire duty officer with his or her decisions. If a sector (area within the fire region) was in Phase 5, the fire hazard class was extreme, and there was potential for multiple fire starts.

PHASE 5

HAZARD CLASS – ESCALATED

FFMC > 90
BUI   > 60
ISI   > 10.0
Intensity Class   4 - 5

> ➤ Potential for multiple starts
> ➤ 50% of resources committed to active fires

CONDITIONS:
> ➤ Fires readily start with potential for spotting
> ➤ Numerous large active fires present
> ➤ High to extreme rates of spread in all fuel types
> ➤ High to extreme fire intensities
> ➤ Control efforts at fire heads may fail

INITIAL ATTACK:
> ➤ All crew on, except those off as per Fire Staff Working Time Guidelines
> ➤ All available crews on red or yellow alert
> ➤ Preposition crews to areas of expected fire occurrence
> ➤ Conduct multiple crew dispatch
> ➤ Consider increasing crew size by supplementing with qualified Extra Fire Fighters
> ➤ Hire Type 2 crews (sustained attack)
> ➤ Consider replacing Type 1 (initial attack) crews with Type 2 on low intensity initial attack fires

---

That was exactly the situation they would be into by tomorrow. Rick knew he was at a stage-two stress level where the messages from the brain to the senses missed turns and ran stop signs. At stage four the messages wouldn't even leave the brainpan, and they would "bag him and boot him out". He looked around the room fondly at the staff that supported him. Some were relaxed, sitting back in their chairs. Some were more intense, leaning forward, but all were all focused. *Geez, I'm supposed to be the alpha male here. I can't let then see me crumbling inside. Time to pull myself together and get on track.*

Chapter 11

DAY 1: 09:30 HOURS, EAST FIRE REGION, FALCON RESPONSE CENTRE

RICK SAMPSON RUBBED A HAND ACROSS HIS FACE as if trying to wash away the weariness and anxiety within. The silence in the room was deafening, and he needed to kick start himself. *Ask a friggin' question.*

"What happened with fire perimeter growth yesterday, Sheila?" Sheila referred to her notes. "SUDBURY 22 put on the most growth, Rick. It went from forty-three hectares the previous day to one hundred and two hectares as of 18:00 hours yesterday. Apparently it got into some C4 fuels and took a run."

Rick instinctively knew that C4 or immature jack pine could crown. Of the six stages of fire spread, smouldering, creeping, running, torching, crowning and spotting or jump fires, it was crowning, or fire being carried through the upper canopy due to wind, that was a fire fighters worst nightmare.

"Rick, WAWA 40 has some potential to be a real problem. It started at a point source ignition due to lightning at 16:00 hours yesterday and grew to twenty two hectares by 18:00 hours. Wawa's TIP (tactical input plan) is late this morning. There's no telling what happened overnight. To make matters worse, it was burning in M4, dead balsam fir/mixed wood fuels, and we have no resources committed to it. It's just being monitored."

"Any values to be concerned about, Sheila?"

"The closest cottage community is on Berford Lake and is six kilometres to the east. There is no cut timber in the vicinity, but

61

Mackey Lumber has a thousand hectares of critical wood supply to the north and west. We're also a little concerned about the town of Hornepayne if this fire runs and puts up a lot of smoke."

The morning briefing was part of the planning process. From it, an updated message would go out to all attack bases in the East Fire Region, the fire duty officer in the West Fire Region in Dryden and the Provincial Fire Centre at AFFMB in Sault Ste. Marie. This updated message was called the Strategic Operating Plan (SOP) Update. A Strategic Operating Plan proper would be developed in the late afternoon and sent out as the fire response plan for the following day. In short, two briefing/planning sessions were held, and two plans were developed each day. Each sector within the fire region also had daily input into the plan. Their input was called the Tactical Input Plan. It provided details on:

- Observed fire behaviour,
- The status of active fires,
- Potential problems for the next burning period,
- Fire crews available for the next day,
- Fire crews required for the next day,
- Fire crew alerts and locations for the next day,
- Other fire staff alerted and locations for the next day,
- Ground tanker (fire truck) status and requirements,
- Aircraft status and requirements,
- Aerial detection requirements,
- Special fire prevention issues or concerns, and
- A contact name and number for after hours.

Although the province was broken up into twenty-two administrative resource districts, the key boundaries associated with the fire program were the sectors. In the East Fire Region, the east half of Ontario, there were six sectors. There were also two areas designated OFR, outside the fire region. The OFR area in southern Ontario had very little potential for forest fire and protection for structural and grass fires were provided through municipal fire brigades. The OFR area north, James Bay/Hudson Bay country, was relatively unpopulated and had limited or inaccessible timber value. Here, when fires did occur, they were monitored. If one of the few First Nations communities in the area was threatened, suppression activity, community protection and, if necessary, evacuation would take place.

One of the visitors, the Southern regional director, looked at the sector map and then raised his hand. Sheila gave a slight nod of approval. "Sheila, how did you determine the boundaries for the six zones?"

"Good question, sir. She looked to the full-wall map behind her.

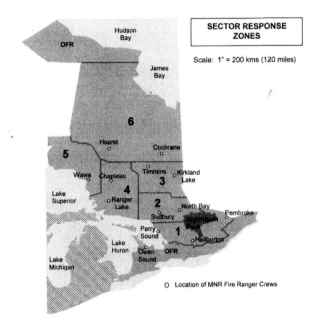

SECTOR RESPONSE ZONES

Scale: 1" = 200 kms (120 miles)

O Location of MNR Fire Ranger Crews

"The key elements associated with the sectors are fire arrival potential largely based on fire history, forest fuel types, fire ranger crew and aerial resource location and subsequently, attack radius and resource access." She pointed to Sector 4 on the map. "Obviously we are limited to locations where we can house fire crews and keep aircraft. We have a camp complete with bunkhouses and a cookery at Ranger Lake where we keep seven crews during the fire season. It also has clear areas for helicopter access. We have an intermediate helicopter there, an A-Star, 350B2.

Chapleau to the north has an airport where we keep a CL415 heavy water bomber and its "lead" or "Birddog" aircraft as well as ten MNR ranger crews and a medium helicopter, a Bell 204B. Given the history of fires in the area, the mixed wood and coniferous fuels available to burn and the fact that this is an active forest harvest area, we feel the locations are a good fit. Having said that, the time to an initial attack is crucial and the sector lines are guideline boundaries that tell us we've reached the effective distance for attack." Sheila looked towards the regional director for understanding. He nodded his approval. It was time to continue with the briefing.

Rick interjected. "Sheila, what have you got for weather?"

"Well, Jack's back from the West Fire Region, so I'll let him brief you on today's weather and forecasted weather."

Rick looked over at Jack. Jack Grossman was one of his favourite people. Short, as bald as a cue ball, slightly rotund with a bushy, steel grey moustache, Jack was always upbeat and brimming with humour. He was the regional weather technician and brought years of weather experience, twenty-five of which were in the Canadian Armed Forces. Rick smiled. *Know wonder he's always upbeat. He's on a pension and also has a job he loves with no pressure. Everyone knows how unpredictable weather is, although he's batting a good average at 75%.*

Rick smiled and inquired with a touch of mirth, "Welcome back, Jack. How was your vacation?"

Jack took the bait. He puffed out his chest to compete with his considerable stomach, looked around for a sympathetic comrade among all the smiling faces and blurted out, "You call that a vacation? Ten days on a project fire, two hundred miles north of Sioux Lookout and sleeping in a prospector tent with five other losers who snored like bull elephants on an air mattress that leaked like a fish net and was no more than six inches wide." He took a quick breath. "And mosquitoes the size of vultures with beaks as long as boat hooks. You call that a vacation?"

The air operations manager jumped into the fray. "I heard from a reliable source that they had to double up on their food orders because you were there."

Jack shot back, "It was like being on a forced diet! I've lost so much weight, that my wife says if I turn sideways, and stick out my tongue, I look like a zipper!"

"More like a penguin with a short beak", someone blurted out.

"OK people, let's get back on track." Rick liked these tension breakers, but it was time to get on with it. He felt a wave of fatigue and nausea wash over his body. *Maybe I'm pregnant.*

Jack began his routine. "Let me start with the obvious". He stepped over to his computer, punched a few keys, and a map of the East Fire Region popped up onto a large screen at the back of the room. A large slash of red, running northwest to southeast, engulfed an area covering fifty by two hundred kilometres, ten thousand square kilometres in all. It stretched through sectors 4 and 5 with its heaviest concentration in sector 5, Wawa. The map was a product of the province's lightning locator system. A series of stations across the province collected lightning data as it occurred, relayed the data to a central computer and extrapolated the inputs to show "real time" lightning. This particular map was selected to show the storm and its resulting lightning as of this morning, 08:00 hours. Jack could punch up another screen that would show the lightning as it struck.

"As most of you are aware, it's the positive strikes, the cloud-to-ground, that concern us." He punched another key. Much of the band disappeared, leaving a series of "plus sign" icons, separate and in groups. "Here are your positives. According to the data, we had approximately ten thousand cloud-to-ground strikes overnight." He punched another set of keys. "Now eliminate the strikes over large bodies of water, and that brings us down to approximately sixty-five hundred."

Rick looked over at Sheila and interrupted. "What does that tell us, Sheila?"

Sheila did not hesitate. "Usually, when the "DMC's", she looked over at the visitors, "Drought Moisture Codes, a relative indicator of how much of the duff layers over the soil will burn, are in the moderate to high range, 21 to 50, we can expect one fire for every five hundred positive lightning strikes on receptive fuels." She turned directly to the visitors and scanned their faces for understanding. There were no blank stares, so she continued. "Right now, the DMC's are, as an average in the area covered by lightning, sitting at 85. 51 plus is extreme. Although this isn't exact science, we believe we can now expect a fire for every twenty-five positive lightning strikes." She could almost hear the cranium wheels grinding, and waited for someone to jump in.

Today's executive officer, Doug Rainville, raised his hand. He knew the answer, but asked the question on behalf of the other visitors who may not have had the confidence to do so. Sheila nodded. "Does that mean we can expect over two hundred and fifty fires from that lightning?"

"Two hundred and sixty to be exact, Doug. But it's not that simple. Depending on the fuels struck by lightning, a fire may ignite and creep, ignite and go to ground, ignite and run, or ignite, lose fuels and extinguish itself. In this scenario, we usually plan that 50% of the estimated number of fires will actually become fires requiring a response."

Rick knew what was coming. *The floodgates are beginning to open.*

The Northeast regional director, Norm Bennett, a tall, thin man, who felt he had the most at stake given the location of the lightning, waded in. "Isn't that risky to ignore the other 50%?"

Sheila looked quickly to Rick, and Rick turned to the executive officer as if to say "it's your round here". The EO took the cue and responded. "It's a risk we're prepared to take. There isn't a province in Canada or a state associated with our neighbours to the south that can afford the resources it takes to organize and prepare for the perfect fire season." He was of course, referring to a severe fire season using the term "perfect" as in the book and movie "The Perfect Storm."

Everyone caught on. "Having said that, we don't ignore that fact that all the stars could line up against us. I sat down with the other fire coordinators and the fire duty officer three days ago. The long-range weather forecast coupled with our drought conditions *and* the fire behaviour experienced in the West Fire Region painted a pretty bleak picture. Rick, so I don't tie up your morning briefing session, I intend to have a meeting with the regional directors and the fire coordinators here after your briefing. Could you join us then?"

"Not a problem. OK, where were we? Oh yes. Sorry Jack, continue with your weather briefing."

Jack took them to the weather maps and data, the short term and long term forecast. He explained how the high pressure system was moving very slowly, almost stationary, and how temperatures were going to peak at the low to mid thirties or high eighties to low nineties, Fahrenheit. Today, however, in Sectors 4 and 5, the situation was critical.

"Weather in sector 4 is a carbon copy of sector 5. Temperatures will be excessive, mid thirties. What concerns me though, is the winds and relative humidity. We anticipate a cross-over." Jack looked around for effect. If his face could talk, it would say "Are we ever in deep shit!" Everyone in the room with the exception of the two regional directors knew what the term "cross-over" meant: when the relative humidity was lower than the temperature.

Rick thought back to his days as a project fire boss, now called an incident commander in the ICS system. As a rule of thumb, as soon as the relative humidity dropped below 40%, a fire would become problematic. It might be active above 40%, but below it, expect movement and perimeter growth if you didn't have a handle on it. He recalled watching fires from the air that, at 11:00 hours and when there was no wind to speak of appeared dormant, little to no flame and light smoke. At 13:00 hours, that same fire, still with little wind, would start to "pop up". Two to four metre flame length, running, torching and dense fingers of smoke would appear simultaneously, as if on cue. The RH had dropped below 40%. With a cross-over, where the RH actually dropped below the temperature, all bets on fire containment were off.

Jack continued. "At 14:00 hours, the RH's will be in the mid twenties." Again, a pause for effect. "Now for the bad news." A collective groan rolled out of ten mouths and dropped to the floor like a wet blanket. "Wind speeds today, at the peak burning period will be thirty kph, gusting to forty-five."

Rick swallowed. A cotton ball lodged in his throat. "Long range, Jack", came out as a dry "croak".

"Well, not much better. This high-pressure system is moving so slowly that we won't be in the centre of the high for at least two days. You can expect the same winds until Saturday at the earliest."

"Any precipitation in the forecast?"

"Nothing in the foreseeable future."

Rick turned to Sheila. He knew that answer to his question, but for the benefit of others, he asked it anyway. "Fire arrival predictions?"

Sheila had already entered the data into the computer. "Based on the predicted fire weather indices, we can expect the following." A last flick of the finger and a coded map popped up on another large monitor at the back of the room. Sheila continued. "For today, Outside Fire Region (OFR), five person and zero lightning caused fires. Sector 1, five person and zero lightning caused fires. Sector 2, five person and ten lightning caused fires. Sector 3, five person and five lightning caused fires. Sector 4, three person and twenty lightning caused fires. Sector 5, three person and twenty lightning caused fires. Finally, sector 6, two person and zero lightning." Then with a wave of her hand, "Tada, a grand total of eighty-three fires predicted today for the East Fire Region."

The worried northeast regional director was not impressed with her attempt at levity and jumped in. "I thought you were predicting around one hundred and thirty lightning fires. I count only forty in the three sectors associated with the Northeast Region where lightning occurred."

A cool Sheila responded quietly. "Your math is correct, sir. We expect the other ninety fires to rear their ugly heads over the next three days."

The RD's eyes widened at the enormity of the situation, and his normal cadaver-like pallor increased three shades to a crimson red. Rick thought he resembled a thermometer with its red mercury busting to get out. *Geez, I could use a drink about now. Have to wait, need to take control.* He interrupted the RD before he became the focus of attention.

"Sheila, escaped fire?"

"We expect three in Sector 4 and two in Sector 5."

Before the RD could become apoplectic and swallow his tongue, Rick continued. "Fire behaviour predictions?"

"Not good Rick. Sectors 3, 4 and 5 are our biggest concerns—M-4 fuels." She looked towards the visitors. "Dead balsam fir/mixed wood, green state with 30% budworm-killed fir, will be into intensity class 5 and approaching intensity class 6. That means aggressive surface fire with torching and intermittent crown fire with a spread rate of eight to ten metres per minute."

The stricken RD regained his composure and squeaked, "In laymen's terms, what does that mean?"

"Well sir, with intensities greater than ten thousand kilowatts per metre of fire, a head fire will be very difficult to control. We can't put people at the head, I mean the front. We can, however, attack the flanks or use "indirect" suppression tactics such as aerial burn-out from a sound control line such as a lake or river."

Rick wanted more. "Sheila, with our present drought conditions, I think those sectors are closer to the M-3 or leafless state for the mixed wood."

"Well, that puts us into continuous crowning where the right fuels are available."

"What's going to happen with a crown fire at those rates of spread in an hour?"

Sheila flipped open her *Field Guide to the Canadian Forest Fire Behaviour Prediction System* and leafed to the appropriate page.

"It will have spread approximately five hundred to six hundred metres or one half of a kilometre in one hour."

Rick knew this would be beyond his span of control and that he would have to beef up his team. He would talk to the EO about a zone duty officer who would deal specifically with Sectors 4 and 5. The mood in the room was sombre; everyone knew there were long, pressure-filled days ahead. The planning session continued.

Chapter 12

DAY 1: 10:30 HOURS,
CHAPLEAU AIRPORT

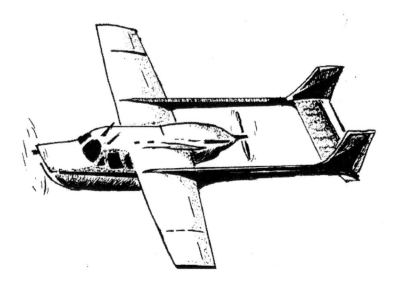

ANDY RADFORD APPROACHED THE CESSNA 337 SKYMASTER sitting on the airstrip with more than a little trepidation. It was his first assignment as a fire detection observer. Armed with an aerial detection UTM base map book and an observer checklist, he looked back towards the airport for the pilot. Andy was a "detail man" and preparation was important to him, so he had done his homework on the 337. Other fire crewmembers had affectionately called him "Anal Andy".

Aerial fire detecting was something new to him. Although his home base was Wawa, this assignment had taken him to Chapleau, a base location for aerial detection at the Chapleau airport. His primary job was second in command, crew boss, on a three-person fire crew. Because of the high fire hazard and significant fire activity and work-load in the East Fire Region, his crew had been beefed up to four people. An *EFF* or extra fire fighter was added a month ago so the crew had optimally consisted of his crew leader, himself and two fire fighters. Because Ron, his crew leader, had broken an ankle on their last fire attack, and Sarah, the EFF person had taken sick, the crew was no longer functional. It was common practice under these circumstances to redistribute staff to other crews or assignments; there was never a lack of work. At twenty-two years of age, Andy was already a veteran with four fire seasons under his belt and twenty-four initial attacks by helicopter. Consequently, he was familiar with spotting smoke from the air and a natural for this assignment.

As second in command on a crew, he was no stranger to the detection mapping system used in Ontario. The Universal Transverse Mercator system was used in many other parts of the world as well. In simple terms, if you could envision a map of the world under the UTM system, it would be divided into numerically identified zones. Across the globe, there were sixty longitudinal zones from west to east, each six degrees wide, and then twenty latitudinal zones from south to north, each eight degrees high. The province of Ontario was comprised of zones 15 through to 18. Wawa and area was in zone 16 U. The 'zone' designation was necessary to make the coordinates unique over the entire globe.

Each zone was represented with a series of maps called base maps. Each base map had grid lines spaced every kilometre. The vertical grid lines determined a block's east-west position. The horizontal grid lines determined that block's north-south position. A fixed point, such as a fire could be easily determined and given a numerical location. With today's technology, global positioning hardware in aircrafts, it was easy to locate and transmit a fire's location numerically both by latitude and longitude or base map block number.

Andy's role was simply to serve as another pair of eyes for the pilot. Andy had convinced the aerial operations manager at Sudbury to allow him to do his own navigation as a learning experience, ergo the base map book. Normally, the pilot would just punch the fire's coordinates in on his console's GPS, but Andy wanted to see if he could "track by map".

His focus returned to the Cessna. The 337 was a unique looking aircraft, not your typical twin engine aircraft with an engine fixed to each wing. The Skymaster had twin Continental IO-360-C fuel injected, flat six piston engines fore and aft of its fuselage. Sometimes called the "push me/pull-you" or "suck and blow" aircraft, it also sported twin tails separated by a flat aluminium-clad frame. With a total length of close to thirty feet and a wing-span of thirty-eight feet, this land based aircraft served well as an aerial fire detection platform.

The wing-over-cab configuration and large windows provided "no-interference", excellent viewing for the observer and pilot. It had an extensive range of over eleven hundred and fifty kilometres, at a cruising speed of three hundred and seven kilometres. It was also capable of low-speed flight, a bonus for aerial fire detection, since the observer had to gather considerable data when assessing a wild fire.

Andy had discovered through his research that the Cessna 337 was introduced in 1964 and a total of nineteen hundred and fifty-one were produced. Five hundred and thirteen of them were used by the U.S. military as Birddog aircraft. Their mission was to direct air strikes and maintain safe air space when other aircraft were in the vicinity. Their predecessor, the Cessna 305, had been getting hammered in South East Asia, and the military was looking for something with multi-engine reliability. Its biggest safety feature was the "engine-out" handling. Lose a power plant on take-off and the 337 wouldn't try to head for the bush. Its biggest draw back was the noise. Engines attached to each end of the cabin created quite a racket at high power settings.

Andy recalled his historical aviation research into Ontario's fire detection program. A lot had changed since the original (and less than reliable) Curtiss HS-2L Flying Boat was used from 1919 to the early 1930's. It suffered from chronic engine failure, and an engineer always accompanied the pilot. Walking out of the bush was a common occurrence. The De Havilland Moth Floatplane arrived on the scene in Ontario in 1927 and was used into the 1940's. It was also a biplane but was considerably more reliable. No engineer was required on board. Over time, a variety of aircraft were used in aerial detection to support the use of fire towers. One of them, the de Havilland Beaver, a high-winged, all metal aircraft was used until 1968.

The use of fire towers for spotting fires ceased in the late 60's. A lone observer would spend the better part of a fire season working in the tower and living in the tower camp. Armed with binoculars, a fire–finder (alidade) laid on the top of a local map and a telephone or two-way radio for communication, he or she must have solved all the problems in the world with the time they had for reflection. Once the district fire headquarters received the fire report (bearing, estimated distance and estimated location), staff would plot the information provided by the "tower man" and take appropriate action. At its peak, Ontario's tower system boasted three hundred and twenty active fire towers. The one hundred foot-high, permanent towers served Ontario well for over forty years, but it was time to move on. Their biggest drawback was geographic coverage. There were vast areas in the province that were inaccessible to fire tower construction. Present day, the Cessna Skymaster was the work horse of the aerial detection program. Ontario contracted fifteen detection aircraft each fire season. If additional aircraft were required, and more Skymasters unavailable, the fire program would default to other twin-engine aircraft like the Twin Commanche.

A tap on his right shoulder startled Andy back to reality. He wheeled around and came face to face with his pilot.

"John Sutter", the pilot announced as he stuck out a rather large, right hand.

"Andy Radford", Andy replied and returned the gesture.

The two men shook slowly, each gauging the other's hand pressure, each measuring the other in the traditional male ritual of forming an initial opinion before familiarity had a chance to right things.

Andy was of medium height, slim, with bird's nest hair and dark, brooding eyes. John was tall, pushing 6'3", head shaved totally bald with green, mischievous eyes supporting thick witch-broom eyebrows. He was likely approaching thirty five years. They both knew where each stood in the pecking order. John was a pilot, likely more experienced, taller (and therefore more imposing) with an easy demeanour. Andy was the antithesis of John.

Score 10 for John, Andy admitted to himself.

The ritual complete, the unspoken acknowledgement of who was the alpha male was telepathically transmitted between the two, John took the offensive with an infectious grin and a "Come on over and meet the best detection aircraft in the business!"

"Thanks, John, I'm looking forward to this."

"Your first time as an observer?"

How did he know? Was it that obvious? "How did you know? Is it that obvious?"

"Elementary, my dear Watson. We normally don't carry observers until the fire hazard or fire load dictates it, and even then it's rare. I haven't seen you before, and I've been doing this for eight years now. Besides, I saw you checking your handy-dandy sample guide. If there's anything I can do to help out, don't hesitate to ask. By the way, you won't need the guide, I've got on-board GPS."

"Thanks, John and don't worry, if I'm not sure of anything, I'm not afraid to ask. I'm just using the guide to practice my mapping. And who is this Watson character?"

"I'll explain that to you over a beer, some day. Climb aboard. I just want to check the prop housings for debris or leaks and pull the chocks so we can get airborne. We can talk about the detection circuit when I get seated". As an afterthought he continued. "And please don't slam the door. Just like in your helicopter training, close, pull and secure the handle while you're drawing pressure on the door."

Andy climbed in and looked around. He had to admit he was a little excited. This could be a good opportunity to prove himself. He was growing a little tired of his fire fighting role and was looking for something different and above all, challenging. He wasn't totally naïve. He had discussed the routine with other staff who were occasionally used as detection observers and understood fully that there were days when patrols were fruitless, even in high to extreme fire hazard situations and when the only smoke in the sky was industrial related such as sawmills and smelters. However, they also spoke of the thrill of finding a fledgling wildfire, assisting the pilot with assessing its activity and escape potential and occasionally being asked to recommend tactics for fire attack. He had been briefed on the purpose of fire detection. It was not only necessary to find a wildfire, but to find it before it reached the potential for escape.

Let's see what I can remember from my half-day information session at Wawa. As I recall, it was delivered by the visiting aerial operations manager from Sudbury. He went into detail on how fire tactics are geared to "fire phases". Right now we're in phase 4, extreme, and approaching phase 5, escalated. Phase 1 is low fire hazard, phase 2 is moderate and phase 3 is high. So the guidelines say that since the areas north of Wawa and White River are considered high value areas because of tourism, cottage communities and forests, a detection observer in addition to the pilot should be considered when the area was in phase 4 or 5.

Now what was that about detection targets? We're in phase 4, so our intention is to discover the fire at less than ½ a hectare, less than an acre.

Andy actually felt sorry for his older peers and supervisors. Bouncing between imperial and metric measurement seemed to be a constant struggle. What compounded the issue was the movement of fire crews from Canada to the States and visa versa.

Andy then recalled that the aerial operations manager had patiently explained to Andy how the targets were tied to *Fire Management Strategy* for the province, the Bible for policy decisions on managing a fire program. He agreed to an extended explanation only after considerable prodding from an inquisitive and ambitious student. He explained that the detection targets were an extension of the performance measures identified in *Provincial Fire Management Strategy*. The performance measures varied depending on the fire management strategy for a given area. Andy was in the *Boreal Zone* within the province—one of six zones, or "eco-regions" within the province. The 'Initial Fire Response Action' objective for this area was one of:

1. Holding the spread of the fire (called "being held" or BHE) by 12:00 hours local time the day following the fire report, or
2. Stopping the fire at four hectares (ten acres) or less, or
3. Keeping the fire perimeter within predetermined boundaries.

Andy was curious enough to question the last one. The aerial operations manager's measured response was challenging. It also made sense to Andy.

The lesson went something like this:

"Let's see, Andy. Here, let me draw you a rough sketch.

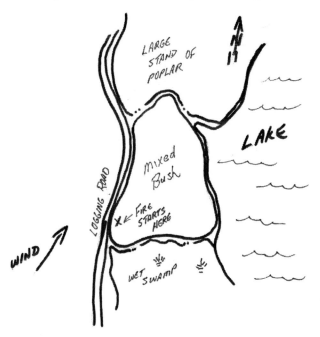

Suppose the fire was started in an area bounded by a wet swamp to the south and a large lake to the east. Now, the fire started near the swamp with a main log-hauling road on its west side. The wind is pushing the fire north into a mixed wood stand made up predominantly of spruce and balsam fir with some poplar. It's summer, and the fire hazard is low and the winds are light. Directly north is a large stand of poplar. The total area within these boundaries is six hectares. Tell me what's going to happen."

Andy was now under the gun and he needed a few moments to collect his thoughts. "Well the fire hazard is low and winds light, so fire spread would be slow and unable to build up into a fast moving fire with the potential to spot or jump."

His supervisor responded, "So far, so good."

"The haul road to the west should hold that flank, and the wind is pushing the fire away from the swamp to the south. Even with the fire back-burning a little, the swamp is wet and water won't burn".

"Go on."

"The lake to the east should hold the east flank, and I've been on enough fires to know that a poplar stand in full leaf provides enough ground cover and therefore, moisture to retard the spread of fire. Again, the hazard is low, and there's little wind. Besides, the total area of burn is only six hectares, not six hundred, and that would be manageable."

"Good. Now what would your attack response be?"

Andy felt his confidence grow by leaps and bounds. "I'd monitor it. No need to commit resources that could be used elsewhere."

"How would you 'monitor' it?"

Think, Andy think! "Make sure the fire location is on the aerial detection route?" The response was more of a question than an answer.

"Well, since the fire hazard is low, there is likely no need for aerial detection."

Andy could feel the heat rise up his neck to his face. "Since there's a road, I guess I'd send a crew to check it out."

"Anything else?" The AOM shot Andy a critical look.

Oh, oh, a loaded question. Shit, think … oh, yeah!

"The crew would have to make sure the fire was out and formally declare it OUT, even if it meant returning later on to do the cold trailing prior to its OUT status"

The questions came faster, now. "What would put it out?"

Yikes. "The next good rain."

"What if we get a drying period, no rain for days, relative humidity drops, wind picks up."

Andy was running out of steam. "I suppose we'd have to send in crews to actually work the fire."

"Anything wrong with that picture?"

A dejected Andy responded, "Yeah, I guess so. It'll still take time and resources."

The AOM knew it was time to salvage the situation. "Andy, your responses were all correct. It's the risk we're willing to take under the circumstances. There is a good chance that we would get the rain. Having said that, one piece of the equation I didn't provide was the forecasted weather. That would have certainly helped in your decision."

It had been a stimulating lesson for Andy. It was the fuel his internal fire needed, and he was excited about this new job. His *shortest* objective was to get noticed by the regional fire organization and this job reported directly to the detection coordinator in the East Region Fire Centre. His *shorter* term goal was to be a Crew Leader, not just a fire fighter. He needed this experience to round himself out. His *longer* term goal was to return to college and take the resource management course. His *longest* term goal was to work permanently for the fire program within the Ontario Ministry of Natural Resources.

Geez, no wonder they call me Anal Andy. Who the hell thinks that far ahead?

Climbing in the Cessna required his focus. *Earth to Andy.* He settled down into the-right hand seat, organized his gear and strapped himself in. He felt the anxiety that comes with being tested. The butterflies in his stomach felt more like F-18 fighters. What had his crew leader told him as a new fire fighter?

Right. *It's OK to have butterflies; the trick is to get them flying in formation.*

Andy attempted to hide his nervousness with questions. "John, what's the 337's threshold for fuel?" *Did I actually say 'threshold'? Making it too obvious that I'm trying to sound like I know what I'm talking about, except I don't?*

John was running up the fore and aft engines and doing his preflight safety checks but took time to reply. "If you mean how long can we stay up with some reserve, I usually count on four hours. This is a 1980 model 337 and we've got eight hundred pounds of fuel on board, that's around a hundred and eighteen gallons. We'll be cruising at three thousand feet when there's an unobstructed ceiling, and we'll average a hundred and thirty knots per hour or approximately two hundred and forty kilometres per hour. We'll burn about twenty-three gallons per hour since we don't have much of a load. When you do the math that gives us about two hours of cruise, a half-hour for fire assessment, if we find one, and an hour reserve. Generally, an average patrol runs two to two and a half hours."

"If I spot a fire, what altitude will you drop down to and what happens to your speed?"

"Andy, it's if *we* spot a fire. I'll be looking as well. After all, that's what I do when there's no observer on board. Don't get me wrong, I haven't got the fire knowledge that you do, but when there's no observer on board, my job is to provide fire location and other rudimentary data. As for circuit altitude and speed, I usually like to drop air speed down to a hundred and ninety kph and fly "on the deck", or five hundred feet up. Now, let's wrap our minds around today's patrol."

We'll be doing the standard "Chapleau west" patrol. Apparently, the regional fire duty officer is particularly concerned about the White River area two hundred and thirty kilometres northwest, due to last night's severe thunderstorms and lots of dry lightning. That's why we're doing an early patrol. There will be another one today."

Andy had done helitack several times in the White River area and didn't have to be told where it was. His lips compressed with a grimace of disapproval, but he checked his temper at the door. His replied tersely, "John, I understand the routine, and I know you'll be calling in a fire if we find one, I guess I'm just curious."

John realized that he was making the boy uncomfortable. "Andy, if we find something, we'll work it together. Now let's get this baby airborne."

Five minutes later, the 337 taxied down the strip. As it lifted off, Andy's anxiety turned to exhilaration.

Andy smiled at no one in particular. *Man, this is going to be fun!*

Chapter 13

DAY 1: 11:00 HOURS, WEST OF SIREN LAKE

THE DRAGON BELLY-CRAWLED THROUGH ITS NEW UNDERGROUND LAIR, consuming oxygen in its quest to rise to the surface. It was growing weaker with time, literally starving for air. A smouldering claw would wind its way around roots, past stone and wither where there was lack of combustible fuel or oxygen. Another appendage would appear on its super-heated body where a morsel of fuel/air could be found. It would soon die without the nourishment required to sustain it.

Above the surface the sun was rising higher, warming any objects that its rays could touch. Forest fuels were heating up and drying since the recent light rainfall. The grasses, twigs and last-year's leaves would be ready for combustion in six hours. Sticks and small, decaying branches and bolts of wood would take less than twenty-four hours to reach the point where they would sustain combustion. The light rain had done nothing to penetrate large fuels such as new fallen trees, dense, shaded foliage or standing trees. These fuels required significant rainfall to reverse their drought-induced conditions.

A light breeze dropped down through the forest canopy and gently stroked the ground. It was followed by a gust of air that sucked up dead leaves and pine needles. It was that same gust that passed over a narrow fissure between two boulders and tugged up the dead air hidden there. The dormant, weak dragon sensed the distant tugging and raised a narrow, crooked finger towards its saviour. The finger wound its way to the surface, tentative but resolute. The bits and pieces of litter it consumed on its ascent barely kept it alive. As it reached the lip of the fissure, it gently felt around the edge, like a blind person feeling for a light switch, until it sensed something small, light and dry. Pine needles! The seduction began.

Prior to actually touching the fuel, the dragon-hand pointed a fiery finger, heating the pine needles to their ignition temperature. Unseen vapours of gas cocooned the needles and ignited. Now there were little waving caps of yellow-orange flame. Where neighbouring fuels still contained some moisture, the preheating resulted in wispy smoke. In other excursions, newborn flames approached their intended victims and seemed to bow and offer a hand. Like music-box partners, the two joined and danced a waltz of death. The dragon gleefully swayed to the minuet, it had its little victory. It had heat, it had oxygen, all it needed was more fuel. The withered hand took on new life. More appendages sprung from its arm and began its soulless search.

THE LOWEST BRANCHES FROM THE TOWERING WHITE Pine suspended over this macabre spectacle began to rise and fall responding to the gentle touch of convective air being pushed up from the dragon's heat. The pine appeared to transform into the shape of a fawning eunuch, fanning its master in abject supplication. Under the dragon's spell, the pine fanned and groaned. It had no will of its own and could only look on with tired resignation. A long time ago, it had seen and been party to this same dance.

THE SOW TOOK THE PATH OF LEAST RESISTANCE, downhill. She had slowed her pace to stay with the distressed cub but kept looking back towards the ridge. Her keen sense of smell picked up something alien. She had smelled it before, in the darkness, and she unwittingly had associated it with the creature that made her most anxious, the ones that most resembled her in stature—man.

This smell was different. It did not bring with it the attraction of nourishment. The odour was more pungent. It irritated her nostrils and awakened a sense of alarm. She and her cub needed cover. Forage could come later. She "woofed" at her offspring as a sign of annoyance, turned back abruptly and continued her descent. She took an angle downhill so travel wasn't too difficult for the cub. Her instincts told her to travel into the wind, in a southeast direction, but a large rock outcrop above a steep drop would force her uphill. She ignored the little tug on her senses and quartered north-easterly. It would be the first mistake she had made in guiding her cub on this critical journey.

THIS MORNING HAD NOT BEEN KIND to Wally. He woke up tired and irritable after his troubled dream. He was out in the workshed trying to get his mind organized but his head was like a cave filled with cobwebs. Restless bats hung upside-down to his skull. Each black flutter, stretch and yawn was an unwanted thought that triggered ripples of anxiety and dread.

His thoughts were like little vignettes. He recalled his last conversation with his girls. Easy and light at first, it had turned into an argument over, of all things, dogs. Hailey had declared, "You need a dog, dad".

He brushed it off. "Look girls, I've been owned by several dogs and I don't want to go there again." They ganged up on him, circled him like coyotes around a wounded badger. He became more defensive. "Remember our last black lab, Tess? You weren't there. She was getting old for a lab, thirteen years old as I recall. Her eyesight was shot and her hearing had deteriorated." *Or became selective. She couldn't hear me calling her but she could hear the dog cookie tin open half a kilometre away.* "I was walking her back behind our place when she dropped. I had to carry her home and she died in my arms." His voice rose and began to crack. "I won't go through that again!" The coyotes were no matched for the badger, they slunk back as the badger morphed into a man, swivelled and stormed out.

A second vignette slid across his brain projector. He reluctantly recalled his first of many visits to his doctor that led up to his predicament. He had always been reluctant to go for the annual physical. It's not that he didn't trust doctors; he just didn't like them. This particular doctor, Dr. Mihn, a small East Asian man, had the examining room manners of a raven at a road-kill. His pokes, prods and jabs were not gentle and his look of concentration was more like a look of constipation. Perhaps Wally had pissed him off in another life, or maybe the doctor had been a VC in the war, and found out Wally had been a marine. The only time the good doctor smiled was just before the dreaded (and in his mind, highly over-rated) rectal/prostate exam.

"Ah, mista McNeil, you ro over on yo side, now." As he snapped the latex glove on and methodically stretched each finger into its scabbard, his lips would stretch like a thin slice of liver, then the ends of his mouth would twitch and curl up and finally his upper lip would lift slowly like a garage door and his newly capped teeth would appear like packing crates. The fingers wormed their way in and poked around, then pressed. Wally recalled thinking, *I hope you're enjoying this, you little maggot.* To deal with the discomfort, Wally tried to think of something pleasant but all his traitorous imagination would entertain was the doctor's hand. His imagination burst onto a brightly lit stage in his brain. *Ladies and gentlemen! What you are about to witness will astound you!* Then Wally imagined the good doctor's whole arm slithering its way up his rectum, crawling through his intestines, then poking around in his stomach, looking for a way out. His throat began to contract when he pictured the arm worming its way up his oesophagus, the hand then forcing open his mouth to escape to the outside. As it broke free, the doctor's hand bent and compressed into a hand puppet that slowly scanned the perimeter. *Ain't imagination grand?*

Wally had returned from his day mare as doctor Mihn declared, "Ah done now, pu up yo pants."

Wally didn't need any encouragement and quickly complied leaving a shirt tail out as he crammed it into his pants.

"Mista McNeil, postate a lil fum. You need mo tests." *Postate a lil fum? Prostate a little fum? Prostate a little "firm"? Oh, now I get it.* It was amazing how a firm prostate, even one a *little* firm had changed his life. Doctor Mihn might have struggled with his English and his manner was, to say the least, abrupt, but damned if he didn't know his stuff. There was more prodding, poking and periscoping over the next two months. Then there was the operation that left him without a prostate. The cancer worm must have seen the writing on the wall, packed its bags and moved into another apartment in his body. Wally would fight the toughest battle of his life, one which in his heart of hearts, he knew he would not win.

Wally forced the history slide show out of his mind and went back to work. For some reason he felt apprehensive but he couldn't figure out why. *Instincts are trying to tell me something.* Wally firmly believed in trusting his instincts and reacting to them but he was having trouble pinpointing the source of aggravation. *Damn, it's like trying to pick up a radio station in on the fringe of coverage. The thought keeps fading in and out.* He smiled when he recalled a Dinero movie where Robert often repeated the phrase, "Forgetaboutit."

Wally would do just that.

Chapter 14

DAY 1: 11:00 HOURS, WEST OF CHAPLEAU

"CHAPLEAU FIRE, THIS IS DETECTION AIRCRAFT 14 OFF CHAPLEAU AIRPORT, bound Chapleau-west detection patrol, do you copy?"

Seconds later, a female voice responded from the Chapleau Fire Management headquarters, "Detection aircraft 14, this is Chapleau fire on channel 15. I copy, bound detection patrol Chapleau-west. And how are you today, John?"

"Any better and I'd have to shoot myself, thanks. I'll check in with the Regional Fire Centre and give you a shout when we leave your area."

"Affirmative. We have your standard patrol on our detection map. Any changes planned?"

"Not today. And if all goes well, we'll be repeating the flight this afternoon."

"Copy that, 14. Chapleau fire out"

In the Chapleau fire headquarters radio room, the radio operator sat in front of an array of telecommunications and computer equipment. Besides the FM base station radio, there was also an HF (high frequency) and VHF (very high frequency) band radio for aircraft without Ministry of Natural Resources' radio equipment. The radios also served as back up should the FM radios malfunction on MNR owned or contracted aircraft. If required, she could even talk directly to high-level, commercial passenger aircraft that occasionally reported smokes directly to MNR.

Besides personnel and administrative data bases, her computer was also networked with MNR computers across the province. It was the delivery mechanism for a decision support system called DFOSS (Daily Fire Operations Support System). All fire information received from public and organized sources was logged into DFOSS. If a person reported a possible fire, it was logged in as an "incident". The incident was given an incident number. Once fire personnel confirmed the incident as a bona-fide fire, it was given a fire number. The number was unique to that fire using a 3-letter code in front identifying the district in which the fire resided. For example, CHA 43 would be the 43rd fire in the Chapleau district for that year. In addition to fire information, the system was a tool for weather reporting and forecasting, lightning information and desktop mapping. The data could be shared from fire headquarters to fire headquarters. As a data base, it also could be queried and had countless "canned" queries developed so that data could be used for analytical purposes, especially fire arrival and fire behaviour prediction analysis.

At this particular time, the radio operator was preoccupied with entering her conversation with the detection pilot electronically in her radio log complete with aircraft identification, the exact time of the call to the minute and a paraphrase of the conversation and her electronic initials. The radio log was not only important for tracking aircraft and personnel, it was also crucial as source data for issues associated with injury, death and liability.

As his aircraft shot through the sky at two hundred and thirty kilometres per hour, John switched FM radio frequencies from 15 to 2 and repeated the call to the Regional Fire Centre in Sudbury. Although it was a pain in the ass to duplicate calls, it was part of the safety protocol and to ignore it would only bring an unwanted reprimand. The Ministry of Natural Resources was a stickler for air to ground radio communication practices.

As detection aircraft 14 was slipping over forest and water in a north-westerly direction from Chapleau, five other detection aircraft were on similar missions across the east half of Ontario. Andy took a glance at a copy of the detection map for the East Fire Region and was amazed at the amount of detection coverage six aircraft could provide in a two to three hour period.

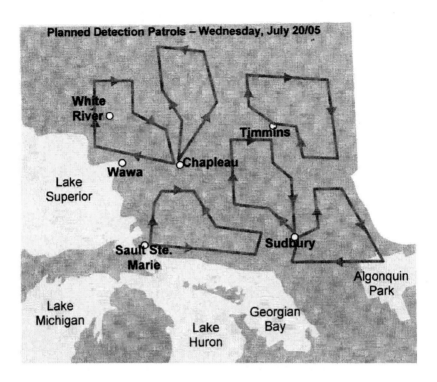

Andy put the map down and focused on his objective. From the moment they took to the air, Andy's priority was looking for smoke. It was his first trip. He sat upright and rigid, his neck craned out with the jugular vein stretched like a bow-string, his head rotating ever so slowly in both directions. His eyebrows struggled to meet, separated by three little ridges of folded skin and two deep fissures. His mouth took on a classic clown-frown, and he was chewing vigorously on his lower lip.

John looked over and smiled. *He looks like Linda Blair from the Exorcist. Hope he doesn't projectile vomit his breakfast.* He spoke matter-of-factly through the live intercom, "Andy, relax. It's a long flight. If you maintain that posture, *rigor mortis* will set in. I'll have to carry you out of the plane like a cardboard cut-out. It's great visibility today. You've got over twenty kilometres. Get comfortable, scan a little and every once in awhile give your eyes about a ten second rest. When you open them, it's a fresh, new picture. I'll make sure you stay awake."

Andy looked down at his hands. They were clenched and his knuckles were white. He could already feel tension in his back and neck. It was hot in the cabin, and perspiration began to form on his forehead and upper lip. His ankles were crossed, and he was flapping his upper foot to some primal beat bouncing around in his head. He became aware of his condition. *Great. It looks like I'm sitting on the porcelain throne. All I need to do is grunt to complete the picture.*

Andy was determined to get along with his pilot. Besides, John was right. "Thanks John, I do feel a little tense." Andy slowly began to relax and enjoy the flight. The aircraft swept over ridges, giant rock outcrops, impenetrable forests and countless lakes ponds and rivers. At one thousand metres, everything at eye level was panoramic, but there was still opportunity to look down and pick out items of interest. Andy was taken with the shapes and colours of lakes—deep lakes a rich blue, shallow lakes, an emerald green. Where sand rose up to meet the shoreline, there were veils of pale blue over tan. Shoreline rocks appeared as white and grey strings of pearls. Reflections of sun bounced and shimmered on the water as if God had cast diamonds like dice across the surface.

Andy struggled to digest his feelings and label them. He wished he had the ability to take each emotion in his hands and wring out the words to describe them. He pictured each feeling as a cloth and as he twisted and squeezed, words dripped down, hit an invisible line and spread out in perfect verse. *God, this country is something else. "Something else", Is that the best I can do?*

John broke his train of thought. "You know Andy, when I'm flying out here, sometimes I feel like I've been given a sneak preview of heaven, and God has reserved this particular scene for me alone. I guess if I could use one word to describe my sense of it, it would be *privileged*. You ever feel that way?"

Andy looked defeated. *I give up. You ARE the king, John.* "I know what you mean, John. I just have trouble verbalizing it."

"Give it a try, Andy. Let's be philosophical since we have nothing better to do. Let's see. How do you feel about life in general?"

Andy began to feel like a loser. *Come on Andy, you can come up with something. "Life sucks" doesn't seem appropriate here. Try poetry.* He dug deep for words, any words, just so he could show this dickhead he had an imagination. Five strained minutes passed without conversation.

"OK, John. Are you ready?"

"Go for it, Andy."

"Well John, this is how I feel about flying with you." He paused and cleared his throat.

"There once was a kid with no luck
Who flew through the air like a duck
The trees he could see
Moved faster than he
And soon he began to up-chuck."

John burst out laughing, a loud, rich, honest, no-holds-barred laughter that took Andy by surprise. Soon Andy joined in. The pissing match was over. A friendship had begun.

They both soon settled down into their respective routines. Twenty minutes later, John called Chapleau to advise they were leaving the Chapleau Response Sector 4 and quickly followed up with a radio call to advise Wawa that they were entering Wawa Response Sector 5. Radio protocol and safety requirements were met.

Chapter 15

DAY 1: 12:00 HOURS, RETURN LAG OF DETECTION PATROL, NORTH OF THE TOWN OF WHITE RIVER

THE DRAGON BECAME ENCOURAGED WITH THE OFFERINGS OF FUEL IN ITS PATH and silently welcomed the stiff surface breeze helping it along its disjointed, slithering journey. The needles, twigs, and other surface litter with any vestige of moisture were sending up small wisps of smoke like visual cries for help. As the wind increased, the dragon began to skip and jump with glee, finding fresh forage to satisfy its appetite. The smoke began to rise and weakly poke through the forest canopy. It was not a robust smoke, and tree top winds would sheer it as it rose, like invisible garden clippers trimming a canopy-hedge. The smoke would disperse, like oil on pond water then filter back down through the trees.

ANOTHER THIRTY MINUTES INTO THE FLIGHT, and heading in an easterly direction now, Andy, who had become complacent with the steady drone of the aircraft, suddenly experienced a surge of adrenalin. He shot straight up in his seat and thrust his head forward. "Did you see that, John? A smoke—on my side—about 2:00 o'clock?"

John turned his head slightly to the right in a southerly direction and spotted a slight drift of something that resembled mist or perhaps smoke. "I see something Andy, let's take a better look."

"Sounds good, John. Can you call in the request?" John was more than aware of the routine. You had to let the Fire Management Headquarters in the local District know you were going off patrol line for both safety reasons and the fact they might already have that fire (if it was one) identified and action had been taken.

John looked over at Andy and said matter-of-factly, "You call this one in Andy. You spotted it. I'll give you our coordinates and you get a fix on the smoke".

All along Andy had been following their flight path on his topographic map, so he had a fix on their present location. He then had to estimate the location of the smoke. He put a mark on his plastic-covered map with a non-permanent marker. "Wawa Fire, Wawa Fire, this is detection aircraft 14 on Channel 6. Do you copy?" His voice jumped an octave and he swore he sounded like Kermit the Frog.

"Go ahead, John", a new female voice said, "We copy".

"This is Andy, Wawa Fire. I'm on board as detection observer." *John must get around.*

"Sorry, Andy. We usually associate that aircraft with John, go ahead."

Andy had no time for banter. It was time to get down to business. "We're presently at base map 64543. Request permission to leave the flight line to investigate a smoke approximately three kilometres south of our position. Do you have anything reported in that area?"

There was a slight delay. Andy waited impatiently for a response. *The radio operator was probably conferring with the sector response officer (SRO). Don't they realize the location puts it about twenty kilometres north of White River?*

The same voice responded, "Detection 14, Negative. We have no report of a smoke in that vicinity. Do you have a visual now?"

Andy looked further to the south and couldn't see the smoke now. He looked at John. John frowned slightly and shook his head. "Negative on that Wawa Fire. But I'm sure I saw something."

"Detection 14, the SRO says to check it out."

Without any further encouragement, John swung the aircraft to starboard and headed for the area designated by the mark on Andy's map.

ON THE SURFACE, the wind suddenly dropped. The dragon was going efficiently about its business, humming an off-key tune to itself and reached to pluck at vertical fuels, young balsam fir and spruce. As it hoisted itself up through the branches, devouring as it went, it attempted to use them as ladders to climb to the top of the forest canopy. Now, without the wind to support it, the dragon was dumped unceremoniously to the ground on its luminous ass. Along with its embarrassing retreat, the tell-tale smoke dropped as well. A disgruntled dragon rummaged around, shrivelled back to its weaker state and pouted.

"RIGHT AROUND HERE, JOHN. But I can't see anything now."

"Andy, let's drop down to two hundred and fifty metres. I'll drop our cruising speed down to a hundred and ninety kph and turn into the sun. Sometimes you can pick up smoke from that angle."

The Skymaster cruised with little effort over the forest canopy and directly over a sedentary dragon, a dragon that, if it could, would look up at the aircraft with a Golum-like smile and slowly raise an incandescent middle finger in its direction.

Three more circuits and no fire, a dejected Andy Radford called the Wawa Fire Management Headquarters and advised of their return to the detection patrol circuit.

"Detection 14, the SRO has requested a fix on the possible fire."

Andy rolled his head and eyes skyward and pursed his lips, admonishing himself. *Right. Still an incident and maybe there's a sleeper there.*

Andy replied, "Sorry, Wawa. I put the incident at base map 61539, block three."

"Copy that. Base map 61539, block three. Wawa clear."

Andy turned to his pilot. "I'm sure I saw something, John. Couldn't be road dust—no roads here. Not likely ground fog, because I don't see any other fog on the horizon and it's too late in the day."

John had been through the same situation. "Don't sweat it, my friend. The wind was up at the time. Maybe it was pine pollen, although it's pretty late in the year for that. The wind could have lifted it as you were looking in that direction. When it clouds up, it tends to look like smoke. Besides, we'll be back here this afternoon sometime between 15:00 and 17:00 hours. Isn't that the highly anticipated *peak burning period*? If it's there, it'll show up."

"Right, John. The pollen's done by the end of June. I only hope it's not too late when we return".

Andy and John were now unwary accomplices to a "detection failure". An early detection patrol was the correct aerial detection strategy. Checking out even the possibility of a smoke and approaching the target site from different directions were the correct tactics. There would be no blame here. This was not the first or wouldn't be the last fire that "went to ground" and couldn't be detected. Andy put a mark on his aerial detection map. They would be back later to check it out. John had already punched it in to his GPS.

WALLY HEARD THE AIRCRAFT before he saw it and was familiar with the overly aggressive engine sound from his days in 'Nam. *Sounds like an old 337 Skymaster. Wonder what it's up to doing all those circuits. No "Charlies" here.* He struggled with a slight tremor in his hands and cursed under his breath. *"Up Country" never really leaves you. It just squats patiently in a compartment in your brain, waiting to crawl out and screw you up.*

He looked above the ridge again. *Probably looking for fire after all that lightning. Wasting his time. I would smell it if there was any smoke in the air.*

The Skymaster seemed to read Wally's mind and lose interest in its task. It banked south and faded into nothing.

TEN MINUTES AFTER THE 337 LEFT THE AREA, the wind
picked up. The grumbling dragon was elated. It began its routine
again. This time, it was able to climb the foliage and reach middle growth. It would crawl into the lowest branches of thirty-foot
spruce and balsam and dance to the tops, creating torches of intense flame. Then it would drop down to the forest floor, begin
to creep where fine fuels were lightest and run where they were
heavier and continuous. On its journey now, the dragon would
consume smaller vertical fuels— three to six foot spruce, balsam
and pine. Where these fuels reached up into larger vertical fuels of
conifers and white birch, the pattern would be repeated—torching,
then down again, then creeping, then running. In this particular
area, one fuel type was particularly susceptible to fire, dead spruce
and balsam fir killed by spruce budworm. The inch-long, reddish-
brown larvae with the distinctive, white-yellow raised spots was
responsible for the destruction of billions of cubic feet of spruce
and balsam fir log material in Eastern Canada and the U.S., leaving
ravaged, standing fuels in its wake.

Now, dense clouds of grey-black smoke began to rise above the
forest canopy. As the thick smoke climbed vertically, and reached
heights of five hundred metres, it would be bent with stronger, upper air currents. The stronger the current, the more pronounced
the bend to the column of smoke. Bright, burning embers of charcoal sized fuel and flat, light birch-bark were carried aloft within
those rolling clouds of smoke to be deposited ten to seventy five
metres away, causing jump fires. The androgynous dragon was
giving birth. The birthing was accompanied by the symphony of
escaped fire, a percussion of crackling, whooshes and snapping, as
each jump fire raced to co-join with its siblings. The dragon was
one, then became many, then fused into one again. Oh, the joy of
it all!

THE SOW HAD FOUND A PLACE OF refuge, a small swamp
well east of the ridge. It was an abandoned beaver pond. The edge

grasses provided a comfortable place to bed down. Black ash trees provided an over-story with shade, and tag alder provided cover. Although most of the pond had withered, there was still water in the lowest area within its perimeter. In the outer perimeter, the ground was hard-baked and cracked. As the sow slowly traversed the swamp in an inward continuous circle, the ground became less firm, then spongy. She sensed that there was nourishment here and she began to turn over logs and stones. Her cub was close behind, picking up morsels of worms, snails and grubs that had fallen out of the decayed material. The sow occasionally dug down into the softer earth and flipped out a crayfish. She and her cub would spend the rest of the day and the night here.

WALLY HAD BEEN PUTTERING all morning in the workshop cleaning traps, sharpening his axe, shovel and assorted knives. For the first time in a long time, his stomach actually growled. He braced for pain. It chose to lie dormant. *Time for lunch.*

He had become a creature of habit. He had very little breakfast, a late lunch, a snack for dinner and tea and cookie before bed. His stomach told him it was around noon. As he walked towards his camp, he took a customary look to the lake and up to the ridge in the west. He had forgotten about the aircraft that had spent some time above the ridge an hour ago until he looked up.

Oh, shit! A large column of smoke rose in the sky at a forty five degree angle in a northerly direction. Below it, a few small ringlets of smoke rose to join the main column. The column hovered over the smaller smokes like a mother protector, biding her children to move on with haste. *Wally, old sod, we have a problem here. Gotta contact MNR.*

Wally raced (at least in his mind) the remaining fifteen metres to the front of the camp and hurried inside. Once he entered the kitchen he went to the fridge, where he kept a list of emergency numbers stuck behind a Winnie-the-Pooh fridge magnet. He had the *Fire Reporting Hotline* number but knew that it got him a robot behind an answering service that didn't know a fire from a frog. Below that number was a direct line to the fire headquarters in Wawa. He was privy to it since he was considered a reliable

source in an isolated area, an area that required immediate attention should a fire occur. Wally then hunted around for the satellite
phone, his curse words increasing in volume incrementally with
each new utterance and his vocabulary reaching new heights of
imagination as he searched in vain for the "friggin phone!" Finally,
there it was, right where "someone else" had left it.

GEORGE WILLIAMS LOOKED UP from the most recent fire report
when his phone rang. "Wawa Fire, sector response officer here."

"There's a fire on the ridge!" Now Wally wasn't so dumb that he
thought the guy on the other end of the line would know who was
calling or would know the exact location of the fire by telepathy.
His marine training had taught him to volunteer as little information as possible and wait for the pros to ask the right questions.

"Who is calling, and where are you calling from, sir?"

"My name's McNeil, Wally McNeil, and that's capital M, small
c, capital N, small "e", "i", "l." I'm calling from Lake Jewel, know
to you as Siren Lake, about thirty kilometres north-west of White
River as the crow flies.

George was already recording the call in his log-book and looking at the map in front of him. He had some recognition of the
name and associated it with one of the trappers to the northwest.
With a little shot of adrenalin, he quickly became alert, his eyes
flicking across the map, pupils dilating, his fingers tightening
around the pencil, knuckles growing white with anticipation.

"Wally, please tell me what you see and where it is from your
position."

"Well, son, I see a large column of smoke on a ridge due west of
my camp."

George's senses became acute. His eyes widened and his nostrils flared out. His mouth became dry and felt like it was coated
with asbestos insulation. He dared not swallow. "Where is your
camp on the lake?" As he asked the question, he scanned another
map where existing fires were located with round magnets, colour-
coded by stage of control. There were no magnets in that location.

"I'm on the east shore of the lake, half way up, and the fire is
about four, maybe five kilometres to the west."

This guy was good. "Can you tell me what the column is doing? Is it solid, is it dark or light coloured, is it bent?"

"Thick as a fat lady, darker than a buzzard's butt, and bent over like a dog fornicating with a football—and pointing north."

George had all he needed. The FRI (forest resource inventory) maps would tell him what forest stand types were ahead of the fire and the values maps would tell him what values such as cottages, lodges and towns were in the vicinity. He also had a data-base as *overlay-on-map data* on his computer. Initially, however, he still liked to look at hard-copy maps. He took Wally's satellite phone number, told him he could expect a visit from MNR district staff and thanked him for his report.

Without hesitation, George picked up the phone, called the Ministry of Transportation yard in White River, briefly talked to the recipient and, as a result, dispatched helitack to the fire. He then called the fire duty officer in Sudbury, Rick Sampson, and requested air attack. He knew right away, that this fire needed water bombing and that a CL415 air tanker with its payload of thirteen hundred and twenty gallons per drop was necessary. He then passed on the information to the radio operator, who in turn entered the data into DFOSS as an incident. The fire crew leader in the helicopter would, no doubt, confirm it as a bona fide fire. His next call was to the district manager upstairs and down the hall. He would give him a heads up. If on-site warnings or evacuations were required, it was the local MNR district manager and his resource staff who were responsible for emergency response while fire staff fought fire.

Let's see, if this is a confirmed fire, then it will be WAWA 43. Let the fun begin.

Chapter 16

DAY 1: 12:00 HOURS, EFR
MEETING ROOM

"RICK, YOU LOOK LIKE A WEEK OLD AIRLINE FOOD. How are you doing?"

"Thanks for the compliment, Brad. I feel like I'm marooned in a toilet bowl that's just about to be flushed."

"Is your day that bad?"

"Nope. But it will be."

The two friends faced each other, both smiling, both knowing full well that they had a couple of months of intense work ahead of them.

Brad Simpson was two years Rick's junior and, at the same time, his immediate supervisor. In physical appearance, if Rick was Stan Laurel, then Brad was Oliver Hardy. Brad's short, stocky frame and balding, round head and face masked his wit, intelligence and confidence. In Rick's words, the man had presence. Both had come up through the fire crew system. They not only respected each other; they liked each other. Right now, Brad was a little worried about his fire duty officer.

"The regional directors will be in soon and they expect an overview of the system. Although Doug is executive officer today, he can't make it—something about a conference call. I think we'll just play the question and answer game. You handle the fire related stuff. I'll deal with program and resource issues. But we have a few minutes. How are things at home?"

Oh, oh, Rick thought, *here comes the "looks like you need a few days off to spend with the family or take a short trip" speech.*

"Could be worse. Beth has taken the kids to summer camp so I'm batching it. Did you know there are a hundred ways to prepare canned tuna?"

Rick didn't want to reveal the fact that he and Beth were having problems. They were becoming more distant with each passing fire season. The two boys were growing up without their father and Beth seemed to be totally immersed in her real estate business. He didn't blame her for giving up; he just didn't know how to handle it, didn't know how to reach out. At times now, his job was a refuge, a comforting patchwork quilt of excuses. The fire program spawned its share of separations and divorces.

"When was your last day off?"

"Let's see, eleven days ago. Ben's sick so I'm working into his stretch. We're looking for a replacement."

"Anything I can do to help?"

"Sure. Do you know how to cook? If you can't cook, then how about lining up a zone duty officer to assist with Sectors 1, 2 and 3? I think we also may require an additional zone duty officer for project fires."

"You think we're going to have some fires take a run on us?"

"Brad, you can count on at least two in Sectors 4 or 5. Remember 1988. We had to deal with four project fires then. This sure feels like *déjà vu* all over again. It's a good thing we've put in those resource requests when we did."

Brad was glad to see that Rick was requesting support for his position. The first law of organizational survival, "do not exceed your span of control", was never more appropriate than in the fire program.

"Rick, promise me that you'll give me a heads up if you start to speak in slow motion or fall asleep in the chair or trip on floor dust."

"We've both been there before, Brad. Cross my heart and hope to spit, or something like that."

"I'll get you the support you need. They'll have to come out of the resource program. There are some real good area supervisors with fire experience who helped us before. I'll start the begging process at our meeting."

Rick couldn't resist a slight smile of hope. "I've worked with Norm Pendleton from Blind River. Or how about Zander Cybulski from Algonquin Park?"

"I'll see what I can do, but you know the drill. Everyone is busy, so you may have to take anyone who meets our requirements. Let's get a coffee before our meeting. And, by the way, this is another fine mess you've gotten us into." His Oliver hardy was pretty good.

Laurel and Hardy headed for their caffeine fix.

"DID YOU GET YOUR SOP OUT OK?" Brad asked the question for the benefit of everyone sitting in the room. Besides himself, Rick and the two regional directors, Brad's admin assistant was sitting quietly taking notes. All meetings required a paper trail.

Rick responded. "Sure did—special emphasis on anticipated fire behaviour and the need for safety."

"How are we for crews and other resources?"

"Well, the West Fire Region can't help us with people. Their one hundred and eight ranger crews are either committed or required for initial attack. Of our ninety-seven crews, two are out of commission due to injuries, fifteen are out west and twenty are committed to fires. That leaves us with sixty ranger crews. There are no crews on days off due to the cancellation, but we have about twenty that are due to be "timexed". They're coming up on their maximum nineteen days on the job without a break. We have them on yellow alert. The remaining forty crews are on red alert. Most of our crews in the West Fire Region are from sector 1. We've pre-positioned ten of the fourteen ranger crews from sector 6 to sectors 4 and 5 and back-filled with type 2 crews."

The RD from the Northeast Region, Norm Bennet, spoke up. "Let's see if I've got this right. You're telling me that my region from Hearst across to Cochrane has only got four Ranger crews for initial attack?" He spoke the last two words as if his throat was filled with broken glass. "And you've got contract crews to back them up?" His voice had just discovered a new octave.

Rick responded, his tone dropping, his words measured and cool. "Not exactly. Although the primary roles of type 2 crews are sustained attack and mop-up once the initial attack is successful, we'll now be using them on initial attack. We have thirty crews inbound to Hearst, Kapuskasing and Cochrane, twenty from Pineland and ten from Horizon. Both companies have a good track record."

"Why am I not comforted here?" This time words were delivered with unmasked disdain.

Brad jumped in. "With all due respect, Norm, most of the type 2 fire fighters working for Pineland and Horizon are hired from our First Nations communities. They've been at the fire business for years and take pride in what their doing. They've had appropriate training and bring lots of experience. They might be reluctant to fill out paperwork, but they know how to fight fire."

Rick backed up his argument. "We don't expect the kind of fire behaviour in sector 6 that we do in 4 or 5. We would not put them in this situation if we didn't think they could handle it."

The RD looked to his counterpart, Mark Delviccio, for support, and receiving none, saved face with a patronizing, "You can continue."

Rick looked down at his strategic operating plan. "We presently have twenty helicopters in the system and have put in a request to the province for another twenty. We have one CL415 "US" right now." He looked up, "Oh, sorry, "US" means 'unserviceable'." That leaves us with two CL415's and two Twin Otters available for air attack. Again, we've put in a request for two heavy water bomber packages, but I'm not holding my breath."

The Southern RD calmly raised a question. "Rick, what's a package?"

Man, I've got to remember I'm talking to civilians. "Sorry Mark, a package is two heavy water bombers accompanied by a Birddog aircraft and officer. Our best hope right now is Manitoba, but they already have a package in our West Fire Region."

Mark continued. "So it sounds like we're in trouble."

"Let's just say we're sitting on a hand grenade with both hands and feet tied and the pin is resting comfortably up an elephant's ass. Now, all you can use to extract the pin to put it back in the grenade are your teeth. That's the kind of trouble we're in."

The image was not lost and everyone laughed. The admin assistant looked up. "Is "elephant" spelled with an 'f' or 'ph'?" Even Norm had a chuckle.

The gentleman from the south offered, "How can we help?"

Rick and Brad looked at each other as if to say "who wants to go first?" Brad gave a slight nod to his duty officer.

"Let's start with the need for compliance monitoring. As you know, we've requested a Restricted Fire Zone for all areas within the fire region. If approved by management board of cabinet, it will start at midnight tomorrow night. I've already put in a formal request to the districts to utilize their conservation officers for enforcement. A complete ban on open fires is not well received by some members of the public. Cottagers and campers like their campfires. We need your support on this since it means other enforcement objectives may take a back seat for awhile."

Norm, ever the sceptic, posed a question. "Why have a RFZ in sector's 1 and 6 if fire hazard is not as high as other sectors?"

Rick continued. "Good question, Norm. First, the fire hazard in those sectors is high and for most areas within those sectors, it will be extreme within a day or two. Secondly, most of our initial attack crews and air attack resources are dedicated to other sectors. We can't afford to redirect them to person-caused fires in sectors 1 and 6. We're hoping an aggressive fire prevention campaign in 1 and 6 will do the trick."

Mark Delviccio stepped in. "Makes sense to me, you've certainly got my support."

The room was uncomfortably silent for a ten second interval that to the Northeast RD seemed like an eternity.

Brad thought, *ah, a Mexican stand-off. How will he save face? Probably defer the decision.*

Norm finally responded. "I'll take it up with my district managers and get back to you."

"Still on the topic of prevention", Rick continued, "we will also need support on the Woods Modified Guidelines. Some of the logging companies out there have not bought into the concept, even after all these years." The guidelines were self-regulating tactics for modifying forest operations in response to fire danger. They were based on two key indices—the "fine fuel moisture code' and the "initial spread index" in a given area. The forest operators were expected to call into or email their respective fire management headquarters on a routine basis to see if restrictions applied. The restrictions might range from limiting types of activities such as road building or log skidding to restricting hours of operation in the bush or even implementing complete shutdowns.

It was Mark's turn. "I can understand their concern. The companies need to provide products, and the employees need to make a living."

Brad responded. "We don't take this step lightly, but if an operator starts a fire and it can't be handled, he could lose five years of cut in a day. That could close a local operation or a sawmill down for good."

"I understand where you're coming from. I guess I'm just venting on their behalf. My District Managers and their staff are the ones who have to deal with them. Having said that, I'll back you up."

It was Brad's turn to take the lead. He pursed his lips and looked at both RD's in the eyes. No words were spoken.

"Oh yeah, here it comes." Even as he said it, Norm tilted his face skyward, his mouth open, his eyes reaching for support from a higher plain.

"We've put in a formal request for two long teams to provide either attack base or project fire service and support. We need one each from your regions." These were twenty-person, non-fire, Ministry of Natural Resources staff that had training in specific fire service roles. Functions like equipment management, administration, transport services, base camp services, helicopter management and fuel management were largely provided by non-fire staff.

"In addition, we've asked our fire management supervisors to negotiate with your district managers for local service support to the fire program."

A flustered Northeastern RD stood up, his hands gripping the table, his eyes wide, the orbs bouncing back and forth in their sockets as if they were frantically searching for the words that had backed up in his throat. *If I swallow, I'll choke. What about OUR programs? What are my options? If I run to the Deputy Minister, he's only going to pat me on the head and back up the fire program. We go through this every bad fire season, and the 'chicken little' stuff never works any-*

way. Got to appear to be a team player. Suddenly, his body relaxed and his colour dropped two shades into a normal range as if he had bitten down on a Prozac and it was kicking in. He suddenly realized how he must have looked. "OK, OK. We've been here before and survived. We'll do what we can to help. Now is there any good news?"

Rick and Brad exchanged a look of relief. Rick continued.

"As a matter of fact, there is. Because of the fire activity in the west and the anticipated activity here in the east, the province has approved a "Fire Emergency Declaration" and fire emergency compensation will kick in."

"So our people will be paid for their overtime?"

"Exactly. When they do return to their real jobs, you won't be dealing with time off issues unless you feel it's necessary to provide time off in lieu of pay. It's been our experience that time off is requested in isolated situations or on a limited basis."

Rick was on a role now, his anxiety level down a quart. "In addition, we put in a request several days ago for suppression support." Rick looked down at his SOP. "The provincial duty officer in Sault Ste. Marie tells me the response has been positive. We're expecting fifteen, 4-person initial attack crews from British Columbia, three, 20-person fire crews from Saskatchewan, ten, 5-person initial attack crews from Manitoba, three, 20-person HotShot crews from somewhere in the States and four engine crews from Minnesota. Engine crews are basically four-wheel drive fire trucks complete with crew. There's a standing request for additional helicopters to all companies across North America. The only thing we'll be shy on is heavy water bombers. We're hoping Manitoba comes through."

Norm had collected himself. "When will that be confirmed?"

"Well, the provincial duty officer is dealing with CIFFC on that one—the Canadian Interagency Forest Fire Centre in Winnipeg—the centre that coordinated inter-provincial and out-of-country resource requests. We should know in a day. We're also going through Montreal River Community Forest, a private contractor to provide service and support personnel. We have a standing contract with them. They have a roster of people across the province to call upon for support. Most of the people they provide are MNR retirees with a wealth of experience and training".

Rick paused. "Wherever we can, we'll use them to lighten the load on your staff."

Brad stood up slowly, a gentle sign of conclusion. "Are there any more questions?"

The room was silent. Finally, the admin assistant put up her hand and said, "You still haven't told me how to spell elephant."

Chapter 17

DAY 1: 12:30 HOURS, WHITE RIVER, MINISTRY OF TRANSPORTATION YARD

SEVEN HOURS EARLIER, AT EXACTLY 05:30 HRS, THE NIGHT HAD PULLED BACK ITS DARK CLOAK like a vampire stepping back from a prize, an orange, wafer-shaped disc that rose over a serpentine ridge of hills to the east. The wafer grew exponentially, forcing the night to draw back further and, as it climbed, threw spears of pale orange light against the side-hills, rock outcrops and cliffs that challenged it. Deep shadows still clung to the west facing slopes and veiled plumes of morning ground fog sprung up like mushrooms in a random pattern where the narrow valleys were their lowest.

Although the evening had been relatively cool, Cindy Corrigan could not sleep, and she had sat cross-legged on asphalt for hours that morning at the Ministry of Transportation yard. She silently encouraged the spectacle, hoping for another hot, record-breaking day. If the sun was any indication, she would get her wish. A fire fighter without a fire was like a boxer without an opponent. To be good, you needed to be tested. To stay good, you needed to be tested often.

Her sleeplessness was not a result of her ambition to fight fire. Cindy was at a cross roads in an unstable relationship, and she needed to come to terms with it. Men had never been a problem for her until she met Rob. To her, they were just the bothersome half of the species, developed with a fifth appendage that often acted as a substitute for their brain. Very few had the courage to come on to

106

her, and those who did usually lived to regret it. She did not suffer fools lightly and would not waste time on sexual sparring.

Cindy was tall and angular, her hands and feet just a little too large, but tapered and elegant. Her bronze skin wrapped itself taunt over a sinewy body, but she did carry flesh in all the right places. High shouldered, she walked unconsciously with the grace of a Masaii warrior, its effect not even lost in the red Nomex jump-suit and work boots. Short, dirty blond hair, cat-like, emerald eyes and a generous mouth made for a striking woman. However, her looks and stature were lost on her. An athlete through high school and college, she was late to bloom and catch the attention of boys and men. At thirteen, while some of her classmates wore puberty and push-up bras with a vengeance, Cindy was still kicking butt on the soccer field. At twenty, with those same girls giving spandex a bad name, Cindy slipped through her metamorphosis and evolved into a goddess. The boys would call her the "model with muscle". She was oblivious to their attention and unaware of her effect. As far as she was concerned, she was one of the two hundred and five fire crew leaders in the province, proud of her role and work. She had no time or patience for male/female ritual—until Rob came along. She had no idea how to battle the alien feelings and emo-tions that inflated in her chest like helium balloons, expanding, rising, and restricting in her throat, threatening to choke her.

Rob Cruikshank was a CL415 pilot and had been with the Ministry of Natural Resources for ten years. At thirty-two, he was four years her senior, and at six feet even, he was only an inch taller than Cindy. Of slender build with an angular face, inviting, spon-taneous smile and restful brown eyes, Rob was easy to be with. He was quiet and put no pressure on anyone in his company. He tended to reserve judgment until he had time to size up a person or situation, and Cindy found it exasperating. She needed a com-mitment now that she discovered that she was a woman. However, he wasn't ready to commit. Two years of circling the wagon was enough. She had approached him with an ultimatum like she would a fire—size it up, set up the pump and attack. His response had been devastating. She was planning a no-holds-barred, take-no-prisoners fight that would lead to an emotional climax and rec-onciliation. He gave her a back peddling, "let's think about this" cop out, spineless retreat. Now, she was frustrated, and he was nervous and they weren't getting anywhere.

It was now 12:30 hours and Cindy was aware aerial detection was inbound to the White River area. She had completed her 5 K run after her sunrise meditation, showered, had a light breakfast and attended the 09:30 conference call briefing with the sector response officer who was in Wawa. She then briefed the rest of the crew, and they prepared for the day's activities.

Because of the previous day's dry lightning, her fire crew and two other MNR fire crews had been pre-positioned to White River along with two short-term contract helicopters. The MTO office and yard had been used often to preposition helitack for the White River area. As a standard operating procedure, a radio operator and base station radio was set up to provide coverage for helitack in the area. Two non-fire, MNR staff had been loaned by the district to provide service and support to this mini forward attack base.

The short-term hired helicopters were from the same company, and they came complete with a pilot each and one engineer to keep them air-borne. Cindy's fire crew was first up and red alert was at 12:30 hours. She and her crew had just loaded Helitack 39, an Aerospatial, A-Star 350 B, and were almost ready for immediate dispatch should a call come in. The A-Star was an intermediate class helicopter. Helitack 76, its sister helicopter was a Bell Long Ranger and was classed as a light helicopter. The classification system was associated with payload—how much weight a helicopter could carry. For all intent and purposes, both machines were suitable for single fire crew dispatch and generally limited to a three-person crew with initial attack gear on board.

The medium helicopters, the Bell 205A's, the ancient 204B's and the 212's could take a four-person crew and all the necessary equipment without breaking a sweat, but they were in short supply and costly. The "heavy" helicopters, like the Bell 214's, could take two crews and equipment in a load. The lights, at an average thousand dollars per hour, could rack up an eight thousand dollar charge in an eight hour flying day. The intermediates averaged fifteen hundred dollars per hour, the mediums, twenty-five hundred dollars per hour and the heavies, three thousand per hour plus. So picking the right machine for the right situation was not only a tactical decision, it was also one of economy.

Cindy had spent seven years in the fire crew system, two of them during the summers while attending the three-year natural resource diploma course at Algonquin College in Pembroke, Ontario. She was considered a veteran in Wawa, and her crewmembers not only respected her, they also trusted her judgment. Lately though, they were puzzled by her recent bout of introversion.

Cindy was in the process of double-checking the on-board equipment when she felt someone watching her. She turned around and looked towards her crew. They were all together, sitting quietly at a picnic table and returning the observation. Two of the three looked away. Only her crew boss, Jim Henderson, maintained eye contact. At forty-two years old with twenty years of fire fighting experience, Jim was her ever-vigilant, silent mentor. He didn't say much. He didn't have to. What she had learned in the bush, she had learned from Jim. He had mentored several crew leaders in his time. He had no ambition for the crew leader position. He was a Wawa local, without post secondary education, who loved fighting fire in the spring and summer and ploughing snow in the winter months. Whenever his crew leaders would move on, and invariably they did, the fire management supervisor would assign a new one to crew 461 (Wawa District number 46, crew number 1), knowing full well that Jim would take the new leader under his wing.

Cindy walked over taking care to appear nonchalant. "What's up guys?" No one spoke. She looked to Jim. "Let's take a walk, Jimmie. I need you to check the load with me." Without a word he stood up and the two walked back to the helicopter. She opened the cargo hatch, turned to him and with her hand on his elbow asked, "What's going down, friend?" The two had a special relationship. Jim had no siblings, and she was the younger sister he always wanted.

Without hesitation he turned to her, gently put two big hands on her shoulders and spoke quietly. "Look, Cin, I'm not one to meddle, but you've been acting like someone spit in your cereal bowl and you found out after you finished it. What's going on with you?"

"Come on, it's personal."

"Cin, I'm not very good with words, so I have to choose them carefully. When you have a troll on your back we feel the weight, too. You gotta shake it off and stomp it into a hair mat. If it's a guy, he's more than likely not worth it, but if by chance he is, then deal with it."

Cindy smiled. "Why Jimmie, that's the nicest thing you've said to me all season. I really like the images of someone else's saliva settling in my cereal and a hairy troll pancake at my feet. Only, I imagine the troll as someone else right now. As always, you're right. I can't let my problems affect the crew. Tell you what, let the boys know that the first beer's on me after the shift."

"I'll let the Continental Inn know they won't have to close down, now." He paused. "Hope it works out for you, Cin. I've just about used up all the brain cells I can afford. Now what's the problem with the load?"

CINDY HAD COMPLETED and signed the load sheet— documentation to ensure a helicopter wasn't overloaded. The pilot was also required to review the sheet because it contained data associated with the specific helicopter weight and fuel load. Each helicopter could be configured differently, but a B2 weighed around twenty-five hundred pounds with a maximum gross weight of fifty-five hundred pounds. The difference, three thousand pounds, sounded like plenty, but a full load of fuel, the pilot and three passengers weighed around twenty-two hundred pounds. That left about eight hundred pounds for an initial attack load (equipment, pump gas, camping gear and food). The bottom line was that there was a maximum payload associated with each helicopter, including its own weight, and it couldn't be exceeded. Because of the extreme drought codes (DC's), an indicator of how deeply a fire would burn, the lightweight Shindawa pump and associated equipment was re-placed with the heavier Wajax Mark-3 fire pump unit. The Mark-3 produced the water pressure required to separate and penetrate soil.

Today, the initial attack load consisted of the Mark-3 pump, a light weight tool kit, a standard intake hose, four nylon bags of light-weight 1½ inch diameter fire hose that provided twenty-four hundred feet, two five-gallon fuel containers for the pump that would provide a day's pumping, a Husqvarna 254 chainsaw and chainsaw kit, one gallon of mixed chainsaw fuel and a litre of chain oil. Hand tools included two back pack pumps, shovel, and an axe. Also on board was a foam kit to inject foam through the pump. This produced penetrating "wet" water. A four-gallon foam container, a four-person food kit, part 1 of the personal field incident kit (personal pack), five gallons of drinking water and a first aid kit completed the load. In addition, the fire crew leader carried an incident commander kit, at one time called a fire boss kit. It included fire diaries, various administrative forms, a field guide to forest fire behaviour prediction, local and regional maps and a grid, a spare radio battery, a "throw-up" antenna to extend radio range, flagging tape, duct tape, rain gauge, pencils and pens and a disposable camera.

A second helicopter load would consist of their forth fire crew-member, a five-person cookery kit, parts 2 and 3 of the personal field incident kit and a tent heater. If necessary, other requirements could be loaded such as extra hose or an extra pump.

The personal incident kits were in three parts and colour-coded to avoid taking unnecessary personal gear on the first load. Part 1(red) included a one-person tent, sleeping bag, air mattress, additional coveralls, rain suit, flashlight and holster, goggles, work gloves, a pocket first aid kit and pressure dressing, insect repellent, foot powder and minimal clothing. Part 2 (blue) contained additional clothing and an extra pair of work boots for long stays in the bush. Part 3 (yellow), contained a tarp, plate, mug and cutlery, additional food for 24 hours, a camp stove and lantern.

Each ranger crew member wore the fire resistant, red, Nomex jumpsuits and orange hard-hats with chin straps and hearing protection. In addition, they were issued safety goggles, compasses, Garman XL12 GPS units and MT1000 hand-held, portable radios. Most carried their own brand of folding knife. In Ontario, the foil coloured space blankets used to protect fire fighters in the event of entrapment were not issued. Unlike some of the more arid parts of North America, Ontario was blessed with over ¼ million lakes, and countless rivers, streams, ponds and wet swamps. Fire entrapment was rare, and when it did occur, crewmembers could usually find escape routes and fire safe areas. It did, however, happen. Stories of narrow escapes have been shared from fire crew to fire crew. The greatest method of protection was information and communication. Knowing where you were at all times, planning where to go in the event of an entrapment incident, and maintaining close communication with other members of the crew usually kept a fire fighter out of serious trouble. The abundance of water, however, did not necessarily limit fire escape and spread. Ontario had its share of large fires.

All fire crewmembers, including those in type 2 crews, were required to take a week-long, intensive fire course called S-100. In addition, the two hundred and five full-time fire ranger crews working for MNR carried out rigorous field and classroom training on a routine basis. The training had to follow a schedule and meet specific goals. Power pump set-up and hose lay as a team was practiced until each member knew their roles explicitly and could be delivered without thought or hesitation.

During the classroom training, Cindy always came up with a little extra. In order to keep crew interest at a peak, she often discussed fire history with her crew with a focus on the big fire seasons. In 1985, Red Lake fire number 150 burned a hundred and thirty-three thousand hectares. In 1980, Thunder Bay 46 burned a hundred and twenty-seven thousand hectares and was so complex that MNR declared it an administrative district with a district manager to oversee activities. In 1985, Red Lake 7 burned a hundred and eight thousand hectares and resulted in a billion dollar loss to Ontario's economy. In 1988, Ontario had thirty-two hundred and sixty fires. And in 1991, twenty-five hundred and sixty fires burned three hundred and twenty square kilometres of forest land. More recently, in 2001 there were fifteen hundred and sixty two fires in Ontario, and in 2003, three hundred and fourteen thousand hectares were burned. Stats would quickly be forgotten, but the fact that doo-doo could happen was never far from the fire staff minds.

Cindy had really piqued their interest when she and Jim discussed the fires they had fought. Today, she recounted stories of her experience on Wawa 16 in 2001 and the two young crew members had "ear antennas" at maximum range. The fire was not far from where they were at this moment. West of White River and only six kilometres away from White Lake Provincial Park and Pic Mobert Indian Reserve, evidence of the fire ran along the north side of highway 17 for twenty kilometres. The landscape appeared now like a giant black sleeping porcupine with dead, spike-like trees for quills and burned off, bald rock for patches of skin. There were large patches of burn on the south side of the highway as well, where jump fires had occurred. For the most part, however, the fire was even-edged along the north side of the highway.

Cindy explained that her crew, along with several others had been assigned the job of burning out along the highway to prevent the advancing fire from crossing and moving south. She recalled discussing the details of the burn-out with the two young crew members, Tim Hogg, a big kid with a tangle of blond hair, and Sam Mendez, a short, dark and wiry eighteen year old.

"We were given a four-kilometre stretch to burn along the Trans-Canada highway. It was a "last resort" tactic. Our job was to conduct the burn-out by hand. Follow-up crews would handle jump fires on the south side of the highway." Cindy paused to allow the young crew members to register the event. She continued. Two pair of eyes, wide like tea cup saucers, were focused on the words as she released them in measured servings.

"We had favourable winds at our backs coming in light from the south. The main fire ahead of us was back burning at around ten metres per minute." She felt like she was telling ominous campfire stories to anxious children.

"The back of the fire coming our way was at least ten kilometres wide and so intense that burn-out was the only option. The fire was two to three kilometres away, so while we were lighting up the highway, aerial ignition with helicopters was being carried out close to the fire perimeter."

Sam, who had been mesmerized, slipped away from the spell and had broken in. "Cindy, how exactly is that carried out?"

"Let's save that for another time, Sam." She carried on.

"Our job was a classic drip torch operation. The one gallon Wajax torches were mixed 80% diesel fuel and 20% gasoline. Three of us used torches; the other crew member carried a fire extinguisher for safety. Forest fuels were dry as a pop-corn fart, so we moved in fifteen metres or so and burned back towards the highway at right angles to the right-of-way."

Again, Sam, always the inquisitive one jumped in. "Why not burn parallel along the highway? Wouldn't it be faster?"

"Good question, Sam. Yes, it would be faster but could lead to more jump fires on the south side of the highway. Right angle burn strips don't run ahead; they converge or join. What you burn-out is more easily controlled."

Tim, who didn't want to be left out, joined the conversation. "I recall in our S100 training, it was supposed to be one on one—one person with a torch, one with a fire extinguisher."

"Technically, you're right, Tim."

Tim looked over at Sam, his pursed smile betraying his smug feeling of one-upmanship.

"However, we were wearing our fire retardant jump suits and time was the issue. It was a safe operation."

Tim's half-mast smile folded.

Cindy continued. "We then retrieved the truck and moved it ahead as required. Other crews were carrying out similar operations along the highway. We tied into their burn outs, and the start and finish of the twenty-kilometre operation tied into a couple of large lakes."

Tim's ego re-inflated. "Cindy, from what I recall in training the torch is started by lighting a little fire in dry fuels and sticking the end of the torch in the fire to get it going."

"Not bad Tim. At the tip of the torch is an asbestos pad. When you tip the torch down, the mixed fuel runs down the nozzle and collects in the pad. Once it ignites, it stays lit. Whenever you want to stop the drip, put the container in the vertical position. Whenever you want to drop fire, tip it down."

Before Cindy could continue, the radio operator stuck her head out the MTO office door, shouted and waved a piece of paper. They had a fire. The helicopter pilot emerged from the office, and Cindy mobilized her crew. She had three minutes from notification to getaway. Tim, the least experienced crewmember, would stay behind until the next load, if there was one. Jim and Sam scrambled into the back and Cindy climbed in the co-pilots position in the left seat. All fire crew members buckled up and put on headsets. The triple blades were already rotating, and the engine on the A-star was accelerating into a high-pitched whine. Within the three-minute target, they were airborne. Tim could only look on with regret as the helicopter disappeared to the north.

Chapter 18

DAY 1: 12:30 HOURS, SIREN LAKE

THE FORTEEN-FOOT ALUMINUM BOAT APPEARED TO GLIDE ATOP THE WATER like a cupped leaf pushed by a quiet breeze. The steady tic-tic of a small motor resonated off the shoreline. About six decibels higher than the ancient motor, the banter of the two occupants rose, swirled and drifted away into the tree line, each unique pitch and volume jousting for anecdotal superiority. The two old, life-long friends faced each other, fishing poles in hand, delighted in the fact they had managed to salvage yet another day to share at this stage of their lives.

To Earl and Henry, each new day in their extensive existence was like unwrapping stolen candy with no consequence in sight. Cheating time was their game, and they considered themselves professionals.

The two couldn't have been more diametrically opposed. Earl was built like Mr. Potato Head with stuck-on, larger-than-life features. Henry continually reminded him that he looked like he climbed out of a cartoon frame.

Henry, on the other hand, had the build, countenance and careful gait of a great blue heron. Earl would often prompt him to pick up the pace. "Hurry up. You're walking like a blind-folded scarecrow in a field of cow pies!" Like most people Henry's age, his face had shrunk with time making its appendages look large; forehead, eyebrows, ears and nose popped out from a narrow, withered face like weather vanes. It was his ears, however, that commanded attention. In one particular moment of enlightenment, Earl had exclaimed, "Henry, if you had a propeller stuck in your ass, you could flap your ears and fly!"

Earl's claim to fame was his poor hearing, and he took pride in his ability to make people repeat themselves. It was his form of control, his hook. If he needed time to respond, he would throw back a "What?", "Pardon?" or, for the ladies, a polite, "Sorry, I've got a hearing problem."

Henry trumped Earl's impairment with his own, a poorly fitting upper plate that dropped repeatedly and chewed up the words as they came out of his mouth giving a whole new meaning to each phrase.

Their dialogue was simply something to behold. They often carried on two completely unrelated conversations at the same time, each of them oblivious to the other's line of thinking.

Occasionally, their words and phrases managed to climb onto the same page, but only when they were short and simple. Over time, they had developed a format for understanding: no long sentences, the use of simple words, no heavy thinking and they avoided topics that triggered emotion. They knew their conversations weren't pretty but considered them functional and economical.

Both were widowers, and their friendship became one of unspoken need, like a quasi marriage, one of easy companionship spiced with an occasional and welcome argument. And, like a marriage, their relationship became instinctive. Earl was the clairvoyant one. He knew what Henry was thinking and would often finish Henry's thoughts for him. Henry, on the other hand, often assumed Earl was pre-cognizant and would verbalize a thought mid-point, leaving the bulk of the idea buried away. It was up to Earl to figure out what he was talking about. This routinely elicited a frustrated, "What the hell are you talking about", from a rotund Earl.

Today was no different than any other day as their disjointed conversation glanced off water and rock, words filtering upward through pine and poplar or bouncing back to them in muted echoes. Their target fish for the day was Walleye, best caught with a slow troll and a fine touch on the rod.

"Pass me a minnow, Earl."

"What?"

"I said, pass me a damned minnow."

"No need to swear, Henry. I heard you the first time. I'm just used to saying 'what'."

"You need your hearing checked."

"And you need to get new teeth!"

There was a moment of reflection after Earl passed the minnow, a minnow that was probably relieved to get cast out of the dysfunctional boat.

"Earl, you using a …?"

"Yellow jig and stinger hook, yup."

There was routine pause in the conversation. Henry shifted on his seat, lifted a bony cheek and passed gas. Earl's hearing was bad but not finished and he still had his olfactory function.

"What the hell was that?"

Henry looked up with a grin and arched eye-brows. "Why, my short, fat friend—that was a barking spider."

"Yeah, well it's got road-kill breath. You been eating tube steaks again?"

Henry became defensive. "Nope. But I had boiled cabbage and beans for supper last night".

With a mild look of astonishment, Earl retorted. "Why didn't you splurge and have pickled eggs for dessert? Your stomach's gonna shove a white flag out your butt and wave it in surrender!"

Henry, who had been thinking about the shot at his beloved hot dogs, counter punched. "And what's wrong with tube steak, er, hot dogs?"

"They're OK if you like eyeballs and arseholes. But then, once again you've proven you can eat just about anything. My problem is, I just can't get up and walk outa this boat."

"No problem, Earl. Just take a deep breath and you'll float on top of the water like a big, circus balloon, one with arms and legs sticking straight out and a fat, round, neck-less head on top."

The two were now spent. They had used up their repertoire of retorts and a reluctant truce of silence followed. It would take some time for their brains to manufacture additional information, put it on a cerebral conveyor belt and ship it to a collection point where it would be ready for delivery.

The 9.9 HP Merc continued its slow, steady tic-tic along the surface. The scratched-up bow of the boat bounced and slapped the six-inch chop in rhythm. Both men rocked with the cadence, each twitching their rods lightly, neither caring if a fish took their bait.

Henry's half-mast eyes rose slightly with the formation of a new thought. "Then we can go there next."

Earl, who was usually good at Henry's thought puzzles, finally gave up. "What the hell you talking about, Henry?"

"Just thinking that after we troll the narrows, here, we can drift to that sunken island out in the big water."

Fifteen minutes later, Winken and Blinken were drifting across open water, motor shut down, both nodding off. Time stood still for the two friends connected by chance, age, loss and pressing mortality. Winds began to pick up and the chop turned into ribbons of wave, white-fringed and aggressive. Henry, who had been thinking about absolutely nothing, opened a reluctant eye. "I smell smoke."

Earl worked up a response like a pelican regurgitating an over-sized fish. "Henry, you know I don't smoke."

"No Earl, I *smell* smoke! Seems like its coming from the north."

Earl, who was sitting in the stern and facing northerly looked up above the tree line. "I can do you one better, Henry. I can see it. Swing around and look over your right shoulder."

A large column of dark grey smoke fringed in white cotton rose and spread like a cone, then bent and flattened out in a north easterly direction.

Earl, whose fight or flight mechanism usually tended towards "flight", grasped the motor throttle and pull cord and croaked, "I think we should vacate the premises, Henry." He gave the ancient motor cord an over-ambitious tug. Two minutes and sixty frantic pulls later, a pale, sweating Earl gave up with a "we're screwed" look in his silver-dollar sized pupils.

Henry responded paternally. "I do believe she's flooded again, Earl—time to get out the spare spark plug."

Earl's response was overshadowed by a rather long, pregnant pause. "This **is** the spare plug, Henry."

Their cross-boat stares spoke volumes. "Don't worry, Earl. The wind is pushing us north-easterly and away."

Earl, desperate to save what little face he had left, pointed. "There's a cabin across the lake and ahead of us. In the meantime,

I'll pull the plug and crank out the surplus gas in the cylinder. Maybe that'll do the trick."

Earl moved around frantically in the boat like a bare-footed bather on hot sand. Henry didn't even shift his position. The boat continued to drift in open water.

Chapter 19

DAY 1: 12:45 HOURS,
NORTH OF WHITE RIVER

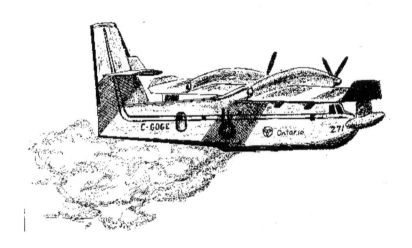

THE CANADAIR CL415 LUMBERED FIVE THOUSAND FEET UP, across a cloudless, pale blue sky, fresh from an initial attack north of its present position. Tanker 271 had been part of an air tanker package—two heavy water bombers and a Birddog aircraft. It had been first on the scene and had to return for fuel, leaving the other tanker and Birddog 12 to continue the battle with Wawa 40, the first of three new fires discovered this day.

The pilot, Rob Cruikshank, now relaxed in the left seat, was at veteran at thirty-two years of age. Three years his junior, the co-pilot, Jamie Verstraten, had four years' experience as a Ministry of

Natural Resources pilot, three of which were on the Dehavilland Twin Otter. This was his second year on the CL415. He had well over the required four thousand hours of total flying and had completed his one hundred hours on type, in this case the 415, to qualify as pilot on the big water bomber. Actual flying was now shared. Rob would act as mentor and share the helm as he saw fit. Both pilots loved their jobs and both professed to be career air jockeys.

The CL415 was the pride of Ontario's air fleet. The total fleet of twenty-eight aircraft was comprised of:

- nine, turbine, twin engine CL415's,
- five, amphibious (combination float and wheel) Twin Otters,
- six, single engine, amphibious Turbo Beavers,
- four, Aerospatial (Astar) B2 intermediate class helicopters,
- three, Bell Long Range (L1) light class helicopters, and
- one, Chieftan Navajo, a twin piston engine aircraft used predominantly for remote sensing.

The ochre yellow 415 weighed in dry at twenty-six thousand pounds and carried up to ten thousand pounds of fuel. With an over-all length of close to twenty metres, a wingspan of twenty-eight and a half metres and a height at one point of nine metres, it could be described (with humility) as formidable. The twin Pratt and Whitney engines each maxed out at close to twenty-four hundred horsepower. It cruised at two hundred and eighty-seven kilometres per hour and could reach a maximum speed of three hundred and seventy-five kph. However, its strength was its range. At a range of twenty-four hundred kilometres, it could stay airborne for close to four hours, pummelling a fire into submission. The 415 could pick up thirteen hundred and twenty (imperial) gallons of water through two small four by twelve inch apertures in ten to twelve seconds. The water was housed in two, large interior tanks. It would eventually be released through four doors, each three feet by two feet in dimension. Both Rob and Jamie were amazed at how thirteen hundred and twenty gallons of water could be forced through a couple of small four inch by twelve inch apertures in twelve seconds or less. It was Jamie's darker sense of humour that once led him to declare, "It's a good thing that humans were born with rear ends that could close. Can you imagine what falling water skiers would look like?"

Once the doors were released, they opened gravitationally. When the load was dropped, they were closed hydraulically. They could be opened all at once or separately depending on drop requirements. With a keel-shaped hull and two, wing-mounted outriggers, the 415 touched down for water and ascended effortlessly. As if a thirteen thousand, two hundred pound water drop wasn't enough, each load was injected with a foam-generating agent to create wet water. Once ejected, it resulted in a blanket of foam. The use of foam reduced the surface tension of water, by allowing air to readily mix with water molecules and form the bubble structure. The effects of the use of foam were two-fold. It acted as a barrier to fire spread by insulating unburned fuels, and it increased the effective life of water by controlling its drainage out of the foam. This stalling effect increased water penetration into woody fuels.

As Rob kept his line of sight on the horizon and Jamie scanned the intimidating array of gauges, their FM radio crackled to life.

"Tanker 271, this is Wawa Fire on channel 6, do you copy?"

Their radio was programmed to scan all District and fire frequencies. Rob depressed his transmission button on the left side of the ¾ pie shaped steering wheel and responded.

"Wawa Fire, this is Tanker 271, we copy."

"Hi Rob, the SRO wants to know how you're doing for fuel."

"Not bad. We've got enough to head to Wawa plus ¾ of an hour's reserve. Chapleau airport was short on fuel this morning so we only took on 2/3 load.

"So you're not returning Chapleau?"

"Not if you want us to continue dropping on Wawa 40. Wawa airport is ten minutes closer one way."

George Williams, the sector response officer at Wawa, looked over at the radio operator, nodded and keyed in his own mic.

"Rob, this is George. Region has assigned you to us and we have another potential target."

"Sounds good, George. Go ahead with details."

"This one was called in by a trapper on Siren Lake. Apparently, it's close to five kilometres west and a bit north of his camp. It's on your flight path at base map 61539."

"We copy, 61539."

I know you're "lone wolf" right now, but can you drop a few loads?"

"Any details on water source?"

"Siren Lake is a good pick-up chance. With this drought, stay away from the narrows. Your best source is deep water two-thirds the way up the lake."

As the radio conversation was bouncing back and forth, Jamie had punched the UTM coordinates into the consol-mounted RNAV GPS (area navigational system that did not require ground based navigational aids to find a location such as an airport) and checked fuel reserve. The GPS converted the base map location to latitude/ longitude, the preferred choice for pilots. The on board VHF (very high frequency) and UHF (ultra high frequency) radios could also be used along with airport ground based navigational aids to assist with navigation. Jamie nodded an affirmative to Rob and scanned the horizon to the south west and pointed. There it was—a vague silhouette of smoke. Rob nodded an acknowledgement and keyed his mic.

"Wawa Fire, we have a visual. We'll see what we can do. Any other aircraft inbound?"

George turned the control of the radio over to the operator. He had achieved his objective—get something on the fire for the time being.

The radio operator responded. "Tanker 271, we have dispatched Helitack 39 with the Cindy Corrigan crew. ETA approximately thirty minutes. H39 will be transmitting channel 6. Cindy is the initial attack fire boss and will call the shots at touch down."

Rob felt the fine hairs on his forearms sit up ever so slightly, a subtle sign of tension. He had a lot of respect for Cindy's abilities' and he knew it was not rational to worry about her, but "caring" equalled "worry". This wasn't the first time he supported her crew with water drops and it wouldn't be the last, but he wasn't inclined to like it. She was a distraction that defied definition, a little butterfly in his sternum. He was definitely more at ease in the cockpit when Cindy wasn't on the ground below him.

Jamie instinctively sensed his discomfort. The two pilots functioned daily as the intellect and heart of their tanker/beast. Like cojoined twins, they responded to stimuli efficiently, their thoughts merged instinctively and their responses were automatic.

Jamie glanced over at Rob. "Give it a rest, boss. She'll be fine. She has a lot more common sense than the two of us combined."

Jamie's words unconsciously transferred his own confidence and calm to his partner. Rob relaxed his stiff posture, and his frame deflated a few inches into his chair. The high profiled tendons joining wrist to hand shrank, leaving only well defined veins as a road map to his heart.

"As always, my friend, you read me like a take-out menu. But don't ever, for one moment think you're right. My ego won't take it."

Tanker 271, at first large and grandiose in a framed sky, shrunk and faded as it rumbled towards the smoke on the ridge in the distance.

"WHAT'S THAT SOUND, EARL?"

Earl was sitting, bent over, his head down, and he was in the process of cleaning and re-gapping a spark plug. He looked at his buddy with a sour look on his face, lips pressed tight, mouth stretched into a 'gas blocking' grimace. Hard work on the motor had given him indigestion and he felt like his stomach was crawling back up his throat.

"Don't hear a damn thing." Conscious of his impairment, the edge-laden words were spat out as a challenge, his eyes locked on Henry's face daring him to verbal battle. *What the hell is wrong with Henry?*

Henry's mouth was agape, like his jaw had suddenly unhinged and dropped unceremoniously to his chest. His eyes were big and bulgy like poached eggs on a plate. One of Henry's arms was thrust straight out with a grim-reaper hand pointed over Earl's head. "Holy sh _ _!!" The words were cut off at the knees as a big, yellow, alien spacecraft scraped the air one hundred feet above them. Earl's pork-pie hat and Henry's ball cap were stripped from their heads and chased the spacecraft in its slip-stream. Thin hair atop gleaming heads stood straight up and waved and tangled frantically as if afraid of losing purchase and being torn away.

Earl dove instinctively to the shallow-bottomed boat, his rear end peaking over the gunnels, his face thrust in oil and minnow stained seepage, with hands covering his head, holding lonely hairs in place.

Henry sat petrified, arm still extended as Tanker 271 passed overhead. He was transformed into a tall, skinny, granite statue unconsciously pissing himself on a worn pine seat in the boat.

Earl was the first to speak, his voice strangled and gurgling as the words were forced through bilge water. "What (choke, cough) the hell (gurgle) was that??"

Henry was the first to gain composure as he looked down at his soiled crotch. *Comes with age*, he thought. "I believe Earl, after some consideration, that it was a water bomber."

Earl peeked over the gunnels, oily water dripping from his nose. Henry cranked his body around, granite joints cracking and popping with the effort.

"Henry, it's dropping. Looks like it might crash."

Henry, the more cerebral of the two, had now connected the smoke to the aircraft. He masked his embarrassment with false calm. "Just picking up water, I suspect."

The impressive ship touched down a hundred and fifty metres to the southwest, its props feathered to decrease speed. As it continued on, engines began to power up again, and in twelve seconds the inconceivable happened—thirty-six thousand pounds of aircraft rose effortlessly, carrying over thirteen thousand pounds of water.

In the meantime, Earl, who was now tuned into to the connection between aircraft and fire, became intent on survival. He cranked the refurbished plug into the motor and gave it a short tug and even shorter prayer, "Oh Lord, start this piece of shit!" The old 9.9 came to life. He threw the motor into neutral, gave it three good revs and rammed it into forward.

"Piece of cake, Earl!" Henry yelled as he covertly covered his crotch with a life preserver.

"What!"

"I said, piece of cake!"

Earl, whose shirt and pants were soaked and smelled of oily fish offal, responded. "Showed that big, yellow tub with wings that we weren't scared, eh Henry?"

"Yeah, we showed 'em, Earl."

As the two sped away, the broken sounds of interrupted and unfinished superlatives rose above the sound of the motor. The sounds eventually faded with distance. It was understandable, so the two brave amigos could be forgiven for unwittingly allowing rods, reels, line and tackle to slip overboard at point of departure, bob, sink slowly and become lake-bottom souvenirs.

Chapter 20

DAY 1: 13:00 HOURS, WAWA 43

"JEEZ, JAMIE, I FEEL BAD ABOUT BUZZING THAT BOAT, but it was sitting on our best target for water."

"Hey Rob, with the wind direction and need for climb, we had no choice." Both men knew that they had to avoid narrows and shallow water and that the big part of the lake closest to the fire was the safest and most efficient choice for pick-up. Although the CL415 could pick up in water as shallow as two metres, it needed just over a kilometre of total distance (decent pick-up and climb out) to escape with a load.

"I do believe we woke them up—probably have to deal with a complaint when we get back."

Rob had just powered on the throttle, and their yellow beast rose, leaving a drift of water behind as the aperture closed. They were now in continuous climb and heading for their intended target a few kilometres to the east. Their FM radio came to life. "Tanker 271. This is Helitack 39 on channel 1, do you copy?" It was Cindy's strong, confident voice.

Jamie switched to the fire frequency. Rob's instinct was to reply with something clever but he chose to follow the rules—keep it short and professional. "Helitack 39, this is Tanker 271, we copy."

"Hi Rob, we're inbound for what is officially Wawa fire 43. ETA, about twenty minutes. You have air space control. I'm going to turn you over to our pilot."

"Copy that, Cindy. Go ahead Helitack 39."

The Astar B2 helicopter pilot keyed the mic on his VHF radio. Most pilots preferred to discuss business on very high frequency. "Tanker 271, what elevation do you want on our approach prior to approval for touch down."

Rob responded. "Three thousand feet on your altimeter will give us plenty of air space. However, we'll probably be on our way for fuel when you get here."

"Copy that, Tanker 271. Let us know when you're out-bound." Cindy's headset was on live mic so she could follow the conversation.

"Affirmative, Helitack 39." Rob had to let his feelings slip away. It was time to get to work.

The heavy water bomber was two minutes out from Wawa 43. There was absolutely no doubt in Rob's mind that targeting the head of the fire was a waste of time. He could see multiple torching and sporadic crowning where standing fuels would carry fire through the canopy. The silhouettes of spruce and balsam fir looked like dark clowns, swaying with the weight of bright orange/yellow clown caps as large again as their bearers. The tips of the caps would twist, turn and pop off as their clown bearers undulated below them in a grotesque dance of withering destruction.

Rob watched the solid column of tornado-whirling, charcoal-coloured smoke rise above his aircraft, bend horizontally, then stretch and grow. Beneath the horizontal shroud, smaller plumes of smoke poked up from the forest below, signally multiple jump fires. He made a pass around the head of the fire and underneath the shroud in order to pick a more appropriate target. The big bird rattled, the steering mechanism shaking in his grip due to the up-drafts and cross drafts created by the heat associated with the column of smoke. Rob keyed his mike.

"Wawa Fire this is Tanker 271 and channel 6, do you copy?"

"Tanker 271, this is Wawa Fire, we copy". This time it was the voice of George Williams, the sector response officer.

"Wawa Fire, I don't think we're going to be of much help here. I've only got enough fuel for two drops. Hitting the head is out of the question."

George responded, his voice up two octaves and even unfamiliar to himself. "What do you suggest?"

"Seems like we have two options here. The smoke column is bent by upper winds at a thousand metres. There's spotting ahead of the fire and under the column. We could kill a couple of those. The other option is to hit one of the flanks near the back of the fire where the crew from Helitack 39 is most likely going to work. Over."

Tanker 271, which direction is the fire moving?"

"There's some strong surface winds, and it's on a ridge, so right now it's taking a long narrow run to the northeast."

"Tanker 271, this is Helitack 39." Cindy broke into the conversation.

"Go ahead Helitack 39."

"Rob, from the sounds of it, we won't have much choice. Can you lay a couple of drops on the southwest flank to get us started?"

"Affirmative, Cindy. Did you copy that, Wawa?"

The SRO had no problem with Cindy's request. In fact, he silently applauded her aggressiveness. "I concur, Tanker 271. Cindy knows what she's doing. It's all yours. Wawa clear."

Rob brought the CL415 around to the back of the fire. Visibility was becoming significantly better so Jamie turned off the FLIR or "forward looking, infrared device" used to help penetrate smoke and target heat. Rob dropped down to a little over thirty metres above the forest canopy and lined up the less active flame front on the southwest flank. His usual tactic was to punch the load just before the target vanished under the nose of the aircraft.

"Jamie, I think we need to stretch the load and lay it half on and half outside the fire edge." A few tense moments slipped by. "On my mark—release!" As he spoke, Rob also gave a firm nod to Jamie who, in turn, flipped the foam injector switch and opened the load hatches in sequence to allow for a slower release. Thirteen thousand pounds of foam-injected water tumbled out of the hatches, one after another, and a fifteen metre-wide band penetrated the forest canopy and fell to the ground as thick, white foam. Black spikes of spruce and balsam fir, their roots weakened by surface and sub-surface fire, were slammed to the ground and arranged themselves like pick-up sticks. The blanket of foam stretched for a hundred and twenty metres. In spots it began to turn a dirty, pale yellow where the intense heat smothered below it, attempted to struggle free to the surface. Three-metre flame heights in finer fuels dropped immediately along the fire edge and trees torching to twenty-five metres were temporarily relieved of their painful fire burden.

The CL415 climbed away and headed for a final load. Rob desperately wished he had an hour of fuel to spare. The distance from the water source to the fire would have allowed for close to eighteen drops. Twenty-four thousand gallons of water and foam would have gone a long way to helping Cindy out.

"Wawa Fire, this is Tanker 271. Off fire 43 and bound for another load."

"Tanker 271, we copy. Be advised that Helitack 39 will be in your air space on your return to the fire."

H39 CLIMBED TO THREE THOUSAND FEET as the tanker dropped its second load. Cindy wanted altitude to get a bird's eye view of the fire, a better perspective of the area outside of the fire and to pinpoint a source of water nearby for pumping. The lake to the east was too far as a water source, but she spotted a dry swamp with a pond in the middle of the ridge about a thousand metres to the east of the fire and about 1/3 of the way up the southeast flank.

Tanker 271 had left for Wawa and fuel about five minutes ago, so she instructed the pilot to drop elevation to a hundred and fifty metres and do a slow circuit clockwise around the fire perimeter. The helicopter bucked and swayed as it worked around the head. Visibility was limited, but the pilot was experienced and Cindy needed to see what they were dealing with. This was no "zero point two" hectare fire that she and her crew could jump on and wrestle to the ground. Her note pad and pencil had unconsciously materialized in her hands and she had crafted a rough sketch.

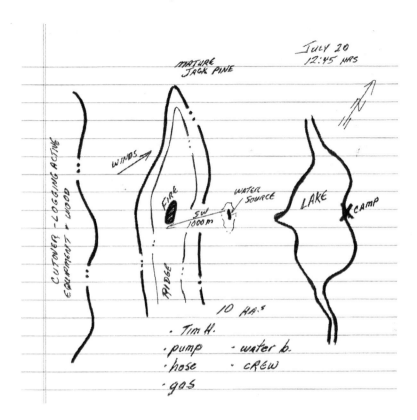

Satisfied with her recon she asked for elevation and talked to her second in command over the intercom. "What do you think, Jimmie?"

"Well, Cin, Rob made the right call. We may even have some trouble with the southwest flank. The fire's pretty intense. It's gonna run and we can't do anything about that but we may be able to delay spread to the west where all that cut wood is piled."

Cindy nodded and Jim continued. "Our real problem is time. From the pond to the back of the fire it's a thousand metres and uphill. We'll need another pump to maintain pressure."

Cindy again nodded agreement and keyed her mic. "Wawa fire, this is Helitack 39. I have a scouting report for you."

"Helitack 39, Wawa Fire. Ready to copy, Cindy."

Cindy began her report. "Size, ten hectares. Fire is running and torching with some spotting at the head and northeast flank. Rate of spread, ten metres per minute. Surface fire flame length, two to three metres." She paused for feedback.

"Copy that, Cindy."

"Values—large stand of mature jack pine two kilometres north of the head. There's a cabin approximately four kilometres to the east on the east shore of Siren Lake. There's an ATV parked outside, so I have to assume it's inhabited. There's a significant logging operation three kilometres to the west with equipment and lots of cut wood. Over."

"Copy that Cindy."

"I have a water source approximately one thousand metres to the east." Cindy took a few moments to collect her thoughts. She knew that this fire was going to escape to the north and that her only strategy was values protection. Priority one was human life. However, at this point the cabin was out of harm's way. The lake could be a significant barrier to fire spread. On the other hand, she also knew that once the fire really started to boogy and if the wind quartered easterly, jump fires across four thousand metres of forest and lake were not out of the question. It would depend on the height and direction of the column and the volume of burning embers imbedded in it. This was no time to second-guess herself.

"Wawa Fire—we can't work the head or east flank, it's just too intense. The two tanker drops have bought us some time on the southwest flank and there's a big investment in equipment and cut wood to the west. That's where our best bet is."

George took over transmission at Wawa.

"Cindy, it's George here. We copied that. It's your fire right now and you're the eyes out there. I agree with your assessment." He began to think ahead. *I'll have to get the District involved to ensure Wally McNeil evacuates his camp.*

Cindy came back on. "If we're going to do any good here, I'll need another pump, ten more boxes of hose, two more sceptre containers of pump gas and my fourth fire crew member. I'd also like air attack ahead of us and another crew behind us."

George was in a fix. He needed Tanker 271 back on Wawa 40. They might be able to wrestle that one down, and it wasn't far from the town of Hornepayne. He had no crews to spare, but he had put in a request for an additional ten. Wawa 43 was a bust. Yes, there was the cut wood to the west but fire 40 to the northeast and its potential to threaten Hornepayne was *the* priority. He could pull Cindy off, but she might be able to buy some time, and besides, he would be hard pressed to justify no action on this fire to Northshore Logging, the operator with all the cut wood.

"Cindy, I can't help you with the crew. We're now up to Wawa 46—three more fires since yours. Air attack is out. We have a priority fire north of you. I will however direct them to save a little reserve time on their way back for fuel. You may get a couple of drops from each tanker when they're going by. Your crewman, pump, gas and extra hose will be loaded on H39 when it returns from dropping you off. Do you need more ground foam?"

Cindy thought, *Man, they keep pushing that shit.* It was a royal pain in the ass. More handling meant more lost time. She also grudgingly agreed that it was effective. "Sure, George. Send us two more jugs."

George handed a note to the radio operator, who immediately got on the phone to the equipment warehouse in Wawa, who in turn called the service people at the MTO yard in White River. The equipment would be down at the helipad in a matter of minutes.

"Look, Cindy. Sorry we can't help you more. Once you're on the ground, you'll have to relay info and requests through the MTO yard. You may need to use your throw-up antenna. Two direct orders: don't be a hero and don't get caught."

"Copy that, George. We're on approach for landing. Helitack 39 out."

George was worried. *Like a mosquito on an elephant's ass.* The "elephant" was the fire and Cindy's crew was the "mosquito". *What else could go wrong?* George no sooner spawned the dirty thought, when the radio operator handed him a note. "George, just got this from Tanker 274 on Wawa 40. They're having some mechanical problems and are returning to Chapleau."

THE SOW LOOKED UP NERVOUSLY to a smoke-veiled sky. Something very foreign and threatening had broken over the fringe of spruce that encircled the dry swamp. The sound and its accompanying reverberation confused her. As the object grew closer, she became agitated and grunted at her cub.

Their haven was being threatened, and it was again time to move on. The rest and nourishment had provided them with some strength, but she sensed that it wouldn't stay with them for long. She required new sanctuary and made the choice to move uphill, the direction from which she had come the previous night. She encouraged her cub with a woof and a push with her nose and broke towards the edge of the swamp. Her cub followed as best it could, but it was no match for the dead stumps and horizontal cedar, black ash and tamarack snags hidden in the high saw grass. Every metre of the cub's advance was impeded by random wall of old stumps and fallen trees. The distance between the sow and her cub stretched and the little bear was losing strength. It stopped, legs quivering and did only what it could do: thrust its muzzle in the air and bawled for the protection of its mother. It was a desperate, high pitched, all-out squawk that stopped the sow in her tracks. She turned her head towards her offspring, then up, towards the threat. Deep down from inside, a primitive, biological message mushroomed and surged through her system to an overwhelmed brain. The message became her focus and triggered maternal instincts that resulted in a vocal, double woof —a command that gave the cub all the encouragement it required as it struggled to shorten the distance to its mother.

Chapter 21

DAY 1: 13:15 HOURS, WAWA 43

THE ASTAR CIRCLED THE DRY SWAMP, its pilot looking for a suitable place to drop off Cindy and her crew. Moments before, the pilot had hovered over the swamp and pointed his helicopter to the back of the fire, the south end. Cindy needed a bearing because once they were on the ground they were at the mercy of a thick, impenetrable forest cover and uneven terrain. There would be times when they would not be able to see the smoke. They had a kilometre of hose to lay to their point of attack, and it had to be dead on. She used the compass on the helicopter to take a bearing of 255 degrees or west, southwest from the swamp. She preferred the reliability of the compass slung around her neck to the sophistication of her hand-held Garman GPS unit. She had already taken a GPS fix where the CL415 had initially dropped foam. She might need it if she had to deviate off her bearing due to obstacles.

Now, all eyes were down. The pilot looked for firm ground and limited vertical interference from trees or high brush. Jim Henderson was looking for a suitable site to set up the pump. He wanted a solid, stable base for the Wajax Mark-3 pump board, at least several inches of water depth along the shoreline for the intake hose, and, as he put it, "shit-free" water so the intake wouldn't suck in debris and fowl the pump. Sam Mendez was assessing the standing trees and snags. He was their chain saw man, and his priority job after helping Jim set up the pump was to take down anything that might pose a hazard to the helicopter. Later on, if it was necessary and when time permitted, he would build a 5X5 metre helipad for the Astar. Cindy scanned the forest fringe and beyond in the direction that hose would be laid. She was looking for a good entry point into the bush and any other obvious obstacles further on that might impede their progress. Ravines, cliffs and blow downs were "time killers" when it came to laying hose.

Jim was the first to spot them. He spoke into his live mike. "Look over there at one o'clock. Do you see them?" Two black objects, one considerably larger than the other had just entered the tree line.

It was Sam who responded first. "A sow bear and cub. It looks like they're heading west towards the fire. We must have spooked them."

Without hesitation, Cindy directed the pilot to pull up and see if he could turn them around. Jim, who had seen this reaction to a helicopter many times with moose, deer and bear, was less concerned. "What about our fire, Cindy?"

"This will just take a minute. We'll know right away if it works."

The pilot directed his Astar to the point where the bears had entered the tree line, reduced speed and walked his machine over the forest canopy. All four occupants were intent on looking down. Cindy thought, *I'll give it one minute more then we'll pack this adventure in.*

"There! At my three o'clock!" Sam couldn't hide his excitement.

The pilot continued thirty metres, turned the machine on a dime and dipped the nose, keeping the Astar in a hovering position. He needed to see the bears himself. Sure enough, they were there, the sow now confused and angry, rocking back and forth on her front paws, the cub tucked in behind her. The pilot had done this kind of work before. With a slight push on the collective, his helicopter dipped even more and slowly progressed towards the frightened animals. The sow had no way of repelling the intruder, and instinctively she turned and bolted back to the dry swamp, her cub not far behind. The pilot kept his machine a respectable distance behind, and herded his charges through the swamp and back into the bush on the other side. They were now headed east, towards the lake and out of harm's way for the time being.

"Not sure that was the best thing to do, Cin. She might have known where she was going, and she can still turn and head west."

Cindy muffled a quiet groan. "As usual, you're probably right, Jim. I felt I had to try. Now let's put this baby down so we can get to work."

The pilot picked a spot and eased the Astar down. When he touched, he kept power on and rocked his helicopter slightly, checking to see if the site was firm. Once satisfied he pulled off power, looked around and advised the crew it was safe to off-load. Everyone knew the drill. Cindy got out of the front port seat, crouched and walked back to the rear hatch. Both Jim and Sam stepped out of the rear passenger area. Jim exited from the starboard, crouching and walking around the front of the helicopter in the pilot's field of vision. Sam exited from the port side and began to off-load the equipment that had been packed in with them and handed it to Jim. Cindy was off-loading equipment from the cargo hold. Once their load was piled properly and there was no danger of anything being pulled up or blown from the helicopter rotor, the team quartered away from the machine and squatted together where the pilot could see them. The Astar ascended smoothly, moved laterally, then cleared obstructions and swept south for another load.

FOR A BRIEF MOMENT, all was quiet. Each crewmember knew his or her role and was internally cataloguing a checklist of personal activity. Movement would be efficient and purposeful. There was no point in rushing; it would only lead to premature fatigue.

Cindy was the first to speak. "Let's do a radio check."

They each pulled out their MT1000 hand-held portable radios, switched to fire channel 1 and in turn, spoke a "test" into the tiny microphone in the centre of the radio. It had a range of two to four kilometres depending on interference. It was a straight "line of sight" transmitter and topography could affect range. It was a five watt radio, capable of ninety-nine channels, and the operator could scan up to eight channels. A coaxial throw-up antenna was in Cindy's Incident Commander Kit and gave the radio significantly more range; the higher the antenna, the longer the range.

Cindy was satisfied. "OK. Let's get started."

It would take the three of them to get the necessary equipment to the pump site. Before they did anything else, they each put two bottles of drinking water in the leg pockets of their jump suits and spare radio batteries in front pockets. Cindy reached into her into her kit and pulled out a 1:50,000 topographic map and the coiled throw-up antenna for her radio. She was already wearing a nylon front vest organizer with an array of pockets and zippers. She put the map and antenna inside. Next, they broke open the pump tool kit. Sam took a hose strangler to shut the water off up the line and two metal hose patches in case a hose sprung a leak. Jim grabbed a nozzle and two metal hose patches. Cindy grabbed the other hose strangler, a spare nozzle and two metal hose patches. The nozzles were stashed in rear pockets, the stranglers came in a pouch and were slid on to belts and the metal hose patches, which could be pried open, were clipped over belts.

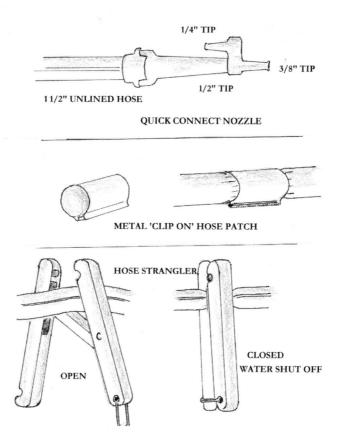

1/4" TIP

3/8" TIP

1 1/2" UNLINED HOSE

1/2" TIP

QUICK CONNECT NOZZLE

METAL 'CLIP ON' HOSE PATCH

HOSE STRANGLER

OPEN

CLOSED
WATER SHUT OFF

Jim swung the sixty pound, Wajax Mark-3 pump onto his back and adjusted the shoulder straps. He then lifted the coupled two and a half metre long, two inch diameter intake hose over his head and on to one shoulder, grabbed the pump tool kit in one hand and a shovel in the other. He was carrying close to ninety pounds.

Sam took the foam kit in a nylon bag with strap and slung it over his neck. He picked up the foam jug and five gallons of mixed pump gas.

Cindy slung a sixty pound bag of hose over her shoulders and around to her back in one fluid motion. She slipped her arms through the harness and picked up an axe.

Jim took the lead. He knew exactly where his pump site would be. The others followed. It was easy walking through the high swamp grass. Normally it would be spongy with ankle-twisting pools of tepid, mosquito-infested water. Now it was slate dry, and the only care required was avoiding holes. Within five minutes, they were at the site.

It was early afternoon now and already thirty degrees. All three fire fighters were sweating profusely. There was no use complaining. They wouldn't call it a day until the sun was down and that wouldn't be until 21:30 hours.

Without a word, they began the process of obtaining water for the fire. Once all the equipment was down, Jim unceremoniously jumped knee-deep into the pond with the 10 foot intake hose. He filled it up with water, threaded it onto the pump end. He then stroked the intake back and forth in the water. This action allowed water into the foot valve and kept it there to ensure the pump end was primed. He then went to the shoreline, found a metre-long dry stick to use as a stake, cut a piece of sash cord supplied in the tool kit, grabbed the axe and jumped back into the water. It was a soft bottom, and in order to prevent the foot valve from sucking in debris, Jim hammered the two-inch diameter stake into the mud, lifted the end of the intake hose six inches off the bottom and tied it to the stake.

While Jim was setting up the pump, Sam had retrieved the axe and found another stake to secure the pump. Once started, the pump could vibrate and shuffle into the water. He hammered the stake into the ground a metre ahead of the pump and tied the pump frame to the stake with sash cord.

Cindy, the hose pack still on her back, had pulled out her Silva compass and, using her intended bearing, picked a tall spruce, well into the bush as her first "walk to" target.

Sam opened the pack of hose on Cindy's back, pulled out approximately three metres of hose and held onto it. Cindy retrieved the axe from Sam and marched to her target spot just inside the tree line. As she walked, four lengths of hose, or four hundred feet, each length connected to the other, slid out of the pack. Once all the hose was out of the pack, Cindy would drop the orange pack and continue on, blazing a trail for the others to follow and lay hose.

Sam set up the five-gallon gas container, inserted the fuel line into it, primed the line to ensure it was full of the mixed gas/oil fuel and connected it to the coupling on the pump.

By this time, Jim had connected the end of Cindy's hose to the pump outlet. Once started, water would be released at a pressure of two hundred pounds per square inch. The pump was now ready to start. The foam kit was set aside for the time being. There was already foam on the first two hundred and fifty metres of fire edge compliments of the

CL415. Jim would set up the foam injector when additional pump gas was required, approximately four hours after start up. The whole operation had taken five minutes. If staking the pump and intake wasn't required, it would have taken three.

Because it was a long haul to the fire edge, and another pump was required in-line due to elevation and subsequent pressure loss, the pump wouldn't be started until hose was laid to the fire and the other pump was delivered and set up. The crew's job was to follow Cindy's trail and lay the remaining five packs of hose. It would give them a total length of over twenty four hundred feet (seven hundred and thirty metres). They would still be shy approximately two hundred and seventy metres of hose, or a little over two packs. Jim knew that it was impossible to lay hose in a straight line. It would take an additional three packs, or twelve lengths to reach the fire. Based on Cindy's equipment order, it would leave them with only seven packs, close to nine hundred metres of hose, to work the fire edge—not enough. As he tilted his head back and took a well earned drink of water, he made a mental note to tell Cindy.

THE SOW WAS CONFUSED and she felt the need for rest. Her anxiety was transferred to her cub, the small, quivering bundle that now sat between her front paws, peering up at its protector. She looked westward where her nose picked up the warning smell of smoke and her ears gathered the unfamiliar sounds of the creatures that had come from above. She looked eastward and downhill towards unfamiliar range. She stepped over her cub and moved away from the threats to the west. Her pace was slow and deliberate. Instinctively, she stopped at rocks and turned them over, using her four-inch claws for leverage. She stopped at punk, rotted poplar and birch lying in the duff and broke them up. Occasionally, she found a standing, dead tree void of canopy, rose up to her full height and rocked it back and forth until either it fell or she had given up. Her spectator cub stayed close and barged in to share any delicacies that might be uncovered. She crisscrossed openings in the forest canopy with exposed bedrock or rock out-crops that would sustain only sporadic ground-cover growth. Her objective, the pale green blueberry bush leaves, were curled inward and fringed and mottled in browns and beiges. The few berries perched on the stems were tiny and shrivelled. She continued downwards during the afternoon, wandering from potential food source to food source, her little companion close behind.

The sow smelled water. She emerged from a cool black spruce grove into another dry swamp. Ochre coloured, thick, saw grass fringed the opening. Curved spikes of dead cedar poked one to two metres above the grass like little umbrellas without fabric. A phalanx of standing, dead, black ash stood randomly, tall and straight. Their bark and branch-free trunks were steel grey, mottled with silver blemishes. These soldiers, daring one to pass, stretched into the distance. An occasional, lonely white or red pine stood with stately prominence on the edge of the wetland—the only signs of life in this micro-ecosystem.

Her point of entry into the swamp was not the source of water that she had picked up through olfactory activity. She flanked the edge bordered with two-metre "tall meadow rue" clusters, some with their greenish-white flowers still intact. She continued easterly, stopping occasionally to test food sources. With her focus on nourishment, she was funnelling herself and her cub to a narrow point of land. In the process of tearing apart a rather stubborn poplar deadfall, she looked ahead and saw her source of water. She was on a rise of land with a thick over-story of ten-metre high white cedar. Straight ahead, flashes of blue peeked through the cedar, showing fringe tops of white and silver, rocking gently. To the south, just beyond the fringe of saw grass, she saw a wide ribbon of blue reaching back into the direction she had come from. She and her cub were on a point of land, with an over-story and cover that provided relief from the heat, at the western shore of a lake that supported a shallow bay to the south.

The bay was the centre-piece of the wetland she had flanked. There would be nourishment here. If not grubs, beetles, slugs and worms, then the shallows would yield crayfish, frogs and minnows. She forayed into the wetland, passing through a tangle of three-metre high redosier dogwood, a bastion of interwoven, deep red branches and polished, dark green, spade-shaped leaves. The wetland's next attempt at defence was a wall of four-metre high, thick-stemmed giant reed with rough-edged leaves, like wide, lightly serrated chopping knives. This season, their wheat-like fruit fringed with silky, fine hair had not materialized.

The sow waded through the layers of growth easily. The ground beneath her paws became spongy, her weight causing a silver fringe of pond water to form momentarily around each paw. As she moved on water pooled into the print. Her cub followed dutifully, stopping occasionally to drink from the bear paw-shaped cups of brackish water. Her next impediment was less formidable. Random stems of common cattail attempted to block her progress. They stood rigid, like stiff royal guards with long, ebony faces topped with narrow, spiked helmets. Each guard was accompanied by several tapered, pale-green leaves each standing tall as lances and spears. She catalogued the cattail in her food data bank. The starchy roots made for a delectable side-dish.

At last she reached open water. She looked briefly across the bay to the other side. A wide corridor of yellow pond lilies hugged the fringe of cattail. Their ten-inch, heart shaped leaves floated restfully on the surface of the water. Each one touched, overlapped or was occasionally separated by a narrow bridge of water. The richly textured, green leaves were raised and curled slightly inward to prevent the intrusion of pond water. Many of them supported bright yellow, multi-pedaled flowers, in full bloom at this time of the day. The sow was satisfied. She has found cover and sustenance.

They would rest here.

Chapter 22

DAY 1: 13:15 HOURS,
WAWA MNR DISTRICT OFFICE

"**S**O LET'S SEE IF I GOT THIS RIGHT. You need ten of my staff to provide service functions to the fire program?" The Wawa district manager sat back in his chair, twirling a pen between both hands like he was trying to role toilet paper back on to the dispenser. George Williams sat across from his desk, leaning forward in his chair, anticipating the usual response—*I'm already short on staff. Who is going to do our work? Are you paying their overtime, or am I going to have to give them time off in the fall?*

Francis DesRoches was not a naive manager. He knew that he didn't have a lot of options here. He also knew George. If George was asking for help, George needed help. He also knew that this had to be played out. The tall, rangy Francis with the thatch of hawk's nest hair, thick, caterpillar eyebrows, dark, penetrating, laser stare and "Duddly Do-Right" chiselled jaw continued. He put down the pen and, for effect, used his fingers as a shopping list of retorts. Placing his left forefinger on his right pinkie, he worked down the right hand to the final and definitive thumb. "One, you already have two of my resource techs up in White River at the MTO yard so I'm already short on staff. Two, we have a shit load of resource work to do and whose going to do it? Three, if you don't pay them for O/T, I have to give them time off. Four, I'll have to cancel vacations."

George struggled to control a smile. *That was a new one.*

"And five." Francis was on the last resort thumb, now and smiling. "When do you want them?"

"How about yesterday? And if that's no good, how about the day before yesterday?"

Francis waved his hands, palms down in supplication. "Consider it done, oh mighty fire person."

The two men were not only co-managers they were also long time friends. Many moons ago both had been students working on the same fire crew.

Francis grew pensive. "Any issues, George?"

"As a matter of fact, yes." A short pause suggested to Francis that some ducks were being lined up. "We're not going to be able to contain fire 43. I can only commit one crew to it. We've had four new fires today, and we're predicting up to ten."

"And?"

"Wawa 43 is in the Northshore Logging license area."

"And?"

"There's a large, active cutover a few kilometres west with lots of tree length material sitting on landings."

Francis now sat up straight. George had his undivided attention. "Oh, oh. Continue."

"According to our values map, just north of the fire is two thousand hectares of mature jack pine. It's a parcel of Northshore's critical wood supply."

With an audible groan, and a voice now cracking with tension, Francis asked if there was any other good news.

"Well, the fire is west of Siren Lake. It was called in by Wally McNeil, who just happens to be at his camp. Can you have someone call him to suggest he leave the area?"

"Sure, I'll get one of the Conservation Officer's on it, but I know Wally, and he's been known to pull a stubborn streak out of his pocket, now and then."

"Well, Francis, because of Wawa 40, I have an MNR Turbo Beaver sitting down at the dock in town. If you need to send a CO out to persuade Wally, let me know."

"How are you doing with Wawa 40?"

"I think we've got a handle on it. We've been pounding it with the air tankers, and I've got three crews holding it at twelve hectares right now. I believe the residents at Hornepayne can stand down."

"How far is Hornepayne from Wawa 43?"

"About thirty-five kilometres, as the crow flies. That's not an issue, yet."

Francis thought a moment. "OK. This is how I see it. I'll get one of my foresters to pull the planning data and maps on the Northshore license. We'll contact the Northshore people right away and get them in for a briefing."

George broke in. "See if you can get them to pull their equipment to one of the larger, fire safe landings. I'll let you know by this afternoon if they need to start pulling the tree-length wood out of there. I hope it doesn't come to that because we both know it's a massive undertaking. Also let them know we may need to hire some of their bulldozers for fire line construction."

Now Francis was making notes and looked up. "You know they'll be howling all the way up the pipes. I'll call the regional director and let him know what's happening. He'll probably want to let the Deputy Minister know. Now, who do you need, and for how long?"

Like a magician, George pulled a list out of his back pocket with a flourish and a "Ta, Da!" He started down the list. "I could use Ralph as logistics chief here at the district. He's great at organizing service staff, equipment and housing. Linda makes an excellent ground support unit leader, or transport officer in the old days, since she already looks after your vehicle fleet. Mary has experience as a radio operator and a time unit leader, so we can use her in our radio room. I can use two people to support our staff in the fire equipment cache and three service staff to work for Ralph. I need Samantha as a fire information officer. We'll be getting a lot of public and media inquiries. And last but not least, Sid could deal with the fire prevention stuff, like managing the restricted fire zone and providing direction on the woods operations modification guidelines. He's done it before and is good at it."

"And?"

"I'll probably need your conservation officers to enforce the restricted fire zone. People think they know better and want their camp fires even if it means burning down their own camp and the neighbours as well."

"And?"

"Right. I would say a minimum of two weeks and probably more like four."

Francis's face dropped as if the muscles supporting the skin had suddenly shrunk and crawled back in facial cavities.

George felt bad. "Look, Francis. I know this is hard on your programs. I'm in the process of hiring people off the street to replace your staff. They'll need to work with them for awhile to get the routines down. I've also requested a logistics team through the East Fire Region. Montreal River Community Forest has the contract to supply the bodies. Most of them are experienced retirees from our noble organization. Once they're on board, they can replace your staff."

Francis, who had been around the horn on this scenario many times, responded. "I'm waiting for the other shoe to drop."

The two men exchanged gun-sight stares.

"Ok, Ok, I won't bull-shit you. The long-range weather picture doesn't look good. Fire weather indices are off the chart. Wawa 43 is likely going to be a project fire. As we speak, the East Fire Region has activated two incident management teams. We're probably going to need everyone we can get our hands on."

"Isn't my planner on one of those incident management teams?"

"Oh yeah. I forgot to mention that. He's on his way to Sudbury this afternoon."

"Thanks, buddy. Anything left on my bones to peck or tear?"

"Well, I have a conference call with the regional fire duty officer this afternoon. Do you want to sit in on it?"

"Can't wait. I really like surprises. Do you think he'll want my first born or maybe he'll just want me to perform seppuku?"

"What the hell's sepoocoo?"

Francis, who was a closet WWII buff, quickly responded. "Japanese suicide."

"Isn't that called harry-carry?

"Yes and no. *Hara-kiri* is a form of suicide. We used to associate it with Japan's kamikaze pilots. For that, I need a Ki-43 Oscar or Zero aircraft and a Canadian battleship worth killing myself over, neither of which is available. Seppuku is disembowelment by sword. I kneel down with the blade of a sword pressed against my sternum and the handle on the floor …"

"OK, wise ass. I get the picture. And, by the way, you're starting to sound like Cliff Claven from Cheers".

"Who?"

"Cliff Claven. You know—the barfly mailman in Cheers who is a veritable dictionary of mundane, useless knowledge."

"Whatever." Francis stood up to signal the meeting was over. His "here-we-go-again" smile was a silent acknowledgement that they both understood it would be burnout time again. George walked out, leaving Francis DesRoches bouncing around thoughts in his head like a pin-ball machine. *Thirty five kilometres to Hornepayne. Wawa 16 in 2001 took a four-day run that ate up eight kilometres a day. There's got to be several thousand cunits of wood sitting on landings in the Northshore cut. The market value would be in the millions. Northshore will probably send in Amos Alfelski, their woodland manager and biggest prick on their corporate block. I'm the one who will have to tell him, with a straight face I might add, that they could stand to lose millions from a fire and we have one crew on it. Seppuku doesn't seem like such a bad idea after all.*

Chapter 23

DAY 1: 13:45 HOURS, WAWA 43

CINDY PUSHED HER WAY THROUGH AN UNDERSTORY OF THICK BALSAM FIR. The two to three metre high balsam stems crowded together, each competing for light. Their lateral branches shot straight out, intertwined, then swept upward. She thought that they were like crowd control cops with their arms locked together to prevent entry. The only saving grace was their needles. They were flat, rounded and soft. If this micro-jungle was white spruce or jack pine, she would end up with a dozen tiny scratches on her hands and face. She hacked a hurried trail through the balsam. Once through, she found some room to manoeuvre and stopped to take a compass bearing. She opened the hinged lid on the compass at a forty-five degree tilt, brought it up to eye level and extended her arm with the compass cradled in the palm of her hand. She then looked into the mirror on the inside of the lid and rotated her body slightly, until the mirror image magnetic needle lined up between the red arrow lines within the compass (the arrow was set on the ring/dial at 255 degrees). She then raised her eyes to the gun sight perched on the top of the lid, looked well beyond and picked a red pine, seventy-five metres ahead as the next target to walk towards. She would repeat this exercise as she progressed.

Before she moved on, Cindy looked through the forest canopy. There was no sky in this visual frame, just dense, black/grey smoke, rolling upward and away. She had been climbing steadily and was relieved to find that there were no significant barriers to laying the hose to the fire. *Yeah, right. No barriers other than fallen logs with sharp, spear-like branches, groups of dead, budworm-killed balsam and spruce holding each other up like crooked tent frames, balsam fir under-story that you could bounce off and tangles of young juneberry and witch hazel where the sun could penetrate pieces of the bush. Man, I hate the leatherwood patches with their super-flexible, springy, tough branches. They come whistling back like bull-whips, across the cheeks, ears and nose. Flies aren't bad today. Black flies are done. Mosquitoes aren't due for another eight hours. Just have to contend with the deer flies, horse flies and moose flies. The bigger the fly, the bigger the chunk they tore from your body.*

She looked down at the back of her hands and wrists. A dozen pin-sized, dried blood spots ran randomly across her skin. *Deer fly bites.* One landed for dessert and with rapier-quick reflexes, she pulverized it. *I take great, unadulterated pleasure in killing the little bastards.*

She had reached her target red pine, pulled out her compass, but before sighting in, looked towards the ridge and the wall of smoke. *Boy, am I glad we'll be on the back end of this thing. Jim was right. When we meet up, the first thing we're going to do is talk escape routes. About another ½ kilometre to go.*

She took her shot and forged ahead. A few minutes later, she broke out into a bed-rock opening about thirty metres in diameter. She could now hear her fire. It was like a large animal warning her off. She thought, dragon, yeah, dragon. It was crackling and hissing. It threw out whoosh sounds, signalling a tree or group of trees torching and exhaling a belch of vertical flame. Her anticipation climbed. She'd been in this situation before and knew how to put things in perspective. *We're at the back of the fire, not the head. We can walk away if we have to. Just keep an eye out for flanking jump fires.* Cindy was still anxious. *Trust your instincts, girl.*

She pulled out a throw-up antenna for her radio from the incident command vest and a roll of cord from a pocket, found a fist-sized rock and tied one end of the antenna section to it, using the cord. She spotted a solitary poplar at the fringe of the clearing. She tossed the rock as high as she could through a series of branches. It came out the other side of the tree and the antenna managed to stay suspended. She secured the cord attached to the antenna to the trunk of the tree. She then reached into a pocket, pulled out a roll of bright orange flagging tape, broke off a one-foot section and tied it to the antenna so she could find it later.

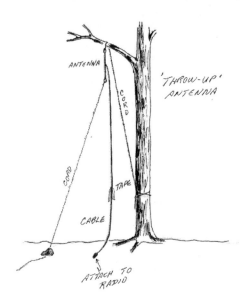

Cindy then sized up the clearing. *Too tight for a helicopter, but Tim could free-drop packs of hose here. It would save a lot of time. I know, I know. It's against policy to free drop, but it's not uncommon and we've had some experience.* She continued on.

While Cindy was scouting the fire, her second-in-command, Jim Henderson was laying hose. It was a touch slower now that he was using part 2 hose. The first two packs laid out from the pump were part 1 hose. Each length was folded in its box and couplings were already connected. Part 1 hose was meant to be run from the pump to the fire edge. The inside of each length was normally rubber-lined to prevent friction loss as the water passed through. This helped to maintain pressure at the nozzle. Stopping to connect each coupling was not required for the four lengths in the box.

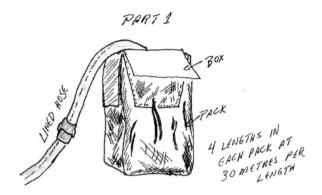

Part 2 however, had a different purpose and was packed differently. It was meant to work the fire edge. Each length was folded in the middle before it was packed in the box and the couplings were *not* connected. When the first length was pulled out, each end of the length, complete with couplings, came out. One coupling of the new length was then connected to the previous length on the ground (already a charged, but strangled hose), and a nozzle was connected to its other coupling. The strangler was released from the previous length, and the nozzle person was ready to apply water.

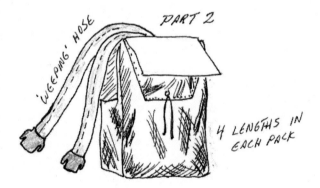

The hose in part 2 packs was percolating or weeping hose. It was designed to sweat or release some of the water outside the lining of the hose through microscopic holes. This would prevent the length of hose from burning if fire crossed it—unless it was an intense fire.

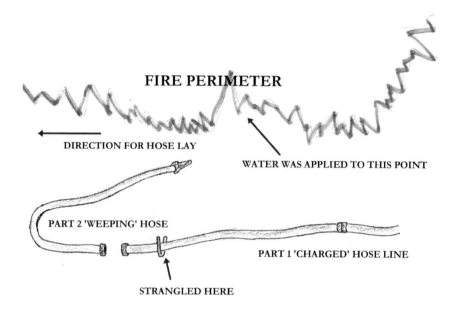

FIRE PERIMETER

DIRECTION FOR HOSE LAY

WATER WAS APPLIED TO THIS POINT

PART 2 'WEEPING' HOSE

PART 1 'CHARGED' HOSE LINE

STRANGLED HERE

Because they had only eight lengths of Part 1, each new length of Part 2 hose would have to be pulled, straightened out and connected until they hit the fire edge. It was a simple process but time consuming.

While Jim was laying hose, Sam Mendez was improving the helicopter landing area. From experience he knew that an area of approximately sixty metres by sixty metres free of vertical interference was required. Looking around, he made a mental note of eight to ten, dead black ash that should be cut down. Also, three thickets of alders close to the helipad site needed removal as well. The site itself was quite firm due to drought conditions, so he only required four, five metre-long logs, six to ten inches in diameter, to set a level landing pad.

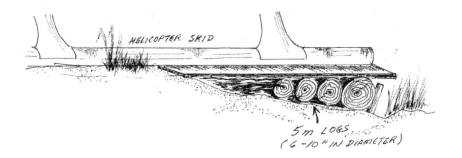

HELICOPTER SKID

5m LOGS
(6 -10 " IN DIAMETER)

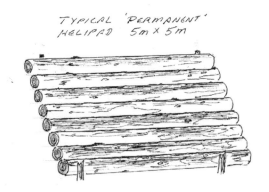

TYPICAL 'PERMANENT'
HELIPAD 5m x 5m

Sam gassed up the Husqvarna chain saw, dropped the screened shield on his hard hat, lowered the ear protectors and in three, short-stroke pulls, had it running. He would be done in fifteen minutes.

CINDY KEYED THE MT1000. "Jim, from Cindy. Do you copy?"

Six seconds later, Jim replied. "Go ahead, Cin."

"Yeah, Jim. There's a clearing about five hundred metres in— too small for a landing zone, but what do you think about Tim free dropping the next batch of hose?"

"Stand by one. I should be at the clearing shortly." In less than a minute, Jim broke through to the clearing, a pack of hose perched on his back with hose strung out behind him. He was sweating profusely, but otherwise showed no signs of fatigue. This is what Jim Henderson was born to do. He raised his radio. "Tim's done it before and it'll sure save us some time. What's it's like up there?"

"Jimmie, we've got some serious fire. We'll need water shortly."

The radio barked in her hand. "Cindy, from Sam".

"Go ahead Sam."

"His breathing came out laboured over the mic. "I'm on my way up with a pack of hose. It's the last one."

Cindy did a quick calculation. *A kilometre total to the fire. We will have laid out around 700 metres of hose. We need that new hose yesterday.* Jim had already done the math.

They shared a silent *"shit"*!!

"Corrigan Crew, this is Helitack 39 on 6, do you copy?"

Cindy raised a fist in the air, "Yes!" She regained her composure and keyed the mic. "Just in time, Tim. Sam, you listening?"

"Go ahead Cindy."

"OK, this is how it is. Tim, we're in a clearing five hundred metres in from the pump—bearing, approximately 225 degrees." She paused.

"I copy, Cindy. 225 degrees."

"I want you to set down at the pump site, off-load the equipment and transfer the hose, and yourself, into the back seat. You're going to free drop it". She thought about the pilot. "Cory, are you OK with that?" Cindy needed the pilot's approval.

"No problem, Cindy. It wouldn't be my first time."

"Sam, lay your hose, then get back to the clearing to guide them in. When Tim free-drops the hose, start laying it. I'll be marking trail for you. I'll rendezvous with you when I can."

"Copy that, Cindy."

"Jimmie, you know what to do."

"I'm on my way, Cin." He knew it was time to get back and start the pump.

"Tim, once the hose is dropped, get back to the pump site. You'll probably have to set up the second pump somewhere up the line and start it once Jim's pump is running."

"Copy that, Cindy."

"This one's a dandy, fellas. We don't have a lot of time. Be safe." Cindy had a gnawing sensation in the pit of her stomach. She didn't like the feel in the air. Her lips were dry and cracking slightly. She reached for a bottle of water, took a healthy swallow. *The humidity must be dropping. This could be a problem.* Cindy turned back towards the ridge top to finish her line running and recon.

Chapter 24

DAY 1: 15:00 HOURS,
REGIONAL FIRE CENTRE

SHIELA MONAHAN LOOKED AT THE FIRE WEATHER INDICES WITH ALARM. All weather stations across the region had submitted their 13:00 hour station data, and the computer had generated the fire weather indices. *Why didn't I pick this up earlier?* She hi-lighted three of the weather stations' compilations and took the long, curled sheet of paper to the duty officer, Rick Sampson. As she approached his desk, she noticed how haggard he looked. His facial tone was pasty. *Looks like drywall compound.* His red-rimmed eyes offered only a blank, distant stare. His hair looked like it had been worked over with an egg-beater. "You OK, Rick?"

He looked up, jolted from some abstract, basement-dwelling thought. "Nothing retirement wouldn't cure. What have you got for me, Shiela?"

"You're not going to like this. Look at Wawa's indices."

Rick knew everything would be off the scale, but he wasn't prepared for this. The warning surge of something deep inside shot up from his scrotum and disappeared in the vicinity of his large intestines. It was the same feeling every man gets when he's about to step on poor footing, like a sheet of ice or slippery rock. It was like a silent, warning shot of adrenalin, not the 'full-monty' rush, just a little atomizer squeeze, a dusting. He immediately reached for his phone and pushed the speed dial button to the sector response officer's phone in Wawa. It only rang twice and George Williams was on the other end.

"Wawa Fire—Williams here."

"George, its Rick." *No time for pleasantries.* "Did you see the afternoon indices?"

"I'm looking at them as we speak. Appears we're going to have the mother of all fire days: three stations reporting a cross-over, temperatures in the mid thirties and relative humidity in the high twenties. That would shrivel a watermelon."

"Who's out there that could be in trouble?"

"We've contacted every crew except Cindy Corrigan. She's on Wawa 43 and out of range. The good news is H39 is in-bound White River shortly for more hose. We can get a message through to her when it returns to the fire."

"How's it look on 43?"

"Not good, Rick. I know that country. There's a shit load of budworm-killed balsam and spruce. Cindy called it in at ten hectares. I know it's not much consolation under present conditions, but she's on the back end of the fire, not the head where you'd need running shoes."

George hesitated then continued. "Our values problem is an active cutover with several million dollars of tree length wood on the landings." Instinctively, the conversation became more cryptic.

"Who's license?"

"Northshore."

Where the hell are those antacids? "Who are you dealing with?"

"Nobody yet, but Amos Alfelski is due in this afternoon."

Hold the antacids, bring on the Malox. "George, you're paying for your previous life."

"That's OK. *His* boss will be coming to Sudbury to see you."

What's better than Malox? Oh yeah, a stomach pump.

"George, I've looked at your resource request and we're working on it. We're also briefing the incident management team you requested, and they'll be on their way to Wawa tomorrow morning on a Twin Otter. Your helicopter request might be a problem. The word's out across North America, and they're at a premium right now. We've got orders in for water bombers but don't hold your breath. The province is running out of MNR ranger crews so we have a request in to Manitoba, Saskatchewan, British Columbia and the States. CIFFC is working on it now.

"Rick, I'd take Type 2 crews if you have them. Once we get a handle on our new fires, I could back-fill with the Type 2 crews and pull out my initial attack crews."

"How many?"

"Give me twenty crews for now and I promise I won't ask for more until tomorrow."

George's attempt at humour went right over Rick's head. "OK, put it in the paper system and I'll get our logistics people working on it. And George ..."

Here it comes. "Yes, Rick."

"I don't want anybody in trouble out there. Pull Cindy out if you're not comfortable, even if she has to come out kicking and screaming."

George had drained his humour barrel. He relaxed his facial muscles and the stress lines deepened on a pasty, stubble face. He responded in a subdued, raspy voice. "No one wants Cindy and her crew safe anymore than me. We'll take care of her."

Rick hung up and was hit with a wave of nausea. He knew this was a sign of stress, but his ego wouldn't let him buckle under. *I've seen it in my staff and forced them to take time off but no-o-o, not me; my damn ego is getting in the way. Things aren't good at home. Beth is hardly talking to me. She wants me to retire but I just can't make up my mind. I sure hope my replacement comes soon.*

Rick decided to call home. After ten rings he gave up. Sheila returned with another piece of paper in her hand and a worried look on her face. "Rick, we could have a real problem."

He kept his head down but raised his eyes. "It can't get any worse."

"I don't want to alarm you. Your phone was busy and George called back. Apparently he can't reach the Corrigan crew through White River."

"And?"

"He's now convinced that they may be in trouble. George wants you to call him right away."

Chapter 25

DAY 1: 15:00 HOURS, WAWA 43

HELITACK 39 APPEARED SUSPENDED OVER THE CLEARING just above the forest canopy like a giant dragonfly. Sam Mendez stood below, his MT1000 up to his mouth. "Good a spot as any, Tim."

Tim Hogg was a big kid and that was a good thing. What he was about to do required significant upper body strength. He sat harnessed in the back seat behind the pilot, his right leg propping open the door as far as it would open. The pilot maintained a steady hover and kept his eyes down to the canopy fringe. Tim's job was simple in concept. He had to reach to his left, hoist the sixty-pound pack of hose onto his lap, lift vertically then thrust it out as far as he could. There were concerns here. One, he had to make sure the hose pack straps didn't get caught on anything associated with the helicopter on its trip to the ground thirty metres below. Two, the pack had to clear the skids, so it required a significant horizontal thrust. If it hit the skids, the pilot stood a chance of losing control. Tim had ten packs to deal with. When the first three had been jettisoned, he would then close the door, pull more packs within his grasp and repeat the process. The exercise took five minutes and went without a hitch. Tim had done this before, and he showed no signs of wear and tear. Helitack 39 rose, turned and shot towards the pump site.

In the meantime, Sam had piled the packs of Part 2 hose, opened the top of one, pulled out the two couplings so that he could reach them from behind and slung the pack over his back. He followed the hose he had previously laid down. When he arrived at the end of the last length, he reached behind, grabbed the two dangling couplings, connected them around a small poplar and walked the fifteen metres required to pull out that length of hose. Since its loop was wrapped around the next length in the pack, that next length came out about two metres, couplings first. This is where he would lose a little time. He had to walk back to the previous length's couplings, connect one coupling to the length before it and then straighten out the looped hose. This was not part 1 hose that was already connected. Once he reached the fire edge it would *not* be necessary to stretch out each length of hose from their loop. One of the couplings would be connected with the previous length; a nozzle would then be connected to the other coupling. Water would be released and the process of fighting fire would begin.

Sam finished laying out the four lengths of hose and went back for another pack. On his return, he met Cindy, coming from the other direction on her way back from blazing a trail to the fire. Sam, who was slightly winded and sweating profusely, could now hear and smell the fire. The look on his face betrayed his anxiety.

"One more pack and we're at the edge of the CL415 foam, Sam." She had sensed his apprehension. "We'll be just fine. Can you handle another pack?"

"Sure Cindy". He hesitated. "It's just that this fire sounds big."

She smiled. "Piece of cake, Samuel. If it gets too hot, we'll back off. Now drop your hose pack and let's go get some more hose."

TIME SEEMED TO STAND STILL. Everyone was focused on their particular routine. Jim had set up the foam regulator at the pump outlet and intake and connected it to the foam jug. The regulator would allow him to adjust the concentration of foam sent up the hose line or stop it all together. Because he had to take the intake hose off the pump end to set up the foam system, he had to re-prime it. It took him one minute. He was now ready to start the pump. "Should have set up the foam in the first place," he muttered to himself. *I just can't get used to working with this stuff.*

Helitack 39 had long gone for more hose, and Tim had taken the second pump, tool kit and gas container up the line to a spot where

Jim had broken some saplings as a marker. This dual pump set up was called *tandem* and was required to maintain water pressure to the fire. He was close to finishing the set up.

Cindy and Sam had run hose past the two hundred and forty metres of CL415 foam drop. She felt the air-dropped foam would hold. Sam had three lengths of hose in the pack on his back and there were two packs on the ground beside them. They were as ready as they were going to be.

Cindy keyed her MT1000. "Jim and Tim from Cindy." They acknowledged her call quickly. She continued. "Yeah, are you guys ready?"

They both replied, "Affirmative."

"OK Jim. We need to conserve the foam. Give me a 0.2 concentration. Start your pumps and get your asses up here ASAP. We've already got a couple of small jump fires about fifteen metres outside the line."

There wasn't a need for a verbal response. In seconds, the first pump started with a high-pitched, whining sound, much like a dirt bike but without the annoying variation due to throttle change. As soon as Tim's pump, the one higher up, received water, he started it. Cindy and Sam could here both engines running at ¾ throttle. Full throttle wasn't required. It would consume fuel too quickly. It would only be seconds before they had water at the nozzle.

Cindy was using the 3/8-inch nozzle tip. Although she would prefer the volume and pressure associated with the ½-inch tip, the hose lay was too long – she needed the smaller nozzle tip to maintain pressure. Sam positioned himself three metres behind Cindy. His job was to help her move the hose along. Cindy was the nozzle handler and set the pace. The hose was tucked under her right arm, her right hand just behind the nozzle, her left on top in order to control its tendency to jump up. Water with a light concentration of foam shot out of the tip at one hundred and fifty pounds of pressure per square inch and it initially forced Cindy to take a step back.

She had to yell. "OK Sam, first things first. Let's hit the closest jump fire."

They progressed quickly towards it, applying water approximately five metres ahead. A group of white spruce was torching, throwing flames six metres into the air and broadcasting intense heat within a three-metre radius. Cindy raised the nozzle and knocked the flames down. She then worked the base of the fire in order to slow its progress. Cindy thought, *the friggin' dragon needed to crawl before it could climb.* The jump fire was no more than a tenth of a hectare or one-fifth of an acre and they had stopped its progress within minutes. They would return later on a back-pass to pressure-wash a trench in the soil in order to hold it.

Sam pointed. "There's the other one, Cindy, about thirty metres ahead." Without encouragement, Sam pulled a hose strangler out of its pouch, bent down, arranged the strangler around the hose and shut off the water supply. They could hear the pumps rev up above the sound of the fire due to the back pressure the strangler created. Sam then walked up to Cindy. She grabbed the two couplings dangling from the pack on his back, dropped them to the ground and stood on them while Sam ran out the next length of hose. Suddenly he went down with a curse.

"You OK, Sam?"

"Yeah, tripped over a snag, couldn't see it because of the damn ground juniper."

He sprang up like a jack-in-the-box, his face flush with embarrassment, walked out the rest of the length of hose, grabbed the loop and stretched the hose out as best he could. He then headed back to Cindy who, by this time, had connected a coupling from the new length to the charged line of hose, removed the nozzle from the charged hose and connected it on to the other coupling of the new length. Sam got to the strangler, placed a foot just ahead of it and with both hands on the strangler waited for the word. He was no sooner ready when Cindy yelled, "Water!" Sam released the strangler slowly. It was under intense pressure to fly open and one of two things could happen. If his foot wasn't against it to stop it, the strangler could run up the hose at lightning speed and take Cindy's fingers off. It could also spring free with such force that it might shoot straight up and catch him in the face. It was made of white metal and depending where it hit Sam, it could break a nose, take an eye out or, worse case scenario, if it hit him between the eyes—kill him. He released the strangler without a hitch. They were on their way to the second jump fire. All this activity had taken three minutes, including Sam's unceremonious tumble.

CINDY AND SAM HAD JUST KNOCKED the second jump fire down when Jim and Tim arrived, each with a pack of hose on their back. Sam strangled off the water supply.

It was time for Cindy to brief the crew. "OK guys. Listen up. I want radios on full volume and batteries checked. You all know the routine but let's talk safety. First, if you didn't see it, I have a throw–up antenna set up in the clearing behind us. Look for the flagging tape. We got three options if we get trapped. Option 1—follow the hose back down to the pump. Option 2—head west away from the fire. There's a cutover and road system two to three kilometres in that direction. It's downhill, so any back burn will be slow. Having said that, we're getting jump fires on the back end here. Option three is a last resort—move into the burn. I'm a little reluctant to even suggest it, still lots of intensity and too much smoke. Last but not least, hydrate yourselves. I don't want anyone passing out on me." Cindy looked around to ensure they all understood. "Any questions?"

Jim responded. "Just a comment, Cindy. I soaked down the pump site real good, just in case."

Cindy nodded and continued. "This fire is hot, gentlemen." She licked dry, cracked lips. "The relative humidity seems to be dropping, and that's not good for us. You see something you don't like, speak up. I'm going to go ahead and do a little scouting. OK, pitter-patter."

The crewmembers knew their roles. Jim would be nozzle handler. Sam would continue to be #1 hose handler, directly behind Jim. Tim was the #2 hose handler. He would lay hose and assist moving the hose at the big loop.

Cindy headed north along the fire perimeter, staying well out because it was characteristically uneven with fingers of fire where there was fire-receptive forest fuel and bays where there were less flammable forest fuels such as stands of poplar. She disappeared into the under-growth.

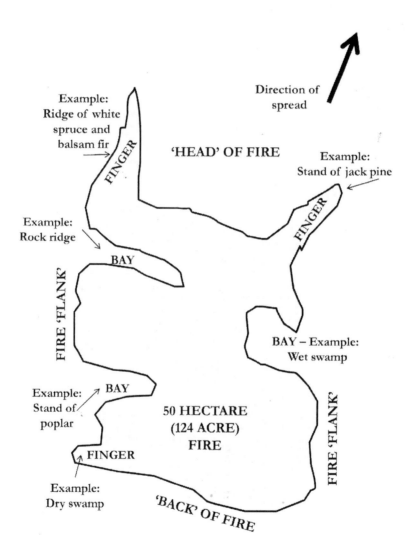

RELATIVE HUMIDITY HAD DROPPED lower than the temperature. The dragon appeared to be beside itself with glee. It was almost as if it tore scabs of fire off its body and merrily tossed them at random. Forest fuels were so void of moisture, that with a little imagination one might envision infant dragons materializing at will. They burst up indiscreetly, ahead, beside and behind their matriarch. They attacked, consumed and grew at a break-neck pace. Mere mortals were no match for the dragon and her spawn.

Chapter 26

DAY 1: 15:15 HOURS, WAWA 43

CINDY KNEW THEY WERE IN TROUBLE when the sun, whenever she could actually see it, appeared to change its location in the sky. As she followed the perimeter in a somewhat northerly direction, the sun had been in front and on her left shoulder. Fifteen minutes ago, it was on her right shoulder. The fire had forced her west. Sure that it was just a long finger of fire, she continued on. Now the sun was at her back and she was heading south. The fire was flanking her position, and the intensity was increasing, signalled by longer flame length. Smoke that had been rising and rolling away was now coming at her. It wasn't thick, at least for now, but she knew it was time to cut her losses and get the crew out of there. She pulled her MT1000 out of its holster. "Jim from Cindy."

"Go ahead, Cin."

"Jim, we've got a problem. I'm being turned back. There's nothing we can do with this fire. I'm returning and should be with you guys in five minutes."

Jim sensed the tenseness in Cindy's voice. He'd been in this situation before and knew she needed something to hold on to. "No rush Cin. We're doing OK here. Progress is really slow, though. This baby doesn't want to cooperate so we can't move ahead too quickly. See you when you get here."

Cindy decided it was time to gather her thoughts. She squatted down to get out of the veiled smoke and took a deep breath. *By my*

*calculations, I should head southeast. If I hit jump fires on the way, I'll
work in a southerly direction around them.*

Cindy adjusted the dial on her compass, stood up and headed
in her intended direction at a measured pace. Rushing would only
get her hurt. As she progressed, she heard the sounds of torching
behind her and to her right. Her apprehension grew. *Our escape
route to the west is being cut off! Where's the crew? There!* She heard
the crackling sound of water at high pressure coming from a nozzle. The crew was a mere ten metres to the east. She was dead on.
She walked quickly up to Jim and he greeted her with a reassuring
smile.

"Jimmie, stash the nozzle, we gotta talk."

Jim found a good sized, double birch sapling with two, six-inch
trunks that joined and formed a notch. He jammed the hose into
the notch and when he felt it was secure, he turned to Cindy.

She opened her arms like a mother encouraging her children to
approach. "Gather around boys."

Sam and Tim joined their mentors. Without encouragement,
they all pulled out a bottle of water.

"Good news, we're getting out of here. Bad news, we can't go
west towards the cutover, we're cut off there."

Both Sam and Tim, who had been taking a pull on their water
bottles, stopped drinking simultaneously, their eyes growing wide
as the message was received and digested.

"We'll have to head back down the hose line."

Tim looked back down the line. His eyes grew even wider, the
whites bulging in disbelief. He pointed and signalled his dismay
with a "Holy Shit!" At the same time as he verbalized his reaction, they all heard an enormous "woosh" and "popping" sound.
Groups of balsam and spruce, some forty feet high, torched within
seconds. Jump fires were now behind them, in their intended escape route.

Jim spoke up in a calm soothing voice." Looks like we'll have to
back-pass our way out." He was talking about the process of doing
a return pass with water, a standard procedure in hose lay. Only
this time it was for self preservation.

Cindy knew he was right, and besides, it would keep the two
younger crewmembers focused. "I agree, Jimmie. When we get

past the jumps, and if the coast is clear, then we drop the hose and get out. In the meantime gentlemen, its time to get wet."

Jim grabbed the nozzle and the crew gathered around him. He pointed it at the base of the birch. There was too much water pressure to hose themselves down directly. Splash back would do the trick. Water pounded against the tree and came back on them as a heavy spray.

The crew then started the return pass. They moved quickly, applying water only where fire was an impediment to their progress. When Jim got close to the next length of hose, Tim was already there with the strangler positioned to shut off water. On Jim's word, water was shut off, Jim took the nozzle off the length of hose he had been working and put it on the next length that was strangled. When he was ready, he called for water and Tim released the strangler. As Jim moved on, Sam stepped behind him to help him drag hose. In the meantime, Cindy walked ahead to see if there were any more surprises. Her target was the clearing and the throw-up antenna, but she didn't want to get too far ahead of her crew.

Ten minutes later, she broke into the clearing, her crew on her tail. She was pleased at their progress and felt good about their chances. She no sooner had the throw-up antenna connected to her radio, when her crew appeared, each person grinning from ear to ear.

"No pun intended, fellas, but we're not out of the woods, yet. We've got about another twenty minutes. I'm going to call for H39." The words were no sooner out of her mouth when the pressure at the nozzle began to drop. In ten seconds, what was once one hundred and fifty pounds of pressure was now a small stream of water coming out of the nozzle from water remaining in the hose.

Jim was the first to react. "I can still hear the pumps, Cin. Looks like the hose has either blown or burned down the line between us and the pumps." Jim looked east towards the pump location. He was pretty sure he knew where the hose ran and a look of discouragement passed his face like a small, single cloud. He saw thick, black smoke, lots of it, to the east and south. "My bet is on burned. There goes another way out."

Everyone was speechless. Cindy looked at her charges, one at a time. All were soaked, their red jump suits had slashes of black criss-crosses from burned brush. Their faces were soot-stained and mottled with streaks of sweat.

Cindy looked towards Jim for support. He appeared pensive. *He's figuring a way out.* Sam was now sitting on the ground, his head down, arms resting on his knees. *He's giving up.* Tim was standing rigid—his face a mask—eyes bulging, mouth drawn down at the corners, eyebrows slanted high on the insides. *He's scared shitless. So am I. Think, Cindy, think. What do I recall in our aerial recon. I remember the clearing we're in now. Anything else? I'm sure there was. Yes! Just north of the clearing, about thirty metres in—a big rock ridge with a stand of poplar below it. But can we handle the smoke?* She looked north. Smoke lined the sky there as well but not as thick or as black. *What choice do we have?*

She quickly explained the option to her crew and got on the radio. "White River, White River, this is the Corrigan crew, do you copy?" Her conversation was now interrupted from short fits of coughing. There was no response, only static. "White River, White River, this is the Corrigan crew, do you copy??" This time her voice betrayed its urgency as it rose in volume and pitch. *Shit, still no response. Looks like it's into the burn we go.*

The enormity of their situation hit Cindy like a hammer between the eyes. Her shoulders sagged under the weight of responsibility. She felt an intense pressure in her head as a wash of stress rose from somewhere inside a hidden place and worked its way up to her face. She recognized the signs from what she had learned in her training. She felt detached, in another place, and was curious that her mind was now processing her body's reaction. *Let's see, the rush of adrenaline increased my heart rate, body temperature and rate of carbohydrate consumption. Then there's a release of hormones and a surge of energy. More sugar is released into my bloodstreams and more oxygen is carried to the muscle. My blood pressure rises by constricting my arteries. Perspiration increases, I become more alert, I stop salivating and my pupils are dilating. My muscles tense. I want to fight or take flight.* Suddenly her whole being was consumed by their predicament. She felt like she was tied and gagged, bound to the front of a fast moving train that was approaching a tractor-trailer on the track. Now, she began to second-guess her judgment. *Am I taking them to their deaths going into the burn? Should we take a chance and force our way back down the hose line? How did I get us into this mess?*

Jim, recognizing the signs of meltdown, walked up to Cindy and spoke quietly. "Look Cin, trust your judgment. You and I both know we've been cut off from the pump. Worst comes to worse, when we reach the poplar, and we will, we can do a little burn out from there. I'm carrying a couple of boxes of matches. It won't be as near as intense, or as smoky as a flame front coming at us."

She looked at Jim intensely, her eyes searching his soul, seeking a grain of truth, of hope. The rational part of her thought process suddenly snapped forward from some distant, dark refuge in her brain. Her laboured breathing became more controlled.

"You're right, Jimmie. Let's try the radio one more time."

THE DRAGON CIRCLED THE CLEARING, moving in for the kill, smug with the knowledge that it had almost trapped its quarry. It slithered to a large cap of open bedrock and reached out an appendage to test for nourishment. When none was to be had, it belly-crawled along the edge and scurrying up balsam and spruce then slipping down when it had consumed needles, cones, small branches, vacant nests and squirrel middens—food caches where nuts, seeds, berries and cones were stashed.

It continued to test the rock outcrop and work around it. Where there was a rise in elevation, the dragon moved quickly. As the slope rose, flame would come into closer contact with the ground, drying whatever moisture was left in the forest fuels. Where ground descended, the dragon slowed its pace, almost if it was afraid to slip. Down-slope fuels were further away from flame, and it took longer for radiant heat to evaporate forest fuel moisture.

The dragon finally cleared the rock but didn't anticipate the next obstacle, shade. A heavy over-story of leaf-laden trembling aspen created an umbrella of temperature-dropping, moisture-holding shade. Shade prevented the sun from baking an under-growth of fire receptive fuels. The dragon could crawl through the cooler area, but it would lose its momentum. Nourishment would be limited and more resistant to consumption. The large, even-aged stand of aspen stood tall and branchless for several metres, with diameters ranging from fourteen to eighteen inches. Each cubic metre of wood bound by a thick, smooth pale yellow bark, contained moisture. If the dragon could reach the canopy, it would have to content with leaves, not needles. The leaves themselves contained moisture. The disgruntled beast would have to carry out a disappointing blind search across a stingy forest floor, at least for the time being.

Chapter 27

DAY 1: 15:30 HOURS TO 17:00 HOURS, WAWA 43

THE COLUMN OF SMOKE WAS MASSIVE. It rose three thousand *metres vertically before it bent and stretched to the northeast.* Now Rob Cruikshank was worried. The CL415 was passing to the west of the column of smoke on its way to Wawa 40 and he knew that where they had previously dropped foam on Wawa 43, it was now over-run by fire. Jamie, who obviously had come to the same conclusion, looked over at his partner.

"They're likely out of there, Rob. Cindy's not foolish."

"Yeah, you're probably right. I just have a bad feeling." His stomach lurched, spring loaded like the gas recoil on a semi-automatic shotgun.

The CL415 progressed north and past the west flank of the fire that, by Rob's estimate, was now pushing over one hundred hectares. Rob decided to trust his instincts. "I'm calling Wawa to see if they've heard from her."

He keyed the mic. "Wawa Fire this is Tanker 271 on channel 6, do you copy?"

"Go ahead 271."

"Wawa Fire, just to advise, we've past Wawa 43 and it's taking a good run. I put it at one hundred plus hectares. Have you been in contact with the Corrigan crew?"

"Negative, 271. White River hasn't heard from them. We suspect they haven't had time to set up a throw-up antenna yet. Helitack 39 is back at White River taking on more fuel and hose. The last time H39 talked to them, it was dropping hose."

What Rob heard next, shocked him, Cindy's voice, raspy and desperate. He felt like someone had reached down his throat, clutched and twisted his heart. "Tanker 271, Corrigan crew, we're in trouble!"

Jamie, sensing the need to intercede, jumped in. "I'll take it Rob. You fly."

He switched over to fire channel 1. "Cindy, this is Jamie. What's your situation?"

In the meantime, Rob had swung the big air tanker west in a tight bank to come around south.

"Thank God you're there, Jamie. We're trapped. We need H39 back here ASAP, no load, and we need you to drop foam to lead us out! What's your location?"

CINDY CLUTCHED THE MIKE, her knuckles white. They were in the centre of the clearing, fifteen metres from a wall of eight to ten metre-high flame. The radiant heat was unbearable, but she was sure it was the smoke that would kill them. Most of it was rising, but a white cloak of choking carbon monoxide drifted through the clearing. Her mouth, throat and nose felt like super-heated sand-paper. She had difficulty swallowing. Her head was pounding. The rest of her crew were huddled together, low to the ground, gasping for fresh air. Jim was telling them a throat-rattling story, intent on keeping them pre-occupied. She overheard him say, "I've been here before guys. We'll get out of this."

She knew they couldn't break through to the poplar stand un-til the fuel on the north edge of the clearing was consumed. Even then, it was less than a 50% chance of survival. *It can't get worse. Oh God, don't let it get worse! I'm sorry, I'm sorry!*

It was then that she heard Rob on the radio. She knew the chances of his being close enough to help were slim to none, but at least she could talk to him. She made the desperate plea for help.

ROB WAS FRANTIC. He took over the transmission. "Cindy, we're a minute out from water and three minutes to you. What's your location?"

Perhaps there was a chance. Two of the three blackened, defeated faces looked up at her, their eyes pleading for hope. Jim just looked tense. "The pump site is at the only swamp east of the fire. We're 225 degrees, one-half kilometre in from the site in a small clearing. We need you to lay foam. We need it from the clearing back to the pump site. We need it now!"

"Cindy, Can you give us a GPS reading?"

Shit, why didn't I think of that? "Standby one."

Cindy no sooner got the words out, when the spruce holding the throw-up antenna burst into flame. Flame candles leap-frogged from branch to branch and shot to the top in a matter of seconds like a vertical flame-thrower. Cindy dove to the ground, smashing the brim of her hard hat against the bed rock. It took the brunt of the fall, but her nose and forehead slammed into the rock when the hard hat snapped to the side. She was dazed, blood poring out of her nose, but she was not done. She lifted her head and looked for the GPS unit. It lay on a grey sheet of granite—in two parts. She looked back to the spruce. No antenna. "Shit! What can happen next?"

Jim leaped to her side and held his friend by the shoulders. "Glad to see you pissed off, Cin. That's the Cindy I know and love. Welcome back. Help me over here, fellas."

The two young fire fighters moved quickly to help Cindy to her feet. She was wobbly but determined.

She recovered sufficiently enough to take stock of their situation. She looked at the boys. For the first time in their young lives, they realized they were not immortal. It came as a complete shock. She knew they required reassurance. With a significant bruise forming on her forehead and blood running down her nose, she managed a crooked, challenging smile. She looked like a hockey enforcer who had just won a thirty-second punch-out and knew it extended his playing career another year. "271 got a pretty good fix on us fellas. Now, let's get into the middle of the clearing. The first person to hear the 415, shout it out. We all stand tall then and start waving our hard hats. They may be able to see them through the smoke."

Tim responded, his voice raspy and broken after a fit of coughing. "What if they can't find us?"

Cindy recognized the sound of desperation in his plea. "The pilot's a good friend of mine. I'll personally kick his ass if he screws this one up."

It was Sam's turn. "What if they hit us with a load?"

"There's nothing in the middle of this clearing to come down on us. Besides, we could all use a bath." Cindy paused. "Good point, though. When the 415 releases its load, remember your training. Flat on the ground, head pointed towards the drop, hands on hard hats."

Jim noticed that Cindy used an optimistic "when" instead of an uncertain "if." *Nice touch, Cin. That's why you're a fire crew leader.*

"WAWA FIRE—WE'VE LOST CONTACT with the crew and they're trapped. We have a fix on them and we're on approach for a load. They want H39 back at the pump site, but ditch any load."

George Williams was now on the radio at Wawa. He looked over to the radio operator who immediately got on the phone to the MTO yard in White River. He looked down at the hand holding the mic. It was shaking, like it had a mind of its own. His voice belonged to some one else, a ghost of its normal volume and pitch. It rolled off his tongue in a muted croak. He couldn't believe it was his voice. *Who is this jerk?* "We copy, 271. Can you find them?"

It was Jamie on the 415 radio. Rob was manoeuvring the aircraft for a water pick up. He sensed the need to instil a little confidence. "There's a good chance. Cindy gave us some pretty specific fixed points."

George knew there was nothing more he could do. "Get them out of there." He looked over to the radio operator. Her eyes were fixed on George and now brimming with tears. George keyed the mic one more time. " Please."

THE BIG AIR TANKER RUMBLED from the east over the swamp just above the forest canopy. Visibility was not the best due to drifting smoke, but it was acceptable. The swamp and the bush just to the west were still intact, but it wouldn't be long before they too were casualties of fire.

"There's the pump!" Jamie was looking down out the starboard window.

Rob corrected his bearing to 225 degrees immediately before they left the fringe of the tall grass. Visibility decreased and Jamie switched on the FLIR. They needed to stay above the heat signature provided by flame. Rob willed his aircraft to find the crew. *Come on, come on! Where's that damn clearing. We should be on it by now!*

The CL415 began to tremble in response to turbulence caused by convection air currents. Rob had to fight the urge to look down. He had to keep his aircraft out of harm's way. He knew it wouldn't do Cindy any good if the 415 went down. He watched the bearing, the horizon and the FLIR screen. Jamie was looking ahead and down, desperate to find the small clearing. He cranked his head slightly to the right. There seemed to be a break in the tree line and the smoke had dissipated slightly. *That's gotta be it!* He immediately punched a button on the GPS unit.

TIM WAS THE FIRST TO REACT. "NO, NO. THEY MISSED US!" The sound of the CL415, loud at first, drifted west and diminished. He stood up slowly, his body rigid, mechanical, as if in a self-induced trance. "I'm getting the hell out of here!" He took slow, even, steps forward. His stiff gate increased in speed incrementally, and he began to run. Sam was on him in a flash. They went down in a heap. Tim pummelled his diminutive friend in a frantic effort to escape. No words were spoken. It was a quiet, unsettling battle, Tim pounding, Sam holding on. It seemed like an eternity, but in mere seconds, both Jim and Cindy were on top of the two combatants. Tim was now pinned and crying. He was no match for Jim, and Cindy was talking him down, her faced pressed to his ear in an effort to get him to focus, her words coming out knife-edged and piercing. "They're coming back! I guarantee it! If they don't, I'll get you outa here, myself! And when we get back, I'll take pleasure in cleaning that pilot's clock! I'm giving them five more minutes!"

Tim was spent. His body relaxed. Jim slowly released his grip. Sam, who was not the worse for wear got up and put out a hand to Tim. "Come on, buddy. Cindy's going to get us out of this."

The crew huddled together, each person silently praying for intervention.

IN CINDY'S MIND it was like watching the last minute of hockey game—one team having a one-goal lead and the other team, with its goalie pulled, pressing for the tying goal. One minute. Sixty seconds. Each second a lifetime in slow motion. Five minutes, three hundred seconds, three hundred lifetimes. Her focus was on counting. Her mind consumed by the count. It was just like hide and seek as a little girl. *A thousand and one, a thousand and two ...*

No more sound of fire, no more smoke, no more sense of panic. *Maybe dying isn't so bad after all. This is almost pleasant. I feel good. Just me and counting. Just me and hide and seek. Shit! What now? What's that noise? Is it a train? Just when I get comfortable. GO AWAY! Why is the crew lying down? Maybe they're sleeping.*

A big hand grabbed her by her jump suit collar and threw her to the ground. *I'm not sleepy, you turd!*

The roar overhead was deafening. Suddenly a twenty metre-wide blanket of foam smashed into the tree line to the south and laid itself down, not with a flutter, but with the unceremonious thump of a giant wet blanket.

Jim was up in a shot, his arm raised to the sky, its fist clenched in victory. Usually a man of few words, he was shouting incoherently. "The wizard of friggin' oz! The yellow brick road, only it's friggin' white!"

Everyone was on their feet now. Tim was the first to react. "It's the wrong direction! They're not following the hose line!"

Cindy realized that he was right. *What's Rob doing?* Suddenly she got it.

"Listen up. They know what they're doing. It can't be far to the back of the fire and it's probably less intense. Once we're out, we can work east around it and make our way to the pump site. Now this is important." Cindy was on a roll. No more counting, time to get out. "We stick together. We don't, I repeat, don't panic. We drop when we hear the 415. And watch your step. That foam is, how do you say it Jim?"

Jim smiled for the first time in a long time. "More slippery than snot on a rooster's lip."

"And remember, where the foam turns yellow, it's hot. Let's go!"

It took four foam drops to get them out of the fire. The heat was intense but their state of mind and surges of adrenaline kept them going. The drops were low and concentrated. Consequently, trees were thrown down like pick-up sticks. Progress was difficult and slow, but with each step and each drop, their confidence grew.

"WAWA FIRE, THIS IS TANKER 271. We have the crew in sight. They're following our drops out to the back of the fire."

George jumped on the mic. "Tanker 271, we copy. And, thank you gentlemen, we owe you one. Also be advised that H39 is inbound and should be in your airspace shortly."

"We copy that Wawa. Do you want us to stick around or head over to Wawa 40?"

"If you don't mind, make sure their out of the burn before you leave."

"Copy that, Wawa." The two pilots looked at each other, both realizing how close to death the crew had been.

Rob continued on the radio. "Helitack 39 this is Tanker 271 on six, do you copy?"

"Go ahead 271."

"We're on you fire, but will stay west and south of the swamp and helipad. Come in from the east and you'll be OK."

"Almost there 271 and I've got a visual on you. I'll be down at the helipad in three."

"H39, the crew should be out to you in fifteen to twenty minutes."

"Copy that, and oh, good work gentlemen."

CINDY AND HER CREW BROKE FREE of the fire perimeter, exhausted and battered, but not broken. "OK guys, it's downhill and northeast from here. If we run into fire, we'll flank it to the south, then work northeast again. Any questions?" Cindy was all business now.

No one answered, all anxious to get out. Fifteen minutes later, Cindy found the swamp and entered the tall grass through the dogwood on the south side. Helitack 39 was a hundred metres north, engine running, rotor on slow rotation. As if on queue, spruce and balsam on the west fringe began to torch.

"Hurry guys, if the grasses ignite, fire will hit the helicopter in minutes."

No encouragement or further instruction was required. Jim and Tim raced to the pump site. Cindy and Sam picked up the empty hose pack, hand tools, chain saw and kit left at the helipad. Once they reached the pump, Tim strangled the hose above the foam injector; there would still be water in the hose up the line that would create a lot of back-pressure. Jim realized they would have no time to come back for all the equipment. He uncoupled the hose and threw the pump, and foam injector into the pond. The rest, the pump gas, tool kit and foam kit, could be carried back to the helicopter by the two of them.

The dry grasses ignited and metre-high flames raced across the swamp, pushed by strong winds. Cindy and Sam were in the helicopter; neither had time to put on their head sets. Cindy was willing the two remaining crewmembers to hurry. *Come on, come on.* It appeared to be a race—flames coming from the west, Jim and Tim running from the east. The pilot had now increased to full power before lift off. Cindy screamed in her mind, *leave the damn equipment!* Realizing their predicament, they threw down the gear simultaneously and lengthened their stride. Smoke was sliding past the helicopter now. *Shit, they're not going to make it! The pilot would have no choice.* The pilot put on more power and the helicopter start to rock on its skids. Cindy looked over at him, her eyes pleading. *What's he doing? He's nodding his head. He's letting off power now.* She looked towards Jim and Tim. She couldn't believe her eyes. They had stopped running and were looking up. *They've given up.*

They've given up! The chilling thoughts had no sooner crossed her mind, when she heard a sharp rumble above and just in front of the helicopter. The big yellow air tanker swept through her line of sight followed by a miraculous wall of foam. In seconds it erased all sign of flame. They would all be OK.

HELITACK 39 HEADED SOUTH. The pilot's instructions were to head straight to the Wawa airport. Cindy was advised that transportation was waiting to take them directly to the hospital. She argued that they were fine. There would be no argument, according to George. The other crew members were in various states of decompression, eyes closed, heads either tilted back or chins dropped on their chests. Even though her head was pounding, her teeth aching and every bone in her body felt like they had taken a beating, Cindy wondered what had taken place. *Was it fate, karma or just plain, horse-shit luck? No, it was good training, excellent people and just plain, horse-shit luck. If Rob hadn't been flying by, we would literally be toast by now. Where did I go wrong? Did I go wrong? This one will be investigated to death.* Thoughts were like butterflies that flickered and tumbled away. Her mind drifted, then a curtain quietly slid across her thoughts. Cindy fell into the abyss of uncluttered, colourless, sleep, her shoulders and head rocking to the rhythm of the Astar helicopter.

Chapter 28

DAY 1: 15:30 HOURS, WALLY'S CAMP

A STARTLED PAIR OF DOVES CATAPULTED FROM THE WALKWAY BELOW THE PORCH raced out over the dock and turned in unison to crest the shoreline cedar. In seconds the fawn-coloured, pigeon-sized birds with their black-spotted shawls and tail feathers fringed in white, disappeared to the south. The catalyst for their flight shuffled out onto the porch with a cold beer in one hand, a pair of binoculars in the other and a bowl of popcorn resting precariously between his forearm and chest. Wally had emerged from his *isolation chamber* camp to take in the afternoon air show at the top of the ridge. However, before he looked towards the far ridge, he had watched the aerodynamic doves with a sense of wonder, something he was prone to do more often of late. He realized this new found curiosity was an anticlimatic surge of appreciation for what the world had to offer. *And what I'm about to leave behind.* He marvelled at their ability to ride the currents at shotgun speed. *And we think we're something special, a higher form of life. Some mornings I can't even tie my boot laces, let alone take to flight.*

He sat down in his 56 Chevy bench seat and focused on the bowl of popcorn with some reverence and a touch of awe. *Lots of butter and salt. Can't worry about the arteries now. They can clog, cry and scream all they want. Hope the suckers close completely. They can move on to hell with me.*

He reached in, scooped up a mitt full of the greasy, inflated kernels, balanced the heel of his hand just below his lower lip, tilted his head back and allowed the fat, white puffs to tumble at random into his mouth. Each kernel found a spot to settle between his cheeks. *Like bingo balls when the air machine is shut down. Popcorn without butter and salt has no flavour. Dieters will tell you, with some desperation, that it does, but real popcorn lovers know it doesn't. Popcorn without supporting calories only has texture, probably like eating those little pieces of packing foam. To declare dry popcorn as 'tasty' is sacrilegious. It's only wishful thinking, the mind playing tricks like an amputee still feeling his missing leg.*

To Wally, popcorn was comfort food. Each mouthful triggered a memory. He took a 'scoop' of his favourite snack food. *I'm ten years old again, hockey night in Canada with Foster Hewitt.*

'Scoop'—*I'm sixteen at a high school basketball game with Sarah Miles. I'm pretending to eat popcorn, but I'm staring at her chest. Popcorn is falling on my lap, staining my crotch with grease. I had to stay seated until everyone else had left the gym.*

'Scoop'—*nineteen years old, sitting around the campfire with Julie. We're sharing a bowl. She let's me eat most of it. We're smiling at each other. She has popcorn between her teeth. Look! There's a golden kernel shell stuck in the front. I think I'm in love.*

'Scoop'—*I'm thirty-three now. Sitting on the sofa, eating popcorn and watching Pete's Dragon on the 'The Wonderful World of Disney' with the girls, three and five years old. One on each side of me, snuggled close. Little podgy ankles and feet poking out from their Winnie-the-Pooh nighties, toes turned in, rubbing and wiggling with glee. They still smell new, with freshly washed hair and a hint of talcum powder. They have their own little bowls of popcorn, without salt and butter. They don't know the difference. Can't let them try mine or the jig is up.*

Wally reminisced. At five, Hailey was already starting to look at the world with a critical eye. "Dad, why is Elliot the Dragon a cartoon and the people are real?"

"Elliot is Pete's imaginary friend, sweetie."

She had looked at him with rich, blue, sceptical eyes and pushed back a straight lock of strawberry blond hair. He looked back with his best poker face until she was satisfied that he wasn't kidding her. She had continued.

"Dad, what's the name of the town, again?"

"Let's see." *I used word association for this one. I remember that it was a tough one.* "Pass-me-a-hot-toddy? Oh yeah, Passamaquoddy, Sweetie." Sweetie was Hailey's "special" name.

Emily would not be out-done for her piece of attention. With her trademark scratchy voice and lazy word delivery she had gone for the sympathetic attention getter.

"Dad, my froat is soy (my throat is sore)."

"Maybe you shouldn't eat your popcorn, Pumpkin (her special name)."

She had gazed up to her father with deep, brown, wide-set eyes, an impish grin and a little shrug of her shoulders. Her naturally curly, light-brown hair was sprouting tips of blond.

"My froat is better now, Dad."

Wally sat alone with his thoughts, a hint of smile on his face and a narrow ridge of tears resting on his bottom eyelids like miniature canoes. *As I recall, Pete grew up and Elliot the dragon passed on. Growing up is the shits, and old friends do pass on.*

The "rat-atat-tat" of a pileated woodpecker woke him from his popcorn trance. *Gotta see this.* Wally stood up and moved quietly to the lip of the porch. He looked south and spotted the huge bird with the eighteen-inch body working the dickens out of an old, dead, poplar chi cot. With a rapid-fire, high-pitched laugh, the woodpecker moved on to a red pine with four quick thrusts of its powerful wings. This was a male with the customary, startling red crest. Both the males and females had black bodies and wing tops with contrasting white under-wings. They also both bore white stripes on their necks and black and white stripes on their faces. He recalled that the females had a grey to yellow-brown forehead. The bird moved on again, his body swooping down, then up with each thrust of his wings. *It didn't stay long—probably "sounding off" his territory with the machine-gun hammering of its formidable beak on the trees. Pretty rare around here. Must be the most northern part of its range.* The woodpecker's hard-headedness reminded Wally of a few of his former supervisors. Whenever he saw the stubborn bird, he called them "pecker heads", the same first name he assigned to Pecker Head Dickson and Pecker Head Sernoski. He was sure they had assigned him a name just as flattering. *My, the old mind is wandering down some familiar paths today.*

Wally decided it was time to do what he had come outside to do—see how MNR was doing with the fire. It was 15:30 hours and the sun was still high. Some of the smoke was climbing slowly down the east facing ridges. *Maybe the wind is swinging a little and coming more from the west?* He looked at the main column of smoke. *Nope, still coming from the southwest.*

He spotted a lone aircraft working the back of the fire and raised his binoculars to get a better look. It was dwarfed by the column of smoke and appeared like a lonely fly circling a picnic campfire. *It's that water bomber. Has to be wasting his efforts on such a large fire. Maybe not. What do I know anyway?*

Wally suddenly heard another aircraft. It seemed considerably closer, and he lowered his binoculars and looked to the south. It came in low, above the lake, passed the camp and turned into the wind for an approach. *Looks like I have a visitor.* The yellow, single engine DeHavilland Turbo Beaver settled gently on the rough water, powered up for a turn and came directly towards Wally's camp. With the winds from the southwest, Wally realized he would have to move his boat. *They'll want the south side of the dock.* He walked down to the dock and pulled the fourteen-foot aluminium boat up on the shoreline. It was light without the motor, the one sitting in the shed begging for repair. *That should give them enough dock space.* He waited for their approach and the grief they were probably bringing with them.

Chapter 29

DAY 1: 15:45 HOURS, WALLY'S CAMP

THE DEHAVILLAND DHC MARK III TURBO BEAVER TOUCHED DOWN on the wind driven lake with little effort. The amphibious aluminium floats, with wheels tucked up and in, pierced each wave in their path with routine precision, creating a series of staccato slaps that might unnerve a novice passenger. The passenger in this case was no novice. Randy Urbanski had spent countless hours in what many considered the ultimate, single engine seaplane, first as a student interior ranger in Algonquin Provincial Park and now as a Ministry of Natural Resources' conservation officer. Randy had used this superb flying machine to do it all, from fish creel census to moose surveys to search and rescue to fish and wildlife enforcement. This particular job was not new to him. However, it was low on the task/satisfaction scale. As part of the District's emergency response duties, he was charged with the job of ensuring those in the path of a wildfire or flood, either evacuated using their own devices or evacuated with MNR's assistance. Randy knew this particular situation was going to be sticky, if not impossible. Getting Wally McNeil to leave his trapper's camp would be as much fun as yanking nose hairs. He had dealt with Wally over trapping issues and respected him, but he also knew that the old guy was as stubborn as a six inch spike in an Ironwood tree. It would take all of his powers of persuasion. Government could not force evacuation; even in a life-threatening situation, it was strictly voluntary.

The MNR pilot sitting to Randy's left, Trevor Gilmore, pulled gently back on the column and the six hundred and eighty horse powered Pratt and Whitney turbine engine relaxed. The staccato slapping of float to water decreased, and the aircraft cut through close to metre-high waves, came about and made its way to shore. Now, floats were being hit broadside, and the fourteen and a half metres of aircraft rocked like a baby crib. Pilot and passenger fell into a comfortable rhythm for the remaining one hundred metre approach.

Trevor had already radioed in his location and landing to Wawa Fire, so the task at hand was simply to dock all fourteen and a half metres of aircraft at a six-metre dock with thirty kph cross winds while avoiding slamming the prop into shoreline boulders and overhanging white birch.

"Randy, I'll come well upwind of the dock, feather the prop and let the waves take us in. If you don't mind, exit out the rear port door and ease the float into the dock. I'll try to give you something to stand on besides lake."

"No problem, Trevor. I could be a little while, so you might as well shut her down and join us if you like."

Trevor was well aware of the trapper's reputation. "I think I'll either sit this one out or take a bit of a walk." Trevor craned his neck forward and squinted towards the 11:00 o'clock position. "I see good bumpers on the dock, so once you're out and comfortable, pull her in tight and hold on. I'll kill the engine, jump out and do the tying off. Can we expect some over-zealous help from McNeil?" Trevor was always worried about someone with good intentions, being "sliced and diced" by a steel propeller cranking out 100 revolutions per second. The graphic signs on all MNR float-plane docks, showing a rotating propeller next to a decapitated stick person were there for a purpose. He pictured one in his mind and smile to himself. *Crude, but effective.*

Randy thought for a moment. "Not likely. He's been around float planes all his life. If he approaches and you're not comfortable, reverse pitch. I'll get out on the floats and talk to him."

WALLY WATCHED THE BLACK AND YELLOW, MNR Turbo Beaver from the comfort of the 56 Chevy bench seat, a glass of scotch in hand. *Wings look like a teeter-totter wagging up and down without kids. Oh well, watching this aircraft sure beats counting shoreline waves.*

He looked above the aircraft to the ridge. Wally closed one eye, extended an arm and measured the column of smoke between thumb and forefinger as he had done an hour ago. It was now a little wider at the base and had risen about two inches. *Wonder what an inch means in feet from this distance. Could mean five hundred or a thousand feet. Wonder what that is in metres?* His American upbringing forced his mind to deal in imperial measure. But then again, he knew he wasn't much different from older Canadians, most of who struggled with conversions to metric on a daily basis.

That water bomber was pounding the fire somewhere. It seemed to be only five minutes between pickups. He thought it was working the back or south of the fire at first. It would head in that direction with a load but disappear over the ridge. A helicopter now appeared to be marking time high above the path of the water bomber. *Probably looking for an opportunity to move in. Wonder if there's a crew down there somewhere? Wouldn't want to be in their boots.* Wally's attention was distracted by the water bomber. After only two drops, it headed away from the fire in a southerly direction. *Fuel or mechanical?* Wally brought his attention back to the Turbo Beaver. *Should I help those guys dock? Nope. I know who's on board and why he's here. Besides, I'll just be a pain in the ass to the pilot.*

RANDY STRETCHED OUT OF THE PLANE, all six foot, three inches in drab green uniform. He stepped down the metal ladder to the float. One short, graceful hop to the dock then he eased five thousand pounds of aircraft into the dock bumpers, applying considerable resistance as the floats pushed towards him due to wind and wave action.

Trevor keyed his mike. "Wawa Fire, this is Oscar, Echo, Romeo on 6. Do you copy?"

"Go ahead OER."

"Wawa Fire, we're shutting down for awhile. I'll give you a shout when we're up again."

"Copy that, OER, down at McNeil's and off the air."

Trevor cut the engine, climbed nimbly out the starboard door with his tie-lines over his left shoulder and tied the aircraft carefully to the dock. He treated his machine more like a grandparent than a baby. OER was one of six turbo beavers owned by the Ontario government but there wouldn't be anymore. This particular aircraft was built in 1967 and at thirty-eight years old, had flown close to sixteen thousand hours. These powerful work-horses (highest power to weight ratio of any commercial float-plane in the world) were obsolete. Out of manufacture, their newest T/B, call sign OPA, was built in 1968. Although their present trade-in value was considerable at eight hundred thousand dollars, MNR wasn't sure that they could be replaced. Someday, maintenance would be an issue when parts became obsolete. Nothing good lasts forever, he thought.

Wally, who was now somewhat mellow, probably due to his third scotch, raised the glass up and viewed the approaching Conservation Officer through it. *Ah, much like looking through stained glass. The tall, green image is somewhat distorted. A tall, thin olive in my scotch … with moving legs … getting larger. Scotch and olives, Sean Connery would never forgive me. I can hear him now with rich, baritone, Scottish monologue flowing slowly over a stretched, lower lip, carefully, with purpose, each word uncovered like a gem in an unfolding palm. "And what, pray tell is this foreign object submerged like a thief and suspended like a lump of shite, mid-depth in the nectar of gods?? Would you also make union with sheep, man? I can only say that my spirit has withered and I'm not well pleased with you."*

Wally felt a little remorse about his increased drinking. The amount didn't bother him; it was the frequency. *So what, I'm dying, anyway. Time to get hold of myself. With the short time I have, I need to be coherent. Good memories are best served with clarity, a by-product of a sharp mind.*

Wally stood up, walked off the porch, poured the remains of his scotch on the yellow piss-patch, and stuck out a right hand to welcome his uninvited guest. In a nano-second, the two sized each other up, their secret thoughts blooming simultaneously.

Young, tall, full of confidence, strong features. Looks a little older since the last time I saw him. Think I'll let him do the talking and run his course, drop his confidence a little before I wade in.

Old, short, tough, I think. Looks a lot older and smaller since the last time I saw him. Eyes have lost a bit of spark. Could be true about his illness? No pushover, so no small talk. Let him start.

Time stood still. Two mannequins in a frozen hand shake. All activity around them seemed to stop, witness to the stand-off.

Just like Clint Eastwood, Eli Wallach and Lee Vann Cleef in The Good, the Bad and the Ugly, Wally thought. *The famous two minute stare. What did the movie poster say? Oh yeah, "for three men the civil war wasn't hell, it was practice." Let's see. I'm the good, he's the bad, so one of us has to be the ugly.* Wally took a close look at his adversary using Clint Eastwood squinty eyes. *Guess it has to be me.* Just then, the pilot appeared and stood just off to the side. Wally took a look at him. *Nope, it's still me.*

Trevor couldn't handle the silence. "Nice weather we're having." He waited. "One hell of a fire up there." The mannequins never flinched. "How about those Blue Jays, Maple Leafs, Raptors and Argos?" The spell was broken with the thought of four loser teams, all out of Toronto. Trevor sensed the tension wither as the stares wavered and the hand shake disengaged like two rail cars uncoupling. "Well, guess I'll take a little walk."

Wally, against his considerable will and bending under the pressure that comes with a good upbringing, was the first to speak. "Randy, can I get you something to drink?" *Say no, say no. Gotta ease the tension.* "Sure Mr. McNeil, anything that's cold and wet."

How about a glass of old beaver piss? "How about a coke?" Before he could respond, Wally turned and shuffled into the camp. Randy followed.

"WHADAYA MEAN, I SHOULD LEAVE!! There's a lake between me and that fire. I can ATV it out to the truck anytime I want. What's the problem here?"

"Look, Mr. McNeil. The fire people tell me that with west or even northerly winds, you could be in trouble. Apparently, one of two situations can occur." Randy paused and looked for a sign of encouragement to continue.

"Right. I could stay or I could stay. Besides, nothing is going to happen here."

Randy's face darkened like a cloud passing a full moon. "With all due respect sir, you're not a prophet."

"On the contrary; I can foretell the past. For example, you're going to come here to try and get me to leave."

Randy began to feel a little frustrated.

Wally noticed his face flush and a hard look in his eyes. *I'm jerking his chain—good.*

Can't let the old bastard get to me. "As I said there are two situations that could threaten you. One—if the piece of bush across the lake becomes the head of the fire, you could get jump fires around your camp."

"Ah, come on, over three kilometres of lake?"

"Yes sir—especially if the column of smoke bends. It'll carry firebrands that far. And second, smoke."

"Smoke? That won't kill me."

"Well, it could prevent you from getting out then the fire will kill you. Or, it could prevent help from getting in then the fire will kill you."

I'm dying anyway, you pecker head! A short upturn at the corners of his mouth produced a shallow smile that didn't quite make it to his eyes. *You don't understand and haven't earned the right to an explanation. Time to send you on your way.*

"Randy, you haven't touched your coke."

Randy reluctantly put the bottle to his lips but didn't take his eyes off the trapper. Wally's glasses had slipped down his nose. Only the flair on each side of the bridge stopped them from falling off. He pushed them back up with a bony finger. "I won't be leaving. If and when I think I'm in trouble, I'll make the decision at that time. I don't owe you an explanation, so I won't give you one. Don't take it personally."

Randy's eye lids closed slightly into a squint and his pupils ratcheted around lightly in the sockets like they were trying to probe the old man's very soul. *He's not going to budge.* "We can't force you to evacuated, sir, but you can expect a fire crew in at any time to protect your camp and out-buildings. Will you at least sign a statement that you've been warned and decline to leave?"

Wally felt sorry for the young enforcement officer. "I'd be glad to." He hesitated. "And for the record, my decision is not the result of a feeble mind or an overly stubborn disposition. I have my reasons, which are very personal."

"I think I understand, sir."

Your lips say you understand but your eyes say otherwise—time to pull out some old guy wisdom. "Look Randy, the trouble with getting old and being a survivor is you find yourself alone at the dance, at the end of the evening. No partner, the scotch bottle is empty and the decorations are in shambles. Just no fun—I'll take my chances."

WALLY WATCHED THE TURBO BEAVER reverse its position away from the dock and taxi out for departure. *An impressive piece of aircraft.*

Was I too hard on him, Julie? I hope not. Some things are best kept to one self. I'm not sure where this is leading, but I'm pretty sure I'll be joining you sooner rather than later. I promise you one thing. I'll let the girls know how I feel about them. I'll start a letter tonight.

The yellow and black aircraft bullied its way off the lake into the wind, got immediate lift and quickly shrunk to the south.

Wally dropped into the bench seat as if his match-stick legs could no longer support his slouching body. *I could use a drink now. Man, I love the amber colour of scotch over fragmented crystals of ice. I enjoy the feel of slippery frost on the glass and take delight when the oc-*

casional cube pops from pressure. I just ran my tongue over my bottom lip. The simple cognition of that gesture should worry me. Perhaps I'm an alcoholic. It just doesn't matter now. However, no more drink today. Have to keep the mind uncluttered to put pen to paper—should eat something so I can take my pills.

As if on cue, Wally felt a twinge in his lower abdominal area. *I can feel the slither-worm approaching.*

Like a series of snapshots placed randomly on the photo album of life, a bent, shuffling old man slipped into his camp and a dragon and its spawn slipped over the ridge and belly crawled in an easterly direction towards the lake. At the same time, a sow bear and cub huddled together for protection and a damaged old pine still stood on the ridge, a ragged sentinel, watching the destruction it could not prevent.

PART 3

ESCAPED FIRE AND SUSTAINED ATTACK

"Have you ever fought a dragon?"
The wide eyed protégé asked the ancient, frail knight.
Through lips cracked with age he whispers,
"I've fought many dragons. Be wary, young knight,
The most formidable are the ones that lie within."

Thursday, July 21st, 09:00, 2005 to Saturday, July 23rd, 17:00 hours

Chapter 30

DAY 2: THURSDAY, JULY 21, 09:00 HOURS, WAWA FIRE MANAGEMENT HEADQUARTERS

"**I** TOTALLY SCREWED UP, JIM." Cindy and Jim sat across from an empty desk in the Fire Management Supervisor's office. The FMS, Darryl Kurtyn, was responsible for all fire management activities in the Wawa District. He had two senior fire officers that reported directly to him as well as eight fire crew leaders, one of which was Cindy Corrigan, and a cast of support staff. One of his senior fire officers was George Williams who was functioning right now as sector response officer and presently had his hands full coordinating fire attack for the Wawa District.

Cindy had finished her incident report the previous night and handed it in at 22:00 hours. The mandatory fire report would not be completed until the fire was declared "OUT", but all fire and cost related data would eventually be collected by Cindy in order to finalize a comprehensive report. At this stage of the game, however, she was expecting disciplinary action, or, at the very least, she expected the FMS to make life miserable for her.

Jim sat awkwardly in the old wooden swivel chair. His butt precariously on the edge, back slouched, arms dangling on each side and long legs splayed out with boots acting like hinges on a worn pine floor. He looked like a marionette that someone had thrown aside. He rubbed a stubble chin with a calloused right hand as if the action alone would stimulate thought. "You're wrong, Cin."

She looked at him with mild surprise. *Is that it? No explanation. No words of encouragement.* She turned to her mentor. "I panicked inside. I thought I was going to lose it. I almost lost it!"

Jim tip-toed the swivel chair around to face her and placed his chin-supporting hand on her forearm. "You didn't panic on the outside. Somehow you cut the bad stuff off at the pass. What came out was some anger and resolve. Bottom line, we're both here and the boys are fine and still sleeping."

Before she could reply, the office door opened and Darryl Kurtyn walked in, coffee cup in one hand and Cindy's incident report in the other. With a curt "good morning, don't get up", Darryl strode around the desk and dropped unceremoniously in his chair. He flipped open the report and hunted around for his reading glasses. "Shit! Where are my glasses?"

Jim smiled and pointed. "They're on your head, Darryl." Once upon a time, Darryl had been a crew member and Jim had been his crew boss. There was good history between them.

Darryl pulled the glasses down through prematurely thinning, corn-stalk coloured hair and perched them on the tip of his nose. He used this little trick to appear wise. He could raise his eyebrows, look over the glasses and throw a laser guided look at an unhappy recipient. "Says here, you lost fifty-six lengths of hose, camping gear, one pump, one intake, etcetera, etcetera." *Laser guided look.* "You managed to salvage one pump, intake, tool box and foam unit, but they're somewhere submerged in a pond." *Laser guided look.*

Cindy felt a fountain of embarrassment rise up through her chest to her cheeks. At the same time she actually felt her body shrivel into a puddle. *I'm like the wicked witch of the west when Dorothy spilled water on her.* She wanted to respond, truly wanted to defend her actions, but there was something lodged in her throat. *Now I know how a cat feels before it coughs up a five pound fur ball—damned if you do, damned if you don't.*

Jim looked at her and in an instant she read his mind. *No defence is the best defence.* "Darryl, I'm truly sorry." *Here it comes. Sorry doesn't cut it! You're sorry! What about the tax payer? Ten thousand dollars worth of equipment down the tube! You think you're sorry now; wait till I quit blowing a main artery and pull my tongue back on its hinge!*

Darryl looked up, paused, took his reading glasses off and pinched a weary nose at its bridge just below his eyes. He put the report down on his desk.

Here it comes for sure. I'm toast.

"There is not a damn thing to be sorry about, Cindy. You and your crew shouldn't have been in there in the first place. We made the wrong call."

Cindy wouldn't accept the absolution. She needed to bring her guilt forward, reveal it in cupped, opening palms, bring it to her lips, savour it like fine wine, wallow in it. The adrenalin surge associated with fight or flight on the fire resulted in behaviour she couldn't wrestle down, at least not yet. "I should have pulled us out earlier."

"And I should have been taller and better looking. But we are who we are, and we do what we think is right at the time. Look, Cindy, hindsight is always 20/20 and always anticlimactic. I'm not here to make you feel better, just to tell it like it is or like it should be."

Darryl needed a thought break. Being a supervisor didn't necessarily mean you had all the answers. He was presently dealing with a significant manure pile of issues. No matter how you forked out a challenge, it always came up smelling like doo-doo. "Step in anytime, Jim."

Jim pulled himself up straight in the wobble chair. "You're right, Darryl."

Darryl searched back in his memory bank of earth shattering, enlightened deliveries. "About what?"

"We shouldn't have been in there."

Darryl looked at Cindy with a head tilting, mouth open, shoulder shrugging "Hellooo. I told you so."

It was approaching a time out, something like in the third period of a one to zip hockey game—the moment for the "let's finish this thing" pep talk. First though, Darryl needed to satisfy a concern. "How are Tim and Sam doing?"

This caught Cindy by surprise. A fire management supervisor with close to sixty staff normally had trouble remembering crew members' names.

"Sam's OK. I'm a little worried about Tim, though." She hesitated. *What cats do I let out of the bag?*

Darryl looked at Cindy and Jim. "Between us, people."

Cindy looked to Jim for help. He slouched even further followed by his best vacant stare.

I guess it's my responsibility. "Tim lost it out there. Sam reeled him in."

"Cindy, dealing with mortality at such a young age, can create— situations. Will he be OK?"

"He'll wrestle a few demons, but I have hopes for him. We're going to watch him closely. He'll be Jim's new project." She looked towards Jim. *That's for not pitching in, oh wise and enlightened one.*

Darryl paused. *This is where I have to be delicate.* "Cindy, you know we have mechanisms in place to get you or your crew some help. When Tim reflects on his actions, his behaviour under the circumstances may be hard for him to face. We have people that can help."

Cindy's reaction was terse and too quick. They both knew it. "Thanks, Darryl, but we can handle it."

"All I'm saying is that instinct is unconscious and it rules. Tim's response didn't have a mind of its own, and reactions would not be expected to be rational. We will have to give the kid a break—and some help."

Both Cindy and Jim looked away. They wanted to avoid looking at a *reality canvas* like it was a surreal, unfathomable piece of art.

Darryl received no further reaction. *Enough said.* "OK. So let's recap. I'm OK, you're OK, the kids are OK. We'll write off some equipment. We'll give you some time off. How about two hours?" *That got there attention.* "Just kidding. How about a couple of days? And by the way, I'm glad you all made it back in good shape. I hate filling out forms."

There was a brief knock at the office door just before it opened. George Williams stepped in, pointed towards Cindy. Small talk was not customary under present circumstances. "Got a real cushy job for you and your crew, Cindy—values protection. We have a camp on Siren Lake that needs protecting. There's a trapper there now that insists on staying. See me when you're finished here." George turned and walked out as quickly as he had come in.

Cindy looked at Darryl with a look that said, "So much for the time off." He was standing, gathering his notes. "Got a meeting with the district manager, Cindy. Stay safe." Like an oak leaf on a blustery fall day, Darryl was gone.

Cindy stood and looked at Jim. "Wow! What just happened here? Eighteen hours ago we had the dragon on our collective asses. Ten hours ago I thought I didn't deserve to run a crew. Ten minutes ago, I thought I'd be looking for a whole new career in basket weaving or folk dancing. Now, we're back at it, and I still have a crew. Go figure."

There was no response, just the typical 'Jimmie' smile. Cindy looked pensively at her mentor. "Jim, you have to stop monopolizing the conversation. Between "You're wrong, Cin" and "You're right, Darryl", you sure delivered one hell of a monologue."

Her tall, weary mentor stood up and favoured her with his best Shaolin Monk, Master Po smile. "Ah, grasshopper, saying nothing takes much discipline and speaks volumes."

Chapter 31

DAY 2: 09:00 HOURS, WALLY'S CAMP

BILLOWY CLOUDS, PINK HAZE, SCENTS OF LILAC AND LAVENDER, *feeling like I'm pulling into the laneway at home. There's Julie and the girls on the porch! Boy they look real? Not another disappointing dream! How can I be dreaming if I think I'm dreaming? A dream within a dream? This one is starting out with promise, though. Think I'll hang around. I wonder if I can make this one up as I go along. What did Julie always tell me? Oh yeah, "Wallace" (she's the only one allowed to call me that). "Wallace, if you can imagine it, you can make it happen." I'm getting off my horse—no, (too much imagination there), getting out of the Chevy pick-up and walking with anticipation to the porch. I'm coming back from Nam. No, the girls aren't born yet. So what! It's my dream, so they can be born. I extend my arms. They appear to stretch twice their length and envelope my family. I smell hair, freshly washed and perfume that triggers the need to step inside Julie, hide in her soul for protection. We are all entangled in a desperate effort to connect and fuse. I hear soft crying and taste salted tears. The girls are so light and delicate, with rapid beating hearts, like hummingbirds. Julie feels tall and strong, taunt at first, then compliant, all of her weight shifting into my body. But my emotions are flat, like a snapped chalk line.*

I don't trust this dream—won't give in to it in case it's a trick dream, one where it would "Houdini" right before my very eyes. But the dream is too real to resist. Julie speaks. "Embrace it, Wallace. We're here. We need to talk." Talk? Who the hell wants to talk? Can we put the girls to bed and, you know?

"No, it's only 9:00 am in this dream. The girls don't want to sleep. They want to tell you something." We turn and move towards the door. We fast-forward into the kitchen, I see our bodies' stiff, jerky and animated like an old movie reel. I sit down with Hailey and Emily. Julie is no longer there. I turn to the girls. They have now morphed into beautiful young women. I hear my voice break. *"Where's your mother?"*

"Oh Dad', Hailey says, "You know she past away five years ago". A little girl voice in a woman's body.

Someone is taking over my dream and I'm getting pissed. I look up past the kitchen to the living room. There's Julie, keeping vigil and smiling at me. My anxiety decreases. My blood pressure must be dropping, if I have blood, or pressure, in this dream. Her lips don't move, but she tells me to pay attention to the girls. When I look at them, their images change like photos in an album. As I flip through the pages, faces and bodies mature.

Emily: "Dad, we know you're in pain."

Hailey: "And we know you won't be with us much longer."

Me: "How long? (Maybe they have inside information—how can I be flippant at a time like this—how can I think I'm being flippant if I'm dreaming)."

Emily: "It doesn't matter. We're here to tell you that we understand."

Me: "Understand what?" (I think I'm being set up).

Hailey: "Why you chose to be alone and not with us for your last days."

Me: (Christ, I'm being psychoanalyzed in a dream. What's next? Is Freud going to pop out of a cake waving a straight jacket?). "Girls, how could you know that? I don't even understand why I'm an asshole."

Emily (smiling): "You're not an asshole, Dad. They're useful."

Me: "Hey, that's my joke. By the way, have I ever told you that you're both beautiful and I'm proud of you?"

Hailey: "You told us that all the time when we were growing up. And don't change the subject."

Me: "It's my dream so I don't have to face the truth right away if I don't have to."

Emily: "Dad, we've come to terms with it. We know that you don't want to share your pain."

Hailey: "And you miss mom very much."

Emily: "And your isolation is not your attempt at making us feel bad, or guilty. We also know that you're really not alone."

They're turning and looking at Julie, and then fade into shadows, then nothing.

Julie is now at my side and she's pressing my head to her chest. God, she smells so good. If she's real in a dream, then she's likely real now, in another realm. Where's my shotgun? The sooner I eat buckshot, the sooner I'll be with her. But wait. If I commit suicide, what if the "believers" are right and I go to hell? And I know she's not there. Maybe I'm going to hell anyway. Can't die now, need to hedge my bets, have to stay alive to do something good. Geez, I'm exhausted from this dream and I'm sleeping! Can't hardly wait to wake up so I can go back to sleep and get some rest.

Wally awoke from his dream, clutching the pillow he had removed from their bed. The covers were tossed and twisted. Sleep crept away and consciousness slowly slipped into its place. Wally squeezed his eyes shut, desperate to climb back into the dream. Just a few minutes more please. Sleep had enough of Wally and he propped himself up.

Must have been that letter I started last night to the girls. I may have to tweak it a little. Time to get up and pay a visit to the facilities. What a way to start the morning—ten minutes in an outhouse before breakfast. Maybe that's where I'll die. I could strain once too often and something could break inside. I can see it now: "We found him dead, sitting on his throne in the outhouse, pants down to his ankles and a Field and Stream magazine clutched in his hand. Don't know whether it was last night's beans that killed him or the article written by an anti-hunter. Funny though, he was smiling."

I know I'm the architect of my own demise. No one else made the little "life altering" decisions for me. Shouldn't have smoked when I was younger. Should have quit drinking years ago. More exercise, fruits and vegetables and fewer fries and fried chicken would have helped. But then, life would not have been worth living.

Wally, old fart, you grew it, you chew it.

THE SOW TWITCHED AND SNORTED in her sleep. Her chestnut coloured eyes shifted randomly in their sockets, semi protected by relaxed lids at haft mast. Thick lips curled up and a long tongue poked out between impressive incisors, searching for phantom food, even as she slept. She was dreaming. Her visions were reflections of earlier years. Unlike the trapper, she had no knowledge of dreaming. The act of dreaming was simply instinctive and would trigger no emotion when she awoke. They were simple dreams, sketches of a cub's activities as she followed and mimicked her protector. She would not dream in colour, but objects within her snapshot dreams appeared bigger than life.

Perhaps the internal, physical action of craving food influenced this particular dream. Grubs and ants appeared bigger and fatter, blue berries hung from their shrubs like large, smoky globes and choke cherry branches bent and hung right to the ground with clusters of dark, ripe, golf-ball sized berries. A large butterfly caught her attention, its erratic pattern exaggerated in haphazard flight. She instinctively chased after it, her predatory tactics hard wired into her genetic framework. Her mother woofed her back into her protective field of vision, ever wary of the threat of a boar or wolf who might exploit her cub's tenuous situation.

The more she moved in her dream, the more her eyes shifted and her body twitched. Now, she was using her little paw to turn over a large piece of decaying red pine. She discovered a cache of writhing fat, white grubs, a treasure trove for a young bear. She gently prodded, lifted and rolled each delicacy with her sensitive tongue, then drew them back into her mouth. If she could rationalize she would likely acknowledge that life for a cub could never be better.

But as the sow lay deep in sleep her olfactory senses picked up something foreign and pungent. She recoiled out of sleep, and her eyes opened completely to see a drift of haze lying within a metre of the ground. This was the thing that had initially driven her from the protection of higher ground. It simply fell into the category of "intruder", and it triggered her defence and protection mechanisms. She rose quickly, startling her cub. She would have to find a safer haven for the both of them.

THE SENTINEL DID NOT HAVE THE ABILITY to sleep or dream, but if it could, what would it dream about? It sat precariously among the barren boulders—boulders that, twenty-four hours ago were shrouded in forest shrubbery and supported by maple saplings and immature birch and pine. Now, all that remained were black spikes balanced on soot-covered, barren ground. The sentinel had been scorched, its thick blue-grey bark now a charcoal black that reached ten metres. Fissures within its bark were weeping a white crystalline resin in a desperate attempt to heal. If it could sleep, dreams might be restless and pain induced. If the sentinel could dream, but not feel, perhaps they would be comforting dreams, dreams of long ago, dreams that bore witness to restoration and growth, not destruction. But dreams were meant for people, and perhaps animals—not three hundred year-old white pine.

Chapter 32

DAY 2: 10:00 HOURS, WAWA 43
AND WAWA DISTRICT OFFICE

THE RED ON WHITE LONG RANGER HELICOPTER cruised along the west flank of Wawa 43, a hundred and fifty metres above the forest canopy at a scouting speed of seventy kilometres per hour. Sitting in the front on the port side of the machine, Russell Gervais scanned intently to the west, away from the fire perimeter. He focused solely on at least fifty rows of cut, tree-length wood. They were piles thirty metres long and five metres high with each limbless and topless tree in the piles averaging twelve metres in length.

Russell had just returned home to Wawa from a fire assignment in north-western Ontario. The short, stocky senior fire officer had literally dragged his ass into the office at 23:00 hours the night before, only to be greeted by an equally exhausted co-worker and friend, George Williams. Wawa's two senior fire officers exchanged hand shakes and back slaps then sat down across from each other at the sector response officer's duty desk. The SRO function was one they both routinely carried out over the course of a fire season. George presently had command and control. He had painted a significantly bleak fire picture to Russell and provided him with his next day's assignment, assessment of their latest escaped fire, Wawa 43.

Now, with only five hours of fatigue-induced sleep the previous night, Russell was in the process of doing a second circuit of the fire and was not optimistic about strategy required to deal with it. As the helicopter crept along the perimeter, Russell made notes and drew the fire perimeter on the map snapped in a clip-board.

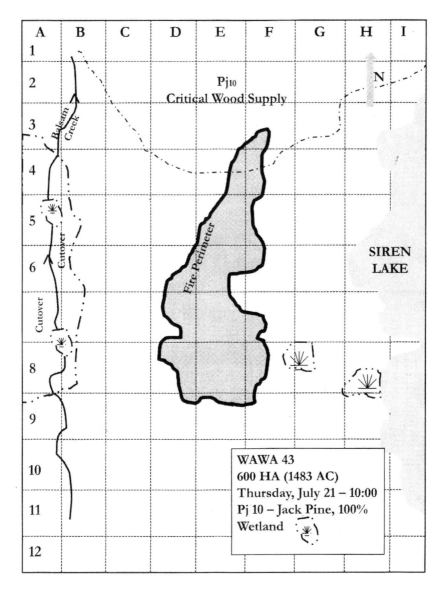

Flying the back and west flank of the fire was easy. The southwest winds were relatively light and pushed smoke to the northeast. Flying the head of the fire was not impossible. The column bent at approximately sixty degrees and provided air space below it. The only issue was turbulence from radiant heat. The helicopter had bobbed around on air currents like a fishing float in choppy water.

The east flank, however, was a different story. Thick smoke, tight to the forest canopy, rolled up and dispersed outwardly, then down, much like the bow wake created from a ship in heavy seas. Visibility was next to impossible, so Russell had directed the pilot to climb. At fifteen hundred feet, he had a bigger picture. He would have to "guestimate" the fire perimeter's location on this flank. Smoke colour and density would provide him with an ill-defined line. The poor division between dark, dense smoke and lighter, thinner smoke would be his perimeter—maybe. He took note of the lake to the east and the speck that represented a cabin on its east shore. He was now ready to send in his report.

Russell keyed his mic. "Wawa Fire this is Helitack 21 on channel 6. Do you copy?"

George Williams, who had been agonizing over the fire location map next to his desk, grabbed the mic on his remote radio perched on the SRO desk. "Helitack 21, this is Wawa on 6. Go ahead Russell."

"Yeah, George. I have a fire assessment report for you. Are you sitting down?"

George looked at the radio operator through the windowless frame in the wall. She was poised with a pencil in hand. "Go ahead Russell, and start with some good news, just to brighten up my already miserable day."

"George, the good news is, and this is the only good news, the cut wood approximately one kilometre to the west of the fire perimeter is still intact." He paused for a response, and when there wasn't one, continued on. "Wawa 43 is presently close to six hundred hectares, running and torching. It's into Northshore's five-year critical wood supply to the north and nothing is going to stop it other than Mother Nature. I expect with this afternoon's winds, we can expect crowning in the jack pine." Another pause.

George looked to the radio operator who nodded that she was keeping up. His face had turned a baking powder white accentuating the furrows and shadows below his eyes. *I'll let my boss, Darryl, deal with Northshore on that one.*

"Go ahead, my friend, but be gentle." *If you could maintain a sense of humour, then work might be bearable.*

"OK George. As I see it, our only target for the time being is the cut wood to the west. We need two of Northshore's bulldozers ASAP to construct a line at the base of the ridge. Get the district to provide one of its techs as a bulldozer leader. We need a couple of their back-hoes as well. There are two potential water sources fed by a dry creek. There's a little water in them, but they may need to be dug out. I need three fire crews complete with pumping units, three drip torches, and aerial ignition capability; either OAID (Ontario Aerial Ignition device) or helitorch will do." Russ preferred the OAID over helitorch. The little ping-pong type balls were filled with combustible chemicals and jettisoned by machine from a helicopter. The helitorch used a napalm-like mixture that required a mixing crew. It was carried in a large drum, suspended from a helicopter and hook up was a little risky.

"Oh, and I'll also need permission to burn-out about five hundred hectares between the cutover and the fire east of it."

George responded quickly. "Russ, I can get you the crews, pumping units and torches. OAID equipment and technician arrived this morning. We anticipated the need for aerial burn-out." He had to choose his words carefully on the next item. "A Northshore rep just happens to be in the district manager's office right now to voice his displeasure over the lack of resources on Wawa 43. We'll hit him up with the bulldozer and back-hoe request. As far as the regional fire duty officer's permission to burn, I'll have to get back to you on that one."

"George, the way I see it is we're going to lose that five hundred hectares between the cutover and the fire anyway, and the winds are in our favour. Besides, there's gotta be a couple of million dollars worth of cut wood laying in harm's way. There's no way Northshore would be able to haul it out in time."

"Russ, what are our time lines?"

"OK, I need the bulldozers and back-hoes up and running by noon. Ferry in the fire crews and equipment starting yesterday." Russell took his thumb off the mic trigger to gather his thoughts. "Give me command of this little operation. I'll return now, and pick up the OAID machine and operator. Have the bulldozer tech ready at the Wawa airport. He or she can come with me. Oh, and get the crews their overnight equipment and throw in an extra initial attack food order for yours truly. I want an early evening burn." He paused, his mind flipping over a new card. "George, have you got a handle on Wawa 40 near Hornepayne now?"

"It appears that way. It's BHE at eighty hectares. Why?"

"I don't think Hornepayne is out of the woods yet. Wawa 43 is definitely going to boogy and put up a lot of smoke. I recommend you get an emergency response coordinator to liaise with the town officials at Hornepayne. And see if you can get an ER team put together from the District and prepared to go to Hornepayne."

George let out an audible grown as he leaned back into his chair for both physical and moral support. *Should have stayed in bed.* He reluctantly toggled the mic. "Any other requirements?"

"How about a 415 in the air when I ignite?"

Would you like the US Army's fifth armoured division as well? "Sorry Russ. We only have one operational right now. It's at the Wawa airport and dedicated to initial attack. We might be able to get a Twin Otter out of the region, though. And wait for the go-ahead to burn, although I don't think it will be a problem."

Russ understood why the 415 heavy water bomber was required for new fire starts. *No sense having additional escaped fires.* He rationalized the effectiveness of a Twin Otter with its four hundred and fifty gallon water drop. *Could work on jump fires.*

"Thanks, George. I'll take the Twin Otter if you can get it. And George, we can't wait too long on the OK to burn."

"Russ we'll be using Helitack 15, a 212 helicopter, to ferry in your crews and some equipment. The rest of the equipment will come in by truck. I'll get the pilot to throw his bucket on board. You can keep him there unless I need him. That'll give you additional water drop capabilities."

"Thanks again, my friend. I *almost* feel better already."

AMOS ALFELSKI STOOD ON THE OTHER SIDE of Francis DesRoche's desk, his considerable frame thrust forward like he was about to leap across and throttle the calm, relaxed district manager. Amos had a head like a car battery, hard, wide and rectangular. His face was presently the colour of a ripe tomato, his anger-laden eyes squinting with menace. Sausage fingers gripped the lip of the desk, knuckles large and white, each a bone and cartilage vice grip.

Darryl Kurtyn stood to his left, leaning against the wall, his arms folded, legs crossed, a "here we go again" look on his face.

Amos's voice rolled out between two snarling lips like gravel being dumped from a tandem truck. "I can't believe you only put one crew on that fire. What the hell is going on around here??" As woodland manager for Northshore logging, he was used to pushing people around. His position, size and confrontational manner were his tools of intimidation. Most employees deferred to his "my way or the highway" approach to managing.

Francis slowly rose from his chair. His smile slipped just a little as he stood erect. "Amos, as I see it, you have two choices. You can walk out now and explain to your supervisor that you don't know what's going on, or you can sit down, act civilly and become part of the solution."

The big man knew his bluff had been called. As he slowly sank in the chair he shot an acid-laced look at Darryl, who had just managed to transform a grin of satisfaction into a half-assed look of sympathy. Darryl had been briefed by his sector response officer, George Williams and was prepared to paint the fire picture for Amos. He pushed himself away from the wall and walked towards the large map on the opposite wall across the room. One of the members of the recently established district fire *service* organization had been keeping the map up-to-date with the latest fire information. Pinned to the permanent map was a rough, eight and a half by eleven inch map of Wawa 43 handed to Darryl five minutes ago by George. Amos, muttering a few of his favourite obscenities, swung his chair around to face the map.

Darryl began. "Amos, the province is presently in the shitter. The West Fire Region has its hands full and our fire region can't keep up with a load of new fire starts. In addition, we have six potential escaped fires across the region, two of which are in the Wawa District." Darryl looked to Amos for a hint of understanding.

Amos wasn't going down without a fight. "Look, I don't give a rat's ass about what is happening elsewhere. What about *our* limits?"

Francis, who now saw his role as mediator/referee interjected. "Last chance to keep it civil Amos then you're out of here."

Amos whipped around like a Rottweiller that had just been stung on the ass. "And how, "Mister" DesRoches, do you propose to make that happen?"

Francis leaned forward ever so slightly on his desk. "I have two conservation officers just down the hall, "Mister" Alfelski, that have full 'peace officer' powers and who are itching to practice their rusty self-defence training on somebody."

Amos realized that his tactics and attitude were failing the situation. *Man, I hate dealing with these sanctimonious pricks.* "OK, OK, get on with it … please."

Darryl now pointed to the smaller map. Russ had provided information concerning the fire perimeter to his radio operator earlier on. "Amos this is Wawa 43. It is pushing six-hundred hectares."

Amos was imperial, not metric. "What's that in acres?"

"Approximately 1500 acres. To the west is your cutover— approximately a thousand metres, or just over ½ mile away. To the east is Siren Lake." Darryl paused. He knew that his next 'point of interest' had the potential to make Amos go ballistic. "As you can see to the north, Wawa 43 is already in that pure stand of jack pine, part of your next five-year allocated wood."

Amos's rather large face turned multiple shades of red, including, but not restricted to crimson. Each shade was associated with a different but related emotion. He struggled to wrestle them down as he looked to the district manager. He wasn't sure how his first words would role out because he had lost control of his vocal ability somewhere along the way. To his surprise, his words came out as whispers, and controlled. "This could put the mill out of business."

Francis understood that some hope was required here. "Amos, I have one of my foresters working on it as we speak. You'll likely get the go ahead to tap into your five to ten-year wood. We'll see what we can negotiate or trade to replace the loss. No one wants a mill shut down."

Amos didn't have the energy to respond. Darryl decided to continue. "Amos, our priority right now is your cut wood to the west and we need your help."

Amos's look hardened, like cooling, molten iron. "What, exactly are you looking for?"

Darryl explained the need for two bulldozers, either D8's or D7's, two back hoes and all complete with operators and the need for them right away. And then he explained the strategy on the duplicate map provided by Russell. He pointed to it. "We need a constructed line running from A4 to A9. The back hoes will dredge for water in those dry swamps at A5 and A7 and 8. We'll burn out that piece within B and C, 4 to 8."

Now I got the pricks. "Let me see if I've got this right. You guys let a fire get away and now you want my equipment to bail you out." His next words dripped with satisfaction. "I don't think so."

Francis had taken enough. He picked up the receiver on his phone and punched in a single speed dial number.

Amos who thought he was about to face a couple of martial artists, responded. "What's the call about?"

Francis threw him a look that would stop a train but didn't respond. He focused on his call. "Hello, this is Francis DesRoches for Ian Miller."

Amos abruptly stood up, a look of surprise and then trepidation sliding across his face. "There's no need to call my supervisor."

Francis ignored him. "Hello, Ian? It's Francis. Yeah, long time. Look we've got a problem that I thought you might be able to help us with." Francis explained their requirements and, without hesitation, Amos's reluctance to cooperate. "He's right here. I'll put him on."

A significantly repentant Amos Alfelski left the District Manager's office a few minutes later with a promise of full cooperation.

CINDY AND ROB STOOD TOE-TO-TOE in the Wawa district office coffee room, arms rigid at their sides as if strapped there, noses a few inches apart, Cindy's pointed up, Rob's pointed down. This was not a mating posture; it was definitely a fighting stance. Words were fired like volleys from a cannon, each one inflicting damage to an already shaky relationship. They had only an hour to win this battle. The requirement to return to work would necessitate a flag of truce, unless, of course, they had destroyed the relationship within their short window of opportunity.

Short, economical retorts were spat in vehement whispers in order to avoid witness from the other room. Point-making emphasis were accompanied by reluctant but unavoidable gestures, (after all, the use of appendages and facial expression had long been ingrained in human communication tactics, long before formal speech was invented).

Without hearing a single word, and with a sound imagination, one could reconstruct the argument just by observing gestures in order of occurrence:

Rob: arms flung out and upward simultaneously, palms facing up, fingers open. Translation; *why the hell did you put yourself in such a predicament?*

Cindy: chin and body thrust forward, feet spread apart for balance, hands high on hips, gripping tightly and pushing in as if to inflate chest. Translation; *how dare you presume you know my business better than me!*

Rob: right hand in front of Cindy's face, index finger pointed at her nose, left hand now firmly planted on hip. Translation; *well someone has to tell you that you screwed up. It's a good thing I was there to save your sorry ass!*

Cindy: steps back a pace, arms crossed, hip shift to the left, pursed smirk on her substantially red face. Loose translation; *my sorry ass! You should have parked your male, fly-boy ego at the door before you walked in here. My ass wasn't so sorry the other night, was it, oh great stud in the air, dud in the bed!*

Rob: arms down to sides, fists clenched, eyebrows pinched in, eyeballs slightly bulging, lips opening/closing, chest heaving for air, flag pole rising between legs ever so slightly – classic male fight or fornicate stance. Translation; *what do I do now?*

Cindy: one step forward, hands lightly on hips, chest thrust out seductively, winner's smile on lips, classic female "you lose" stance. Translation; *typical male, little head thinks for the big head.*

Rob: head bowed, shoulders slumped, arms loosely at sides, face embarrassment-red from a traitorous penis. Translation; *aw shit, I give up.*

Cindy: body turns about face, head swings back, large victorious smile on face, arm up, middle finger extended as she walks out the door. Triumphant translation; *screw you, loser!*

Battle fought. One foe retreats, the other dejected. The prize disappears like a puff of magic-wand smoke.

Winner, neither.

Chapter 33

DAY 2: 12:00 HOURS, WAWA 43

T HINGS WERE HAPPENING FAST. The temperature at White River was already 32 degrees Celsius, the relative humidity was 35%, and the winds were picking up and forecasted to reach thirty kilometres per hour. It was what fire people called a "good burning day", which was, in fact, a bad day to fight fire. At the head of Wawa 43, the dragon was on a role. Now firmly entrenched in a pure stand of eighty year-old tightly spaced jack pine, it raced through the crown at eighteen metres per minute. In one hour, it would steamroll through a kilometre of jack pine. At greater than ten thousand kilowatts of heat per metre of flame front, the heat generated would preclude anyone or anything from being close to it. Air attack with heavy water bombers would be futile. Fire crews would be relegated to the back, or rear of the fire or the upwind flank, using only indirect attack tactics, such as fire line construction and burn out. The strategy for the day would be to protect whatever values might be in harms way.

Just west of the fire's west flank, two D8 Caterpillar bulldozers were constructing fire break in tandem down to mineral soil. They were following a line of flagging tape being laid by a local MNR District technician who was presently two hundred metres in front of them. An experienced tech, he would leave the machines behind shortly in his haste to find a good line location. His line would be approximately three kilometres long and tie into Balsam Creek. He looked down at his map, the same photo-copied map that each fire crew leader would carry. The bulldozer line would run in a

216

northerly direction and generally follow the cutover. His job was to find the easiest line construction chance for the machines and, at the same time, try to avoid designing significant curves in the line. Speed and distance, not width, was the objective, so the operators were instructed to keep the line width a little wider than that of the blade. About three metres wide would do it. The blades were angled, and all material was pushed to the non-fire side of the line. If the debris were pushed to the fire side it would take days, if not weeks to extinguish those piles. They were also extremely dangerous to work on. They contained a lot of air pockets that became super-heated inside. Unseen from the top, an unsuspecting nozzle operator dragging fire hose could break through and be hurt badly, not just from a fall, but also from the likelihood of burns.

ELEVEN THOUSAND POUNDS of Bell UH-1N helicopter, designated the "212", slipped down slowly with a staccato whup, whup, flared and settled down gently on a secondary road in the cutover. The original UH model was spawned during the Vietnam War. It was dubbed the "Huey" after its original acronym "HU-1A". As the large twin blades decreased in rotation speed, the air that was pushed down forced up large pockets of road dust. Rotor and blades came to a halt, and within seconds the twin turbine engines whined down. This was Helitack 15's second trip to Wawa 43, its new assigned location for the day. Two, four-person fire crews jumped out and began to unload fire equipment.

A half-ton truck pulled up to the helicopter to ferry crews and equipment to their specific assignments. Once organized, the fire crews would set up Mark-3 fire pumps in the water sources dredged by the excavators, lay hose to the constructed fire break, test-run their pumps and charge the hose lines. Until it was time to burn out from the line, they would follow behind the bulldozers to throw combustible debris off the fire break.

If one was not standing near the helicopter or bulldozers, one might hear the growl of two Caterpillar excavators. MNR's request for back-hoes was over-ridden by Amos Alfelski. He knew the rubber-tired machines would have trouble working the swamps for water, even though they were dry. He strongly recommended using the metal-tracked excavators with better weight displacement. The long-armed caterpillar 312C's each weighed twenty-nine thousand pounds. They were light-weight contenders compared to the only other tracked excavator available to him, a '325BL' weighing in at an impressive (but unmanageable if stuck) sixty thousand, six hundred pounds. Besides, he didn't need the additional oomph to dredge a few holes.

Russell Gervais was assisting the OAID tech with installation and set-up of the ignition device when he heard the 212 land. He waited for the big machine to shake to a stop, approached it on the pilot's side and waited. The helmet-adorned pilot had his head down, no doubt logging his flight time for this latest trip. When he looked up and spotted Russ, he flashed an award-winning smile below a thick, red, grey-flecked, handle bar moustache.

Russ cringed inside. *Great. Just what I need—an enthusiastic, never-say-die pilot.*

The pilot un-strapped his chest-harness with a flourish, literally trampolined out of the helicopter and thrust a hand out with rapier-like speed.

Russ sized him up. *Geez! He's shorter than I am—must be about five-two—gotta be pushing sixty years. And, is that a pony-tail sticking out of the back of his helmet?*

The pilot, seeing Russell's hesitation dropped his arm and his smile.

Come on Russ, old boy, where are your manners? He extended his had. "Russ Gervais. I'm looking after operations here."

The pilot quickly rebounded with zest and gripped Russ's hand. "John Silver".

Russ looked down at him. *Please don't say 'Long' John Silver. I haven't the strength to control my reaction.*

Without a pause, the pilot continued. "Short John Silver—you know, the short version of the pirate in *Treasure Island*. Call me 'Shorty' for short."

Russ burst out laughing. "Welcome to the temporary base camp for Wawa 43. Do we have work for you! Come on over to my office to discuss it."

Shorty looked around for a building or tent and raised his eyebrows.

"Over to the truck, Shorty. Meet my operator and have a bottle of water."

The MNR truck had a mobile radio capable of reaching White River. An area technician was sitting in the truck with the driver's door open, writing transmissions in a radio log. Fifteen minutes ago, he was running bulldozer line. Now he was radio operator for Wawa 43.

"Any good stuff, Mel?"

"Nothing of note Russ. Just some supplies coming from White River. Mostly camping gear and food."

"Meet, ah …"

Shorty reached in with an open hand. "It's OK. Call me Shorty."

"Well let's sit down in my office and have a cool one." Russ went to the back of the truck, dropped the tailgate, got two waters out of a cooler and sat on the gate.

"Here's a map of the fire and surrounding area. This is your copy." Russ explained the strategy, resources on the fire, other aircraft involved and the pilot's job. Russ had penned crew names, aircraft ID's and radio frequency on the map.

"Do you have your "Bambi-Bucket" and hook ups on board?"

"Sure do Russ. I can be set-up in fifteen minutes. One problem, though, I'm getting low on fuel."

Russ thought for a split second. "Why don't you fuel up now. Head to White River. It should only take you fifteen minutes once you're airborne. We have Jet 'A' fuel set up in a bladder at the MTO yard. Look for a large green dome used to house sand. We have a service organization set up there. They'll help you fuel up. They also have a radio operator, so call her on "White River, fire channel 1" for landing instructions. *And*, I need you back right away. Also, before you depart White River, ask service there if they have anything for me. You can bring it back with you."

Shorty, who had been writing furiously on his map, looked up and grinned. "Wow! Sounds just like my days in "Nam."

"Oh, and one more thing—what size bucket do you have and how much experience?"

"Well, Russ, that's two things. First, it's a relatively standard model for medium helicopters, three hundred and twenty-four U.S gallons. If there's a close water source I can pick up and drop the equivalent of ten tubs full of water in minutes. And second, "lots." The two short in stature, long in experience men looked at each other, smiled and shook hands.

"On my way, Russ."

"See you in a good hour, Shorty."

Chapter 34

DAY 2: 18:00 HOURS, WAWA 43

I N EIGHT HECTIC HOURS, Wawa 43 had doubled in size to twelve hundred hectares. It was now three hours beyond the peak burning period, the daily time at which fire activity would put on its best show. Relative humidity had climbed slightly to 38%. Winds were moderate. Russ would have three to four hours to accomplish his mission. All of Northshore's heavy equipment was sitting in a fire-safe area they had prepared themselves by creating a one hundred by sixty metre fuel break down to mineral soil. It looked like an ochre-brown football field with splashes of black where pockets of soil had been their richest. On two sides of the field mounds and lumps of pushed debris stood two metres high like silent spectators awaiting the start of the game. Operators had been instructed to clean their machines of any flammable limbs, brush or woody debris that might have gotten stuck in the treads or undercarriage, and then leave.

Russ had been given approval to conduct the burn, and he was airborne in Helitack 21, the Bell Long Ranger he now felt was his second home. Helitack 15 was on the ground, its bucket off to one side and hooked up to go, its lanyard snaking from the belly of the helicopter to the relaxed bucket. Shorty sat outside the helicopter near his radio awaiting instructions. A Ministry of Natural Resources' Twin Otter, OPJ, circled overhead at twenty-four hundred feet with over two hundred gallons of water in each float. Powered by twin five hundred and seventy-eight hp turboprop engines, it had a range of approximately fifteen hundred kilometres and a maximum speed of three hundred and thirty-eight kph. It was equally adept at carrying up to thirteen passengers and gear or dropping forty-five hundred pounds of water. It had been MNR's most versatile fixed wing aircraft for over thirty years.

Three MNR fire crews were strategically located along the bull-dozed firebreak, their pumps running and hoses strangled off just behind the nozzles. The normal drone of each pump had increased an octave due to the backpressure caused by strangling the hose. Each fire crew leader carried a one-gallon drip torch to support the aerial burn-out operation. An MNR ½ ton truck sat on the bush road not far from Helitack 15, its operator poised to take down all radio transmissions in his radio log. All escaped fires were subject to a thorough, post-burn investigation. His radio log records would be part of the paper trail.

Couldn't get any better than this. Russ sat in the front left seat with map in hand. The OAID technician was strapped in the back, be-hind the pilot with the starboard rear door removed and the quad-chute (four joined chutes) from the OAID hanging out the side. Next to him, on the seat and floor were three boxes of what ap-peared to be ping-pong balls. On Russ's command, the technician would start the ignition process. It had been awhile since Russ had used the OAID. In other provinces and the U.S., it was called a "DAID" or Delayed Aerial Ignition Device.

He recalled that the concept was simple. *Fill a hopper on the top of the device with the inch and a half diameter, polystyrene balls. Each ball* is partially filled with a black granular chemical call potassium perman-ganate. The balls drop through a hole in the hopper and are fed into a dis-penser that feeds four chutes. As they pass through the dispenser tray into the chutes, they are injected with ethylene glycol, or anti-freeze, through large, piston action needles. The balls drop from the bottom of the chutes to the forest below. Russ looked down. So, let's see. Each ball sits down there somewhere. A chemical interaction is taking place and in thirty sec-onds, the ball burst into a tiny flame. Voila! Houston, we have ignition!

So much for the technical stuff. Now for the tactical wizardry. Russ now went through his mental checklist. Where, exactly to begin ig-nition? He unconsciously did a count on his fingers. What ignition pattern should I use? How high and fast do I want the helicopter to fly? Do I need all four chutes operational? When do I give the OK for hand ignition, and what pattern should the crews use when doing their burn-out from the control line?

Russ carried on with his mental analysis. Helicopter elevation and speed and the number of chutes open would determine the space between each ball. The more difficult the burning conditions, the tighter the igni-tion points. Today's issue would not be the difficulty in starting fire (a combination fart and flame would do the trick), but how do I ensure it doesn't get out of control. Where I start fire and the pattern of ignition I use could make all the difference in this micro forest world.

Random thoughts camera-flashed in Russ's brain. Jump fires west of the bulldozer line? Will more likely be caused by fire crew hand-igni-tion. The Twin Otter and Bambi bucket on the 212 will handle those.

Fire spreading north from the burnout? Can't be helped. My objective is to save cut wood. The escaped fire would go northeast anyway, a given.

What if we lose the cut wood? Move to Southern Ontario and get a job at WalMart as a greeter. Come on, Russ. Trust your training and experience!

The Long Ranger spooned around an imaginary curve in the sky, its main rotor now at a severe angle to the canopy below. Air pressure, driven down from the blades bounced back off tree tops, exaggerating percussion and the "whup-whup" increased in volume.

Russ now had his ignition plan firmly entrenched in the antici-pation/excitement part of his brain. He instructed the pilot on air-speed (about a hundred and ten kph), elevation (three hundred feet above tree canopy) and location. "We're working a backfire close to the Wawa 43's west flank. We'll start on the north-east corner of our burn-out area and vary a pattern southerly. I'll give you specific direction as we progress." He instructed the OAID operator. "Two chutes only. Release balls on my 'Go'. Stop the machine on my 'No Go'."

Russ was completely hard wired to his mission. Without over-thinking his tactics, he knew that burning from Wawa 43 westerly toward the control line was creating a backfire, a burn-out fire that would "back" into the control line slowly while the wind pushed its head towards the Wawa 43. That would minimize fire intensity. With utmost confidence, he rationalized that more than two chutes open for dispersing OAID balls was over-kill. He guided his pattern like a maestro with the Boston Philharmonic Orchestra. *'Mosaic' or patches of fire on rises and hills, might even try centre fire ignition there. I'll lay back fire through flat stands of jack pine, some flanking fire in budworm killed balsam fir and spruce.*

He then had the pilot quickly recon the area to be burned. He talked to the pilot on the live mic. "Sid, you got a sense of the piece we need to burn out?"

The pilot looked over and smiled. "Sure do. Are we OK with elevation and speed?"

"Just about right. We're just about ready. What we *don't* want to do is drop any of those balls in the cutover on the other side of the control line. We'll stay about fifty metres to the east of it and let the hand ignition crews lay converging fire."

"Russ, what about air traffic control?"

"The Twin Otter pilot has been instructed to maintain altitude at twelve hundred feet and to stay to our west over the cutover, that area would be his target area, anyway. His water is east of the fire at Siren Lake. He will depart and approach the cutover area well south of us. If we need the 212 and bucket, he's been instructed to use the same control zone for water and to maintain contact with the Twin Otter. All aircraft, including ours will call in activity and deviations to the radio operator in the truck."

"Are we going to be able to contain this fire?"

Russ smiled. "Nope. Our objective is to protect the wood to the west. Once we lay fire in our piece to the east of the cutover, it will definitely boogy northeast and converge with the main fire. Can't be helped. We're just speeding up the process by a day."

Russ was getting a little anxious from anticipation. He called into Wawa. "Wawa Fire, Wawa Fire, this is Helitack 21 on 1, do you copy?"

"Go ahead H 21. This is George here."

"Yeah, George. We're ready to ignite. Any change in the weather forecast?"

"Negative Russ. Winds are predicted to drop to ten kilometres per hour and the RH climb to 45% shortly."

"Sounds good. We'll have ignition in three minutes. Oh, by the way, I estimate Wawa 43 has doubled in size to twelve hundred hectares. Talk to you later. Helitack 21 clear."

Russ switched to live mic and pointed to a map. "OK Sid, this is my plan."

WHILE HELITACK 21 SWUNG NORTH-WEST to its first point of ignition, three fire crews were busy pre-wetting tinder-dry forest fuels on the non-burnout side of the bulldozer firebreak, the control line. Each crew leader assigned that task to the rest of the crew. The crew leaders themselves were busy preparing their drip torches for hand ignition. They had been briefed by Russ, and each had approximately a kilometre to burn out. Russ was concerned about fire intensity from the hand ignition operation, so he instructed them to use the right angle pattern rather than parallel.

On Russ's instructions, each would begin ignition by walking into the bush on the ignition side of the control line about fifty metres then burn back towards the line. They would continue with these strips until they had covered their target area or were advised to stop by Russ. Because the winds were from the south quadrant, they would cover ground in a southerly direction of their assigned pieces of line, into the wind. The distance between each burn strip would be approximately thirty metres but would vary depending on topography or forest density (some bush you just couldn't walk through). This particular pattern was called a "strip head fire."

Because the aerial ignition would be started first, air created by Russ's fire would draw the hand ignition fire away from the fuel break, supported by southwest winds. Occasionally, however, the strip head fire was ignited first to widen the control line. For Russ, it was all a matter of timing, and he wanted to see how fire would build with aerial ignition first.

The issue here with starting the hand ignition first would be fire intensity. It could create enough radiant heat to start fire on the protected side of the bulldozer line. There was also the issue of fire-brands such as bark or pieces of coniferous foliage being air-lifted and thrown back across the line with the help of convective currents of air. Russ wanted a serious aerial-ignited fire with enough draft to draw the hand-ignited fire. It would be the combined effort of the crews with power pumps and hose, the Twin Otter water bomber and the 212 helicopter with bucket that would deal with any jump fires in the cut over on the protected side—or not.

In order to avoid confusion with crew names or numbers, Russ decided to go with crew leader last name from north to south, and advised all three pilots who would be communicating with them as required.

"SID, THIS IS WHERE WE START IGNITION." Russ had his left index finger on his map at the "C4" area labelled as '1'.

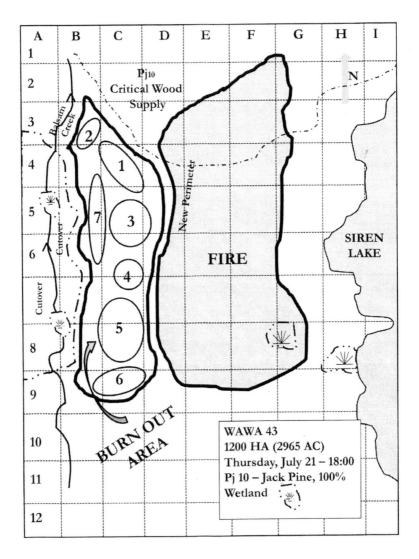

"It'll be a bit of a 'back' fire to start. I'll tell you when to hover to begin ignition lines and I'll give you a fix on your compass to start. My direction will be simple and based on the clock. For example, if I say head your 1:00 o'clock, that's where you'll point your machine."

The pilot nodded his head.

"The numbers within the burn-out area indicate each round of ignition. When we get to each area, I'll show you where to start and the direction and pattern to fly. That will depend on what I see on the ground when we get there, and how our fire is reacting as we ignite."

As Russ looked at his map he seemed to be talking to himself. "I want to ignite the area in '1' before I ignite '2'. I need the fire in 1 to draw the fire in 2 away from Balsam Creek. If it gets across there, we're toast."

"Pardon, Russ?"

The spell was broken. Russ looked up. "Ignitions '3' and '4' are those two hills we just passed over. And by the way, this could all change if I don't like what I see as we ignite."

Sid nodded. He seemed to be doing a lot of that, lately. "Seems simple enough, Russ, you direct, I fly."

"OK. You ready back there?" The OAID responded in the affirmative.

Russ smiled. He keyed the mic. "Twin Otter OPJ, this is Helitack 21 on 1, do you copy?"

"Go ahead 21."

"We're ready to begin ignition. Any questions?"

"Yeah, Russ. Who do I respond to?"

"Anyone of the crew leaders that requests your assistance. I intend to finish burning this piece come hell or high water, simply because we've got nothing to lose and a lot to gain. So my hands will be full. Also, I'd like you to cruise the cutover west of the bulldozer line. You see any jump fires there, don't hesitate to pound them on your own."

"Sounds good Russ. OPJ clear."

"Simms, Rutledge and Brooks crews, did you copy that?" One after another, the crew leaders responded in the affirmative.

"Helitack 15, you asleep down there, Shorty?"

"Just about Russ, but ready when you need me."

"Shorty, we've got good, experienced crew leaders down there. If they request your help, don't hesitate."

"Affirmative Russ, and good luck."

THE NEXT HOUR SOUNDED LIKE CHAOS, or at the very least, organized confusion. From a distance, Helitack 21 appeared to be going on a Sunday drive traveling low and slow, making leisurely turns, then back-tracking. At a closer look, one would see tiny, non-descript ping pong balls being jettisoned from the helicopter, then fall to the ground or get lodged in brush or thickets of coniferous under-story, or even in the tops of balsam or spruce over-story. The helicopter carried on, seemingly without purpose, except that small puffs of black smoke materialized on the ground behind it. The smoke was the product of the ping pong balls. Each of the hundreds of balls launched out of the helicopter would land, then rest, unconcerned, just passing time, sort of, unaware of the fate that awaited them. In seconds, without warning, they would erupt in bright-white, chemically induced flame. Flame would find fuel, combustion would begin and smoke would rise. Each puff then appeared to be pushed aloft by bright, orange/yellow flame. These smoke-capped flame-elves gleefully raced towards each other in belly-bouncing collision; they were *converging*. Russ imagined them doing "high-fives" as they met.

With the exception of areas 3 and 4 on the map, the rest of the areas were generally ignited with back fires in order to keep the helicopter out of smoke. 3 and 4 were significant hills that Russ treated as "islands." He started in the middle of each, then ran con-centric circles of fire to the outside. This centre fire ignition was usually reserved for slash burns in cutover to create a column of smoke that would rise almost straight up and not bend signifi-cantly. It was important to create a vertical column (not a bent one) to avoid jump fires. Here, the use of "centre fire ignition," was sim-ply a matter of topography and personal preference.

When Russ started section 6, he gave the crews the go-ahead to do their hand ignition. When section 6 was finished, H21 swung north to do section 7. There were now three separate columns of black/grey smoke rising from three hundred to one thousand me-tres in the air, all bent slightly northeast. He could also see evi-dence of hand ignition, smaller columns of smoke popping up haphazardly just east of the bulldozed fuel break.

Russ scanned the destruction. *Looks good—so far. But so did I when I was younger.*

Chapter 35

DAY 2: 19:00 HOURS TO
22:00 HOURS, WAWA 43

NOT ALL WAS QUIET ON THE RADIO.
"Simms crew from OPJ, you got a jump in the southwest corner of A4. Stay clear, I'm going to nail it."

"Copy that, OPJ, and thanks."

"Helitack 15 from Rutledge crew, we could use you over here in the west side of B6!"

"Just about ready to lift off, Rutledge. I'll have a load for you in five."

Radio chatter broke in from another crew. "Herb from Derrick."

"Go ahead Derrick."

"Pump's quit on us boss. I'm sending Randy back to see what the problem is."

"What's your PX?"

"We're on a jump fire just off the bulldozer line in the northeast corner of A9."

Russ was up in Helitack 21 watching the drama unfold. This one caught his attention. *That'll get into the cutover from the south!* He practically swallowed the mic and called the Twin Otter. "OPJ, we have a priority for you, do you copy."

"Yeah Russ, I caught that transmission. Just took a load on. I'll be there in three."

"Copy that. Brooks crew?"

"Yeah, thanks Russ. Foot valve on the intake was clogged. We'll be up and running soon, but we still need the help."

It was Rutlege's turn. "Hey 15, we've got torching on the line. Do you see it?"

"Roger that, Rutledge. Bucket and loads on their way!"

Although transmissions were frequent, they were economical, and everyone took care not to "walk on" another's transmission. An untrained listener would cry "bedlam!" It was, however, music to Russ's ears. There was organization and synchronicity in this turmoil. Everyone was relying on their training, instincts and adrenaline. Actions and reactions were quick, decisive and final.

Russ began thinking ahead. "All stations, all stations on the burn out. I'll be finished igniting here in ten minutes and will direct suppression activity from Helitack 21. We'll maintain altitude at two thousand feet. Are you OK with that OPJ and H15?" They both replied to the affirmative.

The final two hours was a flurry of activity. Russ directed crews, water bombing and heli-bucketing with determination and efficiency. He reported back to Wawa at intervals. Eight separate jump fires had been wrestled to the ground. Evening winds were dropping and relative humidity was climbing. It was 20:30 hours and Russ reluctantly released OPJ and H15 back to Wawa for fuel and, as he put it "nighty-night". He had H21 put him down with his crews and sent the helicopter to White River for fuel and its own nighty-night ("The service organization will look after you there") with orders to return at 07:00 hours the next day.

He knew the bulldozed line would hold, but he got on his hand-held portable radio to discuss comfort level with each crew. *If they're satisfied, I'm satisfied.* "When you're ready fellas, rendezvous on the road at B6. All the gear is there and our radio operator slash bulldozer leader has offered to be our radio operator slash bulldozer leader slash cook. The barbeque is on and the steaks are waiting to die."

THE MOON SEEMED TO SPRING UP like a jack-in-the-box into a star filled sky. It was perfectly round, bright and mottled with images of the man across its face. Russ imagined its announcement. *Ta-da. Here I am!*

Its incandescent reflection bounced off of fourteen nylon tents that were scattered in flat spots in the cutover. Not far from the camp fire, a single fourteen foot by sixteen foot, canvas prospector tent stood suspended, its eight poplar poles acting as ridge, frame and support. The crews had set it up for equipment and supplies before retiring to their one-person tents. Russ sat next to a dying camp-fire, a cup of cooling coffee in his hand. He listened to the cadence of soft snoring slipping out from the tents. He hummed a tune to himself but struggled with the words. *Something about a cat in the cradle, a silver spoon and a man in the moon.*

He looked east. The tree line was black against an indigo sky. But separating the tree line and sky a fire phenomenon rivalled, no surpassed the spectacle of a full moon. Yellow flags of consuming flame waved directly above the ragged silhouette of distant trees. As a backdrop and shroud for the flames, the sky literally glowed with an orange/red cloak prodding then diffusing into a black-blue infinity. *Looks like the most spectacular "red-sky at night" I've ever witnessed.*

Russ felt at peace here. His plan worked. The company's wood was protected for now. He was with his crews, and the radio was shut down for the night. He always enjoyed making the 'quit-radio-transmission' announcement himself. *All stations, all stations, this is Wawa 43 going QRT.*

Tomorrow was another day. *Early flight to assess the burn out and main fire. Crews will mop up the jump fires and burn out any pieces of unburned fuels next to the fire break. Meet with Amos Alfelski on site and deal with charge backs for the use of the heavy equipment—and his ranting about how things were screwed up. Organize the crews back into the system. Debriefing at Wawa. Just another sixteen-hour day in the life of a super-hero.*

Time to turn in. Russ dumped the dregs of his coffee on the ground and looked up. *Just like in the old westerns at the end of the day on a cattle drive. Wonder if someone's sitting on one of those stars looking back this way, with a cup of whatever they drink in their—tentacle. Wonder if I'll get haemorrhoids after forgetting my air mattress.*

Big, important fire manager—life has a way of bringing you down to earth.

He stood up slowly, groaned, stretched his aching back and headed for the little tent that would be his shelter for the night.

Chapter 36

DAY 3: FRIDAY, JULY 22, 05:00 HOURS, HORNEPAYNE, ONTARIO (35 KILOMETRES NORTHEAST OF WAWA 43)

A THIN VEIL OF SMOKE CREPT THROUGH THE SLEEPING TOWN, caressing each building, pole, tree, automobile, anything that was stationary with a gentle, possessive touch. Nothing was left to chance. It was as if the dragon consuming forest fuels to the south-west had sent scrawny hands and narrow, pointed, fingers of smoke as probing scouts.

The grey-blue/white spectres slithered over the one thousand-metre runway at the Hornepayne airport without resistance. They ignored the tarmac and short grass that offered no sustenance for mother dragon. The gropers swirled and separated like pond scum in a gentle, confused breeze, now reaching out in all directions, impatient and petulant in their hunt. The arena and curling club with their concrete walls and steel roofs had nothing to offer. The short, yellow/brown grass surrounding the monument might smoulder but had no bulk to carry tiny "dragonettes". The concrete statues of Hornepayne's "three bears" would easily resist fire. They had been a futile attempt to compete for tourists with White River's Winnie-the-Pooh, cartoon-like statue. Times were hard in small town Northern Ontario but bear statues beat skunk, raccoon or porcupine statues hands down.

The dragonettes slithered on. *There! Behind the bear caricatures, a children's play structure—so colourful with its red steel arches and pow-*

der blue plastic slides. Mother might not be able to devour it, but perhaps she could melt the slides.

The wretched hands moved more quickly now, impatience turning to frustration. The CN rail yard and roundhouse with its slightly arched windows seemed to display contempt or at the very least, mirth as the veils blindly felt around the fortress-like structures. This sixty-four thousand square foot, eighty-four year-old monolith stood with contempt, held together by concrete, brick and steel. Although called a roundhouse, it had a rectangular outside structure. The "round" happened inside where rail cars could be housed and sorted from a central hub on to rail spokes.

The veils probed and pried deftly and methodically at the fortress as if to say, "Scoff if you will, but you're old, the houses nearby are frame and clapboard and the forest on three sides of you is tinder-dry. Even the leaf-laden poplar will be nourishment for mother. A breach here and there will do the trick." Having completed their investigation, the fingers advanced.

Ah, what have we here? A church—but not just a church. It wears layers and layers of white paint over ancient clapboard. That farm-shaped spire looks like it should support a weather vane, not a cross. St. Luke's Anglican, nice ring to it. Let's see, "With a little luck, we'll light up St. Luke's."

The veils spread ever so slightly as if relaxing now. They appeared to glide, flatten and curl around opportunities, taking inventory and wordlessly beckoning mother dragon to make haste.

IN A DARKENED BEDROOM that was slapped onto the back of a small non-descript, post World War II bungalow, a mountain of twisted sheets and comforter rose then fell with each ragged, rumbling snore. Ethel Abernathy, an eighty years old widow with a two hundred-pound frame and outer layer of a (as she was not shy to declare) "full-figured" woman, slept soundly and was oblivious to the intruder slinking around her house.

Not so, however, her only family member, friend, champion and defender, Sushi! Sushi was from the "miniature Boston Terrier Sushi clan" (not of the yuppy-favoured, raw meat clan). What Sushi lacked in size or good looks, she made up for in her olfactory ability and willingness to take on any challenger. Her black and white head suddenly popped out from under the covers and periscoped around. At first glance one would think, "How undeniably and completely ugly." A tiny pink nose was pasted against a black and white, flat face. Two wide-set, bulging eyes were suspended on each side of the head, much like those on a grass-hopper or praying mantis. A pouting lower lip rose up, up to the bean sized nose. There must have been an upper lip somewhere. Perhaps she had swallowed it. Just when one would think that she couldn't get uglier, one would see two small teeth protruding upwards and at angles from the lower lip. With any imagination, her nose could represent the sun and the two angular teeth tiny outhouses perched on a lower-lip hill. Of considerable distraction was the protuberance of several 'jowl' moles with complementary hairs, pasted to the sides of her face. If it weren't for the perfect pointy ears one would be forgiven recalling the cult movie *Alien* with the little monster bursting from the space ranger's chest. But as Ethel would declare to any stranger that was at first startled then pretended interest in her proud (but delusional) pup, "She's so friggin ugly, she's cute!" And she was—ugly, that is—and maybe a little cute.

Once Sushi got her bearings, her nose wiggled (as much as it could), and she stepped gingerly out from beneath her cave of covers (she didn't like to be cold) and stretched. Oh, what a transformation! Beyond the less than attractive countenance was the body of a Greek God (or Greek dog—dog is God spelled backwards). She was all muscle and form. Barrel chest tapered quickly to a narrow waist. All four legs were at a challenging 225 degree angle. Her pose silently spoke volumes like the Lion in the Wizard of Oz—"put em' up, put em' up". What a contradiction of body parts! She possessed the body of Arnold Shwarzennegar and the face of Marty Feldman (from Young Frankenstein). Or even more disturbing—the body of Pamela Anderson and the face of Camilla Parker-Bowles (Prince Philips boyfriend).

Wisps of pungent odour seeped through minute cracks in the ancient house. Sushi was not prone to barking like other small dogs. She would snuffle. If that didn't work, she would squeak. So, with her best snuffle and squeak and some insistent pouncing on the mountain of bed-clothes, Super Sushi had triggered a series of events that would give the residents of Hornepayne a cause to rally around for a week and stories to exaggerate for years after—the on-again, off-again emergency evacuation of Hornepayne!

THE MOUNTAIN ROSE UP at the insistence of the little Boston terrier and a puffy, crinkled face appeared from beneath the covers like a puppet apple doll. It was uncanny how the master resembled the dog. The only notable difference was the ears. Instead of perfectly formed pointed ears perched on top, this face had large, rubbery, saucer ears sprouting fine, grey hairs that were pasted to the sides of a generous head. A row of large, multi-coloured curlers curved from ear to ear like little barrels laid down side to side on an arched walking bridge.

Any resemblances ended, however, with their faces. While Sushi was buff, Ethel sported a formidable body wrapped (ever so tightly) in a purple and rose print night-gown. She heaved and rolled unsteadily from the bed, extended two stove-pipe legs and planted two ogre feet on a worn plank floor. Wobbly skin hung from her upper arms like miniature hammocks.

What was that smell? Ethel picked up her little heroine and tentatively checked throughout the house. *Smells like smoke.* Now more determined, she stepped outside and glared up and down the street, ready to challenge any passer-by who might be enamoured by her appearance. *Yup, it's definitely smoke.* She took a healthy breath in and coughed it out in phlegm-laden spasms, just to make sure. Once the magnificent Ethel had been assured that her home was, for the time being, safe, she pounded to the phone and jumped into action, a woman on a mission.

THIS EARLY MORNING BEGAN with a series of rude awakenings. Ethel first called the mayor then followed up with a series of rapid directory-flips and phone calls to her neighbours, friends, relatives and finally, with some hesitation, those people in the community who she didn't really like. At the end of each message she declared that, "they should take down that friggin' statue of the three bears and put one up of a real hero—my Sushi!"

The mayor, after sticking his head out the front door, called the fire chief, the four council members and the township clerk and declared, "meeting, council board room, one hour!"

Fire chief Ken Waal was not one to be easily rattled. He owned and ran the local pub (as well as being fire chief for fifteen years). At 6'3" with two hundred and ten pounds of sinew-wrapped bones, he was impressed infrequently and tolerated little of what he called "horse shit." He calmly called the Ontario Provincial Police (who had a detachment in Hornepayne with five officers and a detachment sergeant) and then the Ministry of Natural Resources in Wawa. A bored, sleepy voice answered the OPP phone. An answering service responded to his call to MNR. Ken knew that a return call from MNR would happen in minutes. He had been made aware of Wawa 43 by their fire organization a few days prior bur was assured that the fire was a considerable distance to the south. *This smoke had to be either associated with another fire, or Wawa 43 was a damn site closer.*

Ken was flipping through the community emergency plan catalogued in his mind when his phone rang. He grabbed it quickly so it wouldn't wake Mrs. Waal. He was big but she was tougher.

"Ken. George Williams here. I'm currently sector response officer for the fire program out of Wawa. It's early, you got a problem?"

"Thanks for calling back promptly, and nope, *we* don't have a problem yet, but my crystal ball and all the smoke in town says we soon will have."

George responded quickly. "We have one fire northeast of Wawa 43 and southeast of Hornepayne, but we've got a handle on it and it shouldn't be putting up a lot of smoke—must be Wawa 43. How bad is the smoke?"

"Our town crier, Ethel Abernathy says it's more satisfying than her two pack a day habit. I figure, on a scale of one to ten, it's a four." Ken paused to wrap words around his thoughts. "If it gets any worse, we may have to look at evacuation. And by the way, how close *is* 43 to us as we speak?"

"Our last mapping puts it thirty-five plus kilometres away. I think the problem is a temperature inversion."

"George, give that to me simply, in either English or French. I speak both official languages."

"OK. As the smoke from the column rises, it usually hits cooler, lighter air and continues to rise. That's good. Occasionally, it hits a layer of air that has a temperature warmer than normal. This layer of air acts like a lid on a pot. The smoke has nowhere else to go but along the bottom of the lid and down. That's bad. I'll confirm this with our weather people."

"So besides coughing, wheezing and hacking up smoke bunnies, what do we do in the meantime?"

"If you can hang in today, you should be OK for another two to three days at least after that. We expect a wind shift from the north tonight. Your smoke will clear off."

"George. Don't want to split hairs bur it's *our* smoke. Then what happens after the two or three day window?"

"Ken, long range doesn't look good. I suggest you dust off you Community Emergency Plan. An evacuation may have to be considered. I know the town. Most of your public buildings are more or less fire safe. Some of the fringe housing could be in trouble. The biggest concern is smoke."

Ken felt a little light-headed. He looked at his reflection in the glass covering a picture of his three kids when they were pre-teen. *Why is my face so red?* He paused. Articulating his thoughts would take a moment. "Whoa, George, slow down and back up a little. First off, our plan is in revision. I'm not even sure how current the contact list is. Secondly, why can't you get a handle on that fire?" Ken knew why, but he figured a long explanation would buy him time to think. "And thirdly, what do I tell our long-winded, short-fused mayor. He'll jettison a haemorrhoid."

George sensed a hint of desperation. *I have to provide something positive to give Ken. Besides, it's in the works already.* "Ken, tell him this. As we speak, one of our area supervisors, Greg Walsh, is being briefed and will be sent to you today. He has lots of experience in emergency planning and response. He'll stay as long as it takes to see you through this. We will also contact Emergency Management Ontario as a heads up. Since you aren't at the point where you might declare an emergency, you won't see them. If, however, things take a turn for the worse, they could send a rep. I know these people. They provide excellent guidance and won't interfere with first responders. That, by the way is you and your community leaders."

Ken couldn't help being a little cryptic. "So refresh my memory. What's MNR's role here?"

Must be 'Emergency 101' for Ken. "We're the lead Ministry for fire, flood and drought emergencies. We'll provide appropriate assistance to a community in a declared emergency."

"It's coming back to me but taking its time. Our mayor can declare an emergency once we've outstripped our capacity to respond, right?"

"Yup. And MNR could, I stress, *could* declare one on your behalf if we feel the response is not appropriate. In the meantime, I suggest you review your existing plan. Information is the first step. People will want to know what's going on and what's being done about it."

George paused. *Good point, be pre-emptive. Just like trouble in the bar, deal with it when it's brewing, not when it's too late.* "Look George, I gotta start this shit storm with the mayor and council. Have your man, Greg, come to the fire hall when he gets here."

"Will do Ken, and have a good day."

Both men hung up. Ken thought about the next step. *Where do I start? Why not with the old plan? The meat and potatoes are still there, it's just the contact list that probably needs tweaking.* He felt a little better about the situation. The adrenalin was dropping and his confidence, having taken a walk earlier, decided to return home. *Could be an interesting day.*

Chapter 37

DAY 3: 09:00 HOURS, FALCON RESPONSE CENTRE, SUDBURY

*O**K. SO THE WORLD IS SPINNING OFF ITS AXIS, and I'm floating to the side in a little paper boat—a confused observer holding on for dear life. Wait a minute, I'm the duty officer and supposed to be in charge. But if I'm in charge, how come I feel like I've lost control? What's wrong with this picture?*

Rick Sampson squeezed the telephone receiver, skin on knuckles translucent, fingers locked in a death grip around the moulded plastic. He wanted to kill it, or whoever was on the other end. He pulled the receiver safely away from his ear, afraid it might ignite in spontaneous combustion. His lips were drawn tight, a fortress gate, holding back a platoon of invectives. If his lips could morph into arms and hands, they would crawl into the receiver, slip out at the other end, and slap down the object of his anger.

"Rick, I can't take it anymore! I'm going home! You're on your own. And until you've decided who you want to be married to, me or the job, don't bother calling! Rick! Are you there?"

He looked around the room, but with eyes only, his head stationary. Everyone was busy, absorbed in their activity, but they knew what was going on, what had been going on for over a year. Words danced around in his head like plastic balls in an overcrowded bingo machine. Each word-ball competed for the little door and chute, bouncing into each other, desperate for release, but nothing rolled out. *Let's see. Do I whine and beg? Will "indignant" work? How about going on the offensive? I'm pissed, right? Calm and rationale? No,*

241

that always cranks her up. Don't say anything? Yeah, I'll just regret anything I let out the barn door right now.

"Goodbye, Beth." Rick gently put the phone back in its cradle. He looked down at his hands with morbid fascination, hands that were shaking, hands that obviously belonged to someone else. *A lot of activity in the room. How come I can only hear the buzzing in my ears. Sheila's walking over. Her lips are moving. She's saying something. Wish I could read lips. Now I'm picking up something. It's faint and broken up.*

"Rick … earth … you…?"

I think I just said "pardon". It's starting to come in clearer, like tuning in a radio station. There it is—no it's gone. Yes! Got it back again.

"Earth to Rick, are you OK?"

No, feel like I've just been served a pâté of earth worms. "Yeah, I'm doing fine, Sheila."

"You lie, Rick. Can I help?"

Rick was slowly gaining control. He managed to shake the world back on to its axis, climb gingerly out of the little paper boat and plant both feet tentatively on terra firma.

"Yes you can, Sheila—how about an update on the Wawa Sector?"

She gave him the "hands on hips, that's not what I meant" posture. "OK, tough guy."

Sheila looked down at Wawa's tactical input plan in her hand. "As of 09:00 hours this a.m., Wawa 43, two thousand hectares. NUC. Values lost: nine-hundred hectares of jack pine, Northshore's critical wood supply. Forecasted size as of 17:00 hours today: thirty-four hundred hectares. Burn out on west flank successful; the cut wood has been protected. Three crews continuing to consolidate the burn-out perimeter. Russ Gervais presently has Incident Command. Helitack 21 is committed to the fire. OIAD tech and machine trucked back to Wawa. The Bill Gorley incident management team is now in Wawa awaiting instructions. Biggest issue: potential need for evacuation of Hornepayne. Wawa district has dispatched one of their area supervisors, Greg Walsh to Hornepayne to act as an emergency response coordinator, if it's required." Sheila paused. "Oh, and Norm Pendleton from Blind River is due in today as zone duty officer for Sectors 4 and 5. Turning over Chapleau and Wawa should take a load off your broad but slumping shoulders. Zander

Cybulski from Algonquin Park is on the hook as project fire duty officer as well. Also, and this is a big also, two tanker packages are inbound from Manitoba and just east of Thunder Bay. ETA Sudbury, 11:00 hours."

The muscles in Rick's cheeks relaxed. His lips, giving up on tight and tense, parted slightly. The colour in his face changed from a waxy, cadaverous pale nothing, to a passable pale. Rick was back in his element. *A little victory. Now this is something I can deal with. A lighter load. Focus on the other sectors. Four more heavy water bombers and two Birddog aircraft to play with.* The erratic thoughts that ran helter-skelter in his head now seemed to slow, role quickly into formation and line up like well-trained soldiers. Wawa 43 would soon be out of his hands. He'd still have over-all command and control, but the fire would now have an incident management team assigned to it, and Norm would provide resource requirements and guidance until Zander showed up.

Rick had no problem with sharing power. Sharing power was sharing responsibility. He believed in the golden rule of fire fighting—never exceed your span of control. Get help. The stress-laden fatigue slipped away like morning fog. *Hell, I'm good for at least one more melt down!* He looked towards Sheila and caught her attention. Sheila had attended to a telephone call during his mental vacation. She now flitted back over to his desk. *A chickadee approaching a feeder.*

"What's up oh frazzled, fearless leader? You really don't look marvellous." She hesitated. Curiosity overcame fear of intrusion. "Trouble at the Sampson castle?"

Rick ignored the question. "Madam intelligence officer, let's get the morning briefing underway." *The chickadee looks hurt by my evasive manner.* "And you are right. Not so good at the castle. Queen Beth has fled to the summer estate."

Sheila's face dropped. "I'm sorry, Rick. I didn't mean to pry."

"Sheila, there's no one else I'd rather have butting into my personal life than you. The good news is the two princess's are away at summer camp. And I guess I'd better learn to like day-old Kraft dinner."

Without missing a beat, Rick looked towards his air operations manager.

"Dale, divert a Manitoba package to Wawa. Call the sector response officer there and make sure someone out of Wawa briefs the two tanker crews and Birddog officer."

Without a word in response, the AOM picked up the phone, punched in a single digit, spoke briefly then headed for the radio room.

Sheila prepared to start the morning briefing when the fire program manager, Doug Rainville, walked in with a gaggle of strangers. Doug was built like a tree stump with hair and immediately commanded attention. The five newbies spread out like they were preparing for a street fight and nervously gazed around the room, taking in the displays of data. As if on silent command, weapons of choice appeared in their hands: pencils, notepads, microphones and tape players. Rick's face dropped as if the weight of gravity was too much for its skin. *Oh no, the media.* The look he fired at Doug spoke volumes. *What! No warning! Just what I needed! I don't need this crap! Have you decided to make this the worst day of my life? Do you enjoy making my life miserable?*

Doug returned the look with a shrug of his shoulders. *Sorry, not my call. I'm as surprised as you are. Let's make the best of it.*

"Rick, I'd like you to meet some media people. I'll let them introduce themselves. But first, lady and gentlemen this is Rick Sampson, our regional fire duty officer. He calls the shots on fire response for the East Fire Region."

As they introduced themselves in turn, the ringing in Rick's ears increased incrementally. He did not hear one name, but instead concentrated on reading faces. *The tall guy with the easy manner will be OK. The perky red head with the microphone looks eager. If she sticks it in my face, I'll bite it off. Two of them looked nervous. Their first assignment? Sheila will make short work of them. The fat guy in the wrinkled suit with the bulgy eyes and sweaty face perched on a series of chins is sitting back. He looks like a grouper fish looking desperately for a meal. Could be trouble.*

Introductions were complete. Rick mustered his best air of authority and announced that a fire briefing would be taking place. "I'd appreciate it if you reserved questions until after the briefing." Rick looked towards Sheila, a Cheshire cat grin on his face. "Our fire intelligence officer, Sheila Monahan, will be glad to answer them, won't you Sheila?"

Thanks scumbag. "Certainly, Rick. I'd be glad to." She looked back at Rick. Her own cat-like grin might as well have had canary feathers poking out through her lips. "But if there's anything I can't answer, I'll certainly turn them over to you, if that's all right with you." Canary-swallowing cat—one, Cheshire cat—zero.

"By all means, Sheila."

Four of five media heads rotated back and forth following the verbal tennis match. The fifth one, the one with the bulgy eyes and sweaty face, unloosened his tie with a sausage finger, pursed his liver-thick lips and grimaced with what appeared to be a rising of acid laden breakfast.

Rick gave the "Michelin Man" a furtive once over. He hummed a tune to himself from an old musical. *Oh, we got trouble, right here in River City, right here in River City. With a capital "T" and that rhymes with "P" and that stands for Press—as in "bad press."*

Chapter 38

DAY 3: 09:00 HOURS, MESCALERO APACHE INDIAN RESERVATION, SOUTH-CENTRAL NEW MEXICO

S IERRA BLANCA MOUNTAIN LOOKED PARTICULARLY IMPRESSIVE this bright summer morning. From five to eight thousand feet high, it was the flagship of the southern Rocky Mountains, the Sacremento Mountain Range. Some locals on the reserve referred to the peaks and valleys as the Apache Mountains, recalling stories from their ancestors and secretly longing for the days when the Mescalero, Chiricahua and Lipan Apache did not have to compete for use of the land.

Nate Ramirez sat on his front porch, his gaze fixed on Sierra Blanca to the north. Striking white patches of ice-laden snow stood out in stark contrast clinging to their rock walls, supported like shields. The early eastern sun created these startling contrasts. Watching the snow patches shrink became Nate's morning ritual—when he was home. He looked for new snow shapes and images that perhaps might provide a sign or message to begin the day. He was not particularly superstitious, but this was his private, little game, one his mother used to play with him when he was a child.

He was the offspring of a gentle Spanish father and a fiery Chiricahua mother. She had named him Naiche after his great, great grandfather, the last chief of the free Chiricahuas. He had spent his last years on the Mescalero reservation and past away quietly in 1919. He did, however, leave a colourful history. His predecessor was the fabled chief, Cochise. Naiche also rode and raided with "One-Who-Yawns", Geronimo. He had three wives at one time and fathered fifteen children. Much of his later years, 1886 to 1913, were spent as a prisoner, a victim of the Apache wars.

Both of Nate's parents had passed on. His father had bequeathed patience, a lighter complexion, warm grey eyes and a tall, lithe frame. His mother's legacy was his thick, raven-black hair, high arched cheek bones and immense pride in his native heritage. He also possessed one of his great, great grandfather's more prolific abilities. At forty-five years of age, Nate had fathered six children and, with the assistance of only *one* wife (although they both knew who was helping whom).

His two oldest children had graduated from college and moved on. Another was attending college, one in high school and one in elementary school. His most recent paternal contribution and his pride and joy, little three year old Nadey, could be heard in the background, playing house with the disgruntled cat. Nate pictured his chubby little daughter walking from room to room with the large orange tabby draped over her short arms like a wet dish towel. *The cat doesn't stand a chance.* Nadey had been named after his great, great grandfather's oldest wife, Nadeyole. Nate wasn't sure if she was his great, great grandmother. The family tree tended to be confusing under the circumstances. In spite of the "interruptions" associated with child-birth, Nate's wife, Celina Ramirez had managed to keep both her figure and job as a teacher at the reservation elementary school.

Nate's gaze flitted from snow shape to snow shape, then fell upon one particular irregularity. Sure looks like an airplane cloud to me. Maybe there's some travel in the future. Nate wasn't a stranger to travel. During the fire season, he worked as a captain on the prestigious Rio HotShot fire crew, a job that took him all over North America when fire resources were in short supply. The Rio crew, stationed in the 3.3 million acre Rio National Forest in south-western New Mexico, was one of ninety such crews strategically located throughout the United States. The typical HotShot crew had a superintendent, captain (or assistant superintendent), three squad leaders and fifteen crewmembers, three of which were designated as senior firefighters.

Nate was proud of the fact that these twenty-person crews were considered the elite of the U.S. fire organization, but he had no illusions. The work was dirty, back-breaking, occasionally dangerous and at times, monotonous, especially in the mop-up stage of a fire. His particular crew was "IHS" or Interagency HotShot and could be dispatched anywhere. He had just returned from a particularly difficult assignment in Oregon and was on his second day of four days off. During the fall and winter, he was a foreman for Mescalero Forest Products, one of the many businesses run by the Apache tribes in New Mexico.

Only five years south of fifty, Nate was in superb physical shape, but he wasn't sure how much longer he could continue as a "ground pounder." It took longer to recover from the aches and pains, and daily doses of foot powder just didn't cut it anymore. He had a standing year-round offer of employment in his foreman position for Mescalero Forest Products, but instinctively he knew that giving up fire-fighting was—giving up. *Decisions, decisions. Maybe I could get a security job at the fabled Inn of the Mountain Gods Resort and Casino. Then I'd probably get fat, breathe in all that cigarette smoke and start drinking, join the millions of Americans whose lifestyle made up the national average. I could play bingo on weekends and suck in more cigarette smoke. Great, great grandfather Naiche would turn over in his grave. He made it to sixty and that's with twenty-five years in prison. The least I could do is push for eighty.*

Nate's thoughts drifted through his mind like slow, summer clouds. He recalled stories his mother shared with him as a child, the same stories Celina shared with their children. His favourite had likely been the reason for working in New Mexico's wildfire program—the Jicarilla Apache story "Origin of Fire." He had heard it over and over again as a child and had committed it to memory.

Now that his mind had turned to fire, Nate grew uncomfortable. Lately, he had only one evil spirit to contend with. He had wrestled many others to the ground over the years, and won. This one seemed to crab-walk up his back and perch on his shoulder. It was the evil spirit of "doubt". The life a fire fighter had been taking its toll. Both his body and mind seemed to be bending under the weight of hard days and nights away from home. Each day now, he found himself looking over to his shoulder and whispering, "Go away little demon. I don't want you in my life. You could kill me."

His thoughts were interrupted by the slamming of the door behind him. Little Nadey burst through the doorway in tears and flung herself at Nate, burying her little, round face in his shoulder. He sensed the tears were of the prefabricated, crocodile nature but dutifully took on the responsibility of concerned father.

"What's wrong little Nadeyole".

She looked up slowly, twin tears suspended from large brown eyes then dribbled down to a pert, runny nose. A quivering bottom lip hid two missing front teeth. "Geronimo won't play with me." The tears broke free, quickly followed by others in order to reinforce the seriousness of the dilemma.

Nate thought a moment, struggling for the discovery of a valid reason for the cat's decision to break free, run and hide from a determined child. "Well, little rabbit, perhaps Geronimo is tired. He is old like your father and needs some rest. I'm sure once he has rested and had time to think about things, he'll want to play with you again."

The cherub face brightened, and a small forearm magically wiped away the tears and some of the nose-dribble.

Nate's banter with his daughter was interrupted by the phone ringing in the kitchen. It stopped and he heard Celina's voice in response. The sound of her footsteps grew closer and Nate immediately thought of the airplane snow-shape. The small hairs on his forearms and the lower back of his neck rose instinctively. I'm experiencing a class 3 premonition. This was Nate's own description of precognition, class 1 being "maybe", class 2 a "probably' and class 3 a "done deal."

Celina opened the door and saw two faces full of anticipation— one with a runny nose and the other sporting a look of feigned innocence. "Nate, it's for you. Apparently, your HotShot crew has a fire."

Nate tried very hard not to look pleased. "Where?"

"Don't look so disappointed." She handed him the receiver. "Some place in Ontario, Canada called Wawa."

Chapter 39

DAY 3: 11:00 HOURS, SIREN LAKE, WALLY'S CAMP

CINDY CORRIGAN WAS PISSED. *What a wussy assignment, setting up protection on a trapper's cabin. What had Darryl Kurtyn offered?* "You guys need a break, and besides, someone has to do it." She felt the last part was a shot. There was no hint of apology.

So here we are, after three hours of road trekking, in the middle of barefoot-banjo country. Cindy stepped out of the truck and told the crew to hang tight. She would walk in from the road and confront the trapper. She had been advised to expect less than a stellar reception.

She walked by his old black chevy truck parked just off the road, and followed the overgrown trail in a westerly direction. The trail wound its way downhill, and occasionally she could catch a glimpse of the billowy, grey/black column of dense smoke through the trees and across the lake. The huge fire across the lake was consuming forest fuels at a torrid pace. The column was at least a kilometre and a half high and bent slightly in a north-easterly direction. The trail narrowed as she descended, broken only by the tread marks of an ATV. *Good—an ATV. Maybe I can talk the old guy into hauling the fire equipment in for us.*

As Cindy walked, she unconsciously swatted at the squadron of deer flies circling her orange hard hat, each looking for a place to crawl under, work its way through her hair and extract its pound of flesh. She suddenly broke out into the open, away from shade and the airborne vampires disappeared. *Wow, some trapper's camp!* She was expecting a Daniel Boone or Davey Crocket model, not something out of 'Summer Homes and Cottages'.

As Cindy rounded the northwest corner for the front, a short, pretzel-thin man surprised her with his presence and stood slowly up on the porch. Aware of his medical condition, she thought to herself that he, indeed, looked frail and cadaverous. *I'd better go easy on him.* She stopped before stepping on to the porch, showing deference for his position as elder and owner.

"Mister McNeil?"

The older man smiled. "None other. What took you so long?"

"Pardon?"

"Well, I sent the young conservation officer packing. Isn't this where they send in the girl to soften me up and change my mind?"

Cindy's face flashed like an emergency red. *So much for frail.* "I assure you ..."

"Just kidding. Excuse my distorted sense of humour. I guess the term "girl" isn't politically correct." Wally extended his hand in greeting. "Come on up and let me pour you a cup of coffee."

Cindy intuitively sensed his smile and offer as genuine, but knew she first had to get business out of the way.

"I appreciate that, sir, but can we talk? I'd like to brief you on why we're here."

"Sure, but let's do it over coffee. I need one and I'll bet you do, too."

Cindy hesitated. "My crew is at the road and waiting for me."

"Let 'em wait. I think I know why you're here and I'll fix them lunch when they get in."

He's made his mind up. I'm getting coffee whether I want it or not. But I sure could use one. Cindy finally took his hand and shook it firmly. "You know what? That's the best offer I've had in the last few days. And by the way, I'm Cindy Corrigan."

"Sit right here, young lady, and relax for a few minutes. I'll be right back with the coffee and my wife's famous peanut butter squares. Did 'em up myself last night."

Wally retreated into his camp with a mission.

Cindy sat down on the old Chevy bench, stretched her legs out and, for the first time in awhile, relaxed. Her shoulders dropped slightly and the muscles in her face retreated, softening her features. She felt the tension that had knotted her muscles and stretched her tendons slip away like morning campfire smoke. She was inexplicably drawn to Wally McNeil and was mildly shocked at a premature urgency to confess the fears and frustrations that had consumed her thoughts and feelings the last few days. She recognized the latent signs of stress testing her defences. *Geez, if he asks me how I'm doing right now, I'll break like a beaver dam in a flood—gotta get a grip on my emotions.* She gazed across the lake. The ridgeline was fringed with a brilliant orange ribbon of fire that snaked down the east-facing slope in several places. A solid wall of dense smoke rose skyward and mushroomed to the north at its apex. A distant CL415 moved in a westerly direction and disappeared behind the column. *I wonder if that's Rob. Not likely going to hear the end of how he saved my ass. Are all pilots condescending and arrogant? Or just the one's I fall for?*

"Pretty impressive." Wally had returned with two steaming cups of coffee and a plate of goodies and had followed her gaze.

Cindy replied with a hint of frustration. "Not when you right beside it."

"Was that your crew in that helicopter two days ago?"

"Yup."

"Well if you don't mind, tell me about it."

Cindy struggled with the decision to tell her story. She looked over to his olive green ATV. There was a trailer attached to it. "OK, Mr. McNeil. But let me radio my crew first. Can we use your ATV and trailer to bring in some equipment?"

"No problem, Cindy. And please call me 'Wally'."

Cindy briefly recounted the experience, including the entrapment. She was, however, reluctant to share her fears and near panic.

Wally listened intently, never once interrupting. He sensed her struggle with the details. Her voice had changed pitch, and he watched both hands gripping the mug of coffee like it was her last. His voice was just above a whisper. "It's a bastard, isn't it?"

Cindy looked at him, her eyelids partially closing, lips tight, mouth drawn down. "With all due respect, Mister McNeil, unless you've been there, you wouldn't understand."

Wally put his cup down. The veins in his temples rose to the surface. His sea green eyes hardened to a flint grey, thunder-clouds passing over ocean shallows. It was the unsolicited memories, not anger that caused the reaction. "Cindy, I've been there—a different time and different circumstances. I was a grunt in Viet Nam, and I know what it was like to face mortality. Organized hype and false glamour doesn't prepare you for the real truth."

Cindy felt her face flush, a trigger to self-defence. "And what is the real truth, Mister McNeil?"

Wally sensed he had offended Cindy. *Oops! Time to diffuse the situation.* He raised his eyebrows and delivered a Cheshire-cat smile. "Is this where I say in my best Jack Nicholson voice, *you can't handle the truth?*"

Cindy laughed, choked on a mouthful of coffee and sprayed the porch in front of her.

"Come on, now. The coffee's not that bad."

"Sorry Mister McNeil."

"Wally."

"OK. Sorry, Wally. And you're probably right, about me handling the truth. But go ahead, anyway."

Wally hesitated, then began. "It's pretty simple, really. In spite of all the rah, rah hype, in spite of all the preparation and training, and contrary to what the movies suggest, all you really want to do is to survive. But therein lies the rub. You will, only if you think you can. And you'll do anything to live." Wally thought for a moment. "Until you know that you've lost."

Cindy groped for the right words to respond. Time seemed to stretch like a bungee cord. She pictured herself organizing words on a scrabble tray. "I thought I had lost. I was ready to give up. If it wasn't for Jim, my 2IC, I would have." Cindy dropped her head in order to mask a single tear sliding down her cheek.

Wally felt her struggle. "Well here's the second part of the truth. That's why the army had squads. That's why you have a crew. That's why baseball and hockey and football have teams. Your second-in-command stepped in and supported you. That was his job. You're here. So it worked."

"Thanks, Wally. But why is it that I don't feel any better about what happened?"

"Because you won't. Not until you have to rescue someone else's soul with such an inadequate explanation." Wally searched for more ammunition. "Look, Cindy, how a person feels and reacts is a mystery. I suspect you feel the way you do because you're a caring, responsible mortal. Blame your parents for raising you properly. But don't dwell on your reaction. Your crew is better off with a confident leader, not one that second guesses her decisions." *I can't believe I'm preaching. She must bring that out in me. Some dumbass need to protect her.*

He's right. It's not about me. It's about the crew. "Thanks, Wally."

Wally sensed it was time to change gears. "OK. That's enough of Wally 101. What can I do for you?"

IT TOOK THREE TRIPS WITH THE ATV and trailer to bring the gear back to Wally's camp. Cindy introduced her crew to the trapper, and as they began setting up camp protection, Cindy explained the process to Wally.

"It's pretty simple, really. We brought in two sprinkler kits, each with five sprinkler heads. They're pretty much like the sprinkler heads you see on a golf course. We'll nail them to roof peaks on your camp and outbuildings."

Wally interjected. "What is their coverage?"

"Each one will give you an effective radius of twenty-two metres or seventy five feet. However, we overlap the coverage so there are no gaps. A single Mark-3 pump can provide water for seven or eight sprinkler heads, depending on distance from the water source or degree of upslope. In this case, one pump will do it. We'll put three heads on your camp, one on each of the two outbuildings and strategically place three others around the openings."

"How's water fed to the heads?"

"Good question. Consider the inch and a half fire hose as a main artery and the pump as a heart. Each length is one hundred feet. Where each one is coupled, a water thief is inserted. They have a half inch outlet and a shut off valve. The sprinkler heads each have a fifty foot length of 5/8 econoflow hose. Think garden hose. These are the "veins" of the system that are attached to the water thieves."

"How do you regulate the distance of spray?"

Cindy smiled. "You're pretty perceptive for a trapper. There are three nozzle tip sizes for the head—1/4 inch, 3/16 and 7/32. The smaller the tip, the more pressure and therefore, the more distance."

Wally was getting into the question/answer rhythm. "What's the other pump for?"

"Either as back up in case the first pump quits or to apply foam to the buildings and bush fringe. The pump and foam will be set up ready to go. Both pumps will be tested and all hoses charged with water."

"Does that mean you're staying?"

"Just for tonight. We'll leave first thing in the morning. My boss figured the crew could use a little R&R." She chose her next words carefully. "And I needed time to convince you to leave."

"So I was right. You were sent to charm me outa here."

Cindy instantly thought of her relationship with Rob. "My feminine wiles are just about as popular as acid reflux or haemorrhoids right now. Besides, I sense that you're too stubborn to change your mind."

"You definitely are intuitive. So when you leave, what happens?"

If the fire looks like it will jump the lake, then the operations chief will send in a crew."

"Operations chief?"

"Yup. This fire, Wawa 43, is now a project fire and will be assigned to an incident management team—used to be called a project fire team not long ago. We've taken on the U.S. Incident Command System."

Wally interjected. "Geez, if it's like their military, you'll need to double the size of your organization."

"Our version is still a little leaner—at least for now."

Where were we? "Anyway, the operations chief is responsible for fire attack strategy and tactics. Then you have planning, logistics and financial chiefs. The head honcho above all these chiefs is called the Incident Commander. You may have heard the term "fire boss", but that's changed. And of course, each one of the chiefs has an organization under him, or her."

"Wow. It's **is** just like the army. Sounds like the organization is worthy of its own discussion tonight around a camp fire."

"No camp fire Wally. We're now under a Restricted Fire Zone."

"OK. Then around the kitchen table."

"We'll set up our tents this evening before "class"."

Wally looked a little surprised. "No need. You guys are staying inside. Four of us will share the bedrooms. You can have the couch."

Cindy had secretly been hoping for the offer, so she put up only polite resistance. *Besides, I like this man. He refuses to leave when threatened. He's been through stuff I've recently experienced.* Her next thought crawled out reluctantly. *And, he seems to be dying with dignity.*

Wally got up from his bench. "I'll fix you guys some lunch."

Cindy rose as well and walked down the steps. "I'll see how the crew is doing."

"While you're at it, see if the two young fellas are capable of catching fish. When they're done work, they can take a couple of my lines and the canoe. I'll point out a good spot for some Walleye."

"Fresh Walleye for supper?"

"Not out of the question. Do they have their fishing licenses? I wouldn't want to be guilty of aiding and abetting hardened criminals."

"Wally, everyone on a fire crew carries a fishing license. We never know when the opportunity will pop up."

Wally gazed back at her as she left. *I like this girl, but she's all tied up inside. She wants more from me. I hope I can give her the answers she's looking for. Hell, I can't even find the answers I'm looking for. Maybe the old 'wisdom well' is dry. We'll probably find out tonight over coffee.*

Wally looked to the ridge. The top of the old pine still peeked out above the grey veiled tree line. For now, it had been spared the ravages of severe fire. A south westerly wind had pushed the fire northerly, away from it. *A new, north wind would finish the old guard. Looks like a bent old man cresting a hill. Hey, old guy! Got any words of wisdom for me? I need inspiration from someone, or something older than me—something I can share with the young lady here. Maybe something I can take with me to bargain with the devil. I can see it now. Satan, old buddy! I have knowledge you don't. And you know what they say, knowledge is power. If I let you in on my secret, do you think you could turn down the thermostat a little? What secret? Well, no less than the secret to a long life. Do we have a deal? Good. The secret to a long life is—don't die.*

Wally chuckled softly at his own morbid humour. *Time to build some sandwiches. The big kid on the roof looks like he could eat a loaf.*

Chapter 40

DAY 3: 13:00 HOURS, WAWA 43

THE RACE WAS ON. The dragon had established a three kilometre head on Wawa 43 and was consuming forest fuels at four hundred metres, or ¼ mile per hour now. Flame lengths reached sixty metres in places, and jump fires were popping up ahead of the main front at a break-neck pace.

Three medium helicopters were frantically racing ahead of the dragon to deposit crews and equipment at camps and cottages in its path. From a distance, the helicopters looked like dragonflies flitting ahead of a shape-shifting, rolling monster. The crews would set up sprinkler systems as required, run up pumps on the camps closest to the fire and get the hell out. They would be picked up by the same helicopters with new equipment on board and continue on further north to other camps. Equipment for this activity was being hauled by cube vans to a central location in the cutover on the fire's west flank. This drastically cut helicopter turn-around time and kept crews safely ahead of the fire.

Russ Gervais was now in charge of the values protection efforts as well as fire suppression on the back and west flank of the fire. He sat in an MNR truck at the staging area, armed with maps showing camp locations and unconsciously clutched the radio transmitter. He was in constant contact with the helicopters. The area tech serving as temporary radio operator sat in the driver's seat next to him, furiously recording the transmissions.

Further north of the fire's head, an amphibious MNR Twin Otter aircraft, OPJ, was being used to carry out the same activity.

Capable of carrying two fire crews and suppression equipment, it would wait while the sprinkler set-ups were established, retrieve the crews and fly back to Wawa for more equipment. At some point, when it was closer to do so, it would get its equipment from Chapleau.

Russ knew where every pump had been set up to protect camps, and when the time came to start them, he would dispatch two fire crew members in a light helicopter with a couple of extra pumps as insurance. His record keeping was vital. When it came time to retrieve the pumping units, he couldn't afford to lose one. It would be needed elsewhere and each unit, pump, hose, intake, tool kit and sprinkler kit was worth around ten thousand dollars.

Once the fire had gone through an area, it was paramount to check the camps for damage and loss. On initial set-up, crews would record the number and state of repair of buildings and any significant equipment left on site and take pictures (each crew leader carried a camera for fire investigation and inventory purposes). It wasn't out of the question that an owner might claim damage or loss to valuables and structures that had initially been in a poor state or not on site at all.

Russ had seen the effectiveness of the pump/sprinkler set up time and time again. 99% of the structures were protected. The 1% loss was usually due to a failed pump. In a post-burn fly-over, he always marvelled at the postage stamp greenery where sprinklers had been set up, in stark contrast to an envelope of black. From his perspective, fires were natural, and people had a tendency to put themselves in harm's way.

It was time for Russ to take a closer look at the situation. He climbed out of the truck and walked directly to a waiting Bell Long Ranger helicopter. The pilot, Sid, who sat patiently on a tree stump, reading a paperback, stood up. Pilots were used to the hurry up and wait syndrome associated with fire fighting.

"Where to, Russ?"

"I need to take a look at fire behaviour at the head and then check in on the crews consolidating the back and west flank of the fire. How's your fuel, Sid?"

"We're topped up. I understand a fuel truck with Jet A will be here shortly, as well."

"Correct. We anticipate the cutover will be used as a staging area for the incident management team so we've taken the liberty of bringing in fuel and equipment. You ready to go?"

"Sure am. My butt and that stump were not a good fit."

Three minutes later, Helitack 21 lifted off into a south-west wind, climbed then banked westerly. The pilot made contact with the CL415 pilot to avoid air space conflict and Russ had cleared departure with the radio operator in the truck.

"Sid, let's see how the crews are doing first. Take it low and slow."

"Roger that, Russ."

The red on white Long Ranger cruised above the forest canopy, skirting the back of the fire on its west side. Three crews were tying in their lines using power pumps and hose. Each was assigned a stretch of fire line that would start from identifiable geographic locations such as ponds, large rock outcrops, creeks or swamps. Each had set up line camps in fire safe areas. They may be there for days, or even weeks. Their initial objective was to put their line in the being-held (BHE) stage as quickly as possible, then eventually get it under control (UCO) with additional hose passes. A piece of line may be worked or passed with hose several times before it could be called UCO. Russ knew that in the case of a large fire, nothing would be declared UCO until every inch of the fire perimeter was at that stage.

Helitack 21 moved northerly along the west flank. Russ had six crews consolidating line along the cutover. Three of the more experienced crews were working the flank north of the bulldozer line— the other three were working into the burn off the bulldozer line.

Russ lifted the radio mic to his mouth. "All fire crews on Wawa 43, this is Helitack 21 on 1. Do you copy?"

One by one, crew leaders responded to the call.

"Looking good down there people. Any issues at this time?"

There was a brief pause. There was always pride-induced reluctance to admit to any problems.

"Helitack 21 from Myers crew. Russ, we had a bear in camp overnight. A large boar and he wasn't too happy about leaving. We didn't get much sleep."

Shit. Here we go again. Russ knew that line camps and bears didn't mix. He also knew that getting rid of the bears was not easy.

You could move a line camp, but the bear would just work its way down to the next camp.

"Dick. I'll contact the District. See if we can get a conservation officer out with a tranquilizer gun to baby-sit. Failing that, we'll fly you out overnight and back in the morning."

"Russ, we can tough it out another night."

"I've been there, buddy, and it's no fun." Russ felt the best scenario was shooting the bear with a tranquilizer and slinging it out by helicopter. That took the availability of a CO (and they had their hands full) and the use of a helicopter (which were presently at a premium). He recalled having a native crew quit on him because of a bear problem. One of their crew-members had previously been mauled by a bear, so they had no tolerance for delay in responding to a bear issue.

"No, we'll either get someone in or get you out." Russ made a note on his personal log. He had three pages of notes already for this particular day.

"Helitack 21 from Dulmage."

"Go ahead Ted."

"Russ, were up in A2 and A3. I think I'm dealing with a large finger of fire on the perimeter running northwest. Can you have a look at it?"

Russ looked at his rough map. Despite its dog-eared, crinkled shape, it was the best information he possessed right now. *Pretty critical area.* "I'll be there in two minutes, Ted. You got a helipad constructed?"

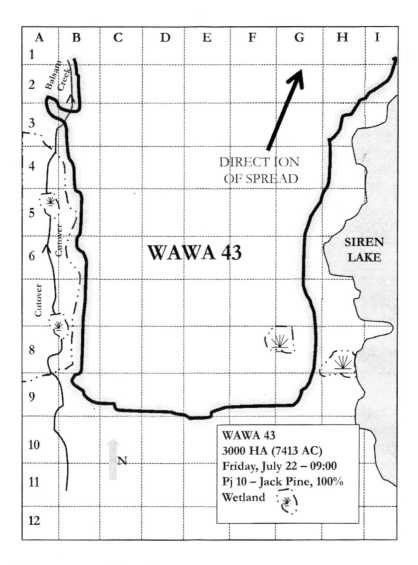

"Affirmative. Follow the creek and you'll see it in the southwest corner of B3."

"Meet me there Ted, and we'll take you up for a look."

"Copy that."

Russ pointed to the map for the helicopter pilot who acknowledged with a nod. The Long Ranger was on course.

"OK, listen up everyone. I've bad news and not so bad news."

Russ paused to collect his thoughts. "First the "not so bad" news. Work on your food orders tonight. We're setting up a service organization at the staging area, and we'll be able to fly in fresh stuff in the a.m."

"Now the bad news. You've got a day to tie in and consolidate your lines. Long range forecast shows a narrow system moving north of us. We can expect northerly winds behind it. It's imperative that your lines hold, or everything we've accomplished to date goes for a sh ... , *Oops* ... is lost." *Gotta watch my radio language. Damn northerly winds. Yeah, a little cooler, but at this time of year they bring strong wind speeds and could last up to three days. The fire will literally turn, run back on us and breach our lines. Then the winds will come from the south sooner or later and flank us. More than one crew has been pulled out of a jack-pot due to north winds.*

Russ heard the keying of several mics and was satisfied they received the message. "Keep up the good work." Russ hesitated. *It's going to be a long stretch and I'll have to pace the crews.* "But I don't want to see more than fourteen-hour days unless you run into a problem."

The pilot looked at Russ, a hint of smile on his face.

"Yeah, I know Sid. Practice what I preach." Russ had been logging eighteen-hour days. *I've probably aged a year in three days.*

"Let's pick up that crew leader with the fire line issue first and show him what he's dealing with, then we'll have to get in front of the beast for a good look."

"I assume you'll want the fire on your side of the helicopter, Russ. When we're done with the crew leader, I'll run east across the burn then swing north and bring you around the head on your side. How's your tummy; there'll be lots of turbulence?"

Russ thought of an old James Bond movie. "That's OK, Sid. I prefer to be shaken, not stirred."

"Keep your day job, Russ. Stay out of stand-up."

The Long Ranger disappeared slowly over a ridge. The stoic old pine, just south of the fire, faced a high, warm sun. A sow bear and cub rested in the high grass of a swamp to the east, and a dying trapper was dispensing a shot of wisdom to a frustrated fire crew leader across the lake. Wawa 43 was now three thousand hectares plus and growing.

Chapter 41

DAY 3: 13:00 HOURS, SUDBURY, ONTARIO, THE RAMPART HOTEL

B OTTOM OF THE BARREL—CAN'T GET MUCH WORSE
THAN THIS. *What did I do to deserve such a crappy existence?*
Richard Head sat alone at the bar, peering through an empty
beer glass and counted the key items on his bad luck scale.

The top of that scale coincided with his birth. Apparently the
nurses were overly polite. His mother had never been reluctant to
remind him (between cigarettes) how disappointed she was. She
had eventually succumbed to cancer, sucking a last cigarette in
bed, at home, on her dying day. With her last breath, she exhaled
the chemically laced smoke. His father (who spoke little and offered an opinion on nothing), had, according to his mother, on seeing little Richard at birth, blurted out his only thought in a whisky
ravaged voice, "What the hell is that?" He had eventually killed
himself with alcohol and a pickled egg, choking on it after several
shots of cheap whiskey. They had both experienced macabre death,
dancing with the devil's two of three favourite enticements—cigarettes and alcohol. Vice number three was sex but Richard was
sure vices one and two took up all of their time.

And there was no denying his father's observation. He was a
huge new born at fourteen pounds and simply, undeniably, ugly.
Not "baby-first-born ugly", but "that baby is going to grow up
ugly" ugly.

Then there was his name. His father had insisted on it. *Probably
payback for the shock of seeing him at birth.* Now Richard, as a name,

is somewhat routine but at least regal. But if you cut to a traditional short version (Dick), then blend it with his last name, voila! Mum, Dad, I'd like you to meet my new boyfriend, Dick Head.

Not that he had ever had a girlfriend (number three on the bad luck scale). He had learned at a very early age that to get what he wanted he had to whine, cry and snivel. As he grew older (and larger), he became the favourite target of school-yard bullies. And, as his father has anticipated, the old axiom of "ugly baby, beautiful child" did not apply to Richard. His father would mutter (just loud enough for Richard to hear), "ugly baby ... uglier kid." So, those special girls who had the ability to get past looks and search for the soul in a personality, found Richard unattractive on both counts.

Richard breezed through six years of high school where the average student struggled through four. He once overheard a teacher talking about him: "That kid 'Head' would be challenged by a three-piece puzzle."

His only joy in life was working on the school paper. He wasn't interested in editing or advertising. Richard fancied himself a reporter. And not just a reporter, but the best (and only) reporter the school newspaper had to offer. Through his extra-curricular job, Richard became the "everyman". Interviews with the football, basketball and hockey jocks automatically rendered him membership into their world, at least in his mind. Interviewing the head cheerleader elevated Richard to "stud" status. Writing reviews associated with the class president or student council symbolically moved Richard to the front of the class. No wonder he struggled between reality and delusion. In his mind, Richard could be the highly intelligent jock who was this close to getting the high school hottie. Or, after one look in the mirror (as he looked up now in the bar mirror), he could be what he was, the fat guy in the wrinkled suit with the bulgy eyes and sweaty face that was perched on a series of chins.

So now, he was, what was he? *Oh yeah, I'm my mother and dad in a loser body with a loser job—a free lance reporter. What a joke! I need another beer with a whisky chaser and a friggin' cigarette. Do I go outside and smoke or do I stay in here and drink?—decisions, decisions.*

Richard laid a critical eye on the bartender who shrugged his narrow shoulders and began to prepare Richard another liquid appetizer.

I need a story. To get a good story, I need a plan. Richard thought back to the briefing he had attended at the regional fire centre that morning. He recalled the way the fire duty officer had looked at him. *Was it my imagination, or did I bother him a little? Maybe he knows a good reporter when he sees one. What was his name? Oh yeah, Rick! Probably short for Richard. How come I get Dick and he gets Rick. If my last name had been "Focker", I'm sure the old man would have named me "Dumb."*

Richard put aside his digression. *I really need to get on that fire. But not with the rest of my loser peers. We'll be herded through their main camp like sheep. I need to either be over the fire, or on it—or both.*

The normally down-turned lip/seam inched up, up, into a weak, struggling, hard-to-hold smile. Fat lips parted to reveal uneven, cigarette-stained teeth. *Yeah, that's it!* Richard pulled on his beer then pulled out a pad and paper from the inside pocket of his wrinkled jacket. A plan was forming and he needed to write it down before the next two rounds at the bar. *Have to stay to take in the "floor" show.* He knew *Crystal Glass was due up on stage and he had been advised by a couple of the regulars that "she could contort her body into a pretzel and still glide across the dance floor, garbed only in a pair of stiletto heels."* The imagery almost sabotaged his original train of thought and his bullfrog smile got even bigger. *This would be a two drink show (at least).*

But first the plan. Shit, my pen is outa ink. How can it be? It's brand new from Harry's Big and Tall Men's Shop. Got it with the three packs of XXL jockey shorts. The ever-watchful bartender reached over and offered Richard another pen. "Your pen deposited its ink in your pocket, buddy." Richard looked down and groaned.

By this time, the bar tender had come to life, obviously enjoying the customer's predicament. "Won't impress the ladies with that. The stain looks like one of them psychiatrist drawings, what do they call them?"

Richard was no stranger to this standard tool used to delve into a patient's mind. A couple of sessions as a troublesome teenager had left its mark. "It's called a Rorschach Ink Blot, asshole." His smile had returned to its normal grouper fish frown.

The bartender didn't miss a beat. "Well, your roar-shits ink blob asshole has taken the shape of either a battleship or a dog turd. I'm inclined to go with the turd. The ladies will love it."

Richard had enough. "Remember that tip you almost got. It'll be used to get this ink stain out at the cleaners." *Swallow that, you dip stick.*

Now both men were frowning.

Back to the plan. A thick, pink, slug/tongue peeked out between the sausage lips as Richard concentrated. *First, gotta get to White River. Easy—take the bus.* Richard was no stranger to bus travel. *Second, rent a helicopter. What's a helicopter going to cost? Didn't the fire people mention around a thousand bucks per hour? Savings are gonna take a beating. Third, rent a car, better yet, a truck. But wait. What of my chances of getting a helicopter or car in White River? Back up. Take the bus to Wawa, then do the renting stuff. How do I get a helicopter to the fire? What about that copy of the fire plan from the Fire Centre? What did they call it? Oh yeah, strategic operating plan.* Richard pulled the folded document from his pocket. He opened it complete with ink-blot. *Does sorta resemble a dog turd.* As luck would have it, the fire location was still legible.

Ten minutes later, Richard had his plan complete with a total cost estimate of twenty-five hundred dollars. He figured a really good story could bring in four times that amount. He also realized that it would have to be spectacular. *Hopefully the fire will grow a lot bigger. Maybe some buildings could be levelled or a couple of fire fighters hurt—not killed mind you. How could I interview them if they're dead? Wouldn't it be great if a town or two was evacuated. There's no end to the possibilities. Hope it doesn't rain for awhile.*

Richard also realized there were some hurdles to overcome. *Flying over the fire to take video wouldn't be a problem—just rent a helicopter and pilot and point him in the right direction.* The tough part would be getting onto the fire itself. First he would have to talk his way onto the fire base camp. *I'll deal with the Wawa fire base on that one.* Then, he would have to find a way to sneak onto the fire. *Need to get a map. Probably wouldn't hurt to pack a lunch and a Mickey of vodka. Do I need bush clothes or boots? Too expensive. Besides, how hard can it be? They're using kids to fight fires, and I'll only be gone a couple of hours. How about the bugs in the forest? I'll bring a can of insect repellent. What about emergencies? Cell phone should do it. Maybe a litre of*

*vodka would be better. Should I bring along a compass? To hell with it. I
don't know how to use one anyway. Tools of the trade? Digital and video
camera would do the trick.*

Richard was now more excited than he had been in a long while.
This could be a big one. *I might even get my fifteen minutes of
fame.* He dabbled with the prospect of being important, being able
to control the space around him, having people watch him—and
knowing it—and pretending to ignore it.

Suddenly, the lights dimmed, the music cranked to an ear drum
splitting decibel level, and another beer and shot materialized before his eyes. He had a plan and the beautiful Crystal glided seductively across the stage. And she was looking directly at him (if he
had bothered to look around, he would discover no one else was
in the bar except the entertainer and the bar tender). He held two,
five-dollar bills in a sweaty palm as incentive for special attention.
He could afford only a dollar or two but you couldn't stick a looney
or tooney in a garter belt, and it was bad form to ask for change.
The grouper fish-frown turned to a bullfrog smile. *Can't get any
better than this!*

Chapter 42

DAY 4: SATURDAY, JULY 23RD, 15:00 HOURS, WAWA 43

WATER!! THE NUMBER 1 HOSE HANDLER RELEASED THE HOSE STRANGLER slowly and carefully on that simple, specific command, and the nozzle operator braced for a surge of water at a pressure of one hundred and twenty pounds per square inch. Number 1 deftly slipped the strangler into its pouch on his belt, grabbed the 1½ inch diameter hose eight feet behind the operator and prepared to march the hose along the fire line at the operator's pace.

The number 2 hose handler was approximately fifty feet ahead at the big loop that had naturally formed in the hundred foot length of hose as it had peeled out of the hose layer's pack, folded in the middle. The number 2 hose handler would push the solid, charged hose at the same pace through and around a tangle of brush, fallen forest debris and trees.

Ahead of this trio, the hose layer was preparing another length of hose to feed out of the pack on his back when the nozzle operator reached him. In this case, he was at his last length, and the original sixty-pound pack was now down to fifteen pounds, for the time being. He would have to go back down the line to get another pack of hose shortly.

All four fire fighters were exhausted, wet from water and sweat, and beyond filthy. Red jump suits, faces, hands and orange hard hats were streaked and stripped black with the ravages of battle. It was as if the enemy was fighting back with bull-whips covered in charcoal. Instead of belts weighed down with pistols, cartridges, scabbards and swords, these warriors carried folding knives, FM radios, hose strangles, metal hose patches, compasses and water bottles. The crew leader also wore a map holder on his chest that appeared much like a Kevlar vest, and a GPS unit on his belt. The nozzle operator moved quickly, gauging his speed against the effectiveness of the water being applied.

To make matters worse, the weak trough of low pressure that had slipped through that morning brought only a trace of rain and strong north-easterly winds behind it. Technically, the crew was now faced with a potential head fire rather than the safer back fire. The crew was in danger of losing all the ground it had gained over the past two days. The fire fighters would have to deal with direct smoke, sub-surface re-burn, fire line flare ups and jump fires from those flare ups. Every crew along the back and southwest flank of Wawa 43 was facing the same dilemma. The dragon was counter attacking with a vengeance.

I DON'T HAVE A GOOD FEELING ABOUT THIS. Wawa 43 had more than doubled its size overnight and now pushed sixty-five hundred hectares. Even in a comatose state, Russ Gervais had the good sense to snatch a topographic map from the radio operator at base camp last night or he knew he'd never be able to map this sucker. *Progressed ten kilometres north-easterly since yesterday evening, only thirty kilometres (and change) from Hornepayne as the crow flies. And that's assuming my mapping is accurate.* He and his helicopter pilot, Sid, had trouble getting a fix on the fire's head. The base of the rolling column of smoke served as a blanket at the head. Russ looked back down at his new map.

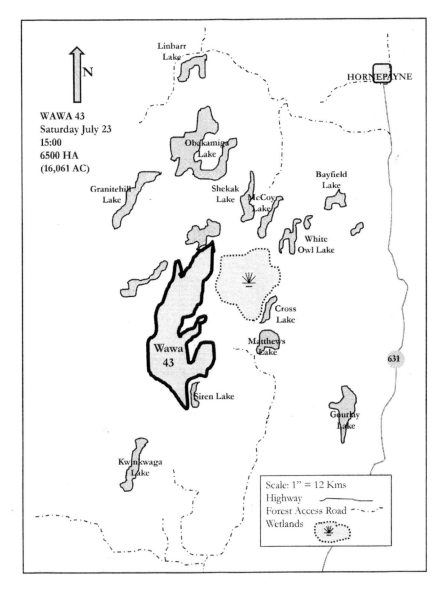

They were now traversing the back and west flank in Helitack 21, and Russ was barking out commands like a desperate general, sensing a shift in battle-ground momentum. From the air, the pattern was typical. Most obvious was the change in the large column of smoke. Instead of a super smoke structure punching through the sky at four kilometres up and bending slightly in a north-easterly direction, this same monolith was now bent significantly in a south-westerly direction. In essence, it now threatened his crews on the ground, the piles of valuable cut wood to the west and the staging area set up to the south-west. *We're probably going to have to move the staging area.*

Russ looked at the pilot. *He looks as bad as I feel right now.* Both men were unshaven and sported blood-shot, red-rimmed eyes. "Sid, take us low and slow, just inside the burn." The weary pilot only nodded and pulled back on the collective. Russ was looking for another tell-tale stage in the pattern of change.

A quilt of charcoal-coloured earth was adorned with countless black spikes of coniferous trees and the whites and grays of burned off rock outcrops. Rings and snakes of green fringes circled swamps and bordered creeks. Clusters of browns and gold scorched poplar and birch appeared as over-cooked popcorn from the air. Plumes of smoke rolled away from the fringes of green and poked up through the poplar and birch. But Russ was looking for something out of the ordinary and there! He saw it, no, *them.* There were lines of smoke in the black, scorched ground cover—not puffy and broken, but solid and stretching with snatches of flame spotted along their base. The enormous area of black stretching for miles to the north had serviced as camouflage for the unburned fuels and hidden fire in sub-surface layers beneath it. Northerly winds were now forcing re-burn to the south and south-west. Russ knew there would be a third stage, breaches on the established fire line, and with those breaches came a forth stage, the potential for escaped fire along the lines they had worked so hard to contain. *And with these winds we're not going to hold it. Time to think about updating Wawa and a crew evacuation strategy.*

AMOS ALFELSKIE SLUMPED in the front seat of the battered Ford 250 pickup, radio mike in hand. A black cloud of anger passed from the top of his head down to his toes. Visual indicators were numerous. Eyes squinted, jaw muscles flexed, a normal dead-fish pallor turned red, then purple, fists clenched and knuckles turned white, back straightened and chest thrust out, feet and legs drawn in. Body slumping came after stark realization had set in. There was a good chance the fire was going to get in the cut-over and

Northshore Logging would lose wood—wood his men had busted there collective asses in cutting, forwarding to landings and piling. His anger mounted, and his check-list of injustices grew. *Not to even mention the mapping, planning, volume estimating, road location, cutting and building. What about the planning and attending of public open houses, the hundreds of public notice letters that were mailed out?*

Then there were days of boundary marking after fighting for countless hours with MNR over nature and wildlife reserves. Haggling with contractors, dealing with native road blocks, fighting with the union and piece workers over wages and rates. Battling with his bosses over production, equipment and downtime issues.

And the handling, oh the handling. First there was cutting the tree using feller-bunchers; then there was moving the material out of the bush using huge grapple skidders. Once you got it to the landing, it was de-limbed using mechanized stroke de-limbers and, depending on the material (log or pulp), it was slashed to log length or left in tree length Then, finally, the loading with tracked loaders and hauling with tandem tractor-trailers. Amos had run out of mental fingers and toes in his counting.

He briefly lamented the old days when a cutter would fell a tree with a chain saw, buck it up into log lengths and a skidder operator would drag a half dozen logs to the landing. He crawled back into his darker thoughts.

And last but not least, dealing with Ministry of Labour over our safety record. All of it, everything, going into the shitter because of a friggin storm and one bolt of lightning. Would have been a lot better for everyone concerned if it had hit me instead.

And where are we at now? Frantically loading thousand of cubic metres of tree-length material onto tractor trailers using every piece of loading and hauling equipment that we could beg, borrow or steal. So the bean counters can take all their "break even analysis" crap and shove it in dark, damp places if we lose this wood!

South and south-west flank of Wawa 43, 17:00 hours

THE FIRE LINE HAD BEEN BREACHED in several places to the south, now the new head of the fire. The crews along the bulldozer line were barely holding their own. Almost without exception in the trouble areas, torching in spruce and balsam fir would occur.

Fire-brands were then lifted skyward with convective currents of smoke-laden air, and jump fires were popping up within 1/4 kilo-metre south and west of the established fire line. North of the bull-dozer line, the pot was brewing but hadn't boiled over yet. It was just a matter of time before the jump fire scenario would be played out within the cut-over.

Time for a change in tactics. One by one, Russ called the crews on the south end of the fire. The message was simple: "Drop what you're doing, head back to your line camps, leave your hose, pull your pumps, pack up your tents, camping gear and personal equip-ment and prepare for evacuation."

To those crews on the south-west flank protecting the cut wood in the cutover, his message was considerably different. "Hold your lines unless you're in big doo-doo. I'm moving the crews from the south over to you. They'll back you up. A 415 package will be on its way shortly to support you with line breaches and jump fires. We can't let the fire into the cut-over."

Russ then contacted Wawa Fire to advise them of the changes and requested that they contact Northshore Logging and tell them to pull out of the cutover if and when he gave the word.

Next, Russ contacted the staging area and told them to get the Bell 212 helicopter ready for dispatch to retrieve crews and equip-ment from the south end of the fire. The medium helicopter's ini-tial load would also include four new packs of hose for the first crew picked up. After dropping off the first crew to the south-west flank, it would automatically return to the staging area, pick up another four packs and then head south to pick up another crew. There would be only three crews to move, and they would be bud-died with the crews north of the bulldozer line.

His final contact was the bird dog officer in aircraft Birddog 18 controlling the two CL415's to the north.

"TANKER 271 and 274—THIS IS BIRDDOG 18, DO YOU COPY?" Both CL415's responded. Terry Dynel, the Birddog officer, Birddog 18 and pilot hovered overhead like a mother eagle watching over her two fledglings.

"We've just been given the word. Pull the plug and head for the west flank of the fire."

Terry had mixed emotions. *What a waste. We've been pounding the head for two hours now and making some progress with that wind switch from the north-east. Russ must be in trouble or he wouldn't have pulled us.*

Five minutes later the small, high-winged Cessna P337 and its two over-sized yellow ducklings were in-bound to the south-west side of the fire. The Cessna raced ahead.

As it approached the target area, Terry toggled his mic. "Helitack 21, this is Birddog 18, do you copy Russ?"

"Go ahead 18."

"Russ, we're east of Siren Lake. Our approach for water will be from the south. Who is out there?"

Russ hesitated for a moment, gathering his thoughts. "Terry, it's like this." As he prepared to carry on, his pilot, Sid, swung the Long Ranger over the cutover and pointed to get Russ' attention. "Standby one, Terry."

Two jump fires sprung up like blankets pulled back from smoke signals. Puffs of black smoke rose, billowed, then drifted south-west. *Oh, Oh.* Russ' first thought had something to do with "shit" and a "fan". *I think I'm about to become a poster boy for the Peter Principle. I've just risen to my level of incompetence. Come on Russ, get your stuff together!!*

Sid, sensing that Russ's alter ego was testing his confidence, toggled the live mic switch, looked towards Russ and smiled. "Could be worse, Russ. You could be down there with the crews instead of up here, floating in the clouds, pushed by a slip-stream, in the cheerful company of yours truly."

Russ looked at his pilot and relaxed. It was as if there was invisible thread running from the corner of his mouth to pulleys on the top of his head then down to his shoulders. When the tension in his shoulders dissipated and caused them to drop, the invisible thread pulled down from the pulleys and caused the corners of his mouth to rise, creating a "you're full of cow manure, but thank you" smile.

Russ then focused on the need to deal with the air tanker package. "Birddog 18. You have Helitack 21, that's us, on the south-west flank of the fire, at five hundred feet. Helitack 15, a 212, is ferrying crews from the south side of the fire to the south-west flank, now on FM 1. You have six crews on the southwest flank, soon to be nine, all on FM 1. They are out of harm's way. Your target is any jump fire in the cut-over just to the west. You can prioritize them yourself. There's equipment loading and hauling the tree-length timber piles. They will be out of there shortly. As you're working the jump fires, if you see any of the piles of wood threatened, nail the closest jump fires first. If your loads aren't doing the trick lay foam on the piles as a protective measure."

A pause allowed Terry to jump in. "Copy that Russ. Now here's what I want you to do. Pull away from the cutover. Stay on top of the fire perimeter. Maintain altitude of two thousand feet. Do you copy?"

"Copy that, 18, two thousand feet."

Terry continued. "We'll be approaching Siren Lake for water from the south, moving north-westerly, swinging around and coming at our targets from the north. I'll deal with Helitack 15. Any other aircraft inbound?"

"Negative, Terry. More crews are coming in, but they'll be driving and will stand-by at the staging area."

As an afterthought, Russ realized he had another assignment to deal with. "Birddog 18. Terry, I'm going to hang around for another fifteen minutes, to make sure the crews are all set, but then we have to head north and check on the sprinkler system set ups. I have a crew leader on top of the situation to the north, but I need to assess some additional cottage protection requirements. Can you cover for me for an hour?"

"Roger that Russ and—good luck."

Town of White River, 17:00 hours

THE TOWN OF WHITE RIVER was no stranger to the threat of wildfire. They had dealt with the need to organize community protection and possible evacuation in 1999 due to another large fire, Wawa 08. However, the reeve and council members who dealt with the challenge then had been replaced twice over by new officials. It was someone else's turn to test the limits of high blood pressure.

MNR had advised the reeve of the probability of winds from the north. Smoke drifting into the town confirmed the wind switch. What really got his attention, though, was the fact that MNR had dedicated limited resources to the south end of the fire, that part of the fire that could threaten the town. The meeting with Darryl Kurtyn, the Wawa fire management supervisor was, to say the least, tense. What was once advertised as the coldest spot in Canada was now one of the hottest. The reeve, Rennie Fullton, represented close to one thousand residents, and he was angry. Darryl was extremely tired and defensive, but resolute. It was a main street gunfight, each verbal salvo intended to do serious harm. A council member, who preferred to remain nameless, said it went something like this:

Rennie was a big man with a big voice. He fired the first shot. "You mean to tell me that the fire is heading in this direction and you're sitting back watching. Taking pictures, maybe. Or roasting marshmallows?"

"Rennie, I'll ignore those last two remarks. As I said earlier, we're shy on resources right now. There's a shit load of crews inbound. Besides the contract crews due here shortly, we also have U.S. HotShot crews and Manitoba crews on their way. We expect the winds to swing and come in from the south in the next day or two. When that happens, and when the crews arrive, we'll be hammering that south end with almost everything we have."

"Whadaya mean, "almost?""

Darryl was losing it. "Rennie, just for a moment, pretend White River is not the only town in the universe. When the wind comes from the south, Hornepayne will be up against it—again."

The three council members seemed mesmerized by the verbal jousting, their heads swinging back and forth between combatants.

"With all due respect to Hornepayne, what do I tell the owners of the Rainbow Motel, or the White River Restaurant or the pastor at Saint Peter's Anglican? You can relax boys. MNR says there's no point in fighting the fire to the south. The winds *may* change and push it back to the north. How far away is it from White River right now?"

Damn. I was afraid he was going to ask that question. "Thirty kilometres." *Here it comes.*

There was dead silence for what seemed an eternity. It was like a movie put on pause. Rennie stood up, his hands gripping the meeting table, his face crimson and fingers splayed to support a potential leap across two metres of oak table top. His bushy eyebrows worked up and down alternately, like a teeter-totter, and the muscles on each side of his face popped then dropped as he struggled to compose himself. His words slipped out in a whisper. "When do you expect the winds to switch?"

Darryl sat back in his chair and flicked his pen between upper and lower teeth. If body language could speak, it would say, "Look, I'm relaxed, you don't intimidate me. Chill out, man."

"Less than two days time, Monday at the latest."

"And how far will the fire progress in that time."

"With forecasted weather, another fifteen to twenty kilometres. Look, I won't bullshit you. There is a chance that the north winds will continue. But I'll say right now that there's a 90% chance they'll swing back to the traditional summer prevailing winds, south-west. I'll also be very candid about attacking the south end while it's the head of the fire. Intensity is so strong, that we won't put people in front of it. All we would be doing is putting them in harm's way and pulling them out again. Flame front is so massive that using heavy water bombers is futile. It's like trying to put out a campfire with a thimble-full of water."

Rennie sat back down. He realized the time for posturing was over. "Well what the hell do we do? I don't mind telling you that I feel like a deer caught in headlights. I know the truck is coming, but I can't seem to move."

"Just, continue with your emergency plan contingencies. We'll keep on top of the weather forecasts. If I was a betting man, I'd bet that you'll feel much better about this by Monday."

"Right, Darryl. It's easy to bet when you personally don't have anything to lose.

Chapter 43

DAY 4: 17:00 HOURS, FALCON RESPONSE CENTRE, SUDBURY

ZANDER CYBULSKI HAD NO SOONER SETTLED INTO HIS CHAIR in the fire centre, when Shiela Monahan, the regional fire intelligence officer, walked briskly up to him and handed him a sheet of paper. After his four-hour drive from Whitney, on the east side of Algonquin Park, he had quickly been briefed by both Rick Sampson, the FDO, and the executive officer, Doug Rainville. Zander's job was daunting. He was assigned with the task of coordinating activities and requests associated with the three project fires in the East Fire Region, including Wawa 43. He would report to Rick Sampson who still maintained over-all command and control of the fire response program. In essence, Zander filtered data and planned for the project fires at the regional level.

"What's this, Shiela?"

"An update on Wawa 43, Zander. You'd better take a good look at it. It's now priority one in the region."

This wasn't Zander's first time in the hot seat. As operations supervisor for one of the largest and most complex provincial parks in Ontario, he was no stranger to pressure. He stretched his six-foot, three-inch, forty-five year-old formidable frame in the under-sized chair. He crossed his left ankle over his right knee, exposing a large, scuffed, unlaced work boot and rolled out a warm smile that was notorious for unhinging knees in women but also reducing the threat index with men. He sported a square jaw with a slight chin cleft, dimpled cheeks, dark, thick, high arched eyebrows over piercing blue eyes and a cap of curly black hair. His only flaw was having no idea what so-ever that he was flawless—and he was happily married.

Perched low on his aquiline nose was a pair of reading glasses that he used to not only to read with, but also to handle, chew on and clean as a delay tactic when he struggled with difficult questions, comments or situations. He reached up and gently pulled the glasses away from his face now.

"Thanks, Sheila. I'll take a good look at it now."

Zander placed the spectacles back on their perch just above the nostrils, scanned the report and ticked off the critical data in his mind. At the same time, he began to write down what he considered key issues and recommendations. He was "in the zone" now, oblivious to the bundle of movement, conversations and telephone ringing all around him. *Six thousand hectares—winds from the north-east—crews unable to contain.*

He looked at the weather display. *Presently north-east at twenty-five kilometres per hour. Tomorrow, north at thirty kilometres, gusting to forty-five. Monday, Northwest at fifteen kph. Tuesday, July 26, southwest at twenty kph—a wind switch.*

Zander then looked at the large, wall-mounted fire map at his one o'clock, pushed his glasses a little higher and did some quick calculation. *Even at a rate of spread of a conservative five metres per minute, that fire will eat up seven kilometres of bush a day. Three days of north winds, twenty closer to White River, eight to ten kilometres away! Very interesting. There'll be a smoke problem, not to mention the cottages in harm's way.* He made a note. "Cottages south of Wawa 43 require protection. White River could be smoked out."

He looked back to the report.

Incident commander and values protection leader, Russ Gervais. Good man. He made a note. "Too much on his plate."

Thirteen crews, two helicopters (a medium and a light), and one tanker package assigned. Crews pulled off the south end of the fire and moved to the south-west flank to protect cut wood. Air attack focusing on jump fires in cut over to the west of established fire line. He made another note. "A little shy on helicopters."

Zander flipped over to the fire map of Wawa 43 attached to the report. He noted the location of the staging area used as a temporary base camp and made a note. "Staging area will have to be moved." *Bill Gorley incident management team on standby in Wawa.* Another note. "Give the Gorley team the fire—now."

Greg Walsh sent to Hornepayne as emergency response liaison/coordinator. Zander then took another look at the long term weather forecast and made another note. "If the winds turn around and come out of the south as predicted, Greg will need his ER team with him. An evacuation of Hornepayne is likely". He continued. "What about White River if north winds continue beyond day three?"

Zander then mentally summarized his notes: Cottages south of Wawa 43 require protection; White River could be smoked out; Russ Gervais—too much on his plate; need more helicopters; move base camp; give the Gorley team the fire; emergency response team to Hornepayne, and, what about White River if north winds continue beyond day three?

Zander knew the fire people in Wawa probably had come to the same conclusions. He hoped sharing his notes in the afternoon briefing would help. He looked towards Sheila, caught her attention and raised a subtle eyebrow. She smiled and walked over. "Sheila, what do we have for resources coming into the region?"

She flipped through her notes. "Let's see, five HotShot and four engine crews from the U.S; ten initial attack crews from British Columbia; ten IA crews, two CL215 tanker packages and four S.E.A.Ts from Manitoba. In addition, we have forty Type 2 fire crews in Ontario on standby and ten ranger crews inbound from the West Fire Region."

Zander thought for a moment. "Three questions. What about helicopters, what's an engine crew, and, what's a S.E.A.T?"

"We have thirty-two helicopters committed, twelve assigned directly to fires and twenty on initial attack. Our air ops people say we have another fifteen coming in. An engine crew is basically a bush type fire truck complete with a crew. And, the acronym S.E.A.T stands for single engine air tanker."

"What's there load capacity and what do they look like?"

Without missing a beat, Sheila responded. "They're Air Tractor 802's with a water/fire retardant capacity of six hundred and sixty imperial gallons and a speed of close to three hundred kilometres per hour. They're also coming complete with a portable reload base. Those are tractor-trailers with water/retardant/foam storage, mixing and loading units and water bladders. They don't have the punch of a CL415, but are good for initial attack on small fires. They can give a crew some time to respond.

As Zander was becoming slightly overwhelmed by the data, he was saved by the bell. His phone rang. Normally an enemy, it became an ally, at least in this particular case. Raised eyebrows and a slight grimace signalled his requirement to answer. *Here's another fine mess I've gotten myself into.*

CINDY AND HER CREW WERE BACK IN WHITE RIVER, along with a dozen other ranger crews, waiting for an assignment. This was typical of any large response effort: anticipate, mobilize, hurry up—and wait. Only this time she wasn't impatient. In fact, she was down-right calm. Her visit with Wally on Siren Lake (or Lake Jewel as he called it) had put some critical things in perspective for her. The few short hours she had spent with the little man with a valley of wisdom had lined up her thoughts and feelings like shooting-gallery ducks. It was time to get her life in order and make peace with Rob. And who knew where that might lead.

Who am I kidding? She had stayed at the Rainbow Motel last night and took the opportunity for a hot shower. When she stepped out, she was shocked by the spectre in the full length mirror. She had lost a lot of weight. *Cripes, my skin is hanging on me like a deflated air balloon draped over a tree.* She decided to do a thorough inspection.

She stepped closer to the mirror and wiped away the steam with a towel. *Mirror, mirror, on the wall, who's the scariest of them all?* Her body was a cadaver white—between white and not so white—except for her face, neck, lower forearms and hands. They were sunburn red—except for her forehead. It was cadaver white where her hard hat had provided protection. *Great, I look like a stop sign with red arms.* The red parts were not without character. They were mottled with welts, bumps and scratches, compliments of heavy brush and flies. A few wet bandages remained as decoration for the collage of pain.

She then quarter turned and twisted to look at her back side. *Wonderful.* A large, purple welt ran across as far as she could see. *That happened when I did the "log rolling contest thing" on a fallen jack pine covered in tanker snot.* Using her hands to support her body in the "twist" position, she noticed several broken finger nails. *Oh great. How am I supposed to gouge Rob's eyes out?* She lifted one foot, then another and pointed her feet upwards at the ankle. They were adorned with quarter-sized flaps of broken blisters. *No more step-dancing for me.*

She turned back to look at her breasts. Not long ago, they had been a source of pride but now *Must have happened when the ground jumped up and hit me in the face when we were trapped. Now I'm a de-fenceless, flat-chested, 'Rocky Raccoon' stop sign that can't dance.*

She saved the best till last—a revisit to her face. To compliment the scratches, welts and bumps, she sported a pair of black eyes, now turning a peculiar shade of olive—and a swollen nose. Must have happened when the ground jumped up and hit me in the face when we were trapped. Now I'm a defenceless, flat-chested, 'Rocky Raccoon' stop sign that can't dance.

As she dressed slowly and with some discomfort she thought, "No centre-fold posing for me."

She went outside for some fresh air and a reality check. A tap on her shoulder brought her back to earth. Her 2IC smiled at her. "Cindy, we've got an assignment."

"Where to, Jim?"

His smile broadened. "Apparently, the north end of Wawa 43— and we're taking drip torches with us. With both hands thrust forward as if presenting a trophy, he announced, "It's burn-out time!"

"WHADAYA MEAN, YOU CAN'T FLY ME OVER THE FIRE?" Richard Head was livid. He had spent a hellish eight-hour trip on the Grey Hound bus, sitting next to an old guy with bad breath who wouldn't shut up, the bus toilet was plugged and the egg-salad sandwich he had purchased at a rest stop was a marvel. *Obviously a new form of egg salad intended to exercise jaw muscles and sharpen teeth.* Then, the bus had dropped him off in Wawa's town centre and he had to walk three kilometres back to the Wawa airport, the one they had passed an hour ago. His "good humour tank" was almost empty by the time he walked through the door at West Wind Helicopters.

The base manager continued. "Just like I said, Mister Head …"

Richard retreated quickly from his offensive posture. *Easier to catch a fly with honey.* "Call me Dick."

The congruity of the name was not lost on the manager, and he suppressed a smile. "All of our helicopters are committed to fires."

Richard looked out on the tarmac and pointed. "What about that one there?"

"It's "US", unserviceable, Mister Head—I mean, Dick."

A young woman behind the service counter shuffling papers quickly got up and rushed into the back room, frantically trying to muffle her laughter.

Richard was offended now. His wide face flushed and his voice rose. "Well, when will it be un-US?"

The manager stood his ground. "It will be serviceable tomorrow."

Ah, victory. "I'll take it!"

"Sorry Dick. We can't take you over the fire."

I can't believe these people. "And why, may I ask, *not?*"

The manager wouldn't take the confrontational bait. "There's a NOTAM on Wawa 43. That's a "notice to air men". We cannot fly within five miles of the fire's perimeter or lower than five miles over it."

Friggin ridiculous. "And why not?"

"It's a safety thing. There's a lot of air traffic on that fire, water bombers, helicopters, fixed wing. Rubber neckers—uninvited observers, could cause accidents and air fatalities. Sorry Dick."

Richard's mouth worked like he was chewing on a busted balloon. "Where can I rent a car or truck?"

The manager, realizing he would soon be rid of Dick Head (*how appropriate*), was more than happy to oblige. "There are two car rental agencies right on the main street in town. Just go three kilometres in that direction. " His pointed arm, hand and finger, held rigid and steady, signalled that it was time for Richard to leave.

"Yeah, I know where to go." Richard looked down at his sore feet encased in a pair of worn oxfords, turned around with as much dignity as his overweight frame could muster, and stocked out of the door.

The manager's words, not without some levity, followed him out. "And good luck, Dick. Probably most of the rentals have been scooped up by MNR." *Poor guy. Looks like a poster boy for a heart attack.*

IN HORNEPAYNE, HEATED DISCUSSION was taking place about the same time. This was the third meeting in a twenty-four hour period between fire chief Ken Waal, Mayor Ted Touluce, the town's four council members and the MNR emergency response coordinator, Greg Walsh. The dynamics of the meeting were as expected. Ken and Ted were at odds, the four frazzled council members displayed an array of non-conforming body languages and Greg sat back in the corner, a spectator at a pissing match. The issue could be summarized as follows:

Ted wanted potential evacuation efforts and resources to stand down. After all, the smoke had cleared, and the fire was heading to White River. He realized his compassion for the other community was a little tainted when he announced, "Too bad for them but better them than us." *So why stir the pot. There was no sense in upsetting my voting public.*

Ken wanted to carry on with evacuation preparation. MNR had convinced him that the reprieve was only temporary and Wawa 43 had the potential to over-run the town.

Their conversation, summarized, went something like this:

"You're over-reacting, Ken, and you can be replaced."

"You're a jerk, Ted and if we lose homes or even worse, residents, you *will* be replaced."

With fingers jabbing, arms flailing and red faces getting dangerously close, Greg knew it was time to step in. He stood up and leaned into the two prize fighters.

"Gentlemen, I really appreciate the entertainment but why don't we all sit down and I'll explain a few things to you."

The two combatants reluctantly went back to their corners.

"First, Ted. I understand your concern, but Ken is right. This fire *will* turn and with forecasted weather, we won't be able to stop it." Before Ted could jump in, Greg held up his hand. "As we speak, the fire people are mobilizing and will try to nudge the head away from Hornepayne a little and buy us some time. They'll do this with aerial and ground burn-out. "

"Secondly, a senior fire officer is assessing your community for sprinkler requirements, and a load of sprinkler heads and three ranger crews are on their way here." Again the "stop what you're going to say" hand went up.

His face hardened to stone. "And thirdly, if I'm not satisfied with your response, we," he looked towards Ken, "the Fire Marshall's Office," he looked back to Ted, "and Emergency Management Ontario, can, and *will* take over the response. How do you think that will look to the voters?"

The muscles in Ted's jaws grew slack, jaw hinges gave out, his chin dropped and his mouth opened. No words came out.

Time to give him some wiggle room. "Tell you what, Ted. Call a town meeting tonight. I'll explain the fire situation, present the options and suggest the best alternative. If, in the final analysis, there was no need to proceed with protection activities and mobilization for evacuation, MNR will have taken on the role of "chicken little". If it's the right call, you'll look like the wise but humble mayor that deferred to a higher authority. If there is a need for you to formally declare an emergency, then the support you require will be there."

Ted needed to save face, and therefore required a last word. "What will this fiasco cost us?"

Greg knew that question was coming. "No charge back for values protection. The province will eat that. Most people can get out on their own steam and have preferred places to stay. They usually don't mind covering their own expenses because they're negligible. Those who don't have a place to go or the where-with-all to get there, will be taken care of in Chapleau, your reception community, either at no cost to you or costs reimbursed where applicable. Community security will be provided by the Ontario Provincial Police at no cost to you. What it will take is your time and effort and that of your fire department and volunteers."

Ted recovered the majority of his composure, looked at Ken and declared, "Well, what are you waiting for?"

❖

THAT MORNING WALLY HAD GAZED WESTWARD at the passing cloud formation. He recalled the thoughts that had tumbled across his mind like dice on a gambling table. *Describing an earlier thought process must be a pre-dying, reflective activity.*

Now, late afternoon, Wally continued sorting his morning observations. Those clouds had been hanging really low on the horizon. They had looked like stretched, furled sails above a hull of forest, earth and rock. He had noted that each cloud-sail bottom was fringed in charcoal. The backdrop sky behind the sails was a veil of plain, white lace with patches of pale blue in the upper corners. *Why has my imagination become so vivid, lately? My creative moments are upstaging my normally dominant, analytical ones and pushing them over like dominos. Not a good sign. Time to stand the dominos up again. So, in retrospect, looks like a change in weather, but nothing significant.* He felt more comfortable now. *Analytical thoughts are considerably more efficient than creative ones.*

Wally not only noted the shift in wind direction, but also a marked change in the column of smoke to the northwest. *It's dropped considerably and not as dense.* In addition, a second, brewing column had sprung up almost due west of his position, not far from the big pine. *The fire's turned. Sure hope they can hold on.*

SHE WAS CONFUSED AND TRAPPED. The alien smell and the increasing discomfort in her eyes, nose and mouth short-circuited her instincts. The sow began to turn in circles. Her malnourished cub sat down on its haunches and watched its protector's behaviour, something new and confusing. The sow's attempts to move to higher ground had proven futile. She looked to her cub with enlarged pupils in chestnut coloured eyes, as if begging forgiveness. The cub only raised its snout and bleated. She had but one choice, retreat to the swamp that had provided protection earlier, and the water she was reluctant to cross.

FOUR DAYS EARLIER, THE SENTINEL HAD BEEN WOUNDED, almost mortally, by a rapier-driven slash of lightning. It had survived the dragon that had scuttled north-easterly, encouraged by south-westerly winds. Since then, it had been left to recover —until this day when the winds shifted from the north and began driving fire back towards it. Unburned pockets of pine needles, juniper and small balsam fir surrounding the old guard now ignited. The fire was unrelenting and its heat intense. Dragon arms leaped up. Dragon fingers caressed thick, fissured bark. Dragon hands stroked and petted its prize and slithered serpent-like, upwards to the tender morsels of green foliage it truly desired. Shadows of wispy smoke followed their liege, cloaking the sentinel in a quilt of intense heat and penetrating flame.

The dragon swayed and undulated around its prey, its hunger temporarily satiated. It felt sensual and sexy and wanted to dance. The old guard stood rigid, hypnotized, with no will to resist.

PART 4

A PROJECT FIRE

The young knight is not sure what to do; who to turn to.
Does he walk away in defeat, head down.
He senses that life could not get worse.

Oh yes, it can.
So desperate times call for desperate measures by desperate people
And he's a desperado.

Sunday, July 24th, to Tuesday, July 26th

Chapter 44

DAY 5: SUNDAY, JULY 24TH, 12:00 HOURS, ACROSS THE PROVINCE OF ONTARIO

NOT ONE OF THE TWENTY-TWO Ministry of Natural Resources' district offices, sixteen area offices or three regional offices could avoid the reluctant staff raid by the fire program. The Minister of Natural Resources had penned his authority to the declaration of an "Emergency Fire Situation" in the province, a declaration recommended by the Assistant Deputy Minister to the Deputy Minister and finally (and with respect) to the Minister.

The three regional directors had quickly lined up to pledge their support, and all other resource programs would have to take a breather. There was nothing new here, or unexpected. In simple terms, the centralized Aviation and Forest Fire Program's job was to plan for, prevent and/or fight wildfire. Resource staff associated with the districts, area offices and regions managed the forests, lands, water and wildlife. In addition, they were expected to provide fire service and support, compliance monitoring (associated with a "Restricted Fire Zone" order), community emergency services, accounting and personnel services, transport services and, in some cases, auxiliary fire crews when there wasn't any other choice.

The only other centralized service within MNR, Ontario Parks, would not walk away unscathed. There would be a lot of soul searching and hand wringing, but, in the final analysis, a good number of the one hundred and twenty-one provincial parks would provide whatever support they could. In fact, parks' staff made the best fire base camp managers and camp officers by the very nature of their jobs.

It didn't stop at MNR. Other Ontario government agencies would be asked to contribute. Emergency Management Ontario staff would be front and centre. Every available helicopter in North America would be brought into the province. Because of resource sharing agreements, fire crews would come from any or all of the western provinces and the United States. Quebec and the Maritime provinces would occasionally lend support, but more often then not, they would soon get the fire weather that routinely moved from west to east and consequently be in the same jackpot. Retirees were brought back into the fold, many with a learning curve due to out-dated notions and skills, but most with an understanding of fire or fire support and many still with common sense.

So, this big army of fire fighters needed to be transported and sheltered, fed, clothed and equipped, first aided and administered. A thousand fire fighters needed half again as many support staff throughout a complex system that started at a base camp in the bush and ended up in a regional office payroll system.

Fighting fire was not cheap. Suppression of a project fire could easily cost one hundred and fifty thousand dollars per day. That was just direct operating costs. Also, the impact of wildfire did not go unnoticed. Stopping a train for a day due to wildfire could cost the company a million dollars in lost revenues.

The loss of five years of critical wood, worth approximately fifty-five dollars a cubic metre at the mill could be devastating. A hectare of productive forests could generate a hundred and fifty to a hundred and eighty cubic metres of wood fibre. The loss of a thousand hectares of mature jack pine would mean a loss of eight to nine million dollars to a company and could force the closure of a mill where there was no wiggle room within a profit margin. Impacts were infinite and in some cases immeasurable.

At this particular time, across Ontario and other provinces and in some of States south of the border, emails were flying, phones were ringing, faxes were being spit out of machines and dropping to worn floors; employees were packing, spouses were cursing and children were crying. The experienced support staff would secretly stuff collapsible fishing rods in their packs, hoping to be sent to a remote location where a day off in twenty might yield a fishing opportunity. Most rods returned still packed and untested—fishing virgins for another year.

On the flip side, grocery store owners were rubbing their hands with glee, rental car, truck and bus agencies were cheerfully staffing up, helicopter company executives were doing their version of River Dance, retirees were doing what they do best, grumbling (and secretly calculating the extra cash they would earn—cash that might buy them an extra month at Senior World, Florida). Hotels and motels from Sudbury across to Wawa and White River were all booked solid as out-of-province crews were being filtered and moved through the big fire-fighting machine. Food caterers were frantically trying to keep up with demand.

Students, who previously couldn't find summer work, were now drivers, food packers, equipment and hose recyclers or just plain gofers. It was cash register "ca-ching" day in Ontario. On this particular day of worship, there were fewer people in churches and many more saying their good-byes and anticipating some excitement in their otherwise routine lives. Now, there was no such thing as a weekend—because wildfire waited for no one.

MNR District Office, Wawa

IN THE MIDST OF ALL THIS CHAOS AND REVELRY, Bill Gorley gingerly replaced the phone receiver on its cradle. He looked at each of the three men sitting down from him at the worn oak table. He peeked down at his notes then spoke quietly but with authority. "We've been given Wawa 43. We get command and control at 13:00 hours tomorrow. Transportation has been arranged for us at 17:00 hours today by helicopter. We'll have a temporary command centre at a MNR camp south-east of the fire. Apparently it will likely be in harm's way shortly. We have the use of that helicopter at 14:00 hours today if we want it. It's waiting at the Wawa airport. Gentlemen, we have exactly four hours to get our collective asses in gear and our best act together. Any questions?"

A hand reluctantly rose to three-quarters mast. A balding, middle aged, middle spread and vertically challenged Bill Gorley shot a stern glance at the extender of that arm and spoke: "Yes, number 1?"

A tall, thin, less than middle-aged Justin Bailey stood up. He was Bill's operations chief formerly known as a suppression boss in the old MNR world. He was responsible for the direct management of all tactical activities or "fighting the fire". "What's with the Captain Kirk routine? You know we've all been on top of this since yesterday. And which one of these poor bastards sitting next to me will be tagged with number 2?"

Bill's best feature, merry green eyes, twinkled and he smiled. "Well, I thought it sounded pretty good, didn't you?" Without waiting for an answer, he looked further down the table. "And how about you, Scotty?"

A florid faced logistics chief (service boss in the old MNR world), Tom Gregory, played along with his best (but terrible) throaty Scottish brogue, each word being coughed up like a fur ball, "Aye Captain, I've given her all she's gut and she's gut na moore." He was responsible for management of food, supplies, facilities, ground support, communications and medical support associated with the project fire.

Justin's chin dropped to his chest in a "here we go again" posture. He was the youngest of the team, the most aggressive (a good thing for an operations chief) and lacked the patience of the rest of the group. Bill not only understood this; he fostered it. He knew that Justin was destined for bigger and better things and he encouraged his enthusiasm.

Bill turned to the last member of the team, "Steady Eddy" Buckner, and raised his eyebrows. You could light a firecracker under Ed's ass, but he would likely sit on it without fan-fare and put it out. "Did we wake you up, Ed?"

Ed looked over the reading glasses perched on a wide, flat nose and in his best farm-laden Prince Edward Island monotone drawl responded, "No, no, it's OK. I was asleep anyway." Ed was the team's planning chief and as such was responsible for the gathering and analysis of all data regarding project fire operations. Key units under his supervision included "Resource" (where are all resources, including personnel, situated on the fire), "Situation" (what's going on right now and what is likely to happen in the near future) and "Documentation" (development of the daily project fire action plan and maintaining all documentation associated with the fire). He was also responsible for demobilization planning (when the fire was UCO and it was time to demobilize resources) and Technical Specialists (such as fire behaviour specialist, meteorologists, environmental impact specialist or resource use and cost specialist).

An observer might be forgiven if he thought this foursome were either not the sharpest knives in the drawer or entirely too frivolous about their assignment. He would, however, be entirely wrong. Their humour was a tool used often to control nervous energy. They were all professionals, hand picked to manage a critical, complex situation. This was their fourth project fire together in two fire seasons. They respected and liked each other. Each knew his role thoroughly, and it wasn't often that Bill had to step in to provide direction.

His team managed the wildfire. Bill guided their activities and dealt with all outside influences that included nervous resource managers, politically pressured program managers and regional directors, threatened communities, impacted industries and information-hungry media. An incident commander had to have confidence and emanate "presence", be strong and clear in his direction, be fair and show compassion, defend his people when they were right and defend (and correct) them when they were wrong. He was ultimately responsible so the buck stopped at *his* doorstep. A little humour never hurt.

It was time, however, to get serious. "Gentlemen, let me lay it out for you." Bill looked to Ed, who had already begun to take meeting notes.

"As of yesterday at 15:00 hours, Wawa 43 was mapped at six thousand, five hundred hectares. North winds have slowed down its progress to the north-east but the fire is now moving in a south-westerly direction. You with me so far?"

Justin jumped in. "Does Wawa fire management have an idea on the present size?"

"I haven't got anything back on that, but under the current weather situation, we can expect it to be double in size today and considerably larger tomorrow."

Bill continued. "Hornepayne is out of the woods—temporarily. White River, however, is another story. They're presently in smoke.

The good news is that the north winds are expected to shift to the south sometime tomorrow, so I don't believe the fire is a serious threat to White River."

Bill's tight-lipped smile indicated he was moving to the "bad news" side of the equation. "The bad news is that north winds are expected to shift to the south sometime tomorrow." Bill paused to let the redundancy sink in. "So the fire *is* a threat to Hornepayne."

"Apparently, Wawa district has an emergency response coordinator with some support staff in there now. An Emergency Management Ontario (EMO) rep is on his way, and the town is evoking their ER Plan. We all know that the protection and evacuation of Hornepayne is in the district's hands. Our job is to wrestle Wawa 43 into submission. However, our strategy and tactics will be greatly influenced by the need to keep fire out of that community."

Justin was anxious to share suppression information. "Bill, I understand Russ Gervais is presently the fire boss—I mean, incident commander. Everyone was still struggling with the changeover to the U.S ICS jargon. "I've talked to the SRO down the hall and he's filled me in. Can we discuss it now?"

Shit, there goes my train of thought—patience, patience, poppa bear. "Sure, go ahead, Justin."

"First off, Russ has managed to protect the cut wood to the west. His hose lines to the south didn't hold, so the crews there have been pulled. Because of the shift in wind direction, he's pulled the staging area equipment out of the cutover. Here's the kicker. Besides taking a run at Wawa 43, he's also looking after values protection to the north and south of the fire. He must be one tired puppy."

Rueful smiles were shared all around. They had all been in that particular boat.

"As we speak, he's preparing to do a burnout north of the fire. He figures he may be able to coax it north-west when the winds come back from the south. Let me show you."

Justin walked over to a new section of map next to the large map on the wall and pointed. "There are two pieces between White Owl and McCoy lakes with a pond in between, a piece between McCoy and Shekak and another piece between Shekak and Obakamiga Lakes. He's hoping the wetlands due east of the fire will slow prog-

ress down there. However, drought conditions make that particular tactic suspect."

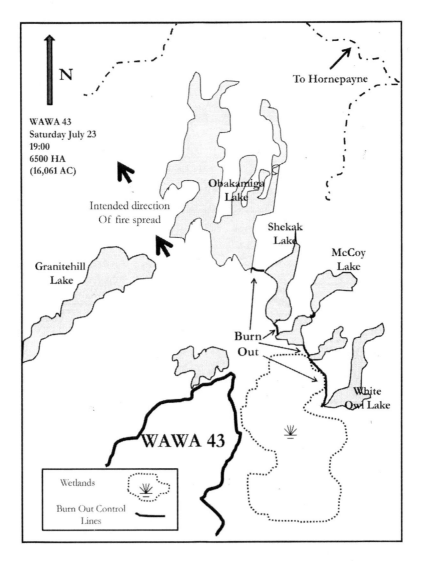

Tom Gregory stepped in. "Likely has no other options."

"I agree Tom, and I would have done the same thing. However,
my confidence metre is registering pretty low. If that swamp holds
back fire, I'll gladly kiss your butt."

With his best rendition of a defeated 'EYOR' voice from Winnie
the Pooh, Ed mumbled in, "I … sure … hope … the swamp …
holds back … fire."

After the laughter subsided, bill continued. "We all know what we have to do, but I want to hear it from you. Keep it short, Tom?"

"Well, I've already touched base with the service section here in Wawa to establish resource protocols, and I'm in the process of finding us a suitable base camp location that we won't have to abandon if Wawa 43 decides to take another big run."

Bill looked to Ed. "Ed?"

"I've got my hands on a slew of maps, a base camp radio to get us started and a list of available crews when you want to draw on them. I also have a good handle on location and availability of air attack resources, including helicopters. Don't know if you already know this, but a long team is here in Wawa at your disposal so that will kick-start us with logistics, planning and finance support staff. I'm in the process of arranging for on-site weather technician and fire behaviour officer."

Bill, as usual was impressed. "Good work, gentlemen. Justin and I will be leaving you shortly to take a look at our new project. We'll be back in two or three hours. Tom, can you arrange ground transport for us? I don't want a driver. I want our own vehicle, preferably a crew cab to get us out to the new base camp, when you firm that up, and ensure were mobile."

"Consider it done, Bill."

"And keep in mind that most of our resource requests will go directly to the project fire duty officer, Zander Cybulski, at the Falcon Response Centre in Sudbury. Ed, I assume you have the SAT phone in your kit."

"All set to go, Bill."

"Good. Justin and I will see you guys in a few hours. I'm sure we'll have plenty to discuss."

14:00 hours, over Wawa 43

THE JET RANGER HELICOPTER PROGRESSED SLOWLY along the south-west flank of the fire, its two passengers focused on the task at hand, updating the existing fire map and assessing its potential for spread and impact. Consequently, the pilot was asked to occasionally take them well outside the fire line.

Justin sat in the front to the left of the pilot, his headset pushing the ball cap with the Aviation and Forest Fire Management logo low on his head, blond curls of hair sweeping up from the sides. He intently scanned the horizon, head slowly rotating, dark brown eyes squinting and firing laser guided looks at an array of targets. At the same time he was making notes on a large scale, 1:250,000 topographic map—notes only he could decipher as the helicopter jigged in a stiff breeze.

Bill sat in the back, right behind Justin with the same configuration of headset over cap, but no hair peaked out. He often bragged that he was follicley challenged. Bill was also taking notes, not so much on the fire (although he made a few mental notes to discuss with Justin) but on management issues. The trip over the area gave him the perspective he needed and the time to pull his thoughts together.

It was hot in the helicopter. Both men had slid their windows open and would occasionally stick a hand out at a forty-five degree angle to catch wind and deflect it back towards the little rivers of sweat springing out from under ball cap brims. Notes were important. When they returned, the team would have to do a thorough assessment of the fire for presentation to the district manager, the person ultimately responsible for resource management in the area. There would be little sleep tonight for the quartet.

Justin turned to the pilot. "If you don't mind, take us north to the area being burned out. I'd like to see the fire behaviour there."

The pilot nodded, took his machine up to a three thousand feet, picked up speed and headed straight for a series of small columns of smoke about fifteen kilometres north. A Birddog, CL415 and a helicopter were working the area, and the pilot cleared approach with the Birddog officer. The smoke in the columns was thick, dark and active. The pilot asked for and received clearance for an approach by the Birddog officer who advised them to fly at fifteen hundred feet.

"Bill, looks like some good fire behaviour up ahead."

Bill looked up from his notes, "I copy that Justin. What are they using for burn out?"

"I believe its aerial, using a helitorch with crews on the ground using drip torches."

"How much are they burning?"

"Apparently, the crews are burning out along five kilometres of hose line. The helitorch is working the interior—close to a thousand hectares all told."

"Will those lines or the wetlands to the east hold when the wind comes around from the south tomorrow?"

Justin swung his head around, shrugged and replied, "Good question boss. That's what we're going to take a look at now."

The jet ranger banked, dropped and headed for the east side of the mountain of smoke.

Chapter 45

DAY 5: 14:00 HOURS, NORTH END OF WAWA 43

T HE GELLED GASOLINE WAS DRAWN THROUGH THE PUMP, past the propane igniter. Globs of fire fell out of the nozzle, dropped and plopped unceremoniously on the ground on dead or decaying logs and branches and in live trees and bushes. One of the mixing crew had ordained the mixture, "hot snot". The gelatinous substance was suspended in a 205 litre drum five metres below Helitack 31, held fast by two cables. The lifeline to the pump and propane heater was through heavy electrical cable. The ignition boss on board controlled pumping, gel combustion and determined the ignition pattern in order to lay the most effective fire. One of the mixing crew was onboard, in the back. The door on the port side had been removed so he could actually see if the helitorch was working properly.

Helitack 31 cruised in lazy circles, a three hundred feet above the forest canopy. Fire was instantaneous and spectacular. Spruce and balsam fir literally exploded with ten-metre tree-tops flung into the maelstrom. The crackle of fire climbing the trees was soon followed by the ear splitting whoosh of the torching. Torching flames joined, then raced through continuous tree crowns. There was no break in forest fuels, and the wall of fire built up momentum. It first sounded like giant stone wheels grinding and fracturing concrete into powder. It then became an enormous, rolling train, climbing grade with a "CHUG, CHUG, CHUG." Brilliant orange and yellow flame sails billowed sixty to one hundred metres into a black, smoke filled sky. Sixty-metre fire whirls danced and twirled like tornado dervishes, picking up whole trees and spiking them into the ground with such force that they were imbedded, like javelins. The dragon must have thought that this was simply marvellous. It stood on a podium of fire, and conducted this overwhelming piece like the "Sorcerer's Apprentice." If this wasn't hell, it was the next best thing.

THREE KILOMETRES TO THE NORTH, Cindy Corrigan had no time to admire the light-show. She and her crew were, as Jim put it, up to their collective asses in alligators. They had laid thirty-two lengths of hose, a kilometre, and completed a back-pass as well to establish a fire line so they could burn out. She was presently in the process of burning out with a hand-held drip torch. Her crew were following her, letting fire run south with the prevailing north winds, putting out fire close to them and keeping an eye out for jump fires behind them.

This time her 2IC, Jim Henderson, set the pace. He was on the nozzle, and there was no point in Cindy getting too far ahead in case he ran into trouble. Four other crews were doing the same thing. It was hoped that the intense heat generated from the heli-torch fire would quickly draw the hand ignition fires southerly—in effect, creating another thousand to fifteen hundred hectares of burned area, but now with an established control line and natural barriers. Russ Gervais had briefed the crews that morning. He rue-fully advised them that this would not stop the fire, only turn it westerly when the winds swung from the south. In his own words, "We're just buying time for Hornepayne."

Cindy's MT1000 crackled. "Hold up Cindy, We've got a couple of small jump fires behind us."

"Can you handle them Jim or do you need air support?"

Jim's voice was strained and she could here heavy breathing coming through the little transceiver on her radio. "We can handle it OK, Cin. Just need ten minutes."

"Jim, don't be too long, my fire wants to back burn in the worst way. If we get torching, we may have more jumps to worry about."

A laboured, "Copy that, Cin" came back to her.

"Jim, you OK?"

"Oh yeah. One of the jumps is on a thirty-metre ridge top. Pulling hose up and through this shit is testing my good will."

"Jim, just give me the word when you're ready."

Jim keyed his mic twice as confirmation. Five minutes later, her radio crackled again.

"Cin, we've got a problem—blew a hose somewhere back down the line. I've sent Tim back with some hose to deal with it."

Cindy's could actually feel the spike in her blood pressure. "How about the jumps?"

"Got one OK. The other could be a problem."

Here we go again. Pull myself together. "Do you need me back there, Jim?"

"Why, so we could both watch water *not* coming out of a nozzle?"

RUSS GERVAIS WAS IN HELITACK 21 taking this all in. Although the crews were talking ground to ground on their own discrete frequencies, Russ had the scanner on and could pick up everything that was said by the four crews doing the burn out.

"Corrigan from Helitack 21 on 2, do you copy?"

The fairy godfather has been listening in. "Helitack 21 from Corrigan. Go ahead."

"Yeah, Cindy, do you need some help?"

"You've been reading my mind, Russ. Can we get a 415 over here to hit a jump fire?"

"Affirmative. Pull your people back. Birddog 18 will lead the tanker in. He'll drop loads at his discretion. In the meantime, keep burning. We'll help you out if it's necessary."

"Thanks, Russ. Corrigan clear."

Similar scenarios were playing across five kilometres of burn out. It was a total team effort. If a crew got into problems, Russ was there to provide direction and the two CL415's provided insurance. Even the wetlands to the east held—with a lot of pre-wetting from the big yellow birds. As Russ had put it, "If you could pick up some of that swamp in your hands, and wring it out, you'd be lucky to get a cup full of water."

IT WAS NOW 16:00 HOURS. The helitorch had long gone and the mixing crew was back at the staging area cleaning the unit and packing up. Lines had held up to this point and crews were exhausted. Russ and H21 were taking a long, slow look at the results of the burn-out and paying particular attention to the areas just north of the control lines. He had released the Birddog and two tankers back to Wawa for fuel and was feeling particularly pleased with himself when the helicopter's radio came to life. Fire crew chatter escalated simultaneously. Everyone was experiencing fire behaviour problems. *What the hell is going on?* What Russ didn't realize now but would find out later, that the forecasted relative humidity of 40% would be wrong. It had dropped to 30%, dramatically reducing moisture content in the combustible fuels and exponentially increasing flash points for combustion and intense fire behaviour.

He looked down. *Oh, no!* Tell-tale plumes of grey-black smoke were popping up along the burn-out fire lines on the wrong side. Now, air attack was out of the question with the release of the CL415 package back for fuel. Conversations with each crew painted the same picture—jump fires behind them with extreme behaviour, burnt hose and lack of water, and retreat to handle flanking fire instead of advancing to tie in the lines. Russ had no choice. He ordered the crews back to their pump sites and called in two of the medium helicopters for evacuation. The dragon had won another battle.

"Helitack 21, this is Helitack 45, do you copy?"

Who the hell is that? Russ keyed his mic. "Go ahead 45."

"Russ, this is Justin Bailey. We've got Bill Gorley on board as well and we're approaching the north end of Wawa 43. Can you clear us in?"

Ah, the new kid on the block. "Come on in, Justin. What can we do for you?"

"Just wanted to look at the burn-out operation. How did it go?"

"It's all over with but the crying. Can't be contained. Have to pull the crews so you'll forgive me if I can't hang around to chat."

Justin wasn't one to stand on ceremony. "This will be our fire tomorrow, so I need a sense of where we're at. Did the swamp hold?"

Russ could feel his face flush. "In a manner of speaking, yes. We added to its water table."

Bill Gorley could read the touch of anger in the response and jumped in. He knew his operations chief and suspected Russ was cut from the same cloth. Ego plus testosterone equalled confrontation. "Russ, it's Bill here. We were given a pretty good briefing on your fire. I understand that you've accomplished a lot with a little and only had to put in twenty-eight hour days. Will you have a couple of hours to spend with us tonight? I'd like to pick your brain on this one."

"Happy to, Bill. I can tell you right now, though, that this one is likely to take a big run north when the winds come around tonight. The burn out was intended to buy Hornepayne a little time."

"See you in Wawa, Russ. Is 20:00 hours OK with you?"

"Fine with me. I'm going to spend a little time here with the crews, then tuck them in. See you at 20:00 hours."

The next hour was a blur. Russ had been working on adrenalin and his tank was running dry. When he talked, his tongue felt out of sync and words fell out of his mouth like pancake batter pored onto a skillet – slowly and in thick, uneven puddles. Crews managed to come out battered and bruised, but intact with pumps, camping equipment and personal gear. Four kilometres of fire hose had been left back on the fire line—there would be little left to retrieve later on. They would collect any unburned hose and couplings they could find from the burned hose, but Russ wasn't optimistic. *There goes about twenty thousand dollars worth of hose.*

Russ felt bad for the crew members. They had given everything they had and failed. He had been there himself, many times. He had taken that same ride home. Slumped and exhausted in the big medium helicopter, head down, shoulders bouncing with the uneven rhythm of main rotor shake. Some would be asleep, chins on chest. Others, especially crew leaders would be flush with either shame or anger at defeat. He also knew that it would pass into resolve once the realization kicked in that they had fought and lost, but would fight again.

The H21 pilot, Sid, looked over at his passenger. *Russ looks like shit.* "Russ, we need to go for fuel. That OK with you?"

Russ smiled. "I'm too tired to flap my arms, so what options do we have?"

A totally exhausted Russ Gervais pulled off his headset, slunk low in his seat belt and immediately fell asleep. The long ranger helicopter banked south-west and floated towards the horizon, a metal and glass hummingbird looking for a perch.

Chapter 46

DAY 6: MONDAY, JULY 25TH, 17:00 HOURS, FALCON RESPONSE CENTRE, SUDBURY

MUCH OF NORTH AMERICA WAS "ON THE BRINK." In Canada, the Province of Ontario had not experienced drought conditions like this since 1988. The east half of the province grappled with four project fires and forty to fifty new fires each day. Burning conditions were spiking in the west half of the province. All of Ontario's two hundred and five initial attack crews were committed, either on fires or on red alert at the forty-five fire headquarters and attack bases throughout the province. British Columbia, Alberta, Saskatchewan and Manitoba had just turned off the resource tap—no more stuff for Ontario. Quebec was holding on tight to what it had. As Ontario goes, so goes Quebec. Only the Maritime Provinces kept the door open—a crack. South of the border, signature fire-prone states, California, Washington and Oregon, were getting nervous. Part of the Great Lakes states, Wisconsin, Minnesota and Michigan were scrambling to keep up with new fire starts.

Sheila Monahan was given the task of explaining the system to a newbee, a university student hired to help out personnel in the fire centre. Sheila realized it was best to keep it simple.

"So given these conditions, one might not be surprised if the head fire guy in Ontario borrowed a quote from a not so famous Jim Carey movie: "We're in a pickle, Dick." However, not so fast. To explain, let's start with the smallest common denominator, the incident commander on a project fire. Let's say he needs ten more fire crews— yesterday. His planning chief would send in a request to the local fire management headquarters. The SRO, sector response officer there, would more than likely declare, "Got nothing here. Pass it on to the RFC, regional fire centre."

The student was nodding her head vigorously with understanding, while at the same time the glaze in her eyes suggested otherwise. Sheila continued. "The RFC's FDO, fire duty officer, my boss, who by now has misplaced his sense of humour, would say to no one in particular, "Are they kidding, add more resources to the request and pass the whole shebang to the head office for fire in Sault Ste. Marie—AFFMB. That's Aviation and Forest Fire Management Branch. Now, the PDO, *provincial* duty officer there, after coming down from a fit of laughter, has to seriously entertain this request from the East Fire Region while reviewing a similar request from the WFR, West Fire Region."

Nod, nod, nod.

Sheila thought, *Yeah, right. I lost you at "pickle, Dick."*

"To keep it simple, let's pretend Ontario needs one hundred additional widgets but only has fifty to spare. Where does it go for more widgets? The PDO picks up the phone and calls CIFFC, the Canadian Interagency Forest Fire Centre, in Winnipeg, Manitoba. The conversation might go like this:

"Hi, George, this is Ed. Can you get me fifty widgets?"

"Let me check, Ed. Let's see. British Columbia, nil, Alberta, no, Saskatchewan, nada, Manitoba, ditto! Quebec and the Maritime provinces, ten! I can get you ten widgets from the rest of Canada, Ed. Gotta go south for the other forty. Get back to you."

Sheila was beginning to enjoy this. "Now George at CIFFC calls Fred at NIFC, the National Interagency Fire Centre in Boise, Idaho." She unconsciously dropped her voice, mimicking a more masculine tone.

"Fred, how's she go?"

"Can't complain, George. What can I do you for?"

"Need forty widgets."

The newbee put her hand up with an "I gotcha" look on her face. "I thought Ed needed fifty widgets."

Oh boy, a candidate for a gene pool cleansing exercise. "Remember? Quebec and the Maritimes could provide ten. Fifty minus ten equals …?"

The newbees eyes flipped skyward, her mouth screwed up and an intense look of concentration crossed her face. After twenty gruelling seconds she declared, "Have you got a calculator?"

A frustrated Sheila declared, "It's forty. Fifty minus ten equals forty! I'll continue." *Who the hell's at NIFC, oh yeah—Fred.* "So Fred checks his inventory and proudly advises, "I can only give you thirty widgets."

'Thanks Fred, we'll take 'em'."

"George reverses the process and advises … what's his name? … ED, the provincial duty officer, that the good old US of A can only provide thirty widgets. Ed decides that will have to do and lets EFR and WFR know." Sheila was proud of her simplification of a complicated process and asked, "Any questions?"

A hesitant newbee replied, "Yes. Who's Jim Carey and what's a widget?"

Same time, north of White River, Siren Lake

WALLY STUMBLED INTO THE OUT-HOUSE completely exhausted. He had slept very little the night before, and the day went downhill from there. The pain had been coming in shorter intervals and the painkillers seemed to have lost some of their punch. To top it off, they were constipating. *Probably die from an aneurysm from all that straining.* To assist the painkillers, last night he had polished off one of the bottles of whisky strategically stashed throughout the cabin. *Just like reading glasses—need them within easy reach.*

While he was passing time in the narrow, stuffy, aromatic building, he dredged up an eclectic array of thoughts. *Head feels like giant, hairy spiders crawling through blankets of cobwebs. It took them twelve years to make that bottle of whisky and only two days for me to drink it.* He looked down. *The older I get the more my scrotum looks like a pair of elephant ears with a short trunk. Oh well, at least my humour hasn't vacated the premises.*

He finished hiking up his pants and drew in the belt. *Dropping more weight. Not a good sign. Can't afford to crap too often … might lose something important next time. Oops! There goes my liver, or is that a kidney?*

Deep down inside Wally knew that his attempt at humour was an effort to mask his fear of the "big sleep." He shuffled to the Chevy bench on the front porch of the cabin and looked across the lake. *Winds finally changed. Coming from the south-west, and at a respectable pace. Geez, the fire is quartering this way. Probably gonna hit the lake and that swamp this afternoon.* He thought about the bear cub he had heard a few days ago. *Well, here I am. Can't move. Can't call for help. No one here anyway. Can't get my face out of the dirt. Congratulations Wallace, the village has a new idiot.*

Wally decided to pour himself a coffee. It was this morning's pot, and he knew he might have to chew it. He stood up and then it hit him. A pain—like something tore inside—a pair of big hands ripping a telephone book in half. Only this book was part of Wally's internal life support system. The bastard worm seemed to crouch, then spring inside his body, throwing it to the ground, like a rag doll cast off by a petulant child. His arms were useless, unresponsive appendages. He managed to scuttle up to his knees, the rest of his body supported by a face that was still firmly planted in the ground on one cheek. The pressure on the dirt side of his head forced his mouth into an ugly kidney-shaped opening. An attempt to scream came without sound. A steady, meandering stream of drool joined rivulets of sweat—and tears. His head buzzed like an angry hornet's nest, and then, a sucking vacuum sound like the closing of a black hole as the pain disappeared. Then—nothing.

Wally could not scream, speak, feel or hear. But he could still see—and think. His face still planted in the ground, he watched fascinated, as the river of mixed body fluids wound its way around tufts of dry grass, pebbles and sticks. Well, here I am. Can't move. Can't call for help. No one here anyway. Can't get my face out of the dirt. Congratulations Wallace, the village has a new idiot.

Look! There's a colony of ants marching this way. Probably crawl up my nose and pick away at my brain. Over here guys! All-you-can-eat brain buffet. He tried to blink the sweat out of his eyes. *Well ladi-friggin'-da! There's a cricket. Can't be more than six inches away. Just sitting there staring. Ha! A staring contest. Let's see who blinks first.*

Pretty embarrassing way to die—my face in the dirt and my ass in the air. How will I ward off the turkey vultures? Maybe I can still pass wind.

That'll do it. How long can I keep it up? As I recall, the longest fart in history was forty-seven seconds. Happened at a baked-bean eating contest sponsored by over-eaters anonymous. Man, the mind works in mysterious ways.

Fifteen minutes had elapsed. The ants ignored Wally as they passed by. *Hup, one, two, three! Hup, one, two, three, foreword Ho-o-o!* Neither Wally nor the cricket blinked. *But we both want to.* And there were no vultures perched on his ass. *Good thing for them.*

Time passes ever so slowly when you can't ignore it by doing something. Then Wally began to feel some sensation in his fingers, then his hands and finally his arms. He pushed his upper body up. *Do I try to stand up now or crawl to the front porch? Crawling is undignified but likely the better of the two options.* Wally shuffled on all fours over to the steps, then up them until he could grab a porch banister. With considerable effort, he pulled his failing body into an upright position.

Then he heard it before he saw it—the 'whup-whup-whup' of a helicopter. It came in from behind, over the cabin, turned at the lakeshore, flared and dropped gently onto patch of yellow grass that had quit trying to be green. The main rotor decelerated and the blades took on a defined shape as they rotated slowly and dropped.

Chapter 47

DAY 6: 19:00 HOURS, SIREN LAKE, WALLY'S CAMP

W ALLY SAT ON THE PORCH STILL CLUTCHING THE BANISTER, his breathing shallow and rapid. *Came in like the angel of death.* He watched as a person stepped out of the helicopter, bent over at the waist to avoid the blades. *The fire crew leader—Cindy.*

"You been out rolling around in the fire, young lady?" Slashes and spatters in ash-black randomly criss-crossed a red Nomex two-piece jump suit. Her face was black streaked and smudged. It was like she had been placed in a bag of charcoal, shaken and tossed.

"Looks like you've gone a round or two yourself, Mr. McNeil. Are you OK?"

Wally faked a grimace. "Indigestion. What brings you here?"

Indigestion, my ass. "I'm going to test run the pumps for the sprinkler system. When the time comes for the real show, your camp is going to be wet. You'll either have to stay inside or head to town. I'd really like you to head to town."

"You'd have a better chance of pushing water uphill."

"Well, you'll be in smoke, and if the fire jumps the lake it could be worse."

Wally screwed up his mouth, a sign of mild exasperation. "Look, Cindy. If I get into trouble I'll take the ATV out to the truck and leave."

Will you? Time for a bit of hardball. "Can we sit down somewhere and talk, Mr. McNeil?

"Sure. The coffee's on. Come on inside."

Cindy looked back to the helicopter and drew her hand past her throat, a signal for the pilot to cut the engine.

Wally poured two steaming cups and they both sat at the kitchen table, across from each other—two boxers waiting for the bell. There would be no sparing, just a simple punch-out. "Mr. McNeil, I'm aware of your situation, and I'm truly sorry. I'm probably too young to understand how you deal with it." *Here goes nothing.* "But if you die here because of the fire or smoke, then I'll be spending the rest of the summer doing paper work—and I hate paper work."

Her attempt at levity did not go over well. Wally leaned forward. *Time for me to be frank.* "Cindy, I know *you* know my situation." He now chose his words carefully. "Just before you showed up, I thought I was as close to dying as anyone could be." Wally's smile turned down and became rigid. "I'm a little fragile right now, and I apologize for being so self centred, but frankly, I don't give a rat's ass about the amount of paper work you would have to do." His hard look softened. "And again, call me Wally."

Well that didn't go so well. "Sorry Wally". Cindy paused to wrestle with a small confession. *Why am I drawn to open up to this shrinking, little man?* "Do you remember when I bared my soul the other day and told you about being trapped by the fire and discovered I wasn't immortal?" *Fierce woman gladiator wasn't so fierce.* "Well, I guess I came as close to death as I really wanted to, and I wasn't proud of my reaction. I know it's selfish, but I'm pretty fragile right now, and I just can't deal with any hard questions if you die on my watch."

Wally remained silent and Cindy wrestled for the right words. "I think you and I are connected in some way. If you die, then I'll face mortality again every time I think of you." She took a big breath, her eyes raised up as if looking for divine guidance. "I'm not a religious person, but I do believe there is a God, and I want to be proud of myself when I face Her."

Her? Good for you. "Cindy, the problem with religion is that it takes itself too seriously. Governments even use it to support immoral decisions with the "God is on our side" card. They can justify almost anything—hate, genocide and rape if they believe God is backing their agenda. I wouldn't be too concerned about being religious. Whenever you run into a dilemma, just ask yourself this question, "What's the *right* thing to do?" Once you answer that question, take your own advice, and you'll be OK. Imagine what the world would be like today if politicians asked themselves that very question before they screwed over some poor shmuck."

Cindy either ignored or didn't digest the little rant. "How the hell do you deal with mortality, Wally?"

He took a slow deep breath. *Not very well, but this girl needs something to hold on to. Maybe she can be a check mark on the "good" side of my ledger. Dying can be as selfish as living.* He took a sip of his coffee.

"I'll let you in on my take on belief, God and a ticket to heaven. But you have to promise not to laugh."

"Wally, I can use anything right now. Things aren't going so well in my corner."

"I'm not used to sharing thoughts lately, let alone the deep, serious ones. So stop me if you think I've crossed the line from stupid to ridiculous."

Cindy nodded her consent to begin.

"I'm beginning to think that life here on earth is the real heaven. However, being here *now* is no guarantee that it's permanent. Why? Let's say we're given notice through revelations or epiphanies. They can be simple and everyday like watching snow melt on an early, warm spring day, or experiencing the comfort of a true friendship or acknowledging that love exists between two people."

He paused to raise a critical eyebrow towards the young woman sitting across from him. *Can you take a hint?* "That last one is called a commitment, and sometimes egos get in the way. Are you with me so far?"

"Yes, but I wouldn't call my last three days as being in heaven."

"Well, here's the conundrum. We get tested. I think we're both in "test" mode right now. Whether we stay after we croak, get reincarnated or get sent down to the minors depends on how we dealt with the testing—how we lived."

"So, are you saying it's the little joys we recognize in life and how we deal with them?"

"Right. But too may people take them for granted. So, God sometimes sends a stronger message, one that's hard to ignore."

"Such as?"

"I'll give you two examples that the certainty of dying has brought to mind." Wally cleared his throat and hesitated, fearing that sharing was somehow weak. "You know that I've been a trapper as a sideline for several years now."

Cindy nodded an affirmative.

"As I was field dressing a large beaver, I was hit with a revelation. With few exceptions, all the creatures on this earth possess the same internal life system as humans—heart, stomach, arteries, intestinal system—all similar in shape and function. I realized that it couldn't be random. It had to be by design, God's design. By the way, that notion seemed to dampen my zeal for trapping."

Wally looked for a reaction from Cindy, a trigger that would tell him either she seriously considered this a gem set in some truth or that he was certifiable.

Cindy's face gave away nothing. "Go on Wally."

"My second example was an epiphany—a really big revelation. It happened in March of 1997. We were at our lodge. My lab pup decided it was time to take me out for a walk. The night was so crisp; each breath was like drawing fine, crushed ice into the lungs. The crust on the snow was thick and rigid, tightened up from the day's thaw. We could both walk across the top, like it was a concrete sidewalk. She was—joyous, yeah, joyous. She skipped, and jumped and wheeled across this crystal playground like Snoopy dancing on top of his dog house. Now picture this—and I'm about to get creative."

Wally paused for inspiration. "The trees threw bold shadows down on the snow and the pup would jump from one to the other, like she was playing hop-scotch. There was a large, full moon—so bright, you would shade your eyes to look at it. That was in one part of the sky. In the other part, the Hale-Bopp comet arched through the night's black like a flaming arrow, at over a hundred and fifty thousand kilometres per hour. At that very moment, I could feel my heart beating and my chest heaving, and I was literally overcome with an overwhelming realization. God does exist! He has to! There is no other explanation!"

Wally had been caught up in his excitement. As he came down, he realized he might have lost his disciple.

Cindy did not respond. She did not know how to respond. She only looked at the little man.

What's in that look? Disbelief? Confusion? Pity? God, don't let it be pity. "Cindy, what I'm trying to tell you is that you survived that fire for a reason. I'm not sure what it is. Only you will know. It was by design. Your instincts will tell you. Whether or not you choose to follow them is up to you. "

Cindy didn't know how to respond. Any words she could design and package would only minimize the value she placed on his counsel. Just as she was about to respond, the MT1000 on her belt crackled, and the pilot's voice scuttled the moment.

"Cindy from Helitack 45."

She slowly reached down to retrieve her radio and place the mic near her lips. Her eyes maintained a connection with Wally's and her facial expression spoke volumes. *I think I understand. I'm only sorry that it takes your dying to start my living.*

"Go ahead 45."

"Yeah Cindy, just got word. We gotta go. All the crews on the south end of the fire have been having a tough time—including yours. Russ wants you back with them."

"Give me five. I'll test the pumps. You can fire up your machine now." Cindy looked at Wally. *I'll run up the pumps. If I show you how, can you let them run for fifteen minutes then shut them down?*"

"No need to show me, young lady. I've run a few Mark-3's in my time."

Cindy put her radio back in its case and held out her hand to the old trapper. "Thanks Wally. It's been a privilege."

Wally allowed a tiny smile on his dirt-smeared face. He felt a wave of peace wash over his fragile body. "No. Thank you, Cindy. For some reason, I'm not scared anymore. I believe I owe you for that." He paused to flesh out another thought. "I'm sixty-four years old, so I've lived close to twenty-four thousand days. In any lifetime, a person is lucky if they can count their meaningful days on two hands. Today might not be in my top ten—but it's not far off."

Their handshake lasted for several seconds. They both knew that this would be a short friendship, one that Wally would hold dear for as long as he could and one that Cindy would never forget. Five minutes later he heard the pump and the water from the sprinkler heads hitting the tin roof on his camp, followed shortly by the sound of the helicopter as it faded in the distance.

Have a good life, young lady.

Chapter 48

DAY 6: 20:00 HOURS, WAWA FIRE MANAGEMENT HEADQUARTERS

"**W**ELCOME BACK TO HOCKEY NIGHT IN CANADA."
I'm Bob Krole and your analyst, Harry Beale, is on
my right. The third period is just about to get underway. Don't go away, folks. It's a dandy. The Dragon, four, and the
Dragon Slayers, two. Harry, do you think the Dragon Slayers can
pull this one out of the hat?"

"I don't know, Bob. They can't sit back. They have to attack. The
Dragon has too much *fire* power."

"Harry, just a recap for any new viewers out there. In the first period, the Dragon was first to score when it escaped initial attack."

"Yes, but the Dragon Slayers came back hard with that burn-out
to save the cut wood, so both teams finished the first period in a
one-one tie. I really thought the Dragon was the better team in the
first, though."

"It came out strong again in the second period when it took that
run to the north and then a huge run to the south."

"You're right, Bob. The Dragon *burned* the Slayers for two goals
there. With only five minutes left in the second, the Dragon Slayers
were down three to one. But then the Dragon seemed to let up a bit
and the Dragon slayers pulled within one with that big burn-out
to the north. It seemed we had a game, three to two. And I thought
the Slayers had some momentum going for them until they lost the
burn-out. Now it's four to two."

"Whadaya thinks gonna happen in the third, Harry?"

"That's a real tough one, Bob. What I can't understand is that neither team has played their big guns tonight. Strong Winds is sitting on the end of the Dragon's bench and he doesn't look too happy. And Heavy Rain isn't even dressed for the Dragon Slayers. I know both coaches haven't been too thrilled with their play of late, but you gotta go with what got you here in the first place."

"Well fans across Canada and our neighbours watching too the south, they're about to drop the puck. Hold on to your hats, this period is gonna be a barn *burner.*"

My imagination is running wild like a nasty kid with overly tired parents. Russ Gervais sat in a vintage wooden chair at the Wawa fire management headquarters with legs splayed out, work-boot laces undone and his face in his hands. He was massaging his eyes with his finger-tips. He knew he had done everything humanly possible to nail this fire. He also knew from the get-go that it was a losing proposition. He looked down at the map on his desk.

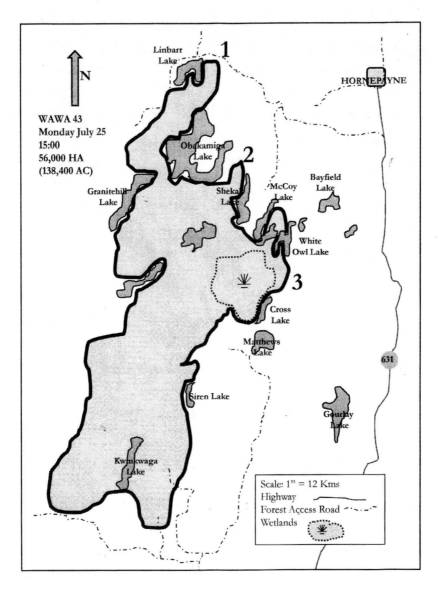

His burn-out had added another fifteen hundred hectares to Wawa 43. However, the two-day run to the south was the kicker. Wawa 43 was now an impressive fifty-six thousand hectares. In acres, it had broken the one hundred thousand mark and climbed to one hundred and thirty-eight thousand, four hundred. This sucker was now fifty-six kilometres long and averaged ten kilometres wide, and only twelve kilometres from White River.

That run to the south was expected, and he knew they didn't have the resources, or the ability, to stop it. They had gambled on a two to three day north wind, and they had won that bet. What bothered him the most was how quickly the fire ran north-west this afternoon when the wind switched from the south.

Yesterday, his burn-out looked like it might hold, but the low RH's had screwed him. Jump fires had popped up late and converged with break-outs on the leading edge of the burn-out. Russ had no choice but to pull the crews and use them on the south end of the fire where they could actually work and do some good. His only piece of advice last night to the new incident commander was simple: initiate the evacuation of Hornepayne.

Today, when the winds switched and came from the south, they did so with a vengeance. Russ could only watch the north end of the fire, a spectator to an impressive light show. Russ looked down at the map again. He had marked the areas of concern as 1, 2 and 3. *Tonight's meeting with the incident management team would be interesting, to say the least.*

The newly appointed incident commander, Bill Gorley, was a low-key kind of guy. He was listening intently to Russ' briefing, asking very few questions and making notes. The operations chief, Justin Bailey was the "Yang" to Bill's "Ying". He was impatient for information and kept interrupting the briefing with questions. Russ could see he was anxious to get at the fire. He reminded Russ of himself when he was younger. He had heard good things about both of them. Besides, it was *their* Albatross now and he was beyond exhaustion. The other two members of the team, the logistics chief and the planning chief had not attended. They were out there somewhere gathering information and networking.

Bill sensed that Russ was in a fragile state at the moment and needed some encouragement. "Russ, it's too bad the burn-out didn't hold, but we both realize it was touch and go, anyway. For what it's worth, I would have used the same tactic."

"Thanks Bill. I'm just sorry I had to pull the crews. Fire was just too intense."

Justin wasn't in the mood for the delicate dance of repartee. "Russ, what's going on with Wawa 43 right now?"

Russ handed them each a copy of his map and pointed to his own. "Well, Justin, I have one of our CL415 packages and a CL215 package from Manitoba pounding those two heads, 1 and 2. I've asked for a third package but resources are scarce. I've got fourteen ranger crews all working the south end of the fire. When the wind swung back and came from the south, my priority was to try to consolidate that area where they could actually work. There's over twenty kilometres of fire line to tie in. That's gonna take some time."

Russ felt a little defensive as he carried on. "There was no point in putting crews at the head today. Fire intensity was off the scale."

Justin ignored his opinion. "Do the crews working the south have any air support?"

"Yes. Fortunately, we have three medium helicopters with buckets. They're moving crews and supporting them with bucketing. As soon as we get the contract Type 2 crews and the HotShots from the States, we can free up our own crews for work on the head."

Justin looked at Bill for support. He knew this next question might ruffle a few feathers. "What if I moved six of those crews to the head first thing tomorrow? With air tanker support, could they work there?"

Russ looked at both men before he spoke. "It's risky—depends on the winds. You would have to be prepared to yank them out and leave the equipment if they got into trouble."

Justin countered. "Winds are forecasted light, five to ten kilometres from the south-west. We both know that air attack alone won't put a halt to this fire. Those three break-out areas on your map can be cut off, but it'll take foam from the tankers *and* pumps and hose on the ground. Air attack will not only help the crews with fire intensity, it'll also knock some of the smoke down. And I agree. We won't put them in there unless we can get them out."

Justin, you've got balls. I'll have to give you that. I only hope you know what you're doing. "As I just said, it's risky, but do-able."

"I'll need the names of your six best crews and the use of two of the medium helicopters. And I'll need them ready, complete with pumping units and lots of hose, by first light tomorrow. I'll deal directly with the two tanker packages tonight. I'll get them overhead by 10:00 hours tomorrow, and I'll personally supervise this operation."

"Look, Justin. It's yours now. Just make sure you keep those crew-members out of trouble. Some of them are from town, here. Some have families and others are friends."

It was time for Bill to step in. "Russ, no one is more concerned than me for the safety of the people on this fire. If I thought it was too risky, it wouldn't happen. And if those winds don't cooperate tomorrow, it won't happen."

That seemed to satisfy Russ. He wrote down the names of six crew leaders on his note pad, tore the page off and handed it to Justin. "Here are the six names I'd recommend. I'll contact them now through their division bosses. They'll be ready at first light. I'll also get the service people on the equipment requirements right away."

Justin stepped back into the conversation. "Russ, if you don't mind, have the crews pull their pumps out with them but leave the hose on the lines in the south. Apparently we're running shy on pumps, and I know the crews like to work with the pumps they're used to."

Bill and Justin were anxious to get on with it, and Russ was relieved to turn Wawa 43 over to them. The other two members of the team, Tom and Ed, had just walked in and sat down. Bill looked back to Russ. "Thanks Russ, we appreciate everything you've done here."

Russ knew a polite dismissal when he saw one. He stood up. "Good luck, gentlemen." *You're going to need it.*

TOM AND ED SAT DOWN. Bill turned to them. "Well, gentlemen, what have you got for me? Let's start with you first, Tom."

Tom Gregory looked down at his notes. "First, the bad news. I've put in our standing order for suppression equipment. Lots of hand tools coming in. No problem with the prospector tents. The base camp cookery trailer from Thunder Bay is on its way, but the province is shy on pumps."

Justin stepped into the conversation. "Nothing new there. Whenever there's a fire flap, we always run out of pumps. We'll just have to recycle our own."

It was Bill's turn. "Before the region tells me this, I'll tell you guys. No stashing or inventory build-up on pumps. Other fires will need them as well. Let's be team players, gentlemen. Tom, what's the good news?"

"Well it's good, and not so good. First the not-so-good part of the good news. There aren't too many opportunities for a base camp location. Any gravel pit or access point remotely large enough is to the east or north. We'd just be in smoke. Or worse, we'd have to pull out if we get over-run. The same goes for lodges. The airport property at Hornepayne is a good fit, but it's in harm's way as well, at least for a full-blown base camp set-up."

Tom looked around for responses. "The good news is that we have the use of White Lake Provincial Park. It's just off the Trans-Canada highway, so equipment from either Thunder Bay or Sudbury can get in easily. We'll have good water, hydro, the use of staff quarters and communications. They have a decent phone system and a base camp radio set-up."

Bill stepped in. "What about conflicts with public use of the park and helicopters?"

"I think I got that covered. There are very few campers in there right now because of two things. One, the threat of Wawa 43 and two, the restricted fire zone prohibits campfires. Most campers can't do without their campfires. Anyone in there is transient and will be out soon. The park superintendent will close the park on our notice."

Tom looked down at a map in his hands. "There's very little room for helicopters. You could get five just before the beach area, but the grass portion is just deep enough for helipad sites. There are, however, two rehabilitated gravel pits available. One is just across the highway, and the other is just two kilometres east off the highway. You can check them out, but I'd pick the one east. It's close to water, so the helipad sights could be wet down when re-quired. We'd have to set up a shuttle service on either one."

Justin raised a hand. "It sounds good Tom, but the north end of the fire is over sixty kilometres away. That's a lot of ferry time and fuel consumption."

"You're right, Justin. As the crow flies, you're at least thirty min-utes by helicopter to the head. But there's nothing else out there.

The MNR forestry camp on the east side of the fire has been run over. The sprinklers saved it. But we can't use it."

Ed Buckner had been patiently waiting his turn, taking the minutes of the meeting and thinking about the situation as well. "Why don't we give the park a try and if we can get a handle on the head of the fire, use Hornepayne as a forward attack base. I know that it would require setting up another service organization there, but the town itself would have facilities we could use."

Bill looked at Justin. "What do you think?"

"Justin smiled for the first time at the meeting. "Sounds good to me boss."

Bill continued. "Anything else Tom?"

"I could write a book, but just a couple of small points. The park superintendent has offered his services as camp manager. His staff would work for him. That way, he can help us out and look after his park at the same time. The bonus is that he's done this before."

"What about the camp manager assigned to the long team that we'll be using?"

"I've already talked to him. The service organization can use him here in Wawa, and he's fine with that."

"What's the next small point?"

"Well, the superintendent wants us to hire three or four people from the Pic-Mobert Indian Reserve just across the river. He says he knows them, could use them and it would help their community out."

"I agree. Go ahead with it."

Tom smiled. "I already have. Oh, and our chariot awaits—got us a rental crew cab."

"OK. Good work, Tom. Ed, your turn."

Ed looked down at his list. He tended to be a check-list kind of guy. "I'll try to keep this short."

Tom couldn't resist. "Yeah, right."

Ed ignored the friendly shot. "Number one. Region will be doing the fire mapping for us. They have a contractor who will map digitally by GPS coordinates, and they come complete with their own helicopter, pilot and technician. We put in our request as required. They'll provide their data directly to Wawa who will download it into MNR's Geographic Information System (GIS). *We need to let Wawa know which data layers we require.* I've already requested the fire to be overlaid on their road access data, values to protect data and Forest Resource Inventory (FRI) data."

"Number two. Our weather technician will be in tomorrow. He comes complete with his own transportation, camper, weather equipment and satellite phone. He'll have extra rain gauges to hand out to fire crews—if we ever anticipate getting rain. I know the crews carry them, but it never hurts to have extras. He'll pick an appropriate location for his own set up and begin providing forecasts to me by Wednesday the 27th."

"Number three. A fire behaviour officer will be in Wawa tomorrow. He'll be looking for me. I'll get him set up with maps. I anticipate he'll have fire growth progressions and fire intensity data for you by Wednesday."

"Number four. The long team is in Wawa now. They have a radio operator, and I'm picking up another one from the district office and setting up shifts."

"Number five. The long team's personnel officer is already getting a handle on all people presently assigned to Wawa 43. We'll have a good picture of existing staffing shortly."

"Number six. The financial manager who came with the long team is already crunching numbers."

"Number seven. I've requested a safety officer for the fire. ETA, Thursday."

"Number eight. I have the Region's SOP update and weather forecasts in my hot little hands."

"Number nine. I'm ready to role with our daily Fire Action Plan and updates. Tomorrow's briefing will be at 07:00. I'll want to talk about our objectives and action items."

"And finally, number ten. It's a bit early to talk about infrared fire scanning requirements, but think about it anyway. It usually takes close to a week to get aerial infrared on line. That's it."

Bill looked at his watch. It was now 22:00 hours. They were staying at the Wild Goose Inn and sleep was a priority. He knew, however, that each of them had a couple of hours of planning ahead. "Let's call it a night. Tom, will you see that we're up at 05:30 and arrange breakfast at the hotel? Everyone, be prepared with your plan for tomorrow."

He looked around at each person for agreement. "Gentlemen, let the games begin!"

Chapter 49

DAY 7: TUESDAY, JULY 26TH, 06:30 HOURS, WHITE OWL LAKE, HEAD OF WAWA 43

FOUR FIRE FIGHTERS SQUATTED IN THE TALL GRASS, heads down, hands on hard hats as the Bell 205A lifted off just above them, turned and raced over a lake/canvas, a mirror framed in broad stokes of greens then splashed with an array of silver and burnt orange ribbons. Cindy looked up. *Red sky in the morn, sailor be warned.*

They had been hastily dropped in on the north-east side of White Owl Lake and could be forgiven if they felt like kangaroos. They had bounced several times from one end of the fire to the other. Even though the previous day's burn-out had failed, the CL415 tankers had returned that evening and pounded a kilometre long stretch of fire starting just a hundred metres south of the crew's present location. Cindy looked in that direction.

The tankers had come in low, leaving a path of destruction now semi-covered by a thin, tattered blanket of brown and yellow mottled foam. Spruce and balsam fir slumped across each other like giant party tooth-picks with green-only heads. Those trees that had the tenacity to remain standing did so, broken and damaged beyond repair. Cindy knew the tanker pilots had no choice. They had a heavy forest canopy to penetrate and required some level of confidence that their lines would hold until the next morning.

Drops had been unrelenting until the huge yellow water bombers reached a point in the evening when they could drop no more.

Working in and around concentrated foam drops was a fire fighters worst nightmare. Many a fire fighter had gone down in a heap after slipping in the stuff. If you could stay to the outside, you were OK. But if a hot spot broke through the foam around or near any vertical fuels such as groups of immature spruce or balsam, torching could occur and jump fires out of the air tanker drop zone might follow. You had no choice but to wade in and deal with it. Now the residue of foam had dissipated overnight beyond any level of effectiveness. Spiral whiffs of thin smoke were rising from several locations.

The crew's objective was simple. They had less than one kilometre of line to hold between White Owl Lake and a pond to the north. Another crew would wrestle with a piece from the pond, north to McCoy Lake. Similar scenarios would occur west of McCoy Lake to Shekak Lake and from Shekak to Obakamiga Lakes. Six crews were required to tie in three and a half kilometres of fire line—and hold it.

Cindy stood up, tore open the velcro-fastened, folding pouch on her chest and looked at the map. *Hmm—six crews*. She was well aware that their collective action was critical to the protection of Hornepayne. If they could contain the fire here and force it west around Obakamiga Lake, then its natural run with prevailing winds would take it west of Hornepayne and they might be able to handle its east flank. *'Could', 'might'—not really confidence boosting words. Well better than 'shoulda', coulda', 'woulda'.*

She was not overly confident that the crews could hold the narrow pieces of land between lakes, but accepted the fact that "no action' wasn't an option. *Besides, this early start might buy us some time.*

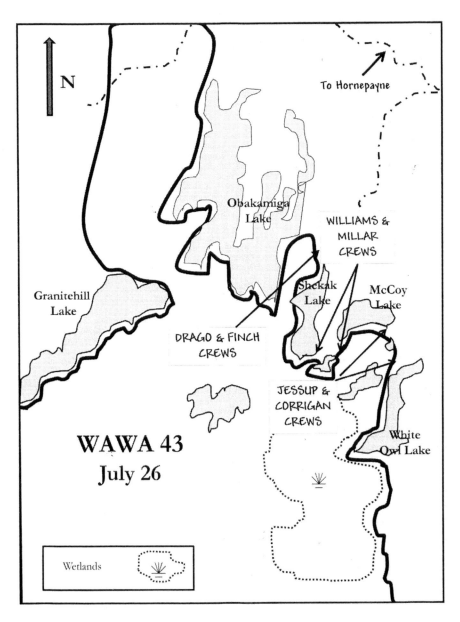

The rest of her crew jumped into action, and in ten minutes, the Mark-3 pump was up and running and hose had been strung to the air tanker foam line. They knew what was required—lay out thirty lengths of hose in miserable country and knock anything down that might flair up along the line. Once they tied into the pond, they would make a back pass, tunnelling the sub-surface duff layer with some serious water. Cindy's marching orders to her crew were simple. "By 10:00 hours, I want two forward and at least one back-pass along our stretch. The tankers are due in around that time. Until then, we're on our own." *Her* job was to scout along the line and well out from it, for signs of any jump fires that would be ready to spring up as the sun rose and winds picked up. If they were there, it wouldn't take her long to find them.

Fifteen minutes into her scouting, Cindy stopped to take as much in as she could. She could hear the comforting sound of the fire pump, its steady drone a sign that it was ready for a full day's work. She could hear her own pulse settle down to something she could manage. Occasionally she could hear the distant, reassuring sound of Jim's voice shouting "water!" when he needed it at the nozzle.

She needed visual reference. Fifty metres to her left, the CL 415's had provided her with a continuous foam break in forest cover. As she looked across the tanker damage, and north, some of the immature spruce and balsam left standing began to torch. *No problem unless bigger stuff ignites.*

Cindy then looked to her right. An unwelcome sphere of brilliant yellow sun was rising behind the dense forest cover not yet over-run by fire. Shafts of light shot through tiny openings. They revealed wispy, dirty-grey smoke, residue of the fire to her left. Her gaze followed the upper contour of the forest canopy, looking for ribbons of smoke that would give away the jump fire hideouts. *Nothing … yet.*

She tilted her head a little to the left, so that her right ear was slightly elevated in an attempt to pick up the crackle, snap and whoosh of torching trees. She consciously sniffed several times to test the dryness in her nostrils. She recalled that, as the relative humidity dropped, her nostrils became dryer. There were times when she could almost predict when forest fuels would burst into flame based on her "feel" of the RH. *Still a bit of moisture in the morning air.* The pungent smell of residual smoke assaulted her senses. *Too quiet—must be what a tiger hunt is like. No sound would be bad news.*

Cindy was not naive. She knew that if she could rise from the ground, straight up like an angel, above the forest canopy, she would see a much more sobering picture. On their flight in that morning, mountainous anvils of dense smoke rose along the one hundred kilometres of fire line like a series of atomic bomb explosions. She could thank the air tankers and the lack of morning wind for her little strip of tranquility. She also knew that within the next few hours, she and her crew would be part of an aggressive battle that, if lost, could mean disaster for a small community that already struggled to survive.

Cindy continued on, zigzagging away from, then into the fire line. She reasoned that two hundred metres outside the line was enough distance to encounter any jump fires. Any further than that would challenge the effective range her crew could work them. As she progressed, she was being forced closer to the air tanker foam drop by a rising cliff. Eventually the foam drop ended up at the base. *Shit! The foam must continue on the top. We've got no choice but to work our way up there.*

Cindy scanned the face for access. She was intimidated by the chiselled fortress. It rose almost sixty metres, close to being vertical. Stunted white spruce and cedar were pasted precariously against the granite walls, their tops bent outwards, like jumpers looking down from their suicide perches.

She worked her way to the top tapping into any reserve energy she might have stored. *What a way to start the day.* She reached the lip of the cliff, pulled herself over, turned around and looked down. The broccoli-topped poplar appeared to be facing up, as if encouraging the cliff hanger trees to jump. Where portions of the cliff were purely vertical and there was no sign of vegetation, giant slabs of flint-grey granite were capped with red-oxide run-off. Below, slides of stone and boulders fanned out from the bottom of the cliff. They were remnants of break-away slabs, forced to topple and fracture over countless winters, by chisels of relentless, prying ice.

The crew would have to access the top from further back somewhere where the rise started. She realized it would leave a significant wedge of unburned, un-foamed fuel. *That will be a problem. Too difficult a target for the tankers because of the cliff. I'll need to burn off that piece. We'll need another pump to maintain pressure. Nothing is ever simple!*

Cindy's mouth was dry, and she sat down on a large flat rock, pulled the bottle of water out of its sleeve, calf-high up on her trousers and took a long pull. Fatigue was taking its toll. Steady sixteen-hour days under brutal conditions were wearing Cindy down and she began to feel sorry for herself. Worse, she even began to doubt her ability to handle the pressure. *What the hell am I doing here? My dad said that this was no job for a girl. Maybe he was right. I'm whipped, pissed at losing battles with this friggin' fire, and my personal life is no life at all. Now, I've got to tell the crew that they're going mountain climbing! Ain't life just ducky!*

SHE HEARD IT BEFORE SHE SAW IT, main rotor cadence from a helicopter. The radio on her belt came to life.

"Corrigan crew from Helitack 45, do you copy?"

Doesn't that guy ever sleep? Cindy deftly plucked the MT1000 out of its scabbard and replied, "Cindy Corrigan here, go ahead 45."

"Morning, Cindy. It's Justin Bailey here. I'm your new operations chief. How are things down there?"

Ah, the new grand Pooh-Bah. Stiff upper lip required here. "Not too bad, Justin—minor problem, though. There's a sixty-metre high cliff in our way. Can you move it for us?"

"I'm crossing it as we speak. Can't move it for you, but I think I can save you the work of climbing it. What's your location?"

Cindy looked up and scanned the canopy fringe. The helicopter came into view moving southerly at a crawl. "You're almost on top of me. If you look down, Justin, I'm at your eleven o'clock." She stood up, took off her hard had and waved it.

"Gotcha, Cindy. Have your crew follow the base of the cliff with their hose. It eventually swings east. The pond you have to tie into is just north-west of it. I'll have the tankers keep an eye on the top. If they can't handle it here, neither can you."

Thank God. "Roger that Justin. Best news I've heard all day."

"Gotta run Cindy. You guys need anything? I've got extra pumps, hose, pump gas and drinking water on board."

"Negative, Justin."

"I don't need to tell how critical your line is, Cindy. Our fire is already starting to boil. We're getting serious torching along some sections of the tanker foam lines. The foams effectiveness is past its best before date."

Cindy felt much better about their chances now and wasn't afraid to say so. "I feel better now that we don't have to go mountain climbing. We'll hold up our end."

"I have no doubt, Cindy. Your reputation precedes you."

The helicopter faded and disappeared beyond the tree line, and a previously discouraged fire crew leader now had a little bounce in her step.

Chapter 50

DAY 7: 11:00 HOURS, SOMEWHERE ON THE SOUTH END OF WAWA 43

"AWE ... DON'T YA JUST LOVE IT!" So far, this was the worst day of his miserable life and yesterday was the worst day until today. *How many 'worst days' can a guy have? I've probably set the record. I could be in the* Guinness Book of World Records *under "most number of worst days in a human's life."* Richard Head slammed the driver's door on the '89 Ford ½ ton, climbed out of the ditch, lit the second last cigarette hidden in a crumpled package and sat on a rock.

It wasn't bad enough that Richard had to get up early. He hadn't seen six a.m. since the time he drank those Tequila shooters and embraced the toilet until the sun came up. He now clutched his throbbing head like he was trying to hold fractured parts together. *Man, there's gotta be a couple of friggin Greeks throwing javelins at the back of my eyeballs.*

It didn't help any that he had been shot down last night by the ugliest woman on the planet. *At least I think it was a woman.* Then he cut himself shaving in three places. *Must have been someone else's shaky hands.* Three little toilet-paper flags were still stuck to his face, held fast by spots of alcohol diluted blood. It had been too early for the zero star hotel he had been staying at to serve breakfast so, to this very point in time, on this very rock, he would be forced to survive on a week-old Hostess Twinkie that he had stashed in his jean jacket. *Have to think positive. It could have been a Joe Louis.*

He fell back into his routine mind-set of denial and despair. He had tried all of the car rental agencies in Wawa—all two of them, only to be told that there wasn't a vehicle to be had. As he turned to walk out of the second agency, the proprietor stopped him in his tracks with the best words he had heard since a new best friend had offered to pay for his drinks some years ago: "I might have something for you, but you're on your own."

Oh, joy of joys, a 1989 Ford ½ ton. Three tone colour no less, orange, white and royal rust. It was all of six cylinders, standard on the column, a veritable power house on wheels. The bench seat had seen better times with a spring poking out of a tear in the driver's side, right where the driver sat. He recalled his thinking on that one. *I could pretend I'm a jack-in-the-box with my body suspended on a spring buried up the crack of my ass. Look on the bright side, no more haemorrhoids because how can you have haemorrhoids when you've reamed out your rear with a spring!* Then there was the brake. *That's right, brake, as in one brake. Probably the reason I ended up in the ditch. But I digress.*

He next thought about his visit to Wawa MNR. No amount of pleading, threatening or grovelling would get him on Wawa 43. He would have to wait until a press visit could be arranged. But Richard was no dummy. When he left the building, he noticed truck after truck being loaded with fire equipment or supplies. He would simply follow the convoy out to the fire. His only concern was keeping up with them in his vintage chariot. But nothing had prepared him for the phantom suspension system. Every bump, every rut, every stone (and there were countless) had transferred the energy associated with the impact right up through *mister* spring, into wonky back-bone and on to gritting teeth and chattering jaw bone. Right now, the rock he sat on felt real good.

Back to my shitty morning. To his utter amazement, Richard had kept up with the other trucks. He had stayed back a respectable distance and had been trampolining inside the cab for just over an hour and a half, when the trucks had slowed down and turned off the well traveled gravel road into what looked like their destination.

It was a fairly large opening, an abandoned gravel pit, with helicopters in various stages of mobility—some shut down, some coming in and some leaving. Richard had recalled movies of the Viet

Nam War that had painted a similar picture. However, he couldn't understand it. *Where was the fire?* He had pulled his truck over to the side of the road and pretended to have a piss. Actually he did have to go. *Nothing's more authentic than the real thing. Inspector Clouseau of the French Sûreté would be proud of my ruse.* He had watched the departing helicopters, his gaze following their general direction and spotted an umbrella of dense smoke just over the tree-tops, but a hellava long way off.

Richard knew he was at a career cross-road. Tuck his tail between tender butt cheeks and retreat. Or ... *be a man, a risk-taker, a cast-your-fate-to-the-winder, er, wind type person.* All of his life he had been a loser. It was time to take the bull by the balls (*or was it horns*). Richard had made his decision. He would find that fire and write his story. With a new resolve, he had wiggled Dick Head Junior back into his pants, zipped up the fly (except it had gotten stuck on a piece of shirt sticking out), climbed back into the Ford and kept on truckin'. Now, two hours later, here he was—sitting on a rock, minus a functioning rectum, internal organs puréed to jell-o, shirt tail peeking out from his zipper and he was choking down a Twinkie. *It couldn't get any better than this.*

FOR FIFTEEN MINUTES, Richard's alcohol-influenced thoughts sloshed around in his head like ship-wrecked flotsam. He wrestled with the possibility that he could be in deep doo-doo. As he saw it, he had two choices, walk down the bush road the way he had come, or walk in the direction he had been going. The two-bite Twinkie was long gone so he pulled out the crumpled pack of cigarettes. *Cripes, only one left!* He shifted his weight on the rock, from one hefty cheek to the other. The precious cigarette was pursed snugly between his lips, his bulbous head turned in one direction then the other, and a fat hand flipped away the persistent, ever circling deer flies.

He thought about all the turns he had made from one road to another. *If I go back, I'll probably walk in circles for days. If I keep going, who knows where it'll take me.* He had both hands waving now. *Friggin' flies. I hate the bush!* Then he thought about his cigarette and put it out. He'd better save half for later. He wrestled his cell phone out of his pocket and flipped up the receiver. *No service. Why am I not surprised.* Frustrated, he looked to the sky and spoke out loud. "Why don't you just finish me now, God? Or do you have more entertainment in store? Give me a sign ... any sign."

Five seconds later, Richard heard it—barely—the high-pitched sound of an engine of some type. He looked up. *No, it's coming from behind me. Might be one of those fire pumps! Yeah, a fire pump. That means fire fighters. Which means interviews. Which means story!* Richard scrambled back to the truck. *Need my pack with the digital and video camera. I know there's a bottle of water and insect repellent in there. Might have another Twinkie. How hard can it be? Just walk to the sound—can't be that far away if I can hear it.* He reflected on his frustrated attempt at prayer. *It's about time!* Now, even more resolute, the big man put on his pack, hiked up his pants, pulled himself through a curtain of evergreen boughs and disappeared into one of the most rugged and desolate pieces of bush Ontario had to offer.

Chapter 51

DAY 7: 11:00 HOURS, HEAD OF WAWA 43, BETWEEN WHITE OWL AND OBAKAMIGA LAKE

JUSTIN BAILEY SAT FORWARD IN HELITACK 45, his shoulders up and tight, his eyes squinting in concentration, his head slowly shifting as he looked for trouble on the ground—a vulture looking for prey. H45 was cruising the three and a half kilometre stretch between White Owl and Obakamiga lakes at an altitude of six hundred metres. Justin took on the mantle of a worried football coach pacing the sideline, wearing a headset and barking out orders, passing information and offering encouragement to a weary team below. His "offensive coordinator" was the Birddog aircraft at twenty-five hundred feet, coordinating the efforts of four, CL415's. The rest of the team was comprised of the twenty four lost and struggling souls on the ground and a medium helicopter that ran back and forth from the combat zone to the most recent staging area for equipment and supplies.

The most important tool in their collective arsenal was the radio. A CL415 drop on a crew had the potential to severely injure or even kill. The biggest enemy was panic. Fear was good. Fear meant adrenalin. Adrenalin kept you going. Giving into panic was bad. Panic meant bad decisions. Crew members depended on a buddy system. Each crew worked their own discreet radio frequency so they wouldn't "walk" on other radio traffic. Too much radio jabber could lead to confusion. They could talk to the boss in the air, if necessary, by selecting the appropriate fire frequency. They could talk to an incoming CL415 on that same frequency. But when push came to shove, they depended on each other. Knowing exactly where each crew members was at *all* times was imperative. They were four bodies with one heart and one mind.

Justin Bailey in Helitack 45 had the FM radio on scan and could hear it all. He had the ability to filter the chatter and pluck out parcels of critical talk. He needed to know who was in trouble. He needed to know what supplies or equipment was required. He needed to know who was winning and who was losing and when to stay or when to pull out.

At this very moment, unburned fuels inside last night's burn area, and there were lots, began to torch. Justin watched the spectacle and he felt a thump in the pit of his stomach. *Maybe my heart just rolled down there like a melon and fell apart. The RH must have dropped and it's only 11:00 hours. We're gonna get lots of jump fires out of this.* He no sooner thought the black thought, when puffs of smoke sprang up at random in the unburned forest … behind the fire crews. Radio chatter sprang into overdrive. *This is just about when shit happens. Think I'll show the colours.*

"Birddog 18, this is Helitack 45, do you copy?"

"Go ahead 45."

"Terry, I'd like to do a fly by on the crews down there."

"OK Justin. Stay fifteen hundred feet on your altimeter and outside the line a half kilometre. I'll give the tankers a heads up."

Justin looked to his pilot who nodded then reached towards the instrument panel to set the altimeter.

As the pilot approached the fire line and dropped his altitude, Justin listened intently at the grab bag of radio chatter. The first shoe dropped.

"Birddog 18, this is Tanker 274, do you copy?"

"Go ahead 274."

"Terry, we've got a problem in our port engine. We're going to head to Hearst. It's the closest air strip. We'll switch over and advise them. If we have to put down somewhere, I'll let you know."

"Copy that. I'll let Wawa know what's going on, and good luck. You copy that, Justin."

"Affirmative, Terry. How's the tanker fuel situation?"

"We're going to let tanker 271 return for fuel to Hearst. He'll baby sit tanker 274 on his way. Where do you want the other package?"

Justin took a moment to collect his thoughts. He looked down at his map.

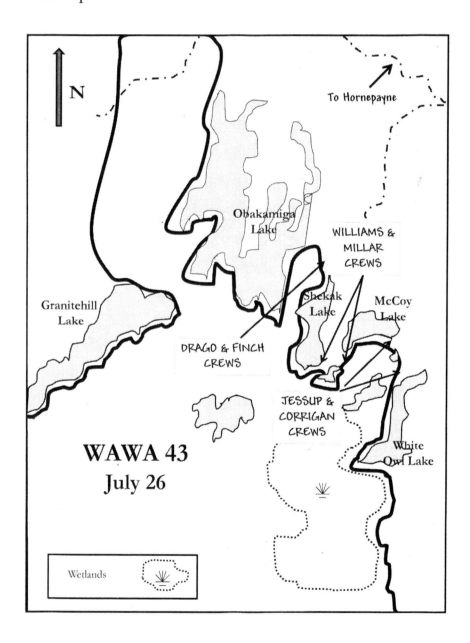

"Break up the remaining two tankers. One should stay with the Drago and Fitch crews between Shekak and Obakamiga lakes. They're having a rough time. The other one can float as required between the other four crews. The priority is jump fires."

"Copy that, Justin. Keep in mind that when Tanker 271 returns, we'll have to let the others go back for fuel and I'll be going back with them. You'll only have one tanker on site."

"Hakuna Matata, Terry. If we can get through the next two hours, I think we'll be OK." *He says with little conviction in his voice.*

Hakuna Matata? The Birddog officer looked at his pilot who smiled and responded. "Lion King—means no worries here."

"Copy that, Justin. I'll talk to the tankers."

Justin checked on his fire crews. The Corrigan crew was holding its own. *Way to go, Cindy.* The Jessup crew kept blowing hose. *Must have had an old batch.* The Williams and Millar crews had there hands full. Four jump fires in the dry swamp behind them were causing problems, but Tanker 274 had provided just enough support to help them keep on top. The Drago crew just had their pump go US on them. He had two onboard and would be there in a couple of minutes. The Fitch crew, tied into the Drago crew, was having a rough time with two jump fires on the hill behind them. The other two tankers would have to stay with Drago and Fitch for the time being. *Man, I love this stuff.*

Helitack 45 flared then dropped gently to the 5X5 metre helipad constructed on the lip of the south-east point of Obakamiga Lake. With the machine still powered up, Justin stepped out, went to the cargo hatch at the widest part of the tail and pulled out a Mark-3 pump and two, twenty-two litre containers of mixed pump gas. In two short trips to the front of the helicopter, he handed the gear to a fire crew member who in turn carried it further back away from the helicopter. Justin motioned the fire fighter off to one side. Once clear of the rotor, they both stood up straight. Justin put out his hand and looked at the name patch on his jump suit.

"Well, how are things going, Glen?"

The kid had been wearing his goggles earlier and the only skin showing behind a layer of black was around his eyes. *He looks like a racoon.*

The kid smiled. *Now he looks like a Cheshire cat.* "Couldn't be better, sir. Once I get water up to the crew, we'll be flying."

"It's 'Justin', not 'sir'. Tell the crew for me that they're doing a fine job. If you can contain this area for another two hours, we may be out of the woods."

"Thanks, Justin. Look, I don't want to be rude, but our crew needs water, so this pump's gotta go in."

Geez, a dismissal. Reminds me of me. Justin laughed. "I can take a hint. Take care, Glen."

The crews are holding there own. Justin turned, crouched and headed for the helicopter. *Now for the other shoe.* Once airborne, Justin instructed the pilot to head westerly. "See that big column of smoke north west of Obakamiga Lake?" *A rhetorical question. Who couldn't see it?* "Take us there. I need to see how much ground we've lost."

Within five minutes, Justin had a fix. It had breached where they had anticipated and grown approximately six kilometres by six kilometres. *Thirty-six hundred hectares—eighty-nine hundred acres. Please God, keep the winds coming from the south west. If they come directly from the west, Hornepayne is done like dinner.*

Chapter 52

DAY 7: 13:00 HOURS, SOMEWHERE ON THE SOUTH END OF WAWA 43

RICHARD HEAD NEW HE HAD MADE THE BIGGEST MISTAKE OF HIS SORRY LIFE. Within a very, very short time, fifteen minutes as a matter of fact, he was completely and utterly lost. Not lost as in "I'm a little lost but I'm sure I can find my way out" lost. Lost as in "I've got no idea where I am and I'm gonna die" lost. It's human nature, and even animal nature, to take the path of least resistance. Nine hundred and ninety-nine times out of a thousand, that path was *not* in a straight line. So now he sat on a brand new rock (his previous rock had been at the road), winded and soaked from sweat, his face a road map of welts and his arms wind-milling around a head used as a landing strip for deer flies. "I'm gonna die!" he shouted at the wall of evergreens facing him like a cemetery hedge.

What do I do now? He thought back to his childhood six-month trial and failure as a boy scout. *What did that dorky book say? Come on, come on.* A battered large head dropped into a pair of grimy hands. *Oh yeah. If you get lost, don't panic. DON'T PANIC! IT'S TOO FRIGGIN LATE! Get a hold of yourself, Richard. What else did it say? Sit down and take stock of your situation. I am sitting down and I'M SCREWED! No ... no, be specific. My situation is as follows:* Richard ticked off each point on a chubby finger and his voice rose in pitch and volume with each revelation.
One, I don't know where I am,
Two, I have no food,

343

Three, I have no water,
Four, I ran out of bug spray five minutes after I left the road,
Five, the flies are using me for an all-you-can-eat buffet,
Six, the forest is using me as its newest whipping boy, and
Seven, now this is a dandy. I have to have a crap and I've got no toilet paper.
    So in summation, ladies and gentlemen of the jury, I'm SCREWED!

Richard's head plopped down into his hands again, his mind flipping through a catalogue of options that included suicide by taking off all his clothes, laying spread eagle on the ground and feeding the creepy crawlies. Suddenly, the watermelon head sprung up. *There's that sound again. The fire pump. Maybe I'm out of the woods. What the hell, how bad can it get anyway? Where there's a pump, there's life. And where there's life, there's hope!*

With new resolve, and forgetting his need to leave a deposit on the forest floor, Richard ploughed through the bush humming a tune from a group that normally caused his teeth to grind, Air Supply and, "Nothing Can Stop Us Now."

TWENTY TORTUROUS MINUTES LATER, a hyperventilating Richard sat down on an old fallen tree, threw the pack down that carried his cameras, and stared up at a thirty-metre cliff. Facial expressions changed uncontrollably as emotions sprung through his mind like ricocheting bullets. He instinctively bent over to prevent nausea, exposing an unsightly butt crack that still sported leaves left over from a recent and very pressing pit stop.

If I have to climb that sucker, I'll probably die. If I don't climb it I WILL die. Wait! Maybe if I follow it, I can find a better route. A pair of black capped chickadees flitted around him looking for tidbits hidden in branches and bark. A red squirrel sat in a limb above him, belting out a staccato "ch-r-r-r" warning. He looked up. A pair of turkey vultures circled high overhead, riding invisible currents of air. *They all want a piece of me. Wait until I'm dead, you little pricks!*

Richard forced his immense body erect and plodded along the base of the cliff. Ten minutes later, thirty metres of ridge became a one-metre rise. *When you're smart, you're smart. Just a minute. No pump sound.* Without realizing it, the ridge had curved back and away from his intended path.

He struggled through the bush for a hundred metres, breaking branches as a guide back to the rise. He repeated this effort in other directions. On his final attempt, he took his one hundred steps and turned around. *Something stinks!* Richard looked down. His left shoe was firmly implanted in a large turd. What made matters worse, what was close to being the last straw, was that it was human, and it was his. *No friggin' doubt about it—there's the leaves I used.* Three hundred pounds of unbridled temper tantrum was not a pretty sight, but it was over in a minute. Richard did not have the strength to completely act out his anger. Sticks were aplenty so he tended to his shoe before plotting the next course of action.

The more he thought about his plight, the more furious Richard became. He was tired, dirty, unbelievably thirsty and pissed. *This is bullshit! I need to find water and I need to find that pump!* Armed with the most determination than he had ever dredged up in his sorry existence, he marched on with purpose and a life's supply of anger.

A half hour later, Richard pulled himself over the lip of the cliff he had abandoned earlier. It took every last ounce of strength and resolve that he could muster. There was no more to give. The big man started crying, muffled at first, but as he surrendered to self pity, snuffles turned to sobs and sobs turned to all out, body-shaking cries of anguish. He was a beaten man. His lower torso dangled from the lip of the cliff, his upper torso was splayed on the top. He was face down in desiccated leaves, his arms outstretched—hands clutching a pair of saplings for support.

It took five minutes for the overwhelming sense of despair to pass. The crying subsided, and Richard looked up and out towards the incessant, irritating sound of the pump. *Holy shit! There's water down there! Some sort of bay or river! And there's the pump on the other side!* A surge of energy snapped through his body, and he pulled the rest of it onto the flat and forced himself into a standing position. He put one foot out in front of the other, slowly at first as if testing their ability to propel him forward, and then he did something he hadn't done since he was a kid— he ran. Like a sumo wrestler, like a dancing bear in a circus, like a toddler towards its mother. But he ran.

Nothing was going to stop Richard. Branches tore at his clothes. Saplings bent and snapped. His huge body bounced off trees but kept on trucking. He was a bull moose in rut. Twenty metres to the water—ten metres—five metres—no metres! He literally belly flopped into a bed of floating bog past the shoreline and slurped in a gallon of brackish, critter-laden water.

Oh God, that's good! I'm saved! Geez! My cameras! He forced himself up onto his knees and checked his pack. *They're OK. Just a little damp.* He looked down at the mat of bog material that supported him. *Wow! It actually floats!* He stood up, turned around and took a wobbly step. His foot broke through and his leg disappeared. *Oh shit!* He went back down to a knee and then his belly in order to pull the trapped leg out. *It's working!* Out came the tree stump leg—minus a shoe. Richard belly crawled to the shoreline. He waggled like a giant, obese crocodile, forcing his body through the web of tag alders he had unconsciously penetrated on his way in.

He sat on the shoreline and attempted to control his ragged breathing. He glared with pursed lips at the red pump across the water. He was a beaten, washed up magician willing a stubborn, uncooperative object to levitate and come to him. His eyes followed the pump hose as far as the bush across the water would allow. Observations and questions clashed in his head like bumper cars. *There's no one there. Where are they? How far does the hose go? There's no smoke close by. When will they come back? How do I get over there?* The pump smugly droned on with an occasional rise in pitch.

Richard re-focused on the pump, his eyelids drooped and his jaw slackened. The steady whine acted like a sedative, soothing Richard into an induced trance until a small stab of pain in his lower abdomen jolted him back to reality. He looked down at the mound of flesh resting on stove-pipe thighs and heard the cauldron-like gurgle buried within. *Oh, oh, rumbly in the tumbly. Must be the water. Gotta get outa here soon or they'll never find me. Correction. They'll be able to follow the trail of crap I leave behind. I can see my epitaph now. "E.T. left a trail Reese's Pieces. Dick Head left a trail of Dia Ria." I gotta get over that water to the pump!*

Richard stood up, took one step and impaled a shoeless foot on a well-hidden dead branch snag. "Ouch! Ow, Ow, Ow!" He fell back down to the ground and examined the damage. *Not too bad, but I need to cover that foot with something.* Five minutes later the big man limped along the shoreline, his tattered shirt now minus a shirt-sleeve. He had used it to tie layers of swamp grass to his foot. *Need to find a place to cross.* Swimming was out of the question. As a kid, Richard had skipped out of his swimming lessons. There was no way he could tell how deep the black, forbidding water was without going in, and he had no intention of going in.

A fifteen-minute hobble took him further away from the pump. What must have been a bay now narrowed to a twenty-five metre wide creek. Things were looking up. Ten minutes later he found his opportunity. A twisty old log spanned the creek. *Jeez, it looks big enough to hold me! I could straddle it and bounce my ass across! Watch out, Circ De Soleil, here I come!*

Richard crawled through the jungle of tag alder, dead branches and giant reed grass, sat on the end of the log, leaned forward to establish a grip and tenuously pulled his large frame ahead. Ten minutes of precarious shinny brought him to the middle of log. From this point on, the bark was gone, exposing a smooth, hard surface. Richard was now sweating profusely. He looked down at the log and watched droplets of sweat fall, bounce a little then run down the sides. *Don't loose your nerve now, old buddy.* He slid his hands forward. *The damn log's slippery!* Richard sat up and took off his shirt, as delicately as possible to maintain balance, wound it into a shirt-rope and wrapped the ends around his hands. He now had a sling to slide across the surface of the log.

Come on, only twenty metres to go! As Richard reached forward, two things happened. The first was a physiological chain reaction. Pain shot through his lower abdomen, his bowels went into involuntary contraction, his sphincter muscles threw their hands up in defeat and he shit himself. This, in itself was not life threatening. In fact, given the present circumstances, it was no big deal. *Oh, surprise, surprise. What more could go wrong?*

The second thing was instantaneous. Richard lost his balance. His centre of gravity had shifted and in a nano-second, the big man was now *under* the log, clutching it with arms and legs. He now fully realized what kind of weight he had been carrying over the years and that his arms were no match for his body. He whipped the dangling shirt-sleeve over the log and grabbed it with the other hand. It was one of those incongruous moments when a person's thoughts did not match their situation. Rather than ponder his plight, Richard's overriding thought turned to how ridiculous he must appear. *Well, here I am—upside down, hanging from a log, my butt skimming the water, no shirt, one shoe and the friggin' flies have settled in for lunch—the great white African hunter being transported to the pot for supper.*

His second thought wasn't so incongruous. *My arms and legs are burning. Can't hold on much longer.* His third thought fell in the "doesn't belong here at this moment" category. *If they find me, my underwear won't be clean.* The forth thought was analytical with a touch of moral certitude. *If I hold on until I can't anymore, and I drown then it's a simple death. If I let go right now, is it suicide?*

In the ten seconds it took for Richard to process his thoughts, his arms and legs gave out simultaneously and his body sank quickly below the surface, leaving only a ring of wavlets expanding away from their centre of displacement. Time and space froze. The deer flies that decided not to go down with the sinking ship, left for greener pastures. Suddenly, like a crocodile bursting out of the water at its prey, Richard came up coughing and sputtering. "I can stand! I can stand!" He attempted to walk out but could not move. His feet were encased in half a metre of mud and decay commonly called "loon shit." "I'm stuck! I'm stuck!" *So I don't drown. I die of starvation. No, I'll get weak, pass out and then drown.*

Richard pondered his day. Every decision he had made to this point brought him one flush closer to the big sewer in the sky. *What's that sound?* He looked back up the creek. *Shit! A helicopter, and it's landing back somewhere near the pump site.* He waved his arms and yelled until his voice was hoarse. He knew that he had to get out. From somewhere within, from a place he didn't know existed, he winched up every parcel of determination and pulled one foot, then the other out of their tombs. He repeated the Herculean task time and again until he had reached dry ground. Richard flopped down like a great grey seal out of water, reached a hand skyward as the helicopter departed, and passed out.

Chapter 53

DAY 7: 14:00 HOURS, HORNEPAYNE

T HE TRACTOR-TRAILER RUMBLED INTO HORNEPAYNE and shuddered to a halt in front of the town office. Four crew cabs and a half-ton with MNR logos trailed like little ducklings behind a fat mallard hen. Not far behind was the mallard drake, MNR pumper 3, a pumper/tank truck that held twenty-five hundred gallons of water.

Hornepayne would soon be evacuated. Twenty of the community's homes and structures had earlier been targeted as risk from wildfire and would require protection. At a community meeting the previous night, it took a considerable amount of discussion and persuasion to convince the rest of the residents that their homes were not likely in harms way. All the shouting, cursing and threats of litigation would not persuade or intimidate MNR's emergency response coordinator, Greg Walsh. His support from Hornepayne's Fire Chief Ken Waal was resolute. Even the mayor, Ted Touluce, was on the same page. He had been the most critical person of the protection plan (one drafted before his tenure) until someone pointed out that his home was targeted for protection.

The caravan that rolled into town would provide the necessary protection. The tractor-trailer housed the equipment and the trucks delivered the personnel to set up MNR's mobile values protection units. The pumper/tank truck was a back-up water source. The closest supply of water came from Lennon Creek and Lennon Creek wasn't in any shape to provide a whole lot of water. Drought conditions had dropped its level considerably. The equipment, four

MNR ranger crews, a division supervisor and a supply unit leader all came out of Thunder Bay. The trailer contained the Mark-3 fire pumps, hose, and more than enough sprinklers and support equipment to protect the targeted structures.

As the crews were getting organized, a township back-hoe was dredging two pools in Lennon Creek close to the community. This kind of activity would normally require a rat's nest of red tape, an individual environmental assessment, before dredging could begin but time was presently at a premium. Environmental impacts and necessary rehabilitation would be determined later. The narrow ribbon of water flowing through the creek would top up the holes, maintain its level in them and continue on its journey. The Mark-3's and the pumper/tanker would have a supply of water. Water retrieval would be slow, however, waiting for the pools to fill. Pumping would have to be managed carefully. The town's water supply, suspended in an ancient water tower could be used as last resort.

The division supervisor had the fire crew gather around, and he handed out specific assignments and site maps showing locations of homes and structures requiring protection. Most of them were on the southwest side of the community, close to the bush. If all went well, pumps and sprinklers would be set up and operational by 18:00 hours.

Throughout the course of the afternoon, crew members set up pumps, ran a main 2 ½ inch water line with numerous lengths of 1½ fire hose running off the main trunk and finished with fifty-foot lengths of econo-flow hose (much like garden hose) at the sprinkler heads. Thirty-two foot extension ladders were shuffled from house to house and crew members scuttled across roof-tops and set up sprinklers either by nailing them to facia or securing them with wooden tripods (roof-pods) on roof peaks.

A final, straight line of sprinklers was established as a fire break to protect structures from the most likely point of fire entry, a three hundred metre stretch of fifteen-metre high jack pine. Sprinkler heads were suspended five metres up using 2X4 studs as tripods. In order to ensure sprinkling overlap, each one hundred foot length of hose was looped in the middle. Consequently, three hundred metres of sprinkler line required four hundred metres of fire hose, or fourteen lengths.

No more could be done. The tractor-trailer, pumper/tanker, division supervisor, supply unit leader and two ranger crews would remain for pump start up and troubleshooting. The other two crews were required elsewhere. If Wawa 43 reached Hornepayne, it would likely overrun the town within a matter of a few hours. As someone put it to know one in particular, "All this work for two hours of fireworks—pretty anti-climatic."

IN SHARP CONTRAST to an efficient and somewhat routine structural protection set-up, the evacuation of Hornepayne was anything but efficient or routine. Simply put, there was a plan, somewhat outdated. There was local, municipal organization but those charged with responsibility had next to no experience in managing an evacuation.

Greg Walsh said it best when he told the mayor and fire chief, who were exchanging volleys in a heated discussion, "Gentlemen, you've got a hellava big learning curve to squeeze into a short period of time." *Like kids fighting in the back seat of a car.* "The EMO rep should be here shortly, and he can help you out with some of this stuff. In the meantime, I can recommend a couple of things you might consider."

Two faces, nose to nose, swung around to face Greg as if on queue. Two "whats!" jumped out of drawn, angry lips simultaneously.

Greg was unfazed. "Ken, you need to get the message out to residents about evac-proofing their homes and registering as they evacuate. You also need to set up a registry. Knowing who is here and who isn't is important. You also need to arrange transport and reception facilities in Chapleau for those who require it. It's all in your plan. I've taken a quick look at it. The only part that's outdated is the list of contact numbers. You're just going to have to get someone to wade through that stuff. Also, get your support organization in place; you can't do it all yourself. That's also in the plan."

Mayor Touluce looked smugly at his fire chief. Greg thought—*he looks like one of two kids caught in a schoolyard dust up that thinks he's off the hook.* "And Ted, you should be thinking about pulling council together if you *think* you need additional provincial support. You'll need to formally declare an emergency. Oh, and you'll need police help with community security and securing evacuation routes."

Both men appeared disillusioned and somewhat chastised. Greg had been in the same situation and felt a little sorry for them. "Look, guys. I've been there before. Trust your plan and your people." He reached in his brief case and pulled out a list. "Here's something from MNR's Emergency Plan. It's a simple "Checklist of Emergency Evacuations Considerations." He gave them a minute to digest it.

* *Up-to-date directory of all emergency support organizations, agencies volunteer agencies and community officials,*
* *Security, maintenance or shut down of utilities,*
* *Planned back-up system for telecommunications,*
* *Community security,*
* *Travel restrictions,*
* *Staging areas/assembly points and alternates,*
* *Hand-out maps of staging areas, assembly points and reception areas and centres,*
* *Be prepared with the most up-to-date information on the emergency situation,*
* *Be prepared with the process to use for those residents who are reluctant to evacuate,*
* *Evacuation routes,*
* *Careful, specific evacuation warnings,*
* *Pre-determined demographics of the population at risk and community locations (e.g., adults, secondary school age, elementary, pre-school, hospital, homes for the aged),*
* *Consider daytime demographics v.s. night. Consider seasonal demographics,*
* *Reception communities and facilities,*
* *Registry of evacuees and inquiry services,*
* *Register volunteers so they are protected from personal liability,*
* *Identifying residents with health problems and special needs,*
* *Staff involved with evacuation should keep an event log,*
* *Identifying damage (recording, pictures, video),*
* *Evacuation checklist for residents (what to do before leaving, what to bring),*

*   *Pre-arranged methods of communicating evacuation warning/notification (e.g., radio, television, street-to-street loud hailers, door-to-door, etc.),*
* *Pre-identified location and availability of temporary shelters, mobile kitchens, generators, privies, trailers, etc.,*
* *State of community institution evacuation plans,*
* *Feed and care of pets and/or livestock,*
* *Early scheduling to avoid extreme fatigue,*
* *Re-entry points and registry,*
* *Transport (e.g., trucks, buses, vans, etc.),*
* *Pre-restoration site inspections with community officials, and*
* *Restoration team to deal with resident issues once they return.*

"And for heaven's sake, let your people and the community know you're on the same page, or at least *pretend* to be on the same page so they have some level of confidence that you'll all get through this thing."

The bluster and fight had abandoned the mayor and chief.

Time to provide some hope. "For what it's worth, I know the incident commander for Wawa 43. He happens to be one of the best in the province. If anyone can manage this fire, he can." *At least I can pretend to be confident.*

THE WORD SPREAD QUICKLY. School buses were lined up to retrieve their charges early. In homes, water was being shut off, air conditioners and hot water tanks turned off, TV's and computers disconnected and important documents and valuables collected. Cars and trucks were stuffed with suitcases, coolers, blankets, sleeping bags, an assortment of emergency food supplies and, of course, children and pets.

A line-up of nervous people cued at the bank machine, gas stations and the municipal office for registration. *Names, address, where are you going, number you can be reached, method of transport, automobile registration, route out of town, is house secured, any pets or livestock left behind to be cared for.* Those who either didn't know about registering or were too panicked to comply were turned back into town.

Vehicles entering Hornepayne were turned back unless they had official need to be there or were retrieving family or friends. If they were allowed in, they would have to register to leave.

O.P.P cruisers were already patrolling streets, stopping from time to time to offer advice or reassure residents. Local businesses were permitted to remain open for the day until residential needs were met and evacuation wrapped up. Town staff was committed to stay to insure infrastructure remained up and running. The local fire brigade, although volunteer, also committed to stay and were preparing for structural fires.

School and contracted buses marshalled at the community centre and were organized to evacuate those who were either incapacitated or had no means of transport. In Chapleau, the town was preparing for reception of evacuees from Hornepayne.

Outside of town, tourist lodges were sending vacationers home, cancelling next week's business and preparing for their own evacuation. These were not happy campers.

As a last resort, some people were watering their roofs without considering that the fire was a day or two off and water evaporates.

Those who refused to evacuate were personally encouraged to do so by the O.P.P. When that didn't work, they were asked to sign a disclaimer taking on full responsibility for the consequences. When that didn't work the O.P.P made note of their unwillingness to cooperate along with other notations such as "to be watched, has potential for criminal activity" or "displays eccentric tendencies."

One such person was Ethel Abernathy. She had no place to go, and there was no way she was leaving her beloved Sushi behind. She put it very directly to the two strapping O.P.P officers, "It'll take more than the two of you to pry me from this home!" They looked at Ethel, then each other. One of them held out a clipboard. "Please sign here, Mam."

Chapleau was a "happening" place. Buses from Hornepayne would soon be arriving at the community centre where they would be registered, given meal vouchers for the local restaurants until a central kitchen could be set up and ferried to their temporary shelters. Where they stayed depended on their state of well-being. Palliative care patients were whisked off to an already overcrowded hospital where hallway beds would be set up. Mobile seniors would stay at the community centre, and everyone else would be bussed to the arena. The numbers requiring lodgings weren't large, only one hundred and twenty-one, but their needs were varied and complex enough to stretch Chapleau's capacity to respond.

By 20:00 hours, Hornepayne was a virtual ghost town. Most of those that remained there did so with purpose. MNR's fire crews, emergency and mobile values protection Staff, O.P.P officers, municipal fire brigade staff, town maintenance workers and the mayor and councillors had jobs to do.

Two security guards nervously roamed the CP rail yard. Rail cars stood abandoned. A handful of residents who refused evacuation, banded together to bolster their courage over a few brewskies. Several neglected dogs slunk from trash can to trash can, and an occasional feral cat sprinted from shadow to shadow.

Not one to overlook any opportunity, the owner of one of the local restaurants decided to stay and keep his place open. Possessing a liquor license certainly helped the cause. By 24:00 hours, it was the only establishment "alive" in the town. A lone O.P.P cruiser sat out on the street across from the well-lit, raucous red brick building. An officer stood outside the noisy restaurant under a black velvet night, looking through a grease-stained window at his charges. A gentle smile of reassurance glided across his face.

Off duty fire crew members rubbed shoulders with local fire brigade volunteers. The mayor was holding court with some of well-lubricated residents who had refused to evacuate.

In the meantime, Ethel Abernathy had cornered two old men in a worn pine booth, her Sushi propped on a wide lap, nose peeking over the table, bulgy eyes transfixed on a half-eaten hamburger. Ethel had a captive audience. Inane words fermenting in a decanter brain poured non-stop through spigot lips. There was no quality control between grey matter and mouth. The words, like cheap wine, had a numbing effect on their recipients. Anyone standing close by managed a subtle quarter turn, covertly searched for an escape route, shuffled to create a disconnect and slunk away in relief.

Across the room, someone in the crowd yelled to the owner, "Hey Ernie! Is this meatloaf or did somebody change a tire!" A fire crew member stood up and walked to the juke box, fingered in a few coins and pushed some buttons. The silent, plastic and metal music troll came to life. A fringe of eclectic colours strobed from top to bottom, and the voice of Johnny Paycheck belted out an international favourite, "Take this job and shove it", sung over the world in thirty different languages, but all with the same heart felt emotion.

It wasn't long before the whole crowd joined in. The O.P.P officer turned around and walked back to the big, white Chevy with the O.P.P logo, humming the same tune. He looked up before climbing in. Dirty brown-grey streamers of smoke slipped across a full moon. One was shaped like a wispy spectre on horse-back, a harbinger bearing bad news. He then looked down the street, in a south-westerly direction. Off in the distance the black, forest skyline was separated from an equally black sky by a soft orange glow, much like the dying embers on a campfire. Only this campfire was fifteen kilometres away with a fourteen-kilometre edge. He smiled as he recalled another song by the Four Seasons, "Oh What a Night, The Summer Of '63."

PART 5

PROJECT FIRE (CONTINUED)

The young knight reflects:

And so it begins,
The beginning of end
Where desperate measures
Show little consequence
But even in the end,
There is a glimmer of a new beginning.

Wednesday, July 27th, 10:00 hours to
Friday, July 29th, 11:30 hours

Chapter 54

DAY 8: WEDNESDAY, JULY 27TH, 10:00 HOURS, WAWA FIRE MANAGEMENT HEADQUARTERS

T HE YELLOW SCHOOL BUS SLOWED TENTATIVELY TO A HALT in the Wawa MNR parking lot, the driver unsure of where to deposit his twenty, travel weary passengers. Not far behind were another school bus and a ½ ton truck. The truck carried additional personal gear that wouldn't fit in the buses. Both buses and the ½ ton were stopped by a small woman in orange coveralls. Without ceremony, she climbed into the first school bus, gave the driver cursory directions for parking and shouted an enthusiastic "Welcome to Wawa, HotShots!"

The six-hour bus trip from Thunder Bay was tiresome and uneventful, but Nate Ramirez could not help but be impressed with the drive along the north shore of an ocean-sized Lake Superior. He remembered an earlier reflection. *One could forgive the ancient mariners for firmly believing that the world was flat.* This day, Lake Superior had let its guard down. Where it met the sky, it was a distinct, perfectly level line that separated the pearl-grey water from an azure blue sky. Many years ago, it would have taken a courageous leap of faith to point a bow out to sea and, at the same time, secretly wonder "When will we fall off and how far is the drop?"

The flight to Thunder Bay on board the twin engine, turbo prop Super 748 had also been uneventful. The powerful two thousand, two hundred and eighty horsepower Rolls-Royce Dart engines

pushed twenty tons of aircraft and payload at a cruising speed
of four hundred and fifty kilometres per hour. With a range of
seventeen hundred kilometres, the two thousand kilometre trip
required a stopover for fuel in Minneapolis, Minnesota. All told,
the trip took six hours.

With a passenger manifest of forty plus gear and a flight crew
of two, the 748 still had room to spare—but not much. With a
two-hour break in Thunder Bay for clearing customs and eating
breakfast, the two HotShot crews had been in transit fourteen
hours. Nate looked around at the other nineteen on this bus. The
"all-nighter" had taken its toll. Some were stretched out in semi-
consciousness with heads back and mouths agape. Others were
leaning forward, chins on chests, heads bobbing in tune with the
rhythm of the bus. And others were like Nate, transfixed in boredom, eyes red-rimmed and glazed. *Man, I need to stretch, and a coffee
would not be out of the question.*

After some jockeying, the bus came to a halt, the door opened
and another stranger boarded. The silver-haired man was short,
chubby, had a full, white beard, sported a pair of round-rimmed
glasses on a stubby nose and was aged on the north side of sixty.
He looked down at the clipboard in his hand. "Is Chester Wilkes
and Notchos Ramirez here?"

Nate's boss stood up. Nate raised his hand, smiled and responded. "It's Naiche, but Nate is easier."

Santa Claus smiled back and pointed out the door. "Kitchen's
open and the coffee's on. I'm Nick Rankin, your shadow for the
duration of this campaign. This next hour is yours, people. Chester
and Nate, I'll join you and provide a briefing, *Reader's Digest
Condensed* version, once you're finished."

It took only a minute for twenty weary travellers dressed in olive green, fire resistant Nomex pants and yellow Nomex shirts to
pile out of their crypt. Santa boarded the bus behind them to deliver the same message.

An hour later, five men sat on a picnic table, four of them clutching ceramic cups of steaming coffee refills. Santa looked from face
to face. "Anyone here *not* know what a liaison officer does?" There
was no response. "Well, I like to talk so I'm going to tell you anyway. First off, my background. I'm retired. What am I doing here?
I'm bored. Thirty years with MNR, seventeen of which was in

the fire program has spawned this restless seeker of thrills and chills."

The audience all smiled, not only because of Nick's sense of humour, but also because their comfort metre jumped several points. They would be dealing with a man with a fire background.

Nick continued. "Shortly, I'll introduce you to the sector response officer here who will turn you over to a fire intelligence officer who will brief you on the location of your 'all expenses paid vacation', Wawa 43."

Four heads nodded.

"Then we'll load you back onto the buses." There was a collective groan. "Where I'll take you out to a group of 'senior' fire instructors to provide some hands on pump and hose lay training with Ontario's famous Mark-3 fire pump."

A hand shot up. "What's a 'senior' fire instructor?"

"A retiree that doesn't know any better. Your trainers are a group of retirees who intend to take you through the paces at 'senior' speed. We understand you can use pumps, but consider this a brush up on our techniques."

Nate chimed in. "Anything is better than more bus. Besides, the crew members could do with a bit of exercise."

Nick was glad to hear this wasn't going to be a "swinging dick" contest. Ego sometimes had the habit of delaying progress. "While you're doing that, I'll be arranging accommodations at the 'No-tell' Motel and meal vouchers. I'll have lunch sent out to you. Tomorrow, we'll be leaving bright and early for Wawa 43 by yellow chariot, where I'll introduce you to 'his majesty' and his incident management team. Any questions?"

"No? OK. Now here's how I like to operate. For the most part, I'll be on the fire line with you. If you're in a tent, so am I. If you crawl through a swamp, so will I. If you work your butts off with hand tools, that's where I draw the line."

The four HotShots smiled, leaned back a little or adjusted position to take in the show.

"If you'd like, I can do a little scouting for you, but my primary role is to see that you're happy. Notice I didn't say comfortable. If I need to square something away on your behalf, I can hop on the service helicopter back to base camp and deal with it. I am *not* your supervisor." He looked around. "See, I've already made you happy. No, that responsibility belongs to your division supervisor, to be named at a later date. I can, however, be your mentor. I've had thirty years with our beloved bureaucracy, know this part of the country pretty well and understand fire behaviour in Ontario's bush. Any questions?"

This time, Nate's boss, Chester Wilkes spoke up. "Yeah, what's left for us to do?"

After a round of chuckles, Nick stood up. "I'm sure we can find something for you. Have a good afternoon, gentlemen."

Chapter 55

DAY 8: 10:00 HOURS, WHITE LAKE PROVINCIAL PARK

S IX SCHOOL BUSES WERE BACKED UP at the White Lake Provincial Park gatehouse. Twenty fire fighters sat on each bus, anxious to get on with business. A personnel officer went from bus to bus and collected their crew information sheets. Within minutes, they were on their way into the park, following a ½ ton truck. They would soon be assigned campsites, directed to the mobile cookery and then briefed. They would stay at the park for a night before climbing back on the buses to be transported to a staging area at Wawa 43, along with their camping gear and fire fighting equipment. From the staging area, they would be ferried to their locations on the fire by medium helicopters where they would set up their own line camps. In effect, they would be parked right on the fire perimeter.

"White Lake Provincial Park was established in 1962. It has been in existence for over forty years. A little bit of trivia. It was declared a provincial park just two years before the last log drive took place from White Lake, down White River to Lake Superior. It's classed as a 'Natural Environment' park, one of six classifications in the Ontario Parks system. The park covers seventeen hundred and twenty-six hectares or four thousand two hundred and sixty-five acres. Our key objective is to provide protection to its landscape and special features. At the same time we offer camping, hiking, boating, fishing, swimming, canoeing, wildlife viewing and natural heritage education to visitors".

The park superintendent delivered his short speech to Bill Gorley, incident management commander and Tom Gregory, his logistics chief. It was delivered from memory, and with some intensity. He obviously was not comfortable turning over his park to an army of fire fighters. He paused, searching for the right words. "I hope you treat it with respect and be 'light on the land'." This phrase was flavour of the month ten years ago, used primarily by land use, resource and park planners within the Ministry of Natural Resources. In essence, it meant "leave no footprint" or sign that you were there. A couple of years later, the flavour of the month was "paradigm paralyses". This phrase was used to challenge staff into accepting new ideas—in this case, major downsizing and organizational change. If you didn't buy into it, your own ideas were paralysed. Governments were notorious for promoting these "mind-trap" nuggets of wisdom.

Bill Gorley stood up. In a calm measured voice, he reassured the superintendent that the park would be left the way it was found and perhaps even better. He handed the super a two-page briefing note. "This is going out to all personnel associated with the fire organization that will be staying here or passing through to Wawa 43. It's a code of conduct specific to the park. When you get a chance, take a look at it. I also understand you'll be staying on as our camp manager. If there's anything going on that you're not comfortable with, see me directly and we'll fix it." This leap-frogged the chain of command, but Bill sensed that the super needed some stroking.

Somewhat reassured, the super left them to their business.

Bill looked to his logistics chief. "Tom, what have you got for me?"

Tom reached across the table and handed Bill a map. "Take a look at this and I'll explain."

Bill Gorley scanned the site map of White Lake Provincial Park's recreational area quickly and looked up at Tom in anticipation.

WHITE LAKE PROVINCIAL PARK

Tom looked down at his notes. "First, an overview. The park has three campgrounds with a total of one hundred and eighty one campsites. That doesn't include the group campground that could take up to one hundred campers. I have plans for it and will get to that later. With a prospector tent at each site, based on five people per tent, we could house over nine hundred fire fighters."

Bill looked at him, his mouth open indicating the onset of disbelief. Before he could say anything, Tom continued. "I know, I know. We won't need that many campsites. And I buy into the concept of getting the troops out to the fire ASAP. But before I continue, at any given time, how many fire fighters will be filtered through here?"

Bill didn't skip a beat. "I want to feed and house no more than one hundred and fifty fire fighters *and* only if we get backed up transporting them out."

"That works for me, Bill." Tom pointed on the map. "I recommend we confine the troops to 'Woodlily' campground. There are sixty-five sites, most with electricity, five vault toilets, a laundromat and six strategically located water taps with potable water. There are two downsides. One, it's the closest campsite to the helicopters, but if we set them up on the west side of the campground, noise shouldn't be an issue. And two, the comfort station with showers is in the 'Moccasin Flower' campground, but it's a short walk."

"And the advantages?" Bill could hazard a guess, but he wanted to make sure Tom had thought it through.

"Many. It's closer for crews to walk to helicopters, if required. It's closer to where we'll set up the cookery. Getting back to the group campground, there's lots of room for the mobile cookery and military shelters for the picnic tables. And by the way, there's no end to the picnic tables the park can lend us. So it's close to the group campground. It's close to the amphitheatre where information boards can be set up and briefings and debriefings carried out. It's close to the swimming area just east of the group campsite when a little R and R is required. Sites with electrical outlets can be used to charge satellite phones and GPS's. And finally, it's the closest and best access for vehicles and buses. Buses can turn-around at 'parking area1' and we can park all crew cabs and trucks in 'P1' as well."

"Sounds good ... so far. Tell me about the heliport."

Tom leaned back in his chair and folded his arms. His body language telegraphed his concern. "This is a tough one. We've got room for three mediums and two lights or two mediums and three lights. Fuelling and maintenance could be an issue. The province has nine fuel bowser trucks, each with a capacity of eleven thousand, five hundred litres. That's a little better than twenty-six hundred gallons for you old timers. Three of them with 'Jet A' fuel are on their way, one for here and two to be located close to the fire. I've arranged for 'Jet A' deliveries by a commercial tanker to top up our fuel trucks as required. Our potential issue is fuelling and helicopter maintenance just above the beach. This is a provincial park and we're damn close to White Lake."

Bill liked to throw it back to his team. "What are the options?"

"Well, we could fuel above the beach, and the helicopter engineers could do their maintenance stuff there as well. We'd have to take precautions. Or, we could use the rehabbed gravel pit across the highway for fuelling and maintenance. In both cases, we'd need to use generators to provide lighting for the engineers. I like the gravel pit option for fuelling and then parking the helicopters in the park for security. It does have a few drawbacks. The pit will need wetting down to prevent helicopter down wash from sand blasting the helicopters. That'll require fifteen hundred metres of hose from the closest water source and a couple of pumps to push it. Probably a half dozen run-ups a day should do it. There's also the issue of security for the pump equipment and the fuel truck. Neither issue is a big deal. But I believe it's better than chancing a fuel spill so close to the lake."

Bill smiled. "I agree with you on that one. What's next?"

"The park is a camp manager's dream." Tom pointed to the map. "The park warehouse, not far from the park entrance, has plenty of room for forest fire suppression equipment (FFSE). There's also room for two reefer trailers. One will be a freezer/cold storage unit. The other will be for dry goods. They're both on their way loaded and should be here shortly. I've also ordered a kitchen trailer and base camp trailer should arrive this afternoon. The base camp trailer will be going up to the fire with a small service organization."

Bill tilted his head slightly and raised caterpillar eyebrows. "Refresh my memory on the base camp trailer."

"Sure. It comes complete with twenty pumping units, one hundred and twenty boxes of hose, chainsaw kits, burnout torches, hand tools, tents, tarps and other support equipment."

Bill changed lanes. "How will people be fed until the kitchen trailer gets set up?"

"The crews have been issued initial attack food kits, cookery kits and propane kits. They'll look after themselves until we're set up. I've got someone on his way into White River for sandwiches, snacks and take-out for the long team, service organization and us for today. The cooks are on their way, and my people tell me they'll be set up this evening to provide supper for up to fifty people."

Bill nodded his approval.

"Now—housing for support staff, pilots, engineers and us." Again, Tom pointed to the map. "Park staff accommodations will be taken up with park staff, who will be working for us. In essence, they'll maintain the park grounds, garbage collection, clean-up, as well as provide transportation throughout the park for staff where required. The Junior Ranger camp in the park has been closed down for some time now, but it has been maintained and is clean and functional. It has rooms for thirty people. We'll put ourselves and the overhead team there. People we've picked up as extra fire fighters (EFF) will be set up with prospector tents at Woodlily campground."

Tom took a breath. "As for the pilots and engineers, we all know they require their eight hours of prone rest and sticking them in the middle of all this commotion won't cut it. So, just five minutes down the highway is White Lake Lodge. This time of the year, it's quiet. Most of their business is in the spring for the spring bear hunt and walleye fishing, and in the fall for moose hunting. I've talked to them. They're more than happy to take us in as tenants. There's plenty of room. They're rustic cabins but in great shape. The best part is that there's room for a couple of helicopters on the grounds if we get pinched for space."

"Sounds good to me, Tom—go ahead and arrange the contract and purchase order."

"I already have. They're giving us a good rate."

Bill smiled. He liked his team to be ahead of the curve. "Anything else?"

"Yup." Tom looked around the park office. "This will be used by the overhead team. It has a base station FM radio, three phones and a fax, two computers with internet and intranet service and a photo-copier. I have an office trailer on its way for us. We can use it for our meetings, and there are six work stations. We'll have the fire behaviour officer and safety officer in here with us as well. I don't think we have cell phone service out here, but we'll have two satellite phones set up. Oh, and let me know when you think we'll need a heliport manager. In the meantime, flights will be monitored from the radio operators here. Besides the FM radio, I've ordered a *very high frequency (VHF)* and *high frequency (HF)* radio and a telecom tech to install them.

"Get us a heliport manager ASAP. I want the helipads organized, fuel managed properly and the pilots looked after. I want zero confusion out there. We'll still do radio traffic out of here, but make sure he's set up with a base station radio to monitor."

"OK Boss. By the way, I have a little something off topic for you. Apparently, one of our helicopter pilots spotted an abandoned pickup near the west flank of the fire just off the cutover. He got in close for a look. The truck was on an old forest access road in the ditch. He was able to land close enough to get the license plate number." Tom knew he had the hook in his boss and waited for a response.

Bill leaned forward. "And?"

"And the district called the OPP who ran it. It's a rental. And it was rented to a 'Richard Head'.

"And?"

"And it gets better. Apparently he's a reporter. He was in the Fire Management HQ in Wawa yesterday demanding an exclusive on the fire."

Bill ran his hand over his face as if trying to wipe away this information. "So we likely have someone wandering around the fire— someone who is lost."

"That about sums it up. However, it's out of our hands. As we speak, the OPP helicopter is out looking for him. Just in case, I've passed the word through the system, so our people will be keeping a look-out for him."

"Thanks, Tom. As usual, you're on top of everything. I'm going to be out of the picture this afternoon. Justin is doing the suppression part of a *fire assessment report (FAR)*. I'll be meeting with him when he returns to finish it. Then we're off to Wawa to present it to the district manager and the fire program manager. I hope to be back by 19:00 hours. You're in charge here while I'm gone. Get Ed to set up a team meeting for 20:00 hours."

"You think they'll buy into your preferred strategy for tackling Wawa 43?"

Bill hesitated. He knew the pressure the district manager was under to satisfy the resource users, especially cottagers and the woods industry. He also knew that the fire program manager was under extreme pressure to prevent damage and impact to the town of Hornepayne. But most of all, he knew that shit ran downhill and he stood at the bottom. "Let's hope so, Tom—and let's hope they find that reporter."

Chapter 56

DAY 8: 12:00 HOURS, SOMEWHERE ON THE SOUTH END OF WAWA 43

RICHARD HEAD WAS IN SHOCK. His short-term memory was playing tricks on him. Recollections were out of sequence. His mind processed his recent experience like it was a book with pages torn and cast aside by a child looking only for pictures. He sat on a log, shivering uncontrollably. He scratched absentmindedly at multiple sores on his rubbery, pink skin, occasionally forcing off a swollen, fat leach. Where a vampire slug dropped off, a trickle of fresh blood followed.

His red face was puffed up like an exaggerated apple doll, eyes hidden by little mounds of swollen flesh. At a closer look, the redness was not a solid cast. It was a random mosaic of a thousand little red pin-pricks, a testament to the previous night's mosquito fiesta. In one horrible twenty-four hour period, his psyche had absorbed and filtered more terror than anyone else might experience in a lifetime. His adrenalin had quick-started so many flight-or-fight responses that his 'emotions tank' was empty. His mind continued to function but it wasn't running on all cylinders. Thoughts flashed and fizzled like intermittent sparks from a fallen power line.

Richard looked down. He clutched the metal coupling attached to a fire hose close to his chest like a security blanket, an unconscious lifeline to sanity. *Where is my shoe? Why am I wet? Where did this hose come from? Where is my friggin' my shirt?* Reality, like an exhausted swimmer crawling towards the beach, began to work its way back into his thoughts. *Nobody's here. Where did the fire crew go? I remember now. I woke up yesterday covered with leaches. I crawled to the pump site but the helicopter must have taken it and the fire crew.* He looked down at the coupling; then his eyes followed the hose until it disappeared into the ground cover. *They gotta come back for this hose, but when? And what if they don't? And last night!* His mind refused to allow his memory to travel back any farther. It instinctively knew his system could handle only so much trauma. *I gotta get out of here. Think, Richard, think!*

Richard began to slowly take control of his panic. *Why did the crew leave?* He looked around, then willed his stiff, battered body up to its feet and looked up past the tree-tops. The massive column of smoke was there, but off in the distance. *They must have done their job here. But why leave the hose? Maybe in case they might have to come back. What would bring them back? I got it! I got it! Of course— more fire!* His glee suddenly turned to abject despair. *But my pack's at the bottom of Vampire Creek and there's no way I'm going back in there to be a one-man blood donor for the slug army.* He reluctantly tapped the pockets of his pants. *What's that? Holy shit … it's my lighter!*

For a big man, Richard moved quickly, his flabby body driven by a massive release of adrenalin. His mind snapped to attention and fired off rounds of despair-piercing thoughts. He had a mission—a mission that could save his life. He gathered up fine, dry grass. He knew his hobble-range was limited, but he needed small branches and then bigger stuff. He would have to venture as far as he dared into dense cover but damned if he was going to let the pump site out of view. *Screw the flies and screw the mosquitoes! I either start a fire, or I die.*

An hour later Richard had built the framework for his fire, and proud of it he was. It was a collage of twigs, sticks and rotten logs. Remembering his scouting days, Richard piled green foliage on top. The structure was two metres square by two metres high. The foliage gave it an appearance of a thatch-roofed shack. Dried grass had been poked into fissures like log cabin chinking. He stood back to admire his work, hands on hips, a large white stomach now covered with scratches and welts, hung over his belt like an apron. His faced beamed with manic pride as he whipped the lighter out of his pocket with a flourishing motion. With one flick of a thumb (he had already tested it), a tiny flame burst forth. *Ta-da. Should I say a few words before the ceremony?*

"Ladies and gentlemen, and children of all ages, I'd like to take a moment to dedicate this 'flame of liberation' to all the losers and jerk-offs out there who doubted my ability to get a story."

And what a story it will be. Richard was now sporting a smile wider than an elephant's ass. *Reporter risks life and limb to tell the real truth about fighting fire—gets lost—engineers own rescue—flies out of harm's way a hero—garners colossal media attention, and … and writes a book! Yeah, writes a best seller! Does the talk show circuit. Live with what's-his-name and what's-her-name! I'll work out first. Go on a diet. There'll be no need to pay for … affection. They'll do a movie! I'll write the screenplay. There's no end to it!*

In Richard's self-delusional reverie, he had not noticed that the flame on the lighter first flickered, then disappeared. He looked down. *Damn! Gotta pay more attention.* He flicked the lighter again. *Nothing.* He shook it then flicked again. *Oh, no!* Frantic shaking and rapid fire flicking produced nothing but dry spark. His face contorted, its muscles losing control like trapped mice in a plastic bag. *This cannot be happening!* Then something gave from deep, deep inside. His mind drawn taunt with fear, snapped and recoiled like a broken barbwire fence strand. The gap now too great to reconstruct, Richard slumped, his face void of expression as he sunk slowly to the ground.

A few hours later, the O.P.P found him that way, like a great, silent Buddha. They helped him to the helicopter. There was absolutely no resistance as they eased him into the back seat and buckled him up. The pilot turned to him and inquired if he was all set to go. A single tear immerged from the corner of a lifeless eye, hidden by a bloated cheek. It fell without fanfare to a white-knuckled fist clutching a lighter, a fat thumb continually flicking the striker without success.

THE SOW WAS ROCKING BACK AND FORTH on her front paws and panting. Trapped and confused, her instincts had abandoned her. She and her cub were back into the swamp—the one they had left several days before. Heavy smoke assaulted her senses.

Flushing tears obstructed her vision. Her cub sat on its haunches, raised its snout skyward and bawled. To avoid the intruding smoke, the sow staggered easterly until she and her cub hit the lake's shoreline. She could go no further. Only the water offered a way out. She had taken to water before, but it would be foreign to her cub. The smoke here wasn't as intrusive, and confusion was replaced by instinct. She sensed she and her cub would require rest before they proceeded on to the next part of the journey. She found a patch of dry shoreline grass, laid down and curled up. Her cub needed no invitation and unceremoniously nestled into her belly, shifting and squirming until it found the protection it required.

Chapter 57

DAY 8: 20:00 HOURS, WHITE LAKE PROVINCIAL PARK

"YOU'RE NOT GONNA LOVE IT" A haggard Justin Bailey sat slumped in the hard, wooden chair facing the rest of the incident management team. Tom Gregory and Ed Buckner both leaned forward in anticipation. Any news that Justin had could increase their workload exponentially. Ed was poised to take notes, this time on his laptop. Bill Gorley sat back. He and Justin had already been through the scenario that afternoon when they presented the FAR to the District Manager and East Region Fire Program Manager in Wawa.

Bill looked around. He never ceased to be amazed at how quickly things came together on a project fire. Their office trailer had arrived that afternoon and was already set up for limited operations. They had lights and power compliments of a 4000-watt generator rattling outside. Ed had a large, composite, digitized map of the fire to date on a huge magnetic white-board fastened to the wall, showing the fire perimeter and values at risk such as critical wood supply, cottages and cottage subdivisions. Based on the information previously given to him by Justin, magnetic strips with the names of fire crews on them were placed appropriately on the map. In addition, small magnetic replicas of helicopters and heavy water bombers, complete with their ID's, were there as well. For safety as well as strategic purposes, it was imperative to know where people and equipment were located at all times.

With the help of his staff from the overhead team, clipboards ran along one wall like soldiers at attention—each one dedicated to information required to make informed decisions. They held the fed's atmospheric environmental services (AES) forecasted weather and actual, strategic operating plan (SOP) and SOP updates from regional fire, Provincial fire updates, project fire situation reports, AM & PM, actual fire behaviour and predicted, and fire personnel summaries. It was important to understand what was happening across the province in order to come to terms with a provincial response to their requirements.

A large fire organization chart had been posted on another wall. Most of the title boxes were blank. It would probably take a week to fill them all. Other equipment was set up to go and included an overhead projector, a computer/projector interface machine, a flip chart, photo-copier and fax machine. The fax would be operational once a Bell Canada tech arrived to run a temporary landline to the trailer. Since cell phone coverage was non-existent for the White Lake area, two battery-operated satellite phones sat on a table. They would get hundreds of hours of use over the next three weeks. The last piece of equipment, and probably the most important, was a coffee maker sitting at attention on a corner table.

Bill snapped out of his reverie. "Justin, before we go over the fire situation, if you don't mind, I'll brief the team up to speed on the FAR we presented to Wawa's District Manager." He rationalized that this would give the high-strung Justin some time to settle down.

Justin straightened up. "No problem, boss. It's all yours. I'll just grab a coffee while you get started."

Bill opened his brief case and took out a document. "Well, there is some good news." This one liner caught their attention. "Wawa 43 is the East Fire Region's number one priority. Consequently, our resource requests will have leverage over other project fires. Having said that, you all know my philosophy, keep things simple, do more with less." Three heads nodded tentatively in reluctant agreement.

"The tombstone data on the FAR is common knowledge at this point, so I won't go into a lot of detail. In a nutshell, Wawa 43 is presently NUC, fifty-nine thousand hectares in size, and the priorities for protection are the town of Hornepayne, private property and critical wood supply, in that order. I advised the DM and program manager of our progress to date. I'll let Justin brief you on that shortly. One obvious but critical point—we'll have to let the fire run north until we get some weather. Any questions? No? OK, I'll continue."

"We then presented our analysis under each of the four options: monitor the fire only, values protection only, limited suppression and finally, full suppression. However, it really boiled down to two options, limited or full suppression. It was a no brainer. With unlimited spread potential, ten's of millions of dollars of wood supply ahead of it, a possible shut down of the CN rail for an extended period and the communities potentially in harm's way around it, White River, Manitouage, Hornepayne, and, conceivably, Hearst, Wawa 43 is the only woman at the bar. She will be given the undivided attention she is due, full suppression. To clinch the deal, we also discussed some cost/benefit stuff."

"Based on long-term weather forecasts, we may have some help in three or four days. It seems there's a low-pressure system that might grace us with its presence. Fire progression analysis puts this fire somewhere around seventy-five thousand hectares by then. *If* the weather materializes, and *if* we can get a handle on it, this will be a four-week fire from this point on to the UCO stage. Costs will average two hundred thousand dollars per day, five to six million dollars all told. Add on the costs to date and costs to baby it from the UCO to OUT stage, this could be an eight million dollar fire. However, the economic potential for losses if we don't get a handle on it, according to the district, is in the neighbourhood of eighty million dollars, and that's just direct costs. It doesn't factor in exponential costs associated with lost jobs, lost tourism revenues, social and environmental impacts. That could conceivably increase the total costs, direct and indirect, by a factor of three." Bill paused to let it sink in. "We'll leave that to the economists. It's at this point that I'll turn it over to Justin."

Justin stood up and stretched his long, weary frame. "Let me give you an overview, first." He looked down to refer to his notes. "The accepted strategy is full suppression. The terrain does not lend itself well to bulldozer line construction, with a few exceptions, so the primary tactics will be power pumps and hose lay, air attack, hand tool work and burn-out in that order of tactical response. This fire will be labour intensive. I can see close to three hundred and fifty fire fighters on it at the height of its curve. Type 1 crews will carry out initial attack, put their lines in the BHE stage, and be moved to other targets. Their original lines will be backfilled with type 2 crews for sustained attack and, hopefully, mop-up."

Justin hesitated, and looked over to Tom, the team's logistics chief. "I anticipate a minimum of eight medium and eight light helicopters on this fire. Consequently, we'll be setting up a helibase and a small forward attack base camp out of the Hornepayne airport. Since a lot of the south end of the fire can be accessed by road, I see two mediums and three lights flying out of White Lake Park. The other eleven helicopters will fly out of Hornepayne. The Hornepayne location is a risk, but if we have to be pulled out, we can do it quickly."

Tom interrupted. "So I'll need a helibase manager, 'Jet A' fuel and a service organization up there."

Justin pursed his lips and ran a hand through dishevelled hair. "Yes. I have a list for you. Believe me, I don't like setting up a mirror organization anymore than you do. It leads to duplication. But I don't think we have a choice. White Lake can't handle the helicopters we need, and ferrying people and supplies from here by helicopter will cost us an additional twenty thousand dollars a day just in tariff charges."

Tom put up his hands in supplication. "I know, Justin. And I don't disagree with your proposal. I'm just trying to get a sense of what's required." Nerves were beginning to unravel.

Justin placed a map on the table. "Let me give you guys a snapshot of where we're at and how I see us moving forward."

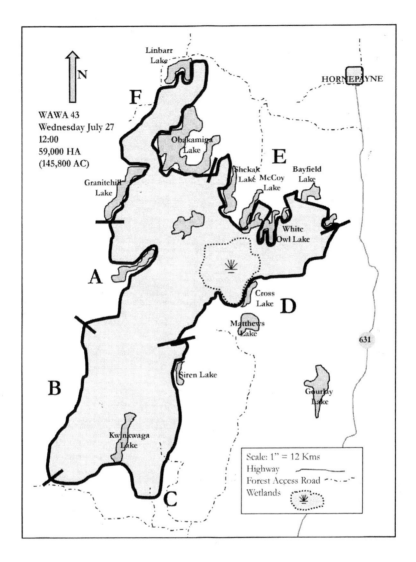

WAWA 43
Wednesday July 27
12:00
59,000 HA
(145,800 AC)

Scale: 1" = 12 Kms
Highway
Forest Access Road
Wetlands

"Right now, I've identified six divisions, A to F. Of course, that could change, depending on fire growth. Let me go division by division."

Justin took a shallow breath. "Division 'A' is unmanned. A lot of dry swamp and some hummocks in the south half, mostly ridge country in the north half up to Granitehill Lake. I won't get into fire crew requirements right now. Suffice to say it's not good terrain for hand tools. When the Manitoba crews get here I'll put them in that division. They're used to pumps and hose. I'll need the OK to do some burn-out in the north half to tie into a series of small lakes—assuming the fire doesn't beat me to it. A division supervisor will be required when the crews show up."

We're just about in the same situation with division 'B', except for approximately six kilometres at the north end." He looked to Tom. "I'll need a good bulldozer leader and four bulldozers, D12 or equivalent."

"Now for division 'C'. I've already got three Ontario ranger crews working the west half. Most of it's off the forest access road. There's little pieces of unburned fuel that they're cleaning up with the drip torches now. I'll have the New Mexico HotShot crews hand tool it from Kwinkwaga Lake easterly as far as they can go. From that point on, it'll be power pumps and hose. I'm using the most experienced fire crew leader as division super right now, but I'll need a replacement shortly."

"Division 'D' will be all power pumps and hose. I'll plug crews in as I get them. It's a big division, approximately thirty five kilometres. I need a division supervisor yesterday to assess it and keep an eye on it. I may have to bust it up into two divisions later on."

Justin's voice became raspy, so he took a mouthful of cold coffee. "The east half of division 'E' is my biggest concern. I've got the six ranger crews working the west half, and they're holding their own. I'm pounding the east half with four air tankers. If it breaks out there beyond Bayfield Lake, then we're back to square one with the threat to Hornepayne. Four ranger crews are going in there first thing tomorrow morning. I'm going to run that one myself for the day. If you can get me a division supervisor tomorrow, I'd appreciate it."

"And finally, division 'F'. Given forecasted wind direction, speed, etc., division 'F' will grow substantially. It is presently unmanned and will be monitored until such time as we can put people in front of it."

"Any questions?" Justin looked around to each face.

Bill spoke up. "Justin, what's your vision for this fire?"

Justin did not hesitate. "My focus is on divisions B, C and E right now. If the winds don't fool us and come out of the north again, give me five days to tie in B and C. I'll know by tomorrow at this time if we can hold onto the east half of E. If the answer is 'yes', then we've bought some critical time for Hornepayne." He looked around to the group, the wrinkles on his forehead projecting anxiety. "Is that all, because I've got another four hours of work ahead of me?"

Bill sensed his angst and smiled. "More like four weeks—but who's keeping track."

Everyone knew that you could second-guess this fire for a millennium, and everyone had lots to keep them busy past midnight, so no more was said. Justin handed his equipment and supply requests to Tom and his personnel requests to Ed. Chairs scraped and tired bodies rose. Coffee cups were topped up and three pairs of legs walked out the door. Bill stayed in his chair and just looked at the map. *Hope I've got the strength to fight this dragon.*

Chapter 58

DAY 9: THURSDAY, JULY 28TH, 05:00 HOURS, WAWA 43, WEST SIDE OF DIVISION E

C INDY SAT ON A SHORELINE ROCK, protecting a mug of hot coffee with a pair of hands that were red, cracked and calloused by countless days of gruelling work and little attention. A bright, yellow bandana covered her short blond hair. She would use this same bandana to protect her lungs from the acrid smoke that had become an unwanted cloak all too often. The bandana was not an Ontario fire ranger standard. It was something that British Columbia fire crews used. Its effectiveness was limited, but she decided to try one a year ago. Since then it became a habit and eventually an old friend. When other crew leaders joked with her about it, she called it her "lucky bandana". From that time on, they had referred to it as her "lucky *banana.*" It had the potential to be a sexist remark, but she had learned to ignore it. Sensitivity eventually dulled in a male-dominated work environment.

Cindy looked out across the lake. The steam from her coffee mirrored the morning fog rolling off the flat water. She could barely make out the other side. Its shadowy shoreline hung back and occasionally peeked through the fog like an elusive spectre. She turned her head and looked back at their campsite, her large, unblinking cat's eyes taking in the outdoor stage props with a forest backdrop.

Perhaps what stood out most, conspicuous by their colour, were the four, red and white, one-person, nylon tents with red nylon tarps, randomly placed to take advantage of terrain. They sat like delicate, shiny turtles in front of a back-drop of drab green. A large twelve-foot by fourteen-foot prospector tent, propped up to a height of close to eight feet by eight, eighteen-foot poplar poles, sat to one side. A slight sag in the dirty white canvas suggested that it had been erected in haste, by people who were too exhausted to care. It was the crew's communal tent, brought in and used only when a long stay was anticipated.

The rest of the campsite was somewhat dishevelled. A pair of large, orange chest coolers, one balanced precariously on top of the other, sat in front of the prospector tent. A lime green, five-gallon water cooler sat next to the chest coolers. A little closer within her peripheral vision, a green propane stove sat on a large flat rock. The stove, fed by a twenty-pound tank, hissed with the effort to percolate the pot of coffee, now bubbling and steaming on top of it. In front of each turtle-tent, three-part personal packs, called "fire incident packs", sat in semi-collapsed states. They were tri-coloured— red, blue and yellow, each one detachable and each one dedicated to carry the essentials of a short to lengthy stay in the bush.

In front of the fire incident packs, boots of various sizes and materials stood up or flopped over on their sides. Boots were not issued; they were personal choices. The only thing they had in common was safety toes and safety shanks. Some were made of leather, while others were ballistic nylon, green rubber or orange rubber chain saw boots. *All* of them had seen better days.

Like a movie camera panning a scene, Cindy shifted her gaze from the 6:00 o'clock to 3:00 o'clock position. A make-shift clothes line was strung between two trees, sagging from the weight of dirty jump suits, an eclectic array of work socks and tea shirts, and one training bra. She smiled at the incongruity.

Her head then panned back to 12:00 o'clock. A loon broke through the curtain of fog and slipped towards her, leaving a shallow, silent wake behind it. She rotated her head to 10:00 o'clock to admire the five-metre by five-metre log helipad they had constructed yesterday. A short vertical stake stood next to it. Nailed to the side of the stake, at the top, was a corrugated cardboard, tent heater box. It was fixed horizontally and functioned as their mailbox. They would place their food and equipment requisitions and miscellaneous memos in it for pick-up by the division supervisor. The super would, in turn, use it for his comments or requests.

At the 9:00 o'clock position, about twenty metres away, the Wajax Mark-3 fire pump sat quietly, waiting to be fired up for another sixteen-hour day. The inch and a half fire hose attached to it snaked its way into the undergrowth like an endless fat, white serpent.

Cindy carefully took a sip of her coffee. She instinctively knew her crew wouldn't be here too long. *Two more nights. No point in setting up a more permanent campsite.* When a large fire was under control (UCO), a crew could spend up to two weeks in one location. A campsite would be transformed to provide a higher level of comfort. Picnic tables and cook tables would be built. Open-air shelters with canvas covers would be erected. Trails would be cut to the helipads and make-shift privies. Cardboard signs would go up announcing the name of their campsites or providing a caustic greeting: "Go away!", "We gave at the office!" "No one lives here anymore!" Furious work days and boring nights lead to bizarre behaviour. She recalled on one fire, flying tree-top from line camp to line camp, seeing a fire crew member standing on a helipad, his arm, hand and thumb up, hitching a ride—wearing nothing but boots, a belt and his MT1000 radio.

Today would be another difficult day. The fire weather report and fire behaviour predictions she retrieved from the mail box, predicted another good burning day. However, she felt confident that her crew had knocked the crap out of the kilometre of fire line they were tackling. Her only concern was the three small jump fires they had wrestled down. There was still some sub-surface fire there and it would receive special attention today.

At this point in the fire season, it was hard *not* to milk the job. She knew that if she advised the division super that they had the line in good shape, they would be yanked to another target and consequently another start to another new piece of fire. The novelty had worn off a long time ago. As Jim was fond of saying, "My 'give-a-shit is broken". She would, however, give her super an honest assessment. Whether or not they moved would be his call.

Cindy's thoughts changed course. *I wonder how Wally is doing. I hope he got out of there. Not likely. His stubborn streak would win over common sense hands down.* Cindy felt a growing emptiness. Tears surfaced in her eyes. She knew she would never see him again. What was even worse was the realization that she just could not understand the connection. *Shit. Get over it. There's work to do. Time to wake the kids up.* She wanted to be on the fire line by 07:00 hours.

Cindy could hear soft snoring coming from the little red and white shrouds. She stood up with some discomfort and picked her way over to three men tucked in their sleeping bags. *Do I traumatize them by yelling and kicking feet? No, they deserve better treatment than that.* One by one, she opened a tent flap and poked her cup of hot coffee inside. One by one, noses twitched to the allure of coffee and one by one crusty eyes opened to the need of a caffeine fix.

Siren Lake, 07:00 hours

WALLY SAT ON HIS PORCH, coffee in hand. Light smoke was drifting through the camp, making his eyes water and triggering an occasional cough. *Probably hack up a lung shortly.* He looked across the lake. The fire was now working its way down to the shoreline, burning slowly downhill. It torched occasionally when it hit a spruce or balsam fir. The shoreline swamp directly across from him was still resisting fire but was veiled in smoke.

Something's there. He squinted to improve his vision. *Can't make it out.* Wally reached over, picked up his binoculars from the corner of the bench seat, pulled them to his eyes and adjusted the retackles. *A sow and cub! They're trapped!* Wally's heart began to race. His palms grew damp, and an overwhelming flood of anxiety surged through his body. *What the hell's happening?* His mind could not compute his body's reaction. He stood up as if to shake out the feelings. *She's pacing back and forth. The cub is right behind her.*

Then it happened. The realization struck Wally like the flash/bang of a cannon. The veil of confusion drew back like a show-stage curtain. His heart beat dropped from a gallop to a cantor then a walk. The adrenalin surge flattened out. His high anxiety immediately disappeared and was replaced by relief, then calm and finally, joy. In a nano-second, Wally assessed the dilemma. *One of us is going to die soon! Please God, let it be me!*

Chapter 59

DAY 9: 13:00 HOURS, DIVISION C

T HINGS HAD HAPPENED AT LIGHT SPEED for the New Mexico HotShots. They had arrived at White Lake Provincial Park at 07:00 for a quick overview briefing, loaded back on to their buses and arrived at the Wawa 43 staging area at 09:00. Their division supervisor was waiting for them, along with packed lunches, camping gear and hand tools. The briefing was short and to the point. He was young—late twenties—tall, and quietly confident. He handed out maps and fire weather information to the two HotShot superintendents. Both had motioned their captains over to look at the maps. After a brief discussion, they were loaded back on the buses, bounced along the road from hell for forty-five minutes and dropped just east of Kwinkwaga Lake.

It was now 13:00 hours and they were in the thick of it. Nate Ramirez took a look at the map once again just to get a sense of the size of Wawa 43.

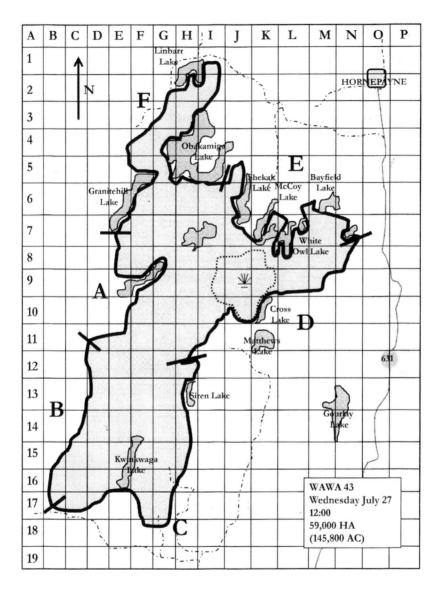

His Rio HotShots were in sector D17 and working easterly. They had been ferried in by a Bell 212 medium helicopter from the forest access road to a dry swamp on the edge of the lake. The eight-kilometre round-trip took only ten minutes. Twenty fire fighters, camping gear, supplies and fire equipment were all in within forty minutes. The other HotShot crew had been ferried in by another medium helicopter to a small gravel pit on the side of a forest access road at the top of sector E18. They would be working west to the Ramone HotShots. Between the forty fire fighters, they had five kilometres, or three miles of fire line to construct with axes, Pulaski's, shovels and chainsaws. Tactics were simple. Scratch a fire line down to mineral soil. Keep the line as close to the fire edge as possible. Keep it narrow—no more than a metre wide. Speed was of the essence. Burn out the narrow piece between the fire line and the fire. Watch for jump fires and hit them aggressively. Be tied into each other by 22:00 hours that evening.

Nate smiled to himself. They had been at it for two hours now. He still had difficulty thinking metric. *So that means constructing three miles of fire line in this shit at a rate of fifteen hundred feet an hour. Not likely. We might get a thousand feet an hour—but we'll get it done sometime tonight.*

Winds were in their favour, brisk at fifteen kph, out of the south-west. The terrain or the humidity was not in their favour. Jump fires would slow them up. The relative humidity, now at a meagre 35%, would almost guarantee jump fires. They wouldn't be getting any help from the air tankers—they were busy in Division E. They did however, have the use of a medium helicopter and bucket. That might just save their asses.

The twenty men in each crew worked like a well-oiled machine on an assembly line. This was not, however, the terrain and cover type they were use to busting. Nate's boss, Chester Wilkes, had moved on ahead, scouting the fire line, doing some cursory over-head clearing with a pulp axe and marking their trail with blaze orange flagging tape. Two chain saw operators and one helper followed. This was heavy chain saw country with a thick under-story of spruce and balsam fir. Anything cut was thrown into the burn side of the line.

Including Nate, that left sixteen fire fighters to bust and protect fire line. They automatically organized into three squads of five, with each one assigned a squad boss. Each squad was given a section of line. Once completed, a squad would leap-frog ahead and pick up another section of line.

The grunt work would start with two fire fighters using Pulaski's. This particular tool had a grubbing pick on one side and an axe head on the other. Duff layers would be grubbed away, the head flipped over when roots required cutting then flipped back for ground pounding.

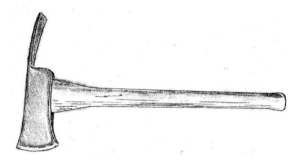

Two more fire fighters would follow up with shovels, throwing any combustible material to the fire-side, and mineral soil would be laid down on the non fire-side.

Nate's job was to inspect the work, jump in occasionally to give a fire fighter a break and eventually follow behind with the drip torch, burning fuels from the fire line to the fire. He would move from squad to squad. Timing was everything when you were burning out.

The fifth member of each squad carried a five-gallon collapsible back pack filled with water, lovingly referred to as a piss-pack. It had a rubberized hose attached to the bottom with a trombone-like piston pump at the end. Water could be shot six metres in a steady stream or sprayed by depressing a thumb deflector. The person wearing the thirty-pounds of bladder and water was required to knock down any fire that snuck to the wrong side of the fire line. The squad worked as a tight unit, but each member worked a safe distance from his or her neighbour. Communication was critical. It was common for a squad boss to halt production and call for help from the other squads, particularly when water was required.

Once the superintendent had flagged his line, he would return, look for jump fires, call in for air support if required, assist with burning out and coordinate the total package. His most critical responsibility, however, was ensuring the line was in the right place.

CHESTER WILKES HAD TWENTY-FIVE YEARS of fire experience and tons of training. His twenty-four mandatory and ten recommended fire courses included "Advanced Fire Behaviour". It was critical in determining the location of the fire-line. Too close and it would be over-run before the line could be constructed. Too far, and the advancing fire could work up a head of steam and fly by, waving hands of fire as it passed over. The distance not only depended upon fire weather, but also on forest fuels and terrain. After awhile, knowing where to run the line became instinctive. However, if one was not familiar with fuel types, one could make mistakes. This was Chester's first time in north-eastern Ontario.

Chester hacked his way through the dense under-story, keeping the fire at a respectful distance by sound, smell and an occasional visual opportunity. An hour into his brushing and flagging, he ran into a huge rock outcrop. It ran for at least sixty metres and rose gradually to a height of twenty metres. There wasn't much to burn on its surface. It was covered with moss, crunchy at this time of year, and some sparse ground hemlock. He knew the moss would easily carry fire and that fire burned faster uphill. He stopped, looked around and weighed the alternatives.

Chester had three options. Option one: he could back track a hundred metres and angle his line to the top. Option two: he could carry on and risk an uphill slope behind his crew. Or option three: he could run his line uphill from this point, then downhill somewhere beyond the rock. Option one made the most tactical sense. There would be no obvious jogs in the line, and the crew would be in a position to handle a slow-moving, downhill burn-out from the top. The risk was that it required burning out a larger area and he would have to back-track. Option two was expedient. It did, however, result in a significant uphill slope behind his people, a recipe for entrapment. He didn't really care for the third option. It resulted in a couple of ninety degree turns in the line—a recipe for jump fires.

Chester was getting tired. He didn't want to back-track. He opted for the second choice. He would keep going. He was confident his people could handle a little fire excursion on moss-covered rock.

15:00 hours

THE RIO HOTSHOTS HAD CONSTRUCTED a kilometre of fire line when they hit the rock face. Nate looked up at the expanse of rock and moss. *Geez, this could be trouble.* It wasn't the main fire he was concerned about—it was back-burning into the wind and moving towards them at less than ½ a metre per minute. It was his *own* burn-out that could cause them problems. Once the standing spruce and balsam fir in his fire's path began to torch, burning embers could be picked up by convective heat and dropped behind them.

He decided to check the slope out and began to climb diagonally to the top. The moss was extremely dry. Each step was like walking on fine crystal. *Tricky if fire gets in here, but nothing we can't handle.* Just before he hit the top of the rise, he turned back. If Nate had kept going, he would have discovered the thirty metre wide strip of two-year-old blow-down, a tangled mess of dead spruce and balsam fir that ran away from the ridge for one hundred and fifty metres. If fire got into the blow-down, the mythical towers of flames in *Dante's Inferno* would pale by comparison.

18:00 hours

THE HOTSHOTS HAD MADE BETTER TIME than they had anticipated. They were used to constructing wider fire lines. Their directive to keep it under a metre, bought time, and time earned them distance. Chester had just returned from a recon of the newly constructed fire line and contacted the Ramone HotShot crew superintendent. Between the two of them, they only had a kilometre of line left to construct. After discussing the situation with Nate, they decided it was time for him to turn back and begin his burn out.

Thirty minutes later, armed with a full Wajax drip torch and two spare gallons of the diesel fuel/gasoline mixture, Nate was ready to burn. He could see the advancing fire twenty to fifty metres away, burning into the wind. He had three crewmembers with him, each with a back-pack pump. Their job was to ensure fire did not cross the line. To make sure that at least two were on site at all times, they would rotate their trips back to the lake to fill up the packs. A small pond was discovered further down the line and about fifty metres away from the non-fire side. That would save a lengthy walk as they progressed.

Nate looked at one of his crewmembers. "Things are really in our favour, in fact, classic. We've got the wind at our backs and a main fire will be drawing in our burn-out." The crewmember understood the principle. As the fire progressed, it would literally be starving for oxygen. Any fire lit in its path would be drawn towards it at a phenomenal rate. Nate thought that in essence it would be like two gladiators charging towards each other in battle. He silently hoped that they would both lose.

Nate finally reached the large rock face. *So far, so good.* He was still uncomfortable with the line location, so he waited for two of the back packers to arrive. As soon as they showed up, he looked towards the main fire. *About fifty metres away at this point.* He walked in towards the main fire approximately ten metres and laid fire back towards the control line. He walked down the line ten metres and repeated the tactic. The control line held. *We're almost out of the woods.* His burn out lines would converge before being pushed towards the main fire by wind.

His anticipation of success was premature. A group of white birch, fifteen metres high and in a leafless state due to drought, suddenly torched. The loose bark ignited and was picked up by swirling convective currents of air. They floated aimlessly in every direction like wind-born candles. Three of them floated above the fire fighters and dropped gently to the moss-covered slope behind them. The dry moss burst into metre-high flames that joined and raced uphill. The two crewmembers ran to cut the fire off at the top. They didn't quite make it.

Nate turned to look at the situation. His mind processed it at light speed. Two, struggling men, dressed in yellow and olive green, black rubber bladders on their backs, cresting a ridge. They disappear. A violent flash of orange, red and yellow flame mushrooms ten metres above the ridgeline. Thick, black smoke rolls up to fifty metres, bends at its apex and curls over him towards the main fire. The next seconds seem like hours. He can't move, glued to his position, eyes transfixed on the ridge. Two men finally appear, each supporting the other, stumbling, getting up, stumbling. A wave of relief washes over him.

Nate immediately brought up his radio. "Chester from Nate."

"Go ahead, Nate."

"We've got a problem—heavy duty fire behind our line."

There was a pause. "Don't tell me. It's that rock face."

The corners of Nate's mouth twitched slightly to form a weak smile. "You got that right, Chester. We'll need the medium and bucket up here ASAP. A tanker wouldn't be out of the question, as well."

"I'll make the call and be over there in ten minutes. Take a look at the situation for me."

"Affirmative, Chester."

Chester didn't even have time to initiate the call. The division supervisor, Derek Saunders, had seen the sudden plume of black smoke from the air and called for the Bell 212 and bucket. In a matter of minutes, he was over the scene in a light helicopter. He contacted Chester and advised him that the medium helicopter and bucket was on its way. As soon as he saw the potential for the fire to trap the hotshot crewmembers as they continued on, he contacted Justin Bailey for tanker support. He was assured that one of the tankers would be on its way shortly. Derek's next message was critical.

"Wilkes from Helitack 67, do you copy, Chester?"

"Go ahead, Derek."

"There's a least one tanker on its way. It'll work in tandem with the medium and bucket." He paused to gather as much calm as he could. "From up here, that big jump fire has potential to flank and trap you guys. I'm going to hang around for awhile to keep an eye on it."

Chester was painfully aware that he had not followed his instincts earlier on. "I'm sorry, Derek. I had a sense that that part of the line could cause us trouble. I should have been on top of it."

"Don't sweat it, my friend. Stuff like that happens daily out here. If you start to get into trouble, your best escape route is to continue along the main fire until you hit the other crew and walk your people out that way. If I have to, I'll get the medium to drop its bucket and pull you guys out."

Derek carefully considered his next words. "But I don't think it will come to that. Keep doing what you're doing and I'll watch your back. And by the way, you guys are doing a hell of a job down there. It would have taken us a lot longer to hand tool that line."

Nate had monitored the flurry of radio traffic and advised his crew by radio to keep line building to tie into the other HotShot crew. He looked towards the source of new fire activity and started walking uphill. He needed to see what they could be up against. *What was it my grandfather used to always say, "You gotta learn to expect the unexpected."*

Chapter 60

DAY 9: 18:00 HOURS EAST FIRE REGION, FALCON RESPONSE CENTRE, SUDBURY

T *WO DAYS OFF AND I STILL FEEL LIKE A WORN OUT INSOLE.* Rick Sampson sat in the Duty Officer's chair and passed a magic wand hand over a rubbery, stubble face, a gesture intended to brush away the cob webs and crawly thoughts hidden in the dark recesses of his brain. He worked hard to resist good feelings or positive urges. Surely a black, spidery thought would leap out, devour them and scuttle around in his head looking for more. Better to conjure up nothing than risk arachnidan thoughts that might dominate his waking day. *Awe, too late. Spent hours on the phone with Beth. Nothing resolved. Worse still, not a trace of warmth in the crossbow drawn conversations. A forty-eight hour diet of bad food, alcohol, anger, and fear with self-pity for dessert sprinkled with a pinch of defiance. Not exactly a winning recipe for 'Good Living' magazine.*

Sheila Monahan approached Rick, her steps light and measured as if walking on broken glass. "You OK, Rick?" *Nothing.* Cindy cleared her throat. "Rick. Are you OK?"

Rick's head snapped up. She caught his look before he could morph a new mask. Pale, cracked lips turned down, face slightly bloating between vertical creases, glazed eyes floating in shallow pools contained in red-rimmed, eyelid-saucers.

Sheila couldn't hide here surprise. *Holy crap! A poster boy for Count Dracula!* "Wow, you look"—*Like shit—cadaverous—morgue fodder?* "Rick, you look terrible."

'Click, click.' Rick was able to skip to a new slide in his carousel of faces—the old, self-assured grin. "Oh, hi Sheila. Doing just fine, thank you. What's up?"

Sheila tilted her head slightly to one side, ratcheted it down a degree, arched an eyebrow and fire a laser guided stare at him. *Can't fool me.* "Afternoon briefing in five minutes. You all set?"

Tight-lipped smile, dimples and all. "Well you see, my one and only friend, it's like this. I've got one little problem. My body's here but my mind is struggling to crawl out of a sewage lagoon. Can you give me the book jacket version before the entire novel?"

Sheila forced a smile. "Sure thing, Rick." She shuffled the stack of papers in her hands. "The nutshell version—only sixteen new starts in the East Fire Region today. All lightning caused, holdovers from the dry lightning storm a week and a half a go."

Rick's look spoke volumes and stopped Sheila's monologue. *Only a week and a half? Seems like a year and a half, no, a lifetime, no, a millennium.* "Sorry, Sheila. Go ahead."

"All initial attacks on new fires today were successful. The largest fire was BHE at one point six hectares, but it took three fire crews and air attack to wrestle it down. That will give you a sense of today's fire behaviour. As of today's date, we have fifty-six fires that are UCO—now for the project fires."

Sheila looked up to see if Rick had digested the situation so far. Satisfied, she continued. "Wawa 42 is BHE at twenty-two hundred and fifty hectares. Sault Ste. Marie 13 is BHE at eleven hundred and twenty hectares. And Sudbury 22 is BHE at sixteen hundred and eighty hectares. No structures lost, no lives lost, no significant injuries to report."

A pause. "Now for our problem child, Wawa 43. Wawa 43 is NUC at—drum roll please—fifty-nine thousand hectares. For those of us who are metrically challenged, that's one hundred and forty-five thousand, seven hundred and eighty-nine acres … and growing. Some details for monsieur le duty officer." Sheila shuffled some more paper.

"Only the back of the fire, the south end has been tied in. There's been some limited progress on the south parts of both the east and west flanks. Concentration of air attack is on a piece to the northeast. The incident management team is trying to plug the dyke with initial attack crews, but they're being dropped in then pulled out with regularity."

Rick put up and hand traffic cop style. "What about Hornepayne?"

"Evacuated. However, the head of Wawa 43 appears to be by-passing the town about eight kilometres to the west. There's a small MNR emergency response team there to help the local first responders."

"What about resource commitments?"

"On Wawa 43 or in general?"

"Big picture stuff."

More paper shuffling. "We have forty-three helicopters across the East Fire Region, ten heavy water bombers, six of which are from Manitoba and the feds, eight Birddog aircraft, one hundred and forty of our Ranger crews, twenty-four out-of-province crews and four hundred type 2 fire fighters committed to fires. In addition we have four incident management teams, one from Manitoba, and four long teams to support them. Three of the IC and LT's are committed to Wawa 42, Wawa 43 and Sudbury 22. One each is in reserve. I don't have the figures on the MNR district and regional staff pulled to support our little party, but it's substantial enough to practically shut down resource programs across the region. Oh, and we're spending money at a rate of close to eight million dollars a day."

Rick smiled. "Impressive. Now, how about weather?"

Sheila, who had subconsciously been standing at parade atten-tion, seemed to relax. "We've actually got some good news, laced with a little bad. A low-pressure system is moving in from the west. The *good* news is like winning a hundred dollars on a ten million dollar sweepstakes. Heaviest precipitation is in the fifteen to twenty millimetre range—and spotty. The *bad* news is like win-ning a hundred dollars on a ten million dollar sweepstakes. The weather system is carrying light precipitation, as low as five milli-metres in some places. We expect it sometime the day after tomor-row." Sheila saw that the time frame didn't register. "The day after tomorrow is Saturday the 30th."

"What are the chances of the heavy stuff hitting Wawa 43?"

Sheila frowned, slumped a little and shifted her weight to one leg. "A crap shoot, Rick."

Rick was chewing lightly on the end of a pencil and twirling it gently like a good cigar. He extracted the substitute. "What is Wawa 43 asking for that we're having trouble supplying?"

"Everything. But high on their Christmas list, and in order of priority, are medium helicopters with buckets, initial attack crews and division supervisors, all of which are standing requests into the province."

Rick began to think out loud. "If Wawa 43 gets the heavy precip, they'll want to slam as many fire fighters into that fire as quickly as they can, so medium helicopters and division supervisors are a must. They'll also need type 2 crews for sustained attack." He looked up at Cindy. "How's Wawa 43 for type 2 crews?"

"Good. In fact we don't have any place to put more crews until they get plugged into the fire. We've got one hundred and twenty fire fighters at White Lake Provincial Park and another hundred waiting in motels from Wawa to Sault Ste. Marie."

Last question. I think I'll throw a curve ball at her. "What about that Wawa 40? Will the two fires join up?"

"Hard to say right now. Wawa 40 is northeast at two hundred hectares. We've got a handle on 40. Even if they join, we don't expect it to act as a buffer for 43. Wawa 40 will just be an appetizer."

For the first time since Noah parked his ark, Rick showed signs of relaxing. He had a sense of the big picture. "Thanks, Sheila, I think I'm ready for the *War and Peace* version of the briefing."

Sheila turned to leave, then hesitated. "Oh. One last thing. Doug and Brad want to see you after the briefing. And no, I don't know what it's about."

Rick watched her walk away. *I can just imagine.*

THE TWO MEN SAT ACROSS FROM RICK at a cluttered conference table, neither one anxious to broach the topic. Rick couldn't help but marvel at their similarities in build. *Two short, square robots—one with hair the other without.* On the other hand, both men noticed some subtle physical changes in Rick. The bags under his eyes looked like under-inflated, black inner tubes. His body had shrunk and his clothes looked several sizes too large. Even his body language reflected inner demons. Once strait and proud, his posture had morphed to that of a puppet with its strings relaxed.

However, there was still some fire in the belly, and Rick was not inclined to make things easy for them as he leaned back in his chair and crossed his arms. If the digital clock on the wall could tick, it would complement the tension in the room. A throat cleared. It was Doug Rainville, the fire program manager, the tree stump with hair.

"Rick, we're worried about you." He looked to Brad Simpson for support then continued. "You're not yourself lately and", a thick finger reached up to loosen a collar. "We've heard rumours that there's trouble at home."

Rick leaned forward and gently placed his hands on the table, supported by spread finger tips, like a sprinter ready to leap out of the blocks. His face darkened. "Are you worried about me or my ability to do the job?"

The two men looked at each other with coincidental "Do you want to take this one?" looks. Brad Simpson's turn. Brad ran a hand over his bowling ball head as if he was checking for hair. "Rick, doing your job has never been an issue, but we think you're almost there. We're also concerned about the situation at home."

Rick's face turned red, his look now deadly. He stood, dry lips parted to speak. Brad raised a blocking hand, his own discomfort turning to resolve. "Sit down, Rick, and count to ten."

Rick exhaled and did as he was told. Brad continued. "I know, your personal life is none of our business, but when it has potential to affect the job we have to deal with the fall out. The cause is not normally our issue. You own it. But Doug and I want to meddle."

Rick looked from one adversary to the other. "Pardon me?"

As if on cue, Doug stepped in. "Neither one of us has been a roaring success in the marriage department. You know the details. We've decided that you're our new project. Consider us your fairy godfathers."

The image of these two fire-plugs in tights and wings was not lost on Rick, and he couldn't resist a smile.

Doug continued. "We hope to spare you the same shit we went through. In a nutshell, if it don't work out, it ain't pretty."

Rick sat back again, his voice now church quiet. "Cut to the chase, gentlemen."

All three men had now entered familiar territory, no pretence, no wagon circling, and no sugar coating. Doug continued. "You're taking two weeks off. What you do with it is up to you, but I strongly suggest you get your house in order—for your own good as well as the fire program's."

Rick's entire body appeared to deflate like a blow-up clown with a sudden leak. "What about the fire situation?"

Brad weighed in. "What have you always told anyone who would listen about the staff here in the fire centre?"

"Yeah, I know—the best in the entire world."

Brad smiled. "Well, you know what? You're right. In fact, just about anyone can sit in the duty officer's chair and do the job because of the support staff. And to prove it, I'm dusting myself off and taking your shifts."

Rick inflated a little and managed a tight smile. "Geez, Louise, the staff will really have to earn their pay now." He paused and dropped the smile. "No options?"

"Nope. And your vacation starts tonight."

Wawa 43

THE PINE WAS NOW A MERE SHELL of its former magnificence. A prince of the forest was now relegated to pauper. Thick, rich-textured bark was black and brittle. Sweeping branches had been stripped of their soft, five-clustered needles for the first fifteen metres. Beyond that, the clusters were now baked to shades of rust and taupe. Thick, blistery rivulets of gummy sap oozed from the fresh spiral wound like fat, white clown tears. The Sentinel was weeping for its children in the valley below. It had failed to warn and protect them.

The canvas of burned-over forest began with subtle shades and shapes of black/grey that contrasted in vertical relief. In the foreground, countless black spikes and spears reached up into a chilled, slate-coloured, indifferent sky. Tightly arranged, uniform stands of jack pine, ravaged by crown fire, stood rigid, like phalanxes of dead, burned soldiers. Surrounding the stands of jack pine, harpoons of blackened white spruce and balsam fir stood randomly or in groups, scorched in staggered agony. But it was the young white pine that the old guard wept for most. They stood tall above the others. Curved, seared branches swept up to the Sentinel, arms reaching, frozen in fear and incomprehension, in eastern prayer, begging for salvation.

As the Sentinel dared to look further out, perspective became less defined. Spikes and spears blended into a rolling sea of black. There was, however, some visual relief. Ribbons and imperfect circles of green crisscrossed and splashed the dark canvas, testaments to unburned perimeters of streams, lakes and ponds. Stark white and muted grey ridges and rock outcrops stood high and naked, burned clean of their protective layers of decaying leaf matter, needles, twigs and branches.

Pale green patches mottled with shades of brown clung like camouflage battle dress to side hills and rested on flats. These were stands of white birch and poplar, at first blush, bastions against fire. A closer look would reveal that underneath an intact canopy of leaves, fire had slowly consumed ground vegetation and vertical undergrowth.

Now raising imaginary eyes from ground to horizon, at mid canvas, the old guard registered random activity. In the foreground, thin wisps and veils of dirty white smoke rose, flattened, dispersed and eventually disappeared—ta-da, magic! Tiny shaped V's patiently floated, circled and occasionally swooped—turkey vultures and bald eagles, searching for victims left behind by the great fire-dragon.

Approaching the top of the canvas, multi-coloured winged shapes flitted and rambled, some randomly, others with purpose. Theses were mechanical birds, intent on doing battle with the stubborn dragon.

Contrary to all artistic rules of contemporary painting, the top one-third of the canvas drew the viewer's eye away from the focal feature. Solid columns of thick, rolling smoke rose, churned and mixed into each other to infinity. Atop the columns, massive mushrooms of dense smoke clouds spread and slipped over the edge of the canvas completing a painting that forced the viewer to flinch and turn away.

The old guard continued to weep blister tears.

Chapter 61

DAY 9: 19:00 HOURS, DIVISION C, SOUTH END OF WAWA 43

NATE RAMIREZ CRESTED THE TOP OF THE ROCK OUTCROP. *Definitely not a pretty picture.* By his estimate, the half-hectare blow down fire was now two hectares and growing. South-west winds were pushing it towards his crew. He looked at the bottom of his map and scratched an 'X' where the jump fire was located.

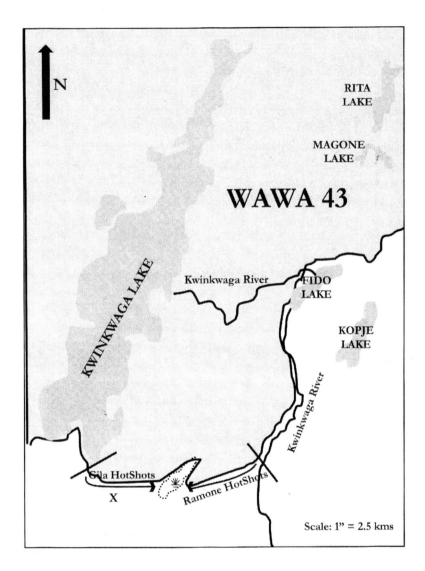

He was not worried about the jump fire becoming a tactical problem. It would eventually run into his burn-out fire. What really concerned him was its potential for trapping his crew. His initial instincts told him to get on the radio and tell them to cut and run. His training and professional pride suggested that they stay and complete their section of the fire line. *Was this the little evil spirit of doubt talking to me?*

He wrestled with a barrage of competing sounds and sights. The whoosh and crackle of animated orange/yellow, fifteen-metre flame was interrupted with the arrival of a huge blue and white 212 helicopter and its thumping percussion. The rotor down wash assaulted the flames' apex, penetrating then bending it out and down. The Bambi bucket suspended below the cable lanyard opened at its base and released two hundred gallons of water and foam on its target. The 212 rose, banked and tore away to get another load.

Shortly after the medium helicopter departed, a huge, ochre-yellow, 415 air tanker skirted above the flames accompanied by its ear-pounding rattle and roar. As it passed overhead, fifty metres to the south and lumbering from east to west, it released its thirteen hundred gallons of foam/water on target. The double whammy of helicopter and tanker made an impact, bisecting an eighty-metre flame-front with a blanket of foam. Nate knew it would take at least another four drops to slow down the fire's advance, then another half-dozen to corral it. He also knew a couple of crews would be needed to tie it into the original fire line. Nate stood for a minute more to digest the results of the battle. *Time to get back to the burn-out.*

An hour later, the two HotShot crews tied into each other. Ten minutes later, Nate arrived, bone weary but upbeat. The burn-out was successful. Their line was holding but would require a day's touch-up and at least three days of mop up, where they would start to work into the fire. He looked to his shoulder. *Good. The little demon took a hike—at least for now.*

Nate explained the large jump fire situation to Chester and the concern that MNR crews would be brought in to handle it. They both agreed that it was their problem and that they should deal with it.

"WILKES TO HELITACK 67, do you copy, Derek?"

"Go ahead, Chester."

Chester responded with a touch of embarrassment in his voice. "How's that jump fire look?"

"Well, the big birds did a job on it, but it looks like I'll have to bring in a couple of crews with pumps and hose to tie it into your line. There's a water source about half a kilometre to the west."

Chester gave it a second to respond. He felt a thickening in his throat that made it difficult to swallow. *Likely fool's pride.* "Derek, we own the problem; maybe we should deal with it."

"I appreciate the offer, Chester, but it's a mess in there with the blow down. It's not a job for hand tooling."

Chester was on a mission. "As I see it, you're about to tie up two of your ranger crews, at least two pumps and a shit load of hose. Give us the pumps and hose and we'll handle it."

There was a very pregnant pause. Chester knew that Derek was wrestling with a concern that the HotShots had little experience with the Wajax pumps, or laying hose. He jumped in. "Derek, we've worked with pumps before and had some recent training at Wawa by a group of MNR retirees. We can do this."

He was right about tying up ranger crews. They were needed elsewhere. "OK, Chester. You should be OK for tonight. I'll get you the equipment first thing in the morning." Helitack 67 was now overhead. The two HotShot crews had tied into a dry swamp. "If that's where you're camping tonight, I'll need a helipad for the morning. I'll probably need a helipad at the jump fire's water source as well."

A relieved HotShot superintendent responded quickly. "Consider it done. We'll need a compass fix on that water source."

"Consider it done as well." The light helicopter turned away and crawled south. In a matter of minutes it was over the pond that would be used as a pump site and rose vertically so it could be easily seen by Chester. "We're on it now, Chester."

Chester took out his compass and took a bearing. "I've got a bearing. Can you give me an approximate distance?"

"No problem." The pilot punched in the coordinates on his consol mounted GPS and helitack 67 sped towards the HotShot crew. He hovered over the crew and punched in another coordinate. With a little digital dickering, he had the distance. "Eleven hundred metres ... or about three quarters of a mile. Do you want the GPS coordinates?"

Chester thought about it for a moment. He did have a hand-held GPS. He accepted the fact that he was a relic and still preferred to do things the old way. "No, that's OK, Derek. Bearing and distance will do. We still have an hour and a half before dark. The crew will set up camp, and Nate and I will wander in to recon the jump and air attack impact. And … thanks."

"I'll bring you guys some grub. Have a good one, gentlemen." Helitack 67 rose, pivoted and flitted away like a big, mechanical dragonfly.

Chester looked at his captain. "What's your take on our situation, Nate?"

Nate had been resting on his haunches. He stood tall and looked at his boss. The sun's rays washed over his face revealing a coppery, leather-tough complexion, a testament to his Spanish/Chiricahua heritage. "Our line is in good shape. We'll get a handle on that jump fire tomorrow. I expect we'll be moving on to another part of this fire shortly."

Chester, eyebrows raised and a slight smile tugging at his lips, looked at Nate. "I see you got your mojo back, brother." Without waiting for a reply, Chester brought his Silva Compass to eye level and picked his path. It ran towards the shimmering, burnt orange, setting sun. He and Nate disappeared into the tangle of spruce and balsam fir.

Chapter 62

DAY 9: 20:00 HOURS,
DIVISION E, EAST OF WHITE OWL LAKE

M AN, IT'S BOILING DOWN THERE. Justin Bailey couldn't
believe it. Just two hours before darkness set in, the relative humidity was still below 40% and they were having
trouble containing two little pieces of fire they had hammered since
Tuesday. His pilot kept Helitack 45 stationary at two thousand feet
while Justin looked down at the flurry of activity below him .

He focused on five critical attack points. Air attack and the
ranger crews had worked like they were possessed but they were
still getting break outs and jump fires. Even as he looked just to the
north and down at a mosaic of forest cover, he could see the beginning "poofs" of new jump fires. *They look like mushrooms growing
through the eyes of a time-lapse camera. Three of the critical points are
in good shape but I really don't love what's happening in the two to the
east.* The helicopter's FM radio was on 'scan' and the ground attack
chatter was at a fever pitch. The four air tankers hammered the
two locations in synchronicity. Tankers 271 and 274 worked the perimeter of the fire. The two CL215's from Manitoba concentrated on
jump fires. Only an hour plus remained before they had to return
to base. Justin wanted to believe that they were the "little train
that could", but the sumo wrestlers rolling around in the pit of his
stomach suggested otherwise. This did nothing for his confidence,
not to mention his disposition.

Then two things happened simultaneously to make him throw
up his hands and almost throw up the contents of his stomach. It

was if the god's were growing tired of the tug of war on the fire perimeter. First, two of the fire crew pumps went US. Justin only had one spare pump on board and had to quickly determine who should get it. The decision would be simple. He turned to the pilot. "Take us down to the deck." He then requested and received clearance from the Birddog officer. There would be two criteria—who was struggling the most to hold their line and which of the two areas had the biggest potential for fire escape?

Justin was not expecting, nor was he prepared for, the second situation.

East of White Owl Lake – Cindy Corrigan crew

WHY ME, LORD? Cindy Corrigan couldn't believe how poorly her Karma was cooperating lately. Her crew was totally spent and on the verge of physical and mental collapse. She had been determined to get them through the next two hours when the "shit happens" axiom crawled out of its hole. Their pump quit. *Jim had gone back for hose and should be close to the pump.*

"Corrigan to Henderson, what's happening down there, Jim?"

"Give me a sec, Cin. I'll check it out."

Five minutes later, Jim came back on line. "It's fried, Cin. I suspect the fuel mixture was too lean. I changed the plug, but it's a no-go."

Cindy immediately called Helitack 45 for a replacement and was advised of the "two pumps down, one available" situation. So there she stood, in the intense heat, smoke building up, blackened and battered hands clutching a nozzle attached to a limp hose, watching fire pop up across her line and wondering what could go wrong next when her question was answered.

Tanker 271

ROB CRUIKSHANK FELT IT the same time as the red warning light went on. He felt a pronounced loss of power as the aircraft yawed to the starboard side.

Jamie calmly announced, "Engine fire, starboard side."

They had just finished a drop and were climbing. Rob felt the blood drain from his face when he realized that if the engine failure had happened during the water drop, they could be down and likely dead by now. Subsequent attempts to remotely extinguish the fire had succeeded but the engine was still trailing oil-laden smoke. They both knew the big yellow aircraft had to be put down somewhere. Their training and knowledge, however, precluded any urge to panic. 271 still maintained close to 60% of its power, over two thousand HP, and could fly on one engine. This was not yet an emergency or "Mayday" situation, so Rob radioed the standard "Pan Pan" urgency signal three times and briefly explained the problem as he gripped the sluggish yoke. He knew one good engine could get them down—if, and this was a big—no, a humongous if, if it could get them out of the valley they were in and over the next rise.

Birddog 18 acknowledged the "Pan Pan" and ordered the other air tankers to cease air attack and stack up from fifteen to twenty-five hundred feet, advised Helitack 45 to climb to a three thousand feet, then followed the stricken CL415.

The tree line, capped in fire and supporting a curtain of dense, billowing smoke loomed in front of, and just above, tanker 271. It would take every ounce of available turbine power in the one good engine and a heavy pull on the yoke to get them over treetops and through a curtain of fire.

"OH, NO!" CINDY SAW THE TANKER lumbering to gain altitude, thick, black, rolling smoke wind-whipped from the starboard engine. *Tanker 271.* It took her a second for her mind to compute. *That's Rob and Jamie!* The heavy tanker seemed to climb only inches and in super slow motion. *Oh, God! I could run faster than that!* The blunt nose of the aircraft began to push through a veil of sixty-metre high flame and a mountain of dense smoke. Cindy's hands clenched the nozzle in tight fists, and she stood on tiptoes as if trying to "will" the aircraft over the tree line. *C'mon! C'mon! You can do it, Rob.* Tears ran down her cheeks and forged clear tracks through the layer of soot. The yellow tanker disappeared and the veil of fire and smoke closed behind it.

JUST LIKE FRIGGIN' MAGIC. Two pumps go US and a tanker blows an engine. And, there she goes! Justin watched the fire jump the control line and advance north like a tsunami wall of fire. *We've lost it—again.* He reached up and drew a hand over a slack-jawed face then depressed the toggle switch to talk to base camp. He advised the radio operator to pass on a message to Bill Gorley. Before he could start, the radio operator replied, "Standby one, Bill is right here. You can talk to him directly." *Wonderful. This is not my finest hour.*

"Bill here—go ahead Justin."

Justin was neither in the mood nor had the energy for preamble. "We've lost her, Bill. Wawa 43 broke through to the northeast and flanked both sides of Bayfield Lake.

The silence at the other end spoke volumes. "Anything else?"

"Yeah, that's the good news. Tanker 271 blew an engine. We're on our way over to check them out."

The voice at the other end rose in pitch and cracked. "Check them out? Are they OK?"

"Don't know yet, Bill. The Birddog followed them over the crest of a ridge to the east. I can only tell you that we presently have no visual of a forced landing."

"OK, OK. We need to know ASAP what's going on there." There was a five second vacuum in the conversation. "What now, Justin?"

"We're done for tonight, Bill. I'm turning back the remaining tankers and pulling the crews with a couple of the 212's. I'll get on the blower to Hornepayne and warn them. We've got a day— maybe a day and a half before Wawa 43 runs over the town. Hold on, Bill. Birddog 18 is calling us."

CINDY'S WHOLE BODY CONTRACTED like an accordion, bracing for the inevitable impact. Her imagination raised flash-card pictures of devastation – the CL415 banking sharply and plunging into a tangle of forest – a violent explosion and mushrooming fireball ascending above the tree line – two bodies being ripped back, slammed and eviscerated into unrecognizable shapes. But there was … nothing. The yoke of fear and dread slipped off her shoulders. From somewhere deep inside, from the place where her soul took up residence, she spoke a silent prayer. *Oh, God. Make it OK. I don't want to lose him. Bring him back to me. I'll do anything you ask. Just make it OK.*

THE STEERING COLUMN SHOOK IN ROB'S HANDS. Jamie kept his left hand on the throttle, ensuring there was full power to the good port engine. They were flying blind, the pupils of their eyes dilating and contracting to the barrage of colours assaulting them. Their minds could not register and sort out the brilliant flashes and swirls of orange, sulphur yellow, pitch black and numbing grey. They were totally focused on an imaginary horizontal line directly before them and hoped, no prayed, that their last visual would *not* be that of rock ridge or trees.

"So far, so good, Rob." Jamie's rattled comments were for his own sake as well as Rob's. Rob glanced down and saw that the undercarriage was barely clearing the spruce and balsam. He looked up and his eyes grew wide with fear. Through a choking mist of smoke, a pine chi cot, dead, straight and devoid of foliage, stood in their path like a sabre—another ten metres above the tree line. Jamie saw it too, cringed and braced for impact. With no more than a few seconds left, Rob instinctively looked to either side. The message transmitted from his eyes to his brain took a millisecond but seemed to register in slow motion. *More bush to starboard—nothingness to port—might be too much smoke to tell. Screw it!* He banked the rumbling machine to port but was concerned that the load on a single engine might be too much.

Jamie's reaction was appropriate given the circumstances. All that he could do at this point was close his eyes. Instinctively, every muscle in his body tightened up, including his sphincter.

The tanker cleared the chi cot—almost. The very tip of this sabre-like can opener severed the port wing tip float from the wing. But that was the least of their worries. When the tanker banked, it naturally lost airspeed and dropped altitude—with very little to spare. What Rob was praying for, and Jamie wasn't privy to, was the possibility, however remote, that the "nothingness" that Rob saw to port was in fact, just that—nothing, diddly squat, no trees— just plain, old air space. He guessed right. That part of the ridge had dropped away drastically. At that location it became a cliff that dropped sixty metres then gradually descended to water. Jamie was born again and murmured three "halleluiahs" to any saviour that might be listening.

Rob wasn't as elated. Without a wingtip float, a landing on water would likely result in the port wing filling up and the aircraft sinking. *I'd have to find enough lake to land, water depth with enough draft to prevent splitting the aircraft in two on rock, a shoreline close enough to beach the monster and enough power to prevent the damaged wing-tip from submarining— like winning the lottery.*

His only other option would be to try to nurse the 415 back to the closest suitable air strip, Wawa. The 415 was amphibious and a wheeled landing wouldn't require the support of a wing tip float. As a last resort, if he was forced to land on water on his way back to Wawa, there were plenty of lakes on the way. *Sure hope we don't have to use one.* After an eternal second, he forced some "cool" into his voice. "Jamie, we're going to nurse the old tub back to Wawa— you up for it?"

Jamie looked like a deer caught in headlights. "I'll agree to anything that saves my ass."

Rob smiled. "I'll give them a heads up. We're sure to get a royal reception."

"CORRIGAN FROM HELITACK 45." There was no response. "Corrigan, do you copy?" Still no response.

"Cindy from Jim. H45 is trying to contact you."

Cindy stood transfixed and slowly looked down at the MT1000 in her hand. *What is this thing? It talks.* She raised it to her lips.

Inside her head, her voice sounded like the batteries were running down on a recorder. "Go ahead 45."

"They're OK, Cindy. They're hobbling back to Wawa."

The news jolted her body like it had been hit by a 300 Kilovolt Tazer. A barrage of questions recoiled inside her head and she fired them at random. "Are they hurt? What happened? Can they make it back to Wawa?"

Justin smiled at the response. "They're not hurt. The tanker's a little bent out of shape, but the guys are perfectly OK. The only thing I'm concerned about, them being pilots and all, is that their egos might have taken a pounding."

Cindy knew it was time to pull herself together. "Thanks, Justin—and sorry we lost the fire."

"*You* didn't lose it. *We* lost it. We're pulling you out. Leave everything but your personal packs and the pump. You'll be overnighting in Hornepayne. We've got a base camp set up there." Justin knew she needed something else to focus on. "And tomorrow, you'll be on values protection. There'll be a lot of pumps to start up, and our VP people will need some help. Gotta run, Cindy—got some planning to do."

Cindy bowed her head in relief. Twin tears dropped and she watched them fall and hit a clump of dry pine needles on the ground. The she looked up to an ashen sky. *Thank you God. I owe you big time.*

22:00 hours, Wally's Camp

RED SKY AT NIGHT, *sailor's delight*. Except this red sky had nothing to do with the sunset and everything to do with the wildfire just west of his camp. "Impressive", Wally murmured to an empty, uncaring cottage. Above an ink-black tree line, the sky was a strip of cadmium orange below patches of diffused orange/gold/red variations that stretched as far each way as the eye could see. It was as if God had dipped a celestial paint-brush in a concoction of pigments and swept it aggressively across the sky in petulant abandon.

Standing at his living room window, Wally drained the last of his drink, twirled the glass as if to irritate the remaining ice cubes and unceremoniously plunked it down on the coffee table. He raised one challenging eyebrow and flung an aggressive look at the half bottle of scotch sitting demurely at the other end of the table. Its cap snuggled next to it, waiting to be either screwed back on the bottle or tossed in the trashcan. The cap looked as if it was betting on the trashcan. So did the bottle.

Screw you guys! Hey, that's a pun. Wally placed an obviously disappointed cap on a reluctant bottle. *Gotta take it easy. My brain cell bank is over-drawn and I need to avoid the ritual comatose state to plan my—what? Worldly departure? Solo bon voyage? Nirvana vacation? Bucket kicking? Journey to the other side? Keep it simple, stupid—to plan my death. "Death"—that's the noun. Alrighty then class, let's go through the tenses of the verb "to die." I'm dying (present/progressive), I will die (future), I'm dead (present), I died (past).* Wally assessed his state of mind and could come up with only one word—morbid. *Time for bed old man. Maybe a good night's sleep will somehow make tomorrow worth the effort of waking up.*

Chapter 63

DAY 9: 22:00 HOURS, WHITE LAKE PROVINCIAL PARK, BASE CAMP

FOUR VERY WEARY MEN sat around a wobbly table in their meeting trailer. In addition to the data already displayed, a blown up map of Hornepayne, showing all structures and street layouts as well as contact numbers, was stapled to the wall. An additional map on the wall showed the locations of pumps in Hornepayne protecting specific structures from fire. Right now, however, a small table set up in the corner with a coffee urn and a supporting cast of cups, milk, sugar and cookies was high on everyone's priority list.

Sitting at the table was the incident management team commander, Bill Gorley, his planning chief, Ed Buckner, poised over his lap top to take notes, Justin Bailey, who had not been long out of the front seat of helitack 45, and Francis DesRoches, Wawa's MNR district manager. Each had a copy of Hornepayne's burn-out plan sitting in front of them.

"There's no other option?" Francis unconsciously did a pretty good facial impersonation of Edvard Munch's painting, "The Scream."

Bill Gorley ran stubby fingers through his thinning hair. Stretched lips were pursed in an effort to contain an indigestion bubble caught somewhere between his stomach and his throat. "There's always an option, but you won't like the outcome. If we let the bastard build up a head of steam when it hits Hornepayne, I can guarantee significant structural losses." The "bastard" was his pet name for all of the project fires he had battled.

Francis wasn't convinced. "What if your burn-out gets away on you?"

"We won't let that happen." Bill knew there was risk, but he also understood the need to display confidence under the circumstances. "Let me paint you a picture." He turned to Ed Buckner. "Ed, give us a run-down on the weather forecast."

Ed stood up and went to the forecasted weather map on the wall behind him. "We have precipitation forecast in the next forty-eight hours. Consequently, the winds will swing around and come out of the northeast and east prior to any rain we might get. That wind switch will happen tomorrow a.m. Winds are expected to be light, no more than five kilometres per hour. Although the RH will go up, the wind will be in our favour for a burn-out, and forest fuels are tinder dry so they'll carry it."

Francis grasped at the single straw of hope. "How much rain?"

"As high as twenty millimetres and as low as five millimetres. We have no way of telling right now what we'll get ahead of, or on, the fire."

"What would five millimetres do?"

"Absolutely nothing. It might buy us half a day, but if we move our people on the fire perimeter, we'll be pulling them out again the next day. We couldn't even use the five mils as an opportunity for indirect attack, with burn-out at the head of this monster. The problem is, we'd have to wait six to ten hours for the fine fuels to be dry and up to twenty-four hours for medium sized fuels, branches, sticks, heavy brush, to be dry. We'd just be delaying the inevitable."

Francis deflated a little, his frame collapsing slightly within itself. "What would twenty millimetres do?"

"Now that's a different kettle of fish. That would buy us two days. We could tackle the head directly—ram as many crews in as possible and jump on it with everything we had. *But*, we can't count on it. We just can't take the risk."

Francis' frame shrank even more and he appeared to have difficulty holding himself up-right.

Bill looked directly at Francis and spoke softly. "Francis, it boils down to this. With the timeline we have, either we burn out now, or we take the risk of the fire running over Hornepayne. We believe we can contain our burn-out fire. We would expect the main fire to converge with our burn-out in …." He turned to Ed for support.

Ed's fire behaviour officer had done the work-up for him. "By tomorrow night."

Francis, the talking cadaver, had collapsed completely. "I've got to call the mayor of Hornepayne tonight. Ted is not going to be too happy about this."

"Tell him Justin will be in to see him tomorrow morning to give him a full briefing."

The cadaver began to straighten up. "That might help a little. How much are you burning out and how are you doing it?"

"I'll turn that over to Justin".

Justin stood up and went to the wall-mounted map. "Francis, first let me say that the bulk of the ignition will be aerial with some hand ignition back-up. We'll be using two helicopters, one with a helitorch, the other with O.A.I.D—the ping pong balls. The machines are in Hornepayne and being set up now. Ignition will take place well outside Hornepayne. We'll need to take advantage of natural barriers— rivers, creeks, wetland, lakes, and man-made barriers such as roads. To contain our fire, we'll be using ranger crews, the three air tankers we have available and two medium helicopters with buckets."

Justin looked him squarely in the eyes. "Now, I won't lie to you, in terms of barriers, there's not a lot to play with, but we're counting on northeast to east winds to help us. This low system arriving in is a fairly weak, so once it passes, the winds will come around from the south again."

Justin pointed to the map. "Now to answer your first question, we'll be burning out approximately twenty five hundred hectares." He looked to Francis for a reaction. The "jaw drop" said it all.

"You can see where Wawa 43 was as of 20:00 hours July 28th— tonight. The "shaded" line represents our forecast of its location by 11:00 hours tomorrow. There will be growth in other parts of the fire but we've concentrated our forecast on this area because of Hornepayne. The piece identified as "planned burn-out" is obvious. Any questions?"

Francis shook his head slowly.

Justin continued. "The arrows identified as "1" will be hammered by air attack starting around 11:00 hours. Crews will be plugged in as required. We expect locations "2" and "3" will give us heartburn in our burn-out. Needless to say, they will be given special attention."

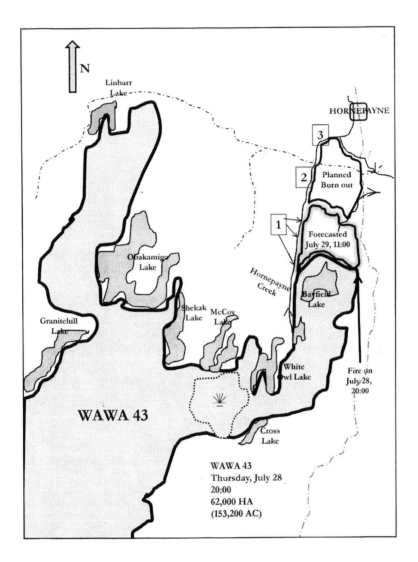

Francis' response lacked enthusiasm. "How can you possibly be ready by late tomorrow morning?"

"Logistically, it's not a real problem. Fire equipment is already to go at the Hornepayne airstrip. Crews have been briefed and will be ready to go by 06:00 hours tomorrow. We're only ten minutes out from areas 1 and 2 by air and thirty minutes out by vehicle from the rest of the control line. My last job for tonight will be passing on air attack assignments to the Birddog officer for the air tankers and to the pilots of the medium helicopters."

Francis gathered his thoughts to arrive at his final question. "Justin, what's your level of confidence on the success of the burn-out?"

Justin did not hesitate. "On a scale of one to ten, I put it at five."

The cadaver collapsed into a puddle.

"WHADAYA MEAN, THEY'RE GONNA BURN-OUT!" The phone in Mayor Ted Touluce's hand would have crumbled if it hadn't been made of durable plastic. "Haven't we got enough fire to worry about already!" he was shouting like there was no conduit between the two phones to carry his voice.

Francis' nerves were stretched to the snap point. *Stay Prozac calm.* "Ted, you won't like the alternative. We have to trust the fire people."

"Trust them! They're the ones that let the fire get so big. Now, they're gonna throw in a little more to what, make it more interesting? Break a world's record for fire size? Roast weenies? Francis, I just don't get it."

Anger erupted inside Francis like a pot boiling over. "The operations chief, his name's Justin Bailey, is coming out to see you in the morning. He'll explain the situation. And as far as "letting the fire get big", you're way out of line, Ted. We've thrown everything at it that we can. Nothing is going to slow this thing down except weather. All the fire guys can do is try to re-direct it away from Hornepayne."

"How? Put up traffic signs?"

Can't take much more of this shit. "Ted, do you work hard at being a jerk?"

"Yes ... I mean no!"

Gotcha! "Well, you either get yourself under control, or this conversation is finished."

Ted was now an 11.0 on the ten point Richter Scale. "I'll decide when it's finished. I didn't get to be mayor by rolling over and playing 'shake a friggin paw'! Hello? Hello?"

Francis had gently placed the phone back in its cradle. *Assehole!* Ted slammed his down like he was killing a cockroach. "Assehole!"

Chapter 64

DAY 10: FRIDAY, JULY 29TH, 10:00 HOURS, SIREN LAKE (LAKE JEWEL)

M*IRROR, MIRROR ON THE WALL, who's the homeliest of them all? Man, I win … hands down.* Wally looked at the apparition staring back at him in the bathroom mirror. It wasn't the stretch marks in his bone-taunt cheeks that bothered him. And it wasn't the funeral home pallor in a complexion-less complexion that shook him up. It was the look of unconscious desperation in a pair of bulbous eyes. He'd seen it time and time again in 'Nam. The "I don't realize it but I'm dying" look. The mind would not accept what the eyes were telling him. *The eyes aren't only a window to the soul; they're also a window to the body.* His eyes were telling him he was dying.

The final look, the opaque, glazed, unseeing look would eventually be witnessed by someone else—unless he died in the cabin. *The mice will get the eyes.* Unless he died outside. *The ravens will pluck them out like grapes.* Unless he decided to end it in the lake. *The friggin' sunfish will nibble away at them. Geez, I'm more worried about saving my eyes than I am of living. Maybe if I pop them out now and put 'em in a tin tea box, the grand kids can use them as marbles or take them to school to impress the other kids. Get a grip, Wallace!*

Last night was a doozy. He had been treated to a kaleidoscope of disjointed dreams. Some were sobering, a few were completely off the wall and one could only be described as hideous. *Let's see what I can remember, in no particular order.*

There was the beaver, crushed in a Conibear trap, that belly-crawled across a polished, ball-room floor and asked me for a dance. Beavers have a speech impediment and slobber when they talk, probably because of the big front teeth. Hid-eee-us!

I changed a baby diaper last night. Can't remember which daughter, but I ended up with a rail car load of baby poop and no place to deposit it. I recall being exhausted from carting it around. That dream started in the "sobering" category but went downhill (or in the shitter) fast.

What else was there? Oh yeah. I was hiking in the bush and could hear muffled sobbing. Someone was having a rough time. As I got closer, the snuffles and shuddering sighs seemed to come from above. It was the old white pine, tears of white resin running down its trunk. Geez, I feel like crying.

Then there was the one at 'Nam. Wally could feel his pulse quicken and his breathing become laboured. *Man, you try to forget. You tuck the memories away in your mind—like stuffing photos of an old girlfriend in a shoe box. Just when you think they're lost forever, they show up out of nowhere in your thoughts or dreams. I don't even want to go there.* And he didn't.

Now I'm a young lad, cleaning fish at the lodge by naphtha lantern at midnight. I feel I'm being watched and look up to see Julie. She's beautiful. I'm suddenly hot. Everything's bouncing around inside like a popcorn machine. I tell her she's beautiful. She tells me I smell like fish. She fades into the darkness as if being drawn away on a low, flat wagon. I reach for her but I slip and slide in fish entrails.

Wally considered the mind a nearly perfect maze. Bad memories had a tough time escaping. Dreams didn't do it—they were false portals that only lead to dead-ends. A bad memory could wander inside forever and occasionally surface in a dream.

Wally had just surfed through giant waves of emotion. It was as if every person, place or thing that meant something to him was taking a last kick at the can. *Wally McNeil, this is your life, in tiny flashbacks, each one an indigestion hiccup. Maybe I'm sub-consciously preparing myself for the inevitable.* He eyed the shotgun in the corner—a double-barrelled hooker, beckoning him with the promise of release. *Nope. Been there, almost done that. Don't need a tee-shirt that says, 'I just committed suicide with a shotgun. See if you recognize me'. It is, however, time to finish the letter.*

This was *the* letter, the one he, until this point in time, lacked the courage to finish—his final letter to the girls. He started out well with it a few nights ago but had trouble with the "no regrets" part. He has a Santa Claus bag full of them. He eyed his good friend, the scotch bottle, licked dehydrated lips, reached out and gently caressed it. Wally jumped between rye and scotch in his bouts of drinking. They were like two girlfriends. At times, it was difficult to choose which one to take out for the night. In a fit of resolve and flourish, he grabbed the scotch bottle by its scrawny neck, rushed it to the kitchen and dumped it down the drain. *Like killing the family turkey for thanksgiving. Didn't want to do it. Had to be done.* He next eyed the stack of paper and the pen. They sat on the kitchen table. In fact they had been there for a couple of nights now—ignored. They had taken a backseat to his best friend, a smoky glass of amber nectar. He sat down gingerly and pressed a shaky pen to paper and began.

THE SOW HAD NO PLACE TO TURN. Acrid smoke was stinging her eyes and confusing her ability to sort out smells. The crackle and snap of burning under-story and whoosh of torching fir, spruce and pine assaulted her sense of hearing. Pirouettes of fire shot up high above the tree line and caused her pupils to grow large. Her normally instinctive thought pattern was now short-circuited. She sensed but one option, take to water. She stepped in without hesitation and began to swim. Her adrenalin-charged cub followed.

A FAT, ORANGE ON WHITE HELICOPTER stayed well out from the east flank of Wawa 43, the pilot intent on avoiding smoke. Cindy sat up front in the 205A-1. Jim sat in the back surrounded by fire pumps and bags of hose. Mixed pump gas was stashed in the tail boom compartment. The other two members of her crew, Tim and Sam were back at Hornepayne, assisting with the preparation of the "last stand." The big 205 rattled and jinked in a south-westerly direction. Winds were already brisk this morning. Cindy and Jim had been running up pumps to supply sprinkler systems ahead of the Wawa 43 for three hours now. Her last assignment was the McNeil camp on the east side of Siren Lake. Cindy stared ahead but with little focus. *Wally calls it Lake Jewel. Wonder if Rob would name a lake after me? I hope the camp's OK. I hope he's OK!*

The pilot looked her way. "According to my handy-dandy GPS, we're only fifteen minutes out. You say there's somebody there?"

Cindy returned the look and smiled. "Oh yeah. He'll be there and probably cranky as ever."

"You know this guy?"

Cindy hesitated, her smile slipped away. "I think so." *And I'm a little worried.*

MY MIND'S A BLANK. Wally had trouble concentrating on the letter. For some reason he was anxious. *Must be the wood smoke drifting in from the fire.* Try as he might, he couldn't drag out the right words from the dark cave that was his mind. Last words seemed so trivial, so lame. *Sometimes how you feel defies description.* Wally looked up, through the living area window and across the lake. The fire was working its way down to the shore. He couldn't see the outline of the old pine now and felt an emptiness inside—a loss—like he hadn't eaten in days and was about to be sick. *Maybe it's a self-centred loneliness. An old friend has gone, and I've got no connection to this planet anymore.*

Wally's gaze dropped and he caught something in the lake— something that wasn't quite right. He walked over to the window ledge, picked up his binoculars and focused on the anomaly. *The bears! They're swimming across the lake!* Wally's first reaction was to leave them alone. *Bears are good swimmers. They'll make it across and be on their way.* But something squirmed around in the back of his mind just enough to trigger some concern. He recalled the cub bawling a few days ago a cry of discomfort and confusion. *Better go outside and get a closer look.* He hesitated. *What the hell's buggin' me?* He scribbled a short note on his letter to the girls. *Bears are in trouble. Might have to help them. If I don't make it back, you'll know why the letter isn't finished. Love, your Dad.*

IN LESS THAN A MINUTE, Wally was down to the shoreline. The sow was two hundred metres out. The cub was not far behind but struggling now in metre-high waves. The sow circled back to her cub to offer encouragement, then turned and changed course about 45 degrees. *Where the hell's she going?* The he understood. Not twenty yards away from her was a twisted, floating cedar, much of it submerged. *Roots must have burned and waves are pushing it across the lake.* She made it to the cedar. Not far behind the cub was now struggling, pawing air instead of water. It would submerge, then surface, paw air and submerge again. *Shit, it's going down!* Wally looked around. His boat motor was under repair so that was out, but his canoe was turned over close to the shoreline, and the paddles were underneath. *But it's too late.* A wave of frustration washed over Wally. He looked skyward, his face stretched in anguish. "God, take me instead!" There was no response. The cub did not resurface.

Wally's shoulders drooped in resignation. Then he heard the distinct bawling again. The cub had somehow made it to the cedar but had trouble pulling itself above the water line. It would pull itself up then slip down. Instinctively, the sow grabbed it by the nap of its neck and pulled her baby up, but it lacked the strength to hold on.

Wally didn't recall the series of activities required to put him in that canoe. But here he was, just below the centre line, tight to one side, deep stroking as fast as his body would allow. *How did I get here. My mind must have taken a vacation while the old body put in overtime.* Every third stroke drove him into wind-driven waves; every wave slammed into the fibre-glass bow and cascaded to each side. Strong winds slapped at the wave tops, sending a volley of spray towards him. *Shit! I'm being pressure washed!* The bow would rise, hover and come crashing down with a resounding 'thunk'. Wally had trouble navigating. In a three-part minute, he looked up at sky, then across at lake, then down in a trough of swirling water. The few seconds he had to look across lake were jam packed with activity: *shake water out of eyes, release one hand from paddle for a nanosecond to push up glasses on bridge of nose, shift weight subtly to control balance, j-stroke paddle to stay on course, look frantically for friggin' bears! There!* The cedar tree, the cub and one pissed sow bear were only twenty metres away. *Now what, Einstein?* The cub was barely hanging on. *Certainly can't hop on board and paddle the tree in. The sow would kill me. Can't grab the cub. We'd both end up in the drink ... and the sow would kill me. Gotta get the whole enchilada in closer to shore.* He'd have to get in close enough to tie onto the cedar and literally tow them in. Through habit, he always carried long bow and stern ropes attached to his canoe. *The trick is to turn 16 feet of partially submerged fibreglass canoe around between swells, tie up to the cedar while being pushed by gale-force winds and avoid a very angry mother bear.* For the first time in a long time, Wally was happy—no, he was elated! This was not only a challenge, but it was an opportunity to do something good. It might kill him, but as far as he was concerned, that was a bonus.

The bow of his canoe slammed into a wave. *A thousand and one, a thousand and two. A thousand and*—at "three" he thrust his paddle blade as far out as he could, leaned, dug deep into the water and pulled it towards him with all the strength he could muster. At the bottom of the trough, the canoe bow swung around to his starboard position. He was now in a very tenuous situation. He needed one more, good stroke to get the canoe around in time to receive the next wave at his stern. If he got hit broadside or quarter-side, he would be swamped.

It was just about this time when the spectator gods became bored and decided to have a little fun. Two things happened simultaneously as he dug in for another stroke: the viper lying dormant in the pit of his intestines struck viciously, causing his body to twist in response, and, as a result, the downward pressure on the paddle caused it to snap in two.

Wally's elation would have turned to despair, if time had allowed. The next wave struck the side of the canoe, forcing it over and throwing the little man, now clutching his stomach, into the lake. The shock must have caused the viper to recoil and slink back into its lair. Wally now considered himself blessed. He had only one conundrum to face. No more pain—just a little shock and the realization that he might drown, along with the cub wailing above him.

Chapter 65

DAY 10: 11:00 HOURS, SOUTH OF HORNEPAYNE

I *LOVE THE SMELL OF BURN-OUT IN THE MORNING.* Justin Bailey recalled a similar line from a vintage movie—only the reference was to napalm. *What was it called? Oh yeah, Apocalypse Now.* He also recalled the follow-up line, "smells like victory!" *Hope this effort smells like victory.* Justin sat in his "fire boss" platform, Helitack 45, a kilometre above "All that I command."

The pilot looked at him. "Pardon?"

The question shook Justin out of his reverie. The long, thin face perched on a long, thin neck showed signs of stress. His pallor was a dirty-dishwater grey, and the lines on his face had grown longer and deeper. "Oh, nothing. Just slipped into my other world for a moment."

Helitack 45 was doing lazy circles while Justin finalized his burn out plan. Behind him sat the OAID tech, the shiny metal OAID machine and boxes of "ping-pong" balls filled with potassium permanganate. The rear starboard door had been removed, and the OAID machine chutes protruded past the doorway.

Justin's daydream had been triggered by the scene below him—twenty-five hundred hectares of forest cover that would soon be ignited. It was bisected by a bush road and highway 631. Justin looked down at his hand-drawn map.

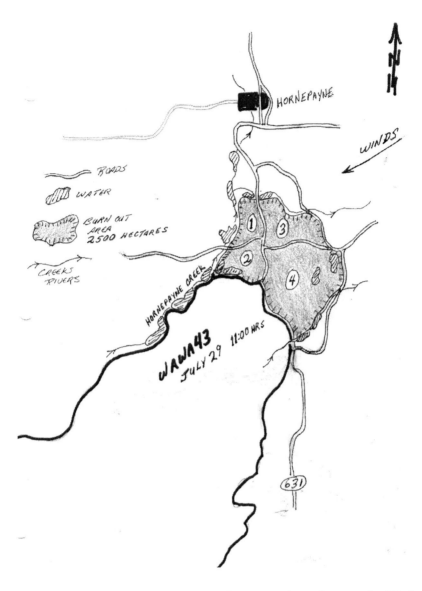

The town of Hornepayne stood exposed to the north. He had divided up the burn out area below him into four sectors. They would be used for ignition sequence and to simplify communications. Everyone involved in the effort had been given a copy of his rough map. He could see trucks and green MNR fire tankers on the roads, evidence of the crews assigned to contain the burn-out. Very close and south of the burn out, the main fire was almost in a holding pattern, advancing slowly because of higher humidity and northeast winds. Also, south of the burn out area and on the northwest flank of on his map, three yellow air tankers were going about their business, attempting to keep the fire contained to the lake and creek system. They looked like three yellow moths attracted to light, flitting by the glow, then leaving, then returning. If the air tankers were moths, then the Birddog aircraft circling above them was a tiny fruit-fly, mesmerized by their antics. Justin smiled. *Three very fat moths and one tiny fly.* Although he couldn't see them, Justin knew there were a half dozen ranger crews down on the ground working with the air tankers. Not far below him and just to the east, another helicopter circled, towing a large drum suspended by cable. This was his second source of ignition, the helitorch, the closest thing to napalm that he would ever encounter *this* morning.

Justin looked down at his map again. He would start by igniting sector 1 on the west flank close to the water system, Hornepayne Creek, and then work back towards the road running north-south. This would ensure a less intense fire near the lakes where crews were waiting to do a little hand ignition and contain the fire. He would use the same tactics with sector 2. Once he began sector 2, the helitorch would drop its globs of gelled gas in sectors three and four simultaneously starting from the road system on the east and work west. Once Justin was finished igniting sector 2, he would cease ignition and orchestrate fire fighting tactics from his flying command centre.

Earlier that morning, Justin had advised all air attack people and ground crews that once they started ignition, there would be no turning back. This was their last stand—their final "rabbit-out-of-the-hat" to save Hornepayne. He had nothing left in his bag of tricks.

Justin keyed the toggle switch to the FM radio. "All stations, all stations. Ignition begins *now*."

AT THE SAME TIME as Justin was dropping ping-pong balls north of Wawa 43, Nate Ramirez was pumping water on a jump fire sixty kilometres to the south. His boss, Chester Wilkes, was three metres behind him, helping with the charged, 1 ½ inch hose line. They had already completed a first pass around the three hectare jump fire and were in the process of starting a back pass. Two other HotShot crew members were helping them with the hose, and another three were patrolling the jump fire for break outs.

"Man, this water is great stuff!" Nate had shouted out his admiration to no one in particular. Back home in New Mexico, they didn't have the luxury of Ontario's un-countable sources of water, hence the need for direct and indirect fire attack with hand tools. *And hence the need for twenty-person crews.* It had quickly dawned on Nate that four fire fighters and a pumping unit, under the right conditions, could accomplish as much as a twenty person hand tool crew in half the time. He recalled his discussion with Chester not half an hour ago. Chester was a traditionalist and somewhat pragmatic.

"We don't have Ontario's water, Nate."

"Yeah, but imagine if we did."

Chester had screwed up his mouth and raised his eyes as a prerequisite to developing thought. "But a pumping unit costs about eight thousand dollars. Then there's gas and oil and maintenance and parts and who knows what else."

Nate liked a good discussion and couldn't let it go. "So in a days work … twelve hours …, twenty HotShots might construct a mile of fire line. Let's say a four-person ranger crew could lay two miles of fire-holding hose in the same time. Simple math tells me that four people could do double the work of twenty. So, we wouldn't need a regiment, just a platoon. Think of the money we would save there!"

There had been a protracted lull in the conversation. "We don't have Ontario's water, Nate."

"Yeah. But imagine if we did."

Now, they were in good form and quite pleased about it. They had a handle on the jump fire, got to use a Mark-3 pump—and quite efficiently to boot—and their burn out line was BHE. What more could a fire fighter wish for?

BACK IN HORNEPAYNE, things were not so ducky. Mayor Touluce was apoplectic. Fire chief Waal was distracted. And MNR's rep, Greg Walsh, was becoming impatient. His trademark "good humour" had taken a vacation and gone south.

Terrible Ted was shouting. "I can't believe they're lighting fire!"

A "not too sympathetic" Ken Waal jumped in with renewed enthusiasm. "I can't believe you can't believe it!"

Two red faces squared off, lips turned down in disagreement, jaws thrust out in confrontation.

"OK, gentlemen." *Jerks!* "Can we continue with the summary review?" Greg did not wait for agreement. "From MNR's perspective, crews are in place, sprinklers are up and running and a service organization is at the airport." Imitating a news reporter to an anchor person, "Over to you, Ken."

Ken Waal caught on. "Thanks, Greg. Let's begin with breaking news."

Ted Touluce had all but short-circuited. Both Ken and Greg were sure he would soon foam at the mouth, compress and "accordion" to the floor. However, there was no more vitriol left in the tank. He sat back, his arms fell to the side and his shoulders slumped. "You guys win. Carry on."

Ken's flippant persona changed to Mr. Businessman. "First, my people. All volunteer fire fighters are in town and assigned to our two fire trucks. One's outside here at the fire hall. The other is on the south side of town near the CN rail roundhouse. Both are ready to move wherever they're required."

Ken looked at both men and continued. "Our two doctors and a skeleton staff are on standby at the hospital. An Ontario Medivac helicopter is on standby at the airport. The O.P.P is patrolling the town and have the highways blocked. They're supported by MNR conservation officers. We have a list of people still in town and their locations."

He paused for questions. "Finally, Chapleau reports they have taken in one hundred and forty-eight Hornepayne residents and have room for more. The rest of our residents have looked after themselves." He turned his attention to Ted.

Ted was now pouting and reluctantly offered his input. He finally conceded. "I've got two volunteers here as receptionists. All calls are being logged. There's not much more this office can do."

Greg looked at him with a critical eye, one brow flat, and the other arched. "Ted, your work will grow exponentially when people come home. I suggest you read your plan."

Ted's ego required a final word. "OK, gentlemen, we're good to go. I feel confident that all will go well. If it doesn't, jobs are on the line."

Both Greg and Ken rolled their eyes skyward, as if beseeching a greater power to intervene—or strike the little prick dead.

Chapter 66

DAY 10: 11:00 HOURS, WALLY'S CAMP

W HERE'S THE BEAR WHISPERER WHEN YOU NEED HIM? Wally had surfaced close to the floating cedar. He held onto a gnarled root with one hand and a sweeping branch with the other. The cub was only two metres from him and in a panic. The sow was on the other side of the cedar, half in and half out of the water, three metres away, snapping her jaws in anger. *If I could just get this piece of floating crap closer to shore.* Wally began to scissor kick. The wave action and the scissor kick created a little momentum. It also really, really ticked off the sow. She let herself down in the water and swam towards him. *Now what? I could let go and drown, or I could try to reason with her. Screw it. Let's play this one out.* Wally turned and kicked harder.

He no sooner looked back to check on his adversary, when the sow struck out at him. A warning, weak glance, but the contact was powerful enough to drain any strength Wally had left. The blow caught him on the side of his head. There was an immediate buzzing, starting from a distance then increasing, like the approach of a model airplane. This was followed by sharp ringing. He swore he was down for the ten-count. This was definitely not *his* head. It belonged to somebody else ... someone much larger than Wally, someone with a pumpkin for a head. He turned his face away. It seemed to move like the ratchet on a half-inch drive, click, click, click. The subsequent message of pain that traveled to the brain through the optic nerve came in stuttering flashes.

As Wally reluctantly lost his grip on the tree, he intuitively used his remaining dribble of strength to push it, and its tenants towards the shoreline. He slipped down below the surface but felt an irritating need to ascend. He needed some assurance—a desperate desire to confirm that he had given something back. He broke through to the surface. The picture changed from liquid stained glass to crystal clear images and back again, until he stretched his neck and thrust his chin to the sky. He took a few rattled breaths and looked around. His thick white hair was matted randomly around his head, like a bad toupee. His reflection in the water triggered a single wry thought ... *Hero Wally, king of the self-delusional, loser dummies.*

Head back, chin up, eyes down, Wally rotated his whole body clockwise, moving his hands at the wrist and scissor kicking his legs. *I feel like a synchronized swimmer in bush clothes. I should probably raise both arms and perform a pirouette.*

With each blink, his eyes seemed to record vintage, movie-like scenes. The ring/buzz in his head became the rattle of an old 16 mm film. *Cue the blue/green chop of the lakes surface with veils of wood smoke drifting across in pale, translucent sheets. Next, the steel-grey shoreline rock outcrops. Quiet on the set! Take 3. Shoreline white cedar, winter browsed by deer. Cue the red pine above the line of cedar, not yet people ... there!—blackened by the ravages of ground fire. Man I love red pine. Focus you old fart!*

Finally, a last look to the far ridge—an awesome patchwork of fire whirls, dense black smoke, orange/red fingers of flame and patches of verdant forest still untouched by the carnage. And, now visible , standing alone and defiant, the white pine, its branches flaying in the fire-induced maelstrom as if swatting at itself to ward off a barrage of heat and flame. *What a contender! Focus, back to the sow and cub. Where are they? There!—in front of his camp, the sow breaching the shoreline. Oh, God! Where is the cub?*

His film production seemed to be in freeze-frame. *Take another breath, open up the eyes, be there you little fur ball. Yes!—a little, black, staggering furbee, not far behind momma now.*

Close to the bush line, the sow shook herself and looked back towards Wally, with perhaps an acknowledgement of primitive gratitude. Then both sow and cub vanished into a cloak of green and olive.

Now what? Not much strength left. Wally realized his situation was just another example of the law of unintended consequences. He had not intended to die this way. It was the unforeseen consequence of his intention to save the bears.

Then it happened. The little pain worm strolled in and registered, preparing to take a room somewhere in his lower abdomen. It moved at a snail's pace, tentatively looking for the right floor, then the right door, humming a morbid tune, "Ready or not Mr. McNeil, here I come!"

Wally knew what was coming. *Great timing, you turd!* He looked skyward and thought about the worm. It was a soulless coward. He imagined it sneaking around in supplication, as if to apologize but at the same time washing its armless hands in anticipation while sporting a shit-eating grin on its scabby face. "Hurry up you fucking weasel! You don't have the guts to take me head on!"

His challenge seemed to hit home and turn the worm into its alter ego, a scum sucking monster with a terrible appetite. It was a shape shifter—from bottom feeder to snapping, tearing spectre in a millisecond. Wally doubled over, completely forgetting the need to stay afloat. His frame literally appeared to shrink within itself. He was doubled over as if the worm was riding on his shoulders like a bronco buster intent on beating him into submission. Wally slipped down, down.

Shit! Shit! Shit! What do I know about drowning? Let's see. I reflexively start to breath, lungs fill with water. I become asphyxiated, simply because I'm unable to breath. Why am I rationalizing this shit? Can't hold my breath much longer. Pain can't be any worse than what I'm dealing with now. How come this is taking so long?

What Wally didn't know was that his body was in its energy saving mode. It needed to maximize the time it could stay under water. His heart rate reduced by close to 50%. He could actually hear it slow to crawl like a train coming into a station.

Then his throat began to spasm and a dull pain in his chest began to grow, slowly at first then swell incrementally like a helium balloon.

Because Wally had neither the strength nor the will to react, he did not panic. In his remaining few seconds, he was determined to recall images of his girls and his wife. Their last Christmas together— laughter, smiles, music, good smells, warmth, and love—above all, love. *I think I'm OK. Time to go.* His lips, pressed survival-tight, began to part. *Simple, Wallace. At the count of three: one, goodbye girls, two, fuck-off pain, three, hello, Jewel.*

Quick, numbing upper body pain, then, miraculously, a wash of relief. Now a kaleidoscope of images. Wally's life in a second, each image like a playing card in a deck falling through time—each card with a colourful scene and act, each with meaning and joy. One card in particular rotated more slowly than the rest and came to a full stop, the ace of hearts—the day he met Julie.

Chapter 67

JULY, 1961
THE ACE OF HEARTS

IT WAS WALLY'S FIRST DAY on a summer job in Windy Lake Lodge, a fishing/tourist camp north of Thunder Bay, Ontario. The owner, Neil Martin, was proud of the camp motto and used it to challenge his tourists. With a tongue squarely lodged in his cheek and a sparkle in his eye, he would announce, "If you can't catch fish here, then you just can't catch fish!" As a favour to Wally's father, a long-time client, Neil had taken on Wally as the lodge gofer. Jobs included fuelling and cleaning boats, transferring equipment, hauling garbage, cleaning and packaging fish and anything else that Neil could find for him. The fact that Wally was an American was of no account. As far as Neil was concerned, he was just another tourist who happened to be paid in food, lodging and a little cash.

About two weeks into the job, Wally was filleting Walleye by lamplight. The night air was humid and the mosquitoes relentless. Each time he swiped a platoon of blood sucking vampires off his face, he left a new smear of his own blood mixed with fish blood, scales and tiny pieces of fish gut. His dirty Minnesota North Stars hockey cap was cranked down low on his head in a side lock position. Shocks of red hair stuck out in disarray, some curled up, some curled down. It was almost midnight, and he had been cleaning fish for three hours. This stringer of six Walleye belonged to a particularly obnoxious tourist, and Wally cursed under his breath with each stroke of the filleting knife.

A young girl heard the muttering and stepped gingerly into the fringe of light from his lantern. She appeared to be close to Wally's age. The muttering continually changed in volume and intensity, and sounded like a child playing with a radio dial. She stepped closer and saw the young man from the back by lamp-light, elbows in rhythm, frequently rising up to support the arms and hands swiping at mosquitoes. She caught an occasional glint of a knife as blade met artificial light. She moved up behind him quietly, not sure about his cursing and the weapon in his hand.

"What's your problem?"

Wally jerked with a rush of adrenalin. "Damn! Owe!" the finely honed knife, nicked him on a knuckle, drawing blood immediately. He swung around prepared to launch a whole new round of invectives at the intruder. What he saw stopped a particularly favourite curse word mid-stream. Forgotten were the mosquitoes, forgotten was the slime and smell. His heart bounced around in his chest like an agitated canary in a cage. He couldn't speak—just bleed. And bleed. He didn't feel a thing, though. He just kept staring at the vision before him, transfixed on her eyes. They were soft chestnut like a doe fawn, protected by long, velvet auburn lashes. Her eye-brows arched in permanent mirth. Full smiling lips revealed almost perfect teeth, the top two front teeth separated by a slight gap. Her face was narrow, making her eyes and mouth slightly large and even more appealing. Her hair was cut short, the colour of summer wheat. She wasn't tall, he guessed about 5'2" and was slim, but not boy slim, definitely girl slim. He had neither the time, nor the nerve to analyze the rest of her physique. He wanted to reply, really wanted to speak but doubted that he could hear his own voice over the tidal wave in his head.

"You're bleeding."

Wally looked down at his hand as blood ran from his knuckle, down his forefinger and dripped on his pant leg.

"Here, let me take care of that." She seized him by his slimy hand and pulled him towards the lodge. He stumbled behind like a toddler. He knew then that he would follow her anywhere, anytime.

"My name's Julie. What's yours?" Wally searched in vain for his tongue. It was there somewhere, supposed to be between his teeth and his tonsils. There!—a large, unresponsive lump like a dead toad on the road. With maximum effort, the toad came to life and the reply finally came out just like he hoped it wouldn't, a fractured squeak: "Wally" with a squeak.

Aw jeez. Bad enough to have the name Wally, let alone let it out like a mouse with laryngitis. I hated "Wally." My parents probably couldn't make up their minds and ran down the alphabet to the 'W's'. Forget the 'X's', 'Y's' and 'Z's'. Short of 'Xavier', 'Yvon' or 'Zorro' there wasn't much there. In his case 'Wally' was not short for 'Walter' but 'Wallace'. His mum once told him she named him after the actor, Wallace Beery. He thought it was something to be proud of until he saw him in the old 1934 movie Treasure Island, an overweight, leering pirate with a squinty eye, one leg and a ratty parrot on his shoulder.

Julie walked with confidence and seemed to glide, like a dancer, while Wally stumbled and tripped behind.

Need to get some control, man.

As they climbed the stairs to the main lodge deck, Wally saw his reflection in a window. *Who the hell is that?* He looked in horror at the hat, the hair, the "fish" makeup on his face. *Dam, the village has found a new idiot! Pull yourself together, Wallace!*

At this moment, Wally didn't trust his body to walk and talk at the same time. Once through the lodge great-room and into the kitchen, Julie sat him down at a worn pine table.

She put her hands on slim hips and tilted a reflective head. "I'll be right back." Wally detected a spattering of humour connecting the well-enunciated words. He already loved her voice, and he pictured the bouncing ball skipping on top of each phrase accompanied by illustrated musical notes.

What should I do? Try something novel, like conversation, dummy. Take off my ridiculous hat. Wait! No telling what lies beneath. Maybe my hair will explode like furniture springs through a worn couch. I'll look like Clarabel the Clown on Howdy Doody. Maybe it'll be an improvement over village idiot. What about the disaster called my face?

Wally looked around. *Halleluiah! A box of Kleenex sat on the counter.* He reached over, grabbed a mitt full and vigorously wiped his face. Unaware that little, torn pieces of white in various shapes and sizes stuck to the fish slime and clung precariously to his face, Wally let out an audible sigh of relief. *This has to be an improvement.*

Julie returned with a first-aid kit; her eyes widened, and she laughed, with some reserve at first, but uncontrollably when she saw the stricken look on Wally's face. Her laughter had destroyed any resolve to salvage some self-respect that he had mustered in her absence. His anger faltered as he was consumed by the sound of her laughter. It was the timbre and resonance of a thousand wind chimes touched by a light evening summer breeze.

Wally had to take the upper ground. "Will you marry me?" *What the hell was that?* His toady tongue, the lump that didn't work when it should have, the red-bellied traitor that normally took no prisoners, even on a bad day, came back to life, popped up and blurted out his first full sentence, without the benefit of guidance from his brain. *Why don't I just pull out the filleting knife and slit my throat right now?*

Julie's laughter came to a screeching halt. The shocked look on her face became pensive, somewhat withdrawn as if she was really considering an answer. She took a long, hard look at him. Time stood still. All things mobile became suspended and the air seemed to hum like a power line on a hot day.

"Maybe. After University. I'll have to ask Dad first. Bye the way, he owns this place".

Maybe? Maybe. Maybe is close to "probably." "Probably" is really close to "more than likely." And "more than likely" really means "yes!" After university? Four or five more years? Long courtship? That could work. Mr. Martin is her dad? Shit! That means I have to make a good impression.

Wally responded. "Then it's settled. I have to get back to work. See you tomorrow." He was his old confident self now, a man/boy in charge, a man/boy with a plan and a destiny. Wally strutted back into the night—un-bandaged. His face was a road map with streaks of blood and slime for roads and fish scales and pieces of Kleenex for towns and cities.

Day 10 -Siren Lake

WALLY SLIPPED BACK INTO TERROR. Julie's features faded from colours to sepia, then slipped behind frosted glass. Her profile morphed from three dimensional to two. She was now a vague cartoon character. The 'here and now' rushed back into his brain like a cat escaping the rain. *As I'm dying, Julie is fading. Time to get on with the business of drowning and join her.*

Chapter 68

DAY 10: 11:30 HOURS, SIREN LAKE

"**D**ID YOU SEE THAT?" The pilot was pointing to the drama unfolding ahead and below his helicopter. Cindy had witnessed the attempted rescue and just couldn't believe it. *What the hell is he doing down there?* Jim was in the back seat, craning his head forward to see what was going on.

In a kind of time warp, Cindy saw the canoe flip over in a narrow series of cresting waves. She saw the sow bear and cub clinging to a floating tree. Her eyes widened when the sow emerged close to the lone figure who was attempting to push the whole flotilla closer to shore. What happened next was at light speed. The sow struck the man with a quick, glancing blow. Then she saw the man turn face up. *It's Wally!* Then he sank slowly below the waves.

"Get us down there!" The pilot needed no further encouragement and put the medium helicopter into a steep bank.

The scene below had not immediately registered for Jim. "What's the hell's happening, Cin?"

"It's Wally, Jim. He's going down. We've got to save him!" Something deep inside rose up to wrestle with her instincts. *Wally is going to die anyway. In fact, he wants to die. So we bring him back to what? Shrivel up in a hospital? Suffer for another six months? Deal with pity and heartbreak from his friends and family? He won't be a happy camper.*

The pilot interrupted the little devil perched on her shoulder. "Can't land. I'm on skids."

441

Cindy absorbed his comments through the haze of thought. *Sorry, Wally. It's not my call. Remember what you told me, "The easiest choices in life are just not fun or interesting." No choice here.* Cindy reached down to undo her boot laces.

I'M SLIPPING AWAY. THANK YOU, GOD. The final card in the deck had fallen and spiralled away. Wally took a last, semi-conscious breath. His spirit left his body, a body wasted and no longer useful, a body that when it died, would take the cowardly worm and his pain with it. He watched himself fade and pirouetted down into the cold abyss. *Good riddance.* His last, self-induced thought was of the sow and cub. *Hey! I think I did something good back there.* He turned, looked up and smiled. *I'm coming, Jewel.*

THE PILOT HOVERED over the angry water just about where he thought the old guy had gone down. The passenger front and rear doors opened. He was worried about pitch. "One at a time or we're all going in!"

Cindy stepped out first with nothing on but an athletic bra and panties, stood on the skid then let herself drop the two metres to the lake. Jim wasn't far behind her, clad only in underwear and wool socks. Later he would explain the socks by saying he didn't want his feet to get wet. When he surfaced, Cindy was facing him treading water, a look of determination on her face. Over the sound of the helicopter above them she yelled, "We stick together, Jim!" He nodded in agreement. She raised one hand, yelling and signing with her fingers at the same time, "One, two, *three!*" They both porpoised and disappeared below the surface.

The pilot looked down. He counted thirty seconds. *Nothing! How am I going to explain three drownings?* Suddenly two heads appeared. *The old guy's gone.* The two swimmers side-stroked five metres towards shore and dove once more.

Where the hell are you, Wally? Two metres down, Cindy looked at Jim. Her eyes spoke volumes. *Where is he? I'm about finished. This is our last try.* They both looked down through increasingly darker water. *Nothing!* Cindy's heart sank. The adrenalin rush began to subside. Jim tapped her on the shoulder then shook his head in resignation.

Why isn't she looking at me? Jim's signal of defeat was being ignored. Cindy was looking past him. He tried to corral her attention. *What now?* Cindy's eyes widened and she did two things. She pointed behind him and at the same time mouthed a single word and released a stream of air bubbles. *There!* Jim turned around and saw the suspended body, up and just below the surface, rocking in time to the current like a bundle of seaweed.

Now the pilot was in panic mode. It had been a full minute since the last dive. He imagined the paper work. He dreaded the prerequisite inquest. He loathed the thought of dealing with the pond-scum sucking news media. *How much longer do I wait before I call this cluster-fuck in?* He looked down once more. Two heads popped to the surface. *Thank God. Too bad about the old man. What the hell? It's the big guy and someone else. Where's Cindy?* He no sooner asked himself the question, when another head popped up three metres away. *Well, whoda thunk it? They got him. Time to earn my pay.*

WALLY FIGURED HE WAS DEAD. *This ain't so bad. There's the much talked about bright light. Whoa! This must be something new. Two angels are taking me up. Well, one looks like an angel, the other, I have to say, is big, and butt ugly. Don't hear a choir though.* The light grew bigger and brighter, brighter and bigger. It shimmered and undulated like a migration of waves was passing by. *What the hell? What's a helicopter doing in heaven?*

THE PILOT DROPPED HIS HELICOPTER just above the water, taking particular care to watch the apex of cresting waves. They had very briefly discusses this part of the rescue. "Remember, when you come up, I can't have all the weight on one side."

That was the plan in a nutshell. Jim had a headlock on the old guy and reached for the skid. He was able to lock his free arm around it. The pilot looked over at Cindy. *Now it gets tricky.* He slowly manoeuvred his helicopter over to her position, dragging his two hitchhikers with him. His machine yawed to one side. He had to avoid the metre high waves with the skids *and* the rotor blades. He was close to Cindy now. She reached over and grabbed the skid. Before she could hook her arm over it, a particularly aggressive wave hit her broadside and she lost her grip. The pilot could see that she was struggling.

Jim looked across the underbelly of the helicopter. *Come on, Cin.* If he had to choose between letting Wally go to save Cindy or holding on to save Wally, there would be no contest. *Goodbye old guy. Hello, boss, best friend and young person with a future.*

I got enough in the tank for one more stab at it. Cindy reached up and hooked her arm around the skid. The pilot pushed the collective forward ever so carefully and towed his charges across the lake to the shoreline slowly, like they might fall apart like wet newspaper if he picked up speed. He knew now that there was a very fine line between dirt bag and hero. *Glad to be on the right side of the line!*

PART 6

THE FIRE IS CONTAINED

So the dragon has crawled back into its lair,
To lick festered wounds and recover unnatural strength.
"What you must do young page is not for the feint of heart.
Enter his dark and rancid hole at your peril.
Draw your sword and sever its demon head from its lizard body.
To do less, will invite certain disaster."

Saturday, July 30th to Monday, September 12th

Chapter 69

DAY 11: SATURDAY, JULY 30TH, 08:30 HOURS, FALCON RESPONSE CENTRE

T HE RAIN DROP FELL TWO THOUSAND METRES, like a single tear from heaven. It hit the ash covered earth with significant force, a testament to the momentum it had gathered from such a distant journey. The impact caused the drop to penetrate the ash. It became a micro-meteorite, first compressing, then breaking up, then creating a shock wave and, finally, a rim of sodden ash. The water drop fragments sat in suspension for a millisecond then disappeared slowly into the parched earth. Countless more raindrops followed. They were raindrop "lemmings" rushing en masse, uncontrollably, to certain death.

SHEILA MONAHAN WATCHED THE WEATHER RADAR SCREEN, one of many screens in the EFR Response Centre. A narrow band of precipitation was tracking across the screen—and, more importantly, across Wawa 43. The precipitation was being pushed ahead of a warm front, part of the low pressure system chugging its way across Ontario from west to east. The federal government's Atmospheric Environment Service's (AES) weather forecast had predicted a range of precipitation from five millimetres to twenty millimetres for the area north of White River. Sheila knew the forecast wasn't received with rave reviews. She recalled the standard response of her four year old niece when a treat was met with mixed reviews. *I don't really love it.* She looked over at the lightning locator monitor. If anything was there, each strike would show as a flash on the screen within a minute of the actual strike. *Nothing showing; I really love it.*

Sheila knew better than anyone that the level of fatigue for staff across the province was peaking. In the Response Centre, the mood had digressed from one of "good humour" to one of "no humour." They weren't at the "get off my ass" stage, but they were getting close. Staff had reached the point where really good news was needed. *Better to have no rain at all then a teaser.* They would know better by 13:00 hours what rainfall occurred on or near the fire through their system of weather stations and the rain gauges set up by fire crew leaders actually on the fire. It was standard operating procedure that each crew leader carried a rain gauge in his or her incident fire kit.

Requests for resources from the incident management team on Wawa 43 had spiked significantly. *I like their optimism— just hope it's not misguided.* The project fire duty officer, Zander Cybulski, was vetting the requests and had discussed them at length with the new "queen bee", Brad Simpson. Rick Sampson had been given some time off so his boss, Brad, had climbed into the fire duty officer's chair, better known as the "hot seat." Brad then discussed the aggressive nature of the attack strategy and the need for additional resources with the provincial duty officer in Sault Ste. Marie. All three had come to the same conclusion: they were confident in the incident management team, and it was time to either "fish" or "cut bait." Fishing was the preferred option. Bill Gorley and his team would get everything that could possibly be provided.

WHITE LAKE PROVINCIAL PARK was a "happening" place. Bill Gorley and his team had two ways to anticipate the impending weather: either there would be enough precipitation to jump all over Wawa 43, or there wouldn't. Bill and Justin chose to gear up for the former. They had sat up a good part of the previous night with their team and division supervisors planning the positioning of fire crews along one hundred and eighty kilometres of fire line.

Given the resources on hand, only the priority areas along the perimeter would be attacked.

Yesterday's burn-out had been a measured success, at least for the time being. As Justin had put it, "We had a few minor fire excursions but the air tankers saved the day." Crews were holding fire line associated with the burn-out, but he needed to jump on the main fire to prevent those crews from being flanked. Most of the ranger crews available and assigned to Wawa 43 had been ferried up to Hornepayne the previous night. Justin had also driven up there after last night's strategy session. Consequently, deployment preparation was now happening on two fronts, Hornepayne and White Lake Provincial Park. The respective division supervisors were rallying their troops at the park. Justin and two division supers would deploy crews for the north end, or head, of Wawa 43 from Hornepayne. Justin stood on the airport tarmac and reviewed his map.

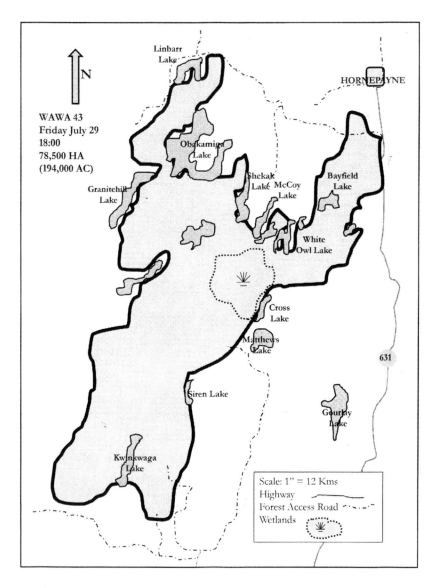

He still marvelled at how much area this fire was able to consume in a relatively short period of time. Since Wednesday, three days ago, Wawa 43 had added another seventeen thousand hectares to its already significant frame. He added another twenty five hundred hectares yesterday afternoon with the burn-out. Now this porker weighed in at seventy-eight thousand, five hundred hectares. He looked down at the map again. *Looks like a lobster.*

What's that in acres? Let's see ... it's pushing two hundred thousand.
Justin still recalled discussions of the 1980, Thunder Bay 46 fire at
three hundred and thirteen thousand acres. *Well, we haven't set a
record—yet.*

His strategy was simple. He knew he would never get the resources to tie in the entire fire line with fire fighters. It just wasn't
realistic. So, he had to prioritize. His marching orders were precise
and clear. One, protect Hornepayne to the north and White River
to the south. Two, protect private structures in harm's way. He
looked down at his map again. Consequently, his priority target
areas would be the right lobster claw, the left lobster claw and the
lobster tail in that order. He had a good head start on the "tail" and
a bit of leverage on the "right claw" but nothing on the "left claw."

Once divisions and sectors within the divisions were BHE, he
would move type 1, initial attack crews, to other areas requiring
attention and backfill their vacancies with type 2, sustained attack
crews. He wanted to keep suppression forces at the three hundred
and fifty person level. Beyond that, he could see the east fire region
breaking the fire in two and bringing in another incident management team, if they could find one. It was all a part of a time hon-
oured philosophy: do *not* exceed your span of control. The only
caveat to this "best laid plan of mice or men" was rain. It was spit-
ting now, and he wasn't about to wait to jump on Wawa 43 with
both feet. He hoped the dragon could not rise up and bite them in
the ass.

Chapter 70

DAY 11: 09:30 HOURS, HORNEPAYNE

T WO, OLIVE GREEN MILITARY 212 helicopters lumbered off the tarmac at the Hornepayne airport. The
large 212's and their flight crews were on loan from
Canada's Department of National Defence and could ferry a
four or five person crew complete with suppression and camping gear in a single trip with room to spare. Unlike a commercial medium helicopter which flew with a single pilot, the
212 crew consisted of a pilot, co-pilot and load master. The
load master made sure that personnel boarded safely, that the
load was balanced and lift-offs and landings associated with
the rear of the helicopter were obstruction-free. You could tell
a military helicopter in lift-off by the person conspicuously
leaning out an open side sliding door, sporting a flight helmet
and mic, with one foot on the skid, reporting on clearance as
the helicopter rose. Justin watched the drab green dragonflies
disappear over a ridge. The co-pilots had maps complete with
GPS coordinates and would deposit the crews as close as they
could to their target areas.

Justin mentally reviewed a typical first day for a fire crew. One
of the first things the crew would do was set up their pump, run
hose line and begin fighting fire. Sometime during the day, they
would build a helipad large enough for the 212's. If all went well
on the fire line, the crew would be there for at least three days and
could expect daily deliveries of food, water, pump gas and any
additional equipment they required. At the end of their fourteen

hour day, they would set up camp, cook supper and retire for the night. Before the crew leader crashed, he or she would make out a food and equipment requisition, a short fire report and either radio it in to base camp, put it in a makeshift mailbox, or turn it over to the division supervisor if he or she showed up by helicopter before dark.

At the same time as the helicopters were taking off, two rented school buses departed the airport property, bound for road accessible areas on the fire. Typically, each bus would carry two crews and as much equipment and supplies as it could handle. More often than not, a half-ton truck would follow, carrying overflow equipment.

Justin marvelled at the service organization required to deliver and support fire fighters. It provided transportation services, administration services, daily fire information, base camp set-up and maintenance, a base camp cookery, helicopter management, telecommunications, first aid services, and equipment retrieval services. Because of the size of this particular fire and the distance from one end to the other, approximately sixty kilometres, a mirror service organization was running out of White Lake Provincial Park to service the south half of the fire. Although necessary, a duplicate service organization compounded the complexity of service delivery.

Justin reluctantly agreed that the fire should be managed by two incident management teams, but they just were not out there. Everything in Ontario was committed, and other provinces were stretched to the limit.

AT WHITE LAKE PROVINCIAL PARK, Justin's boss, Bill Gorley had two significant issues to deal with. The Region was on his ass due to delinquent daily tactical input plans (TIP's—what are the team's tactics today, how many people are associated with the fire, what's the fire behaviour like, what are the issues, how much has the fire grown, etcetera-infinitum). He realized that there was a bottle neck. Justin's TIP's from the north end of the fire had to go to him before his planning chief, Ed Buckner, could merge the data with the south end of the fire and develop a single TIP for

Wawa 43. Since fire suppression information came to Justin from his division supervisors, he would have to routinely work out of White Lake Provincial Park and have the info called in over sat phone. He knew Justin wouldn't be too happy about being away from the north end. *Screw the Region. They can wait for their information for two or three more days. It's more important that we get a handle on the north end of the fire. I need Justin on top of it.*

The second issue was a logistics nightmare. Many of the ranger crews were approaching their nineteen day duty threshold. Personnel were not allowed to work more than nineteen days straight without a break and bringing them into base camp for a day's rest and hot shower did not constitute a break. Many of their schedules indicated they were due for four days off. If he gave them only two days, the remaining two would be worked entirely on overtime, a very expensive proposition. His planning people had a handle on who was approaching the threshold. His best option was for the Region to ferry in replacements and bring the "19 dayers" home for their break. Failing that, he would have to arrange for them to take R and R in Wawa. They would not be happy campers with this option. He had also heard that there might be a possibility of the 19 day threshold being reduced to 14 days. *Now that will be hard to manage. Requests for replacement crews have been sent in. We'll just have to wait and see.*

THE WAWA MNR DISTRICT was a hot-bed of activity. Fire personnel, suppression and service, were coming in by transport aircraft, buses and vehicles. The service organization at the district had three options: put them up in tent city at the district, send them to motels, all of which were committed to fire "housing", or put them on buses to White Lake Provincial Park. All fire suppression crews were destined for Wawa 43. They would eventually be ferried by bus to White Lake Provincial Park where they would be briefed, assigned and distributed. Incoming service personnel were bound for either White Lake or Hornepayne. Others were to remain in Wawa to help out at the district office. It was only human nature to lighten your own load and therefore get them on the road. The problem was that White Lake was approaching its threshold. The issue boiled down to "here, you take them" and "not yet, we don't have room."

Heated discussions between the district logistics chief and the incident management team logistics chief at White Lake were settled by Bill Gorley over a conference call. "Get me two more medium helicopters, send them to Hornepayne and bus all the suppression personnel you have directly to Hornepayne. I'll have someone there brief them. Now this is important. They have to be in Hornepayne each day *no later* than 13:00 hours. That'll give us time to get them into the bush that day." There had been a collective sigh, agreement all around, and a few apologies to round out the conference call.

13:00 hours

OF THE ONE HUNDRED AND SEVENTY SEVEN MNR WEATHER STATIONS strategically located across Ontario, none were given more attention than the two associated with Wawa 43. They were located at White Lake Provincial Park and the town of Manitouage. There was also a portable weather station set up in Hornepayne. Of the three, Manitouage would likely tell the story that the fire people wanted to hear. Although it was twenty-two kilometres directly west of Wawa 43 "as the crow flies", the low pressure system was tracking from west to east. What Manitouage got for rainfall, Wawa 43 would likely get as well. The definitive story was on the fire itself. Ranger crews at the head of the fire, or north, and those on the back, or south, all had their plastic rain gauges set up. One fire crew leader at the head probably said it best for all concerned. As he looked up at a dirty grey sky, he murmured to himself, "Come to Momma."

THE FIRE RECETIONIST AT THE EAST FIRE REGION IN SUDBURY depressed the button on her phone cradle and called Sheila Monahan. "Fifteen millimetres in Manitouage and still rain-ing." Sheila, in turn, wrote it down, got up from her desk and took the note to Brad Simpson, the current fire duty officer for the East Fire Region. He was on the phone, so she dropped it in front of him. Brad quickly read it while he was talking and pumped a victorious fist in the air. He hung up his phone, swivelled his chair around to face Sheila. "What is the probability of that precip reaching Wawa 43?"

Sheila smiled. "They're getting some rain there now. Not a lot, mind you, but I'd say there's a ninety percent chance that the fire will get fifteen mills plus this afternoon.

Brad was practically beaming. "It looks like Gorley and his team made the right call with the burn-out. Now's the time to drop-kick Wawa 43 into the next century."

18:00 hours

FIRE CREWS WERE REPORTING LEVELS IN THEIR RAIN GAUGES from a low of seven millimetres in the south to a high of twenty-two millimetres, or almost an inch, on the head of the fire. It was time to make hay, and crews were being plugged in along the fire line at a frantic pace. Service organizations were almost to the breaking point. Occasionally, an equipment or food order didn't come close to matching the request. However, most fire crews had been in this situation before and, if anything, were creative. They could deal with a food order or camping gear order that in no way resembled what they had requested. Didn't get the hose or pump gas they requested? No problem. A quick radio call to their division supervisor would clear that up. He usually made his rounds with a spare pump, spare gas and spare boxes of fire hose on board. Yes, it was a mad, convoluted dash, but everyone knew what he or she had to do. They also knew what little time they had.

The numbers said it all. Due to the rainfall, the Fire Weather Indices had dropped from 'extreme' to 'high' and 'moderate' ranges. So the rainfall had bought some time for the fire people—but not much. It would only take a day of hot temperatures with moderate winds to bring critical indices back up to extreme. Translation:

fine fuels exposed to fire would readily ignite (again) and the fire would spread rapidly (again).

Justin's message to his division bosses: "Time is at a premium. Let's knock the snot out of 43!"

Chapter 71

DAY 12: SUNDAY, JULY 31ST, 06:00 HOURS, WAWA 43

C INDY SAT ON A BRIGHT ORANGE CHEST COOLER, PUSHING THE COLD BACON AND EGGS around her tin plate with her fork. She looked down at the coagulated bacon fat spread out on the plate, fought the urge to gag, and put the plate down on the ground.

They were now back in the thick of things on Division 'E'. *Did we do the right thing?* Much like the scrambling of her food, she pushed around events two days ago—events she hoped she would not regret. The helicopter had towed Cindy, Jim and a likely dead Wally to the shore. While the pilot landed his helicopter on Wally's front lawn, she and Jim performed CPR. The five minutes they worked on him seemed like eternity. They were certain they had lost the old guy until he convulsed, spewed up a cupful of water like a mini-fountain, coughed vigorously and pronounced his return to the living with a resounding "Damn it to hell!" Cindy had instructed Jim to get to the helicopter and call in the MEDIVAC helicopter from Hornepayne. While Jim was calling in the MEDIVAC helicopter, Wally looked up the smiling angel cradling him. He had enough energy for only one word: "Why?" The tormented look in his face had been sobering, and she was now left with a sinking feeling of recrimination.

Cindy stood up, walked over to a green garbage bag and scraped the remains of her breakfast into it. *Yesterday's news, and I've got a job to do right now.* Cindy went from tent to tent and enthusiastically rallied her crew with a "Waky, waky, rise and shine. You lazy old pricks, it's breakfast time!"

WINDS WERE NOW FROM THE SOUTH, and the dragon was again crawling out of its lair. The rain was an old, formidable enemy. But this time, it lacked the clout to put the dragon down for good.

Within the interior of the fire, on the highest points of land, bedrock had been burned naked, standing out from pockets of surrounding top soil as stark, white knobs and mounds, like overturned bowls and platters. Fringes of surface fuels around the outcrops began to smoulder, sending up vertical, wispy smoke signals. Smoke began to puff up alongside and inside ribbons and belts of unburned tag alder and hazelnut that surrounded or fringed ponds, lakes, wetland, rivers and creeks. Mottled green and brown islands of poplar, birch and brushy under-story—some a hectare, others approaching hundreds of hectares—were made conspicuous by the black sea of total burn around them. Heavier funnels of twisting smoke began to rise from within these islands breaking free above the poplar and birch.

Of most concern were areas along the fire perimeter, especially where the dragon could burrow deeply into sub-surface fuels. Rain had cooled them temporarily, but there was still fire in pockets, deep down below the surface. As it dragged and clawed its way upwards, searching for oxygen, the dragon found new, unburned needles, twigs and moisture-barren leaves. These would ignite, producing "infant" flames that would mature rapidly as new forest fuels were consumed in their paths.

The dragon was energizing. It seemed to rise out of the earth with a conductor's baton in hand, directing its offspring to play a symphony of destruction again. Only this time its enemies were strategically placed and waiting for them. The dragon's offspring would be allowed to attack with abandon in some areas, but no ground was to be given on the lobster fire's "right claw" or its "tail."

13:00 hours, Hornepayne

"WHAT ARE YOU PLANNING FOR DIVISION G?" Bill Gorley had flown up to Hornepayne by helicopter to meet with his operations chief, Justin Bailey. A few minutes earlier, from the airport tarmac, looking west, he could see a solid column of black-grey smoke busting through a flotilla of billowy, white clouds that were drifting across a benign, pale blue sky.

Now, Bill and Justin were in a construction trailer and were looking down at a large map spread out on a wobbly card table. Another division had been added to the fire since last Wednesday, four days ago. This was the largest fire Justin had ever had the "privilege" of tackling, and it was taking its toll. With little rest, no appetite for food and no time for hygiene, other than the bare essentials, Justin looked like a withered scarecrow, propping itself up with stick-arms on a rickety table. However, in contrast to his frail posture, Justin's eyes glowed with laser-like intensity. He was "on his game," and there was no reluctance or hesitation in his response.

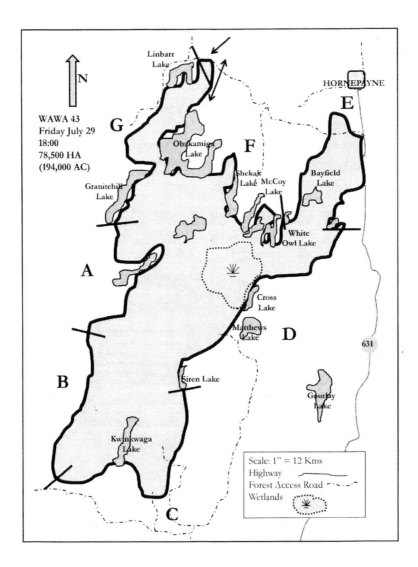

"Bill, let me give the good news first." Justin pointed down at the west side of the lobster tail. "Division B is manned and all line construction—bulldozer, hand tool and pumps, are tied in. I've pulled all Type 1 crews and backfilled with Type 2 crews. Division B is going nowhere. Any questions?"

"How many of the Type 1 crews are our own ranger crews?" Like any fire manager, Bill tended to have more confidence in his own people.

"We've salvaged seven ranger crews from B. I'll tell you about them in a minute." He paused for additional questions, pointed to the lobster tail and continued. "We've got two-thirds of Division C tied in. I've pulled three ranger crews from there and back-filled with Type 2's from Pineland." Pineland was a contract outfit that provided Type 2 crews, mostly from First Nations communities across north-western Ontario. " American HotShot crews are working the east side of Division C, hand-tooling and using our pumps and hose."

Bill interrupted. "And how are they doing?"

"Their division supervisor couldn't be happier. They've caught on to the Mark-3 pumps and hose handling without a hitch. We're going to hopscotch them northward and finish tying in Division C. We'll backfill on their present lines with Pineland crews." Justin couldn't get enough of the "lobster" to "fire" analogy. "The lobster tail should quit flipping within two days."

"So, are there any divisions where the fire is BHE?"

"Yes. Some areas, like Divisions B and part of C are BHE. Other areas are crewed up but not tied in." Justin pointed to the right lobster claw. "As we speak, we've put in all the crews we'll need on Division E. The most important factor here is that the tip of the lobster claw is close to BHE. I anticipate all lines in the division to be tied in by Tuesday at 13:00 hours. At least, that's the objective I've given the division supervisor."

Justin quickly looked up at Bill who nodded slightly with guarded approval. "Now for Division F. As you already know, we're holding our own on the lobster's eyes." Justin pointed to the narrow bulges, one just to the left of the letter F and the other lower and to the right of it. These had potential for fire break-out. If we hold these areas, and I believe we can, then we can prevent fire excursion between the two claws, an area I estimate to be about twenty-five thousand hectares, give or take a few thousand."

Justin unconsciously took in a hefty breath, puffed out his cheeks and released it. "Now to answer your first question about Division G. The ten ranger crews I pulled from Divisions B and C will have the dubious honour of dancing with Division G. See the arrows on the left lobster claw'? Those areas are being pounded by the CL215 package fresh in from Manitoba."

"Is that the smoke column I could see west of here?"

"That's the bastard, all right. Those crews are going in there today, soon after 17:00 hours."

Bill smiled. "So if we can cut off the two lobster claws, we should be in good shape."

"Barring any surprises, we'll put a lid on this fire. Having said that, I expect the lobster to put on some weight in Division D and a little in Division A. We'll just have to live with that until it's their turn for attention."

THE CANVAS BAG OF FIRE HOSE SAT ON THE TARMAC at the Hornepayne airport among many other similar boxes, along with an eclectic array of other equipment. Fire pumps and their tool boxes, ground-based foam kits, chain saw kits, shovels, axes, Pulaski's, back pack pumps, sprinkler kits, tents, tarps, propane stoves, lanterns and tent heaters, cookery kits, burn-out torches, prospector tents and canvas tarps, chest coolers, water jugs, boxes of MT1000 radio batteries. All sat there, playing the fire game called hurry up and wait.

So this particular bag, containing a corrugated box that contained four lengths of hose at one hundred feet each, if it could feel anything, would be suffering from traveller's fatigue. It first boarded a transport truck at Lac Du Bonnet, one of Manitoba's Regional Fire Headquarters for a leisurely eight hour drive to an MNR fire cache (warehouse) in Thunder Bay, Ontario. There it was off-loaded to wait patiently for its next assignment. Sure enough, it was loaded onto another transport for an all-expense, eight-hour, paid vacation to beautiful Hornepayne. But its travel agents were not done with it yet. It would soon board a luxurious Bell 205A helicopter for a thrilling ride to its final vacation paradise, Division G, line camp three, or six, or whatever. From there, it boarded a pack mule called a "fire fighter" and bounced and twisted its way into eco-tourist heaven called the bush. There, it would be eviscerated, its box top torn open and its hose unceremoniously pulled out and dragged like a participant in a pagan disembowelling ritual. This single bag of hose was certainly not alone. It represented the transfer and transport of thousands of pieces of equipment within and across provinces and even the Canada-U.S. border.

FOR THE NEXT TWO DAYS, fire fighters would labour under intense heat and in hostile environments, eat when they could and sleep the sleep of the dead in small nylon tents. Helicopters would rack up their maximum eight hours of flying, moving equipment and fire fighters and assisting crews with bucketing. Air tankers would pick up and drop thousands of gallons of foam-injected water. Tiny Cessna Birddog aircraft would circle overhead making sure fixed-wing aircraft and helicopters kept safe distances and ground crews wouldn't be pounded with thirteen thousand pounds of water in a single drop. Where they could be worked, bulldozers were constructing fire line close to the fire perimeter and crews were burning out from the lines to the main fire.

Back at base camps, service people would be loading equipment, mixing pump gas, hosing down helipads, receiving food and equipment, packing chest coolers, keeping generators running, and carrying out a million other duties. Security staff would be patrolling base camp perimeters, and cooks and cookees would be preparing and serving countless meals.

Ensconced in construction trailers and large canvas prospector tents, planning staff would be producing maps, keeping track of all resources associated with the fire on maps, "T-cards" and lap-top computers, collecting and displaying weather information, producing updates to send out to the crews along with their food, faxing out Wawa 43 TIP's and receiving Regional SOP's, collecting time sheets, keeping track of crews approaching nineteen days without a break and on—and on—and on.

And on Wawa 43, on the eve of the thirteenth day, eighth month of the year 2005, among all the organized confusion, a lone figure sat on a picnic table in White Lake Provincial Park sipping on a cup of coffee. Bill Gorley, the CEO of all this turmoil, was in the moment, in his element, and couldn't be happier.

Chapter 72

DAY 14: TUESDAY, AUGUST 2ND, 19:00 HOURS, HORNEPAYNE

TIM FELDMAN WALKED INTO THE PLANNING TRAILER at the Hornepayne airport. He handed his map to the nearest planning officer. Tim was division supervisor for Division F and had just returned from a recon of his division. He had advised his helicopter pilot to get a bite to eat and that they would be doing another run at 20:30 hours to tuck the kids in, his euphemism for making sure his fire crews were OK before they called it a night. Prior to dropping off the map, he had submitted crew food and equipment orders to the food unit leader and equipment manager respectively. Tim would deliver these orders to the fire line in the morning. Now it was time to play "Twenty Questions" with the planning officer who had brought Tim's map up to the large fire map on the wall.

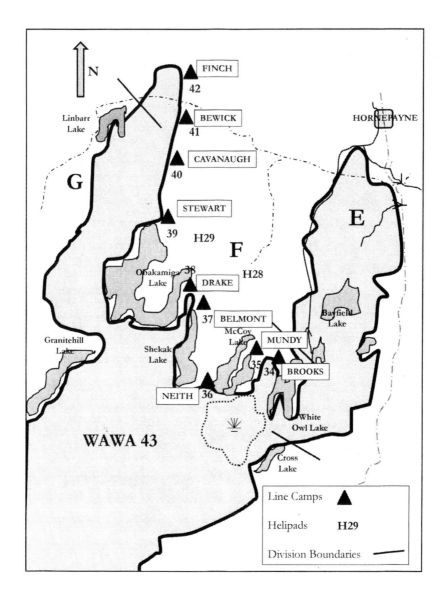

"I haven't got the Neith Crew at line camp 36 or the Cavanaugh at line camp 40 on my map." The planning officer was anal, and his announcement was slightly confrontational.

Tim, on the other hand, was laid back and smiled. "I just put them in the bush today, Fred. They're replacement crews. The Jessop and Gaudry crews have maxed out their nineteen days and are going home."

Fred, the "Officer" with a capital O, frowned and thrust out his chin. "What about H28? Is that a new helipad?"

"Brand new today, Fred." *I'll give him some info to stroke his ego.* He pointed to his map. "See, the helipad is at the end of that forest access road. When we start to demob, I'll be slinging equipment there by helicopter to be picked up by truck."

This revelation gave Officer Fred an opportunity to demonstrate his wealth of knowledge. Using his best conspiriatorial tone, he murmured, "Makes a lot of sense, Tim. A lot cheaper to truck equipment out than use a helicopter."

Using the straightest face he could muster, Tim replied, "It's plain to see you know your stuff, Fred. Any more questions?"

"Well, what about your fire lines?"

"Good question, Fred." Now Fred was positively beaming. Tim continued. "As of today, at 17:00 hours, all lines are tied in. I'm going to give the crews one more day and will likely declare Division F BHE by 17:00 hours tomorrow. But don't tell anyone else yet. Shit can happen."

Fred was now beside himself with this explosive piece of information. Better yet, it now reached the dizzying level of "shared secret." He raised bushy eyebrows, pinched a thumb and forefinger together and ran it across his lips like a zipper. "My lips are sealed."

"If they were sealed, how could you just say that?" Tim smiled and Fred laughed at their little joke. "Can I have my map back in an hour, Fred?"

"You certainly may. Better still, I'll photo-copy it right now, and you can have the original back."

Tim walked out the trailer door with his map. *Man the guy is good at what he does, but it certainly takes all kinds. Time to get some chow.*

A reinvigerated Fred, transferred the data onto his map and put the photo-copy in a mail slot. It would be courriered to White Lake Provincial Park to update the map there. A copy of the latest version of Wawa 43 would be then courriered to the Wawa MNR District office where the information would be fed into a computer. The final product was a fully digitized map showing line camps, fire crews, stand-alone helipads (each line camp would likely have a helipad) and fire line progression by type (bulldozer, hand tools, power pump). In addition, the map would overlay the GIS data in the computer. The final, final product would also show recreational camps, lodges, protected areas such as ANSI's (Areas of Natural and Scientific Interest), other protected areas and the newest forest access roads. If the incident management team required it, the fire could also overlay the latest forest resource data showing forest cover by type, age and density.

Fred was a happy camper. He was where he needed to be—part of the equation.

JUST ABOUT THE SAME TIME THAT TIM WAS HANDING IN HIS MAP, Bill and Justin were digesting the image on the high-level infra-red map on the table in front of them. The map had been obtained from the United States Department of Agriculture, Forest Service, National Infrared Operations at Ontario's request, through CIFFC. The USDA provided the service at cost.

"OK, Justin. What does this do for us?" Bill was 'old school' and Justin was 'new school'.

"Well, I've had a little training on this stuff, and this is what I can tell you." Justin was subconsciously pulling on his chin. "First off, the image of Wawa 43 before us was probably taken from a twin engine aircraft at approximately ten thousand feet. Likely a Cessna Citation Bravo, since the USDA owns one."

"On board would be a 2-band Nadir infrared unit, one that could penetrate smoke, airborn water vapour and radiation. So basically, what we see is a snapshot of Wawa 43's perimeter, in fact a thermal image."

Bill wanted to cut to the chase. "Yeah, so what?"

Like any "tecky", Justin did not want to be rushed, and he pursed his lips in discomfort. "Well, it does have its limitations. First off, it only picks up fire on the surface. It won't show us anything burning deep. It has trouble penetrating forest canopy, so that's why the bands showing yellow around the perimeter are broken up."

"Yeah, so what?" Bill was now smiling and having fun.

"Well, it certainly gives us a good picture of the fire perimeter."

"We have that now. We've done our own mapping."

Now Justin became a little indignant. "*Well*, now we can truth our fire map against this image."

Bill couldn't resist one last shot. "And it's in colour and it's glossy. I wonder how much this has cost us?"

Justin was pensive and hadn't caught Bill's last remark. "I'm a little concerned about what's brewing below the surface of this fire. I wish this map could tell us."

Bill echoed his concern. "I'll second that, Justin."

Chapter 73

DAY 15: WEDNESDAY, AUGUST 3RD, 11:00 HOURS, WAWA 43

A S PREDICTED, THIS WAS TURNING OUT TO BE A GOOD BURNING DAY. What was especially disconcerting to Justin was the forecasted wind speed. Already kicking up at thirty kilometres per hour with gusts up to forty kph, it was expected to peak at sixty kph that afternoon. Combine that with temperatures reaching a high of thirty-three degrees Celsius, and their work to date, and resolve, would be sorely tested. Justin had advised every division supervisor to warn their crews of the potential for four situations.

Of the four, the number one concern was the potential for overhead hazards such as branches and tree-tops snapping off and blow-down—falling trees. Their burned roots would provide little support in high winds. This was a recipe for serious injury or even death.

The second concern was the probability that the air tankers couldn't provide water bombing support with significantly high winds.

The third issue was that the high winds might prevent helicopters from flying. If a crew got into trouble, they would likely be on their own.

The fourth issue, the potential for re-burn, was a deal breaker. Although Wawa 43 had burned fairly deeply into the duff layer, there were still expansive pockets of sub-surface fuels that had not burned. Many of these areas were well within the fire perimeter, but that didn't make them any less of a threat. Even though an area had been burned over, the combination of high temperatures, high winds and existing sub-surface fire was a traditional formula for re-burn. The fuels in the duff layer would ignite readily and the strong winds would push this sub-surface fire towards, and then beyond, the fire perimeter. All the hard work and accomplishment up to this point could be lost with just one break-out location. Each and every crew had to be extremely vigilant. Fire line patrol, instant crew communication and a quick response to flare-ups and break-outs were the tactics of the day.

AT 13:00 HOURS, THE TELL-TALE SIGN OF RE-BURN REARED ITS UGLY HEAD. It initially started with new smoke popping up throughout the burn area, followed shortly by flame. As the smoke grew in volume, the strong winds pushed it parallel to the ground. From the air, it appeared as smoke-waves, pushing their way towards a fire perimeter. In some of the old cut-over areas within the burn, where there was little or no forest cover, lines of smoke seemed to appear like wounds, bleeding thick grey smoke that drained over a blackened landscape skin.

Justin was watching the scenario unfold in Helitack 45, on the north-east corner of the fire, the right "lobster claw", Division E. *We have to hold the lines here.* With south-west winds, this was the likeliest area for fire escape and his highest priority because of its proximity to Hornepayne. The north-east side of Division D on the left lobster claw, would also be a problem. It was priority number two. He had been advised that the air tankers could still fly, so he had assigned a CL215 package there and three CL415's to the area he was watching now, Division E. Further south, the east flank of Wawa 43 was still unmanned, and would likely put on more growth, but Justin couldn't worry about that now. The air tankers were pounding the re-burn closest to the fire perimeter in order to slow down its advance.

17:00 hours

NOT ALL NEWS WAS BAD NEWS. What was causing this present weather system of strong wind was the approach of a narrow cold front behind it, followed by a massive warm front that held the promise of heavy precipitation. Justin had his fingers and toes crossed. *If we can just hold this sucker for another day, we could be out of the woods.* He no sooner thought this good thought when he received a radio call from the Birddog officer.

"Helitack 45 from Birddog 18, do you copy, Justin?"

Justin's premonition metre spiked. The pilot in Helitack 45 was having a tough time controlling the Long Ranger in the strong winds. The machine was being tossed around like the "ball" part of a paddle board. "Go ahead Birddog 18."

"Yeah, Justin, we're going to have to pull the pin. The air tankers are having trouble with the turbulence. We came close to losing one during a drop."

Justin hesitated in order to develop an appropriate response. "I copy that 18. And thanks for the support today. If the winds cooperate later on, we could use you back here."

"Consider it done. We'll stay on top of the weather situation and be back if it cooperates."

Justin looked down and watched as the three yellow dragonflies and mother fruit fly headed east in formation.

Justin knew that the division supervisor was somewhere below in Helitack 76, looking after his crews. "Helitack 76 from 45. You copy all that, Eric?"

"That's affirmative, Justin. I guess we're on our own."

Justin knew he had to project "positive." "Eric, we've got this dragon right where we want it." *If only.* " If we can hold the reburn, there won't be much sub-surface fuels left to burn when we go into mop-up mode in a few days."

"I'll be sure to pass that on."

Justin noted a sprinkling of sarcasm in the response. *Can't say as I blame him.*

As the re-burn reached the fire perimeter, radio chatter became more intense, a sign that crews were being severely tested. All Justin could do was provide an eye in the sky to those crews who needed it, some much appreciated direction and morale-boosting encouragement.

Helitack 45 was being bounced around by gusty winds but Justin paid no attention to the rough ride; he was totally focused on holding the line. His pilot, on the other hand, had just about reached his tolerance level. Justin noticed that his reaction time to the helicopter's "jinking" was slower and his response to direction not as sharp. Justin looked over to the fuel gauge. His pilot needed a break, and the helicopter needed fuel. *And I want to live.*

"Helitack 76 from 45, do you copy, Eric?"

"Go ahead, Justin."

"Man, I hate to leave you holding the bag, but we have to return for fuel."

"We'll do our best. Are the 212's available if we need to pull crews?"

Justin didn't even want to consider that option, but he knew he had no choice. "That's affirmative, Eric. They're on red alert at the Hornepayne airport. They could be up and over to you within fifteen minutes. Don't hesitate to give them lead time."

"Okee-dokee. Do you think they might be able to assist with some bucketing?"

"Negative. Too windy." Justin waited for a response but got only dead air. He looked to his pilot who pointed to the fuel gauge. "Eric, we're outa here."

Helitack 45 banked to port and headed north. Justin wasn't thrilled about leaving. *Wonder what's in store for us when we return.*

JUST ABOUT THE SAME TIME THAT JUSTIN LEFT, Cindy and her crew were right in the thick of things on Division E. She had three quarters of a kilometre of line to hold, and her strategy had been simple: break up her crew and work in pairs. Jim was up ahead working the nozzle with Tim to assist him. She and Sam were patrolling the line behind them. Because they were dealing with re-burn, she didn't expect jump fires, unless the fire breached their line and got into standing spruce or balsam fir. They each carried a fire nozzle and hose strangler. If either one of them ran into problems, they could radio Jim and tell him that they were tapping into the water. It was a simple matter of clamping off the hose near the problem area, uncoupling it above the strangler, putting on the nozzle then releasing the strangler. In the meantime, Jim and Tim would carry on with line patrolling.

In the last few weeks, Cindy had been faced with enough life-altering experiences to last a lifetime. She had been trapped by fire, damn near lost Rob in an airplane accident, saved a man from drowning and forced that same man to face another, more insidious form of death. *Way to go, Cin. What else can I do to win a popularity contest? Maybe allow this fire to get away on me—again.* The very thought pissed her off. *That is not an option! Give my head a shake. I'm becoming a drama queen. Just do my job and all will be well.* Her mind continued to drift. *My jump suit is either growing or I'm losing weight* .She had managed to squeeze in a shower at base camp. When she caught herself in the mirror her reflection confirmed previous observations. *Holy cow. No, holy snake! I could be a runway model. If I stood sideways and stuck out my tongue, I'd look like a zipper.*

Now, here she was again— in a "be careful what you wish for" situation. She was exhausted and thirsty. Every joint in her body felt ancient and arthritic. The pair of feet in her soaked leather boots were blistered, raw and pressure-point sore. *And frankly, I stink. I'm an unwashed cave-woman who has spent too many days standing over a cook fire, rendering dinosaur fat into candles or building shelters from dried mammoth turds.* What alarmed her the most, though, was the realization that her recovery period after a night's sleep was growing shorter each day. Instead of stumbling on her feet (and her tongue) by 18:00 hours, she would start to become spastic by noon.

This thought pattern didn't sit well. She was thinking too much and reacting too little. Cindy shook her head. *Gotta focus.* Then she heard it, the whooshing and crackling sound of torching. She looked behind her. Fifty metres away, she saw a rolling cloud of dense, rolling smoke punch through the tree line followed by a spiral of intense orange-yellow flame. The novelty of fighting fire had long since worn off. *Shit! Here we go again.*

Chapter 74

DAY 16: THURSDAY, AUGUST 4TH, 08:00 HOURS, DIVISION 'E'

A T CLOSE TO TWO HUNDRED POUNDS PER SQUARE INCH, the solid stream of water smashed its way through the decaying layer of needles and leaves into mineral soil, creating a narrow trench. The kickback of water, soil, moss and other forest litter would occasionally ricochet off rocks and trees, layering the nozzle handler with a fresh coat of slime. Cindy was at the receiving end of this mud bath. She didn't mind. She and her crew had held their own the previous day and were in their second back-pass with the hose, forcing water into the duff layer as deep as they could and creating a fuel break.

All divisions on the north end of Wawa 43 had held against the re-burn. There were a few nagging fire excursions, but crews jumped on them right away. Of course, it helped this morning that the sky was low-overcast and the relative humidity was pushing sixty percent. Cindy felt the rain coming. It was just a matter of time. Her secret smile was incongruous with her appearance. She was in "camo-mud", including her face, goggles and hard hat.

Five minutes later, Jim showed up in similar attire. "Now the real work begins, Cin."

Cindy looked up at her tall 2IC. "My, don't we look dashing to-day, Jim. Got a hot date?"

"Well, if she looks like you, I'll probably stand her up."

Cindy worked up a crooked smile. "That bad, huh?"

"Yup."

The banter stalled. "You're right about the real work thing, Jim." They would soon start to work into the burn from the perimeter, a metre at a time, widening the control line. Once they were confident that their line was UCO, then mop-up would begin. It was tedious, back-breaking work. They would use hose, hand tools, back-pack pumps and chainsaws. Killing pockets of open flame was a no-brainer. Dropping trees that still harboured fire within, much like a chimney, was touchy but doable. Logs or piles of brush that might conceal fire were a royal pain but unavoidable. You had to bust or separate them with axes, Pulaski's or shovels, then pour the water to them.

The most difficult part of mop-up was "cold-trailing" for sub-surface fire. Once you reached this point, there would be few visible signs of fire. The dragon was down there somewhere but wasn't about to show itself in such a weakened state. Cold-trailing basically used the senses of smell, touch and sight.

Using *smell* meant picking a target area and staying downwind, hoping the nose would pick up the more intense, pungent odour of fire, then tracking the smell back to its origin. *Touch* meant finding a likely source of sub-surface fire and sliding your hand slowly into the duff layer. If that particular spot became hotter with the depth of your prod, you had found fire. *Sight* was best served in the morning as the sun came up. Looking towards the rising sun made it easier to pick up wisps and veils of obscure smoke. In each and every case with cold trailing, once the source was found, it had to be dug up and drowned. No one liked mop-up, but it had to be done. Imagine spending five or six million dollars on combating a project fire, then letting it get away when you had it all but beaten down.

Cindy gazed skyward. "The rain will be here soon. If we get enough to knock us to our knees, we may get a little down time— enough for serious R and R. We could actually take time to lick our wounds."

"Don't think I'll do any licking until I've had a shower." Jim looked serious, now. "I'm kinda leaning that way, and my bones say we'll get the rain—and lots of it. But do you really think we'll stay on this line?"

Getting slow, Cin. Jim's right. Cindy let out a long, slow breath. "Not likely. We'll be moved somewhere else, and they'll backfill with a Type 2 crew." Her smile was a brilliant white against a facial backdrop of mud. "And here I thought our all-expenses paid vacation would be on Division E. Well, duh!" Cindy looked up again. The first rain drop smacked her on the goggle, a big, fat, beautiful one. It was soon followed by a cast of thousands. Working in a light rain was OK. That's what rain suits were for. But working in a downpour wasn't an option. Visibility was poor, chills and hypothermia could set in when a body was over-worked and footing was a problem.

Jim looked at the sky and grinned. Using his best "the Price Is Right" voice, he bellowed, "Shit load of rain … come on down!"

Cindy looked at him and smiled. "Time for some wound licking, shower or no shower."

10:00 hours

DARK CLOUDS ROLLED IN THICK AND LOW to the tree line. They looked like old wool blankets held up by tree-top spikes. Helicopters and air tankers were grounded. Base camps were still active, but people in orange rain suits moved with a purpose rather than panic. All along the fire perimeter, crews were hunkered down. Ranger crew members crawled into single person tents while other crews, contract Type 2, HotShots, Manitoba, Saskatchewan and B.C., stretched out in canvas prospector tents—five or six weary souls per tent. For two hours, pushed by solid winds, rain came across the landscape in sheets. As the wind subsided, the rain became steady and less intense. Ground fog rolled up like a ghost crawling out of grave, spread and gently covered everything. Across the eighty thousand plus hectares of Wawa 43, there was a silent, welcome truce.

13:00 hours

BUT NOT EVERYWHERE. It was time to drive a sword through the dragon's heart. All of the Bill Gorley incident management team sat around a table at White Lake Provincial Park, planning their strategy with grim determination. It was time to put this fire to rest. It was naive to think they could circle the fire perimeter with personnel, so they remained true to their original attack strategy. Where possible, pull Type 1 crews and back-fill with Type 2. Rally the Type 1's to Hornepayne and White Lake Provincial Park and prepare them for re-entry into unmanned divisions.

Right now, Justin and Bill were at odds with pulling Type 1 crews from Divisions E and F at the head of the fire. Justin rolled out a map on their table.

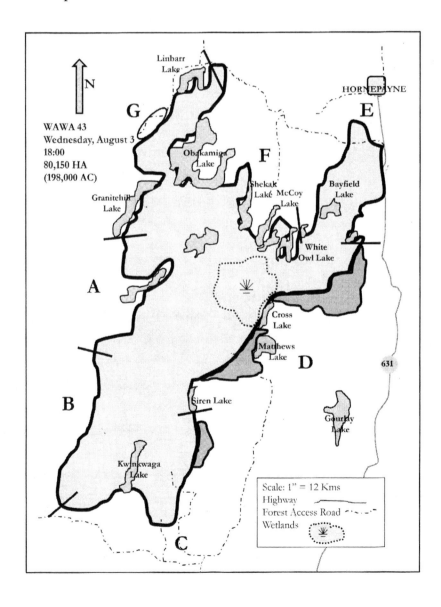

"Bill, I'm comfortable with divisions E and F. I think we can pull the Type 1's and replace them with Type 2's. I need them on Division G—we're not tied-in there yet. I also need to start plugging in crews on the top end of Division C, and I've got nobody in Divisions D or A."

Bill recognized a hint of desperation in Justin's voice. "I don't disagree with your thinking, Justin. I do, however, suggest we wait for low-level infrared. We've got two flights planned for 05:00 hours tomorrow morning. That will tell us a lot."

Justin's impatience began to show. "At least let me pull some crews from F and plug the hole in G." He pointed to the circled area to the right of the letter G. "I've got five kilometres of un-manned line there."

Bill could see the logic. "I've got no problem with that, but I'd be more comfortable if we left the Type 1 crews on Division E for one more day." Bill and Justin had worked together before. Justin recognized the "I'd be more comfortable" as closure. The decision had been made. Bill pointed to the darker areas on the east side of Wawa 43. "Now tell me about the new fire growth in C and D."

"Well, the two divisions put on new growth before the first rain, a few days ago. Our mapping has just caught up with it. They put on an additional sixteen hundred and fifty hectares, but it's a real mess. There are burnt fingers and patches of bush surrounded and crossed by swamp and laced with a countless jump fires. The rain has knocked open flame down, but you can bet the farm that fire is still there."

"So the conundrum is?"

"The conundrum is that we need experienced people in there to sort it out and a good, experienced division super to guide them. And, it's definitely not bulldozer or hand tool country."

"Can you sit on it for a day?"

Justin pursed his lips and, under the table, his left leg was shaking, an unconscious sign of impatience. "Yeah, I guess so, but I'll lose sleep over it."

Bill smiled. "What is "sleep"? Is there a definition we can look up somewhere?" Before Justin could reply, Bill jumped in with another question. "And how are things in Hornepayne?"

"Well, there's a sense of relief there, but I've cautioned them not to drop their guard yet." Justin looked around the room. "Any questions?"

Ed Buckner, the planning chief, raised his hand. "Justin, where do you want tomorrow morning's infra-red?"

19:30 hours

THE BLACK SATELLITE PHONE IN THE CORNER OF HER TENT came to life. Instructions were to leave it off except from 19:00 to 22:00 hours each night in order to conserve battery life. Cindy threw open her sleeping bag and reached for the phone. This simple action reminded her of the pounding her body had taken. *Must be the div super.*

"Whoever it is, I put you on my 'do not call' list".

There was brief hesitation. "Is that any way to greet the love of your life?"

Cindy bolted up in her sleeping bag. "Rob! My God! How are you doing?" She paused to allow the link to complete its vocal transaction.

"Good, but better if I was there next to you. Were you asleep?"

"Yes, and trust me. It would be like sleeping next to a cadaver."

"Probably better than sleeping alone. Listen, I met your arch-enemy today, 'Water Man'."

"Water Man? Who the hell is Water Man, and why is he my arch-enemy?"

"Wally McNeil, and he's not too happy about waking up in a hospital room. It seems you weren't supposed to save his life."

Oh, no. "What were you doing in the hospital? Trolling for nurses?"

"Nope. We had a bit of a rough landing in Wawa. The aircraft is fine, but Jamie suffered a little whip-lash. They have him in for observation. He'll likely be out tomorrow."

Cindy became frustrated and cut in, which was somewhat futile with a satellite phone. "What about you!" *My voice just went into another range.* She toned it down. "And what about you?"

"Just bruised my ego."

Cindy couldn't help herself. "Must have been a whale of a bruise."

This pause was considerably longer. "Anyway, I heard about your heroics and that the grateful and gracious victim was in the hospital, so I paid him a visit."

"So he was pissed, eh."

"Royally. He also mumbled something about a sow bear and cub were going to outlive him and that his best friend was a tree that had died so he might as well be dead and that he should be up there with "her" and not down here with "dipstick", meaning me. The man's quite delightful."

"You know his medical history?"

This time Rob's voice came through somewhat subdued. "Yeah, I don't know how he looked before, but right now, he looks like a skinny, apple-head doll with buggy, desperate eyes. I guess we can't blame him for being pissed. But just about the time he was working his way up to full volume, his two daughters showed up and I slipped out of there. Their appearance seemed to have a sobering effect on the old guy."

I've got to get in there to make peace before it's too late. "So you called to tell me I blew it?"

Rob now sounded surprised. "Geez, no. I called to invite you out on a date—when you can pull yourself away from your echo adventure." There was hesitation on both ends of the call. Rob dropped the levity. "I think we have to talk, Cin—about us."

"What about *us*?" The volume in her voice cranked up a notch.

"I'd rather talk face to face. No telling who is listening out there in outer space."

All of Cindy's prodding and threatening couldn't pry anymore out of Rob. *If I was Elastowoman, I'd stretch all the way to Wawa and throttle the jerk.* With as must frost in her tone as she could muster, Cindy replied. "Our nineteen days are up in three days. I'll catch you in Wawa."

They said their goodbyes and cut the connection. In a hospital room in Wawa and a tent in the boondocks, two people were now highly agitated.

Chapter 75

DAY 17: FRIDAY, AUGUST 5TH, 05:30 HOURS, FIRST LIGHT, DIVISION 'E'

H ARRY PAGE LEANED OUT FROM THE SIDE OF THE ASTAR 350B2 HELICOPTER, pointed his infra-red camera towards the ground at a thirty degree angle and slowly panned the target area below him. The sleek red helicopter was two hundred feet above the forest canopy, flying at a respectable speed of seventy kilometres per hour. Harry had one foot on the skid for support and was prevented from tumbling out of the helicopter by a lap belt and a 4-point shoulder harness. A compact man in his early sixties, Harry had retired from the MNR fire program and now worked for Hawkeye Fire Services out of Beardmore, Ontario. Although it was August, Harry was sporting a two-piece snowmobile suit, toque and gloves. The toque was held in place by a headset. At 05:30 hours it was a balmy five degrees Celsius. Hanging out of a helicopter travelling at seventy kilometres per hour with a temperature not far above freezing tended to make one dress for the occasion.

Harry had a tendency to express his feelings in short bursts and was often overheard saying, "Who needs this shit?" With thirty plus years of fire experience under his belt and at an age where most men fixated on golf or fishing and warmer climates, Harry had earned the right to a little cynicism. But right now, he was a man in conflict. He really didn't need this work but was too stubborn to admit he loved it. So it was no surprise as he leaned out of his seat, bulked up in a snow-suit and watching the canopy of trees fly by him that he routinely muttered, "Who needs this shit?"

Harry had forgotten he was on live mic. The division supervisor sitting up in the left, front seat with a monitor on his lap responded. "What was that, Harry?"

Jeez, caught again. "Need a better place to sit Eric," was all he could come up with. *Pretty good response, though.* The B2 was not the best machine to use for low-level infra-red. It had lots of power, so with three people on board it could get close to three hours of flying before fuel-up. The problem was the rear door that had to be removed. It was called a "pocket" door and for good reason. It was small and therefore the opening was small. In order to get a good field of vision, the Agema Thermovision 510 operator had to practically hang outside the helicopter. If he had his choice, Harry would have been in the back seat of a Bell 206-III. The rear door (removed) was bigger, the back seat was roomier and there was still plenty of power to operate in any condition with a pilot, mapper/recorder up front and the scanner in the back.

"Beggars can't be choosers."

"Pardon?"

"Oh, nothing, Eric." *Change the topic.* "What's showing up on the monitor?" Although Harry could see what Eric was seeing through his eye-piece, he had been focusing on shooting and needed to confirm what passed quickly before him.

Eric's job up front was three-fold. As division supervisor, he provided direction to the pilot on where to fly, and when to hover. He watched the screen for the tell-tale sign of close-to-surface fire—bright, white spots. And today, he was plotting the clusters of hot spots on a map. Even though they had received an inch and a half of rain, Eric wasn't surprised at the results. "All kinds of clusters, Harry. There's lots of work down there."

Harry wasn't surprised either. The planning chief had provided a simple scanning mission. "We're not at the stage of identifying single targets yet. We want to get a sense of where the concentrations of fire still remain around the perimeter." Harry understood the strategy. Given the recent rainfall, there would be areas along the perimeter that harboured very little fire, and areas where there would still be plenty. This was a great tool in assisting the operations chief in distributing his limited resources. It wasn't cheap by any means. The helicopter alone was running at fifteen hundred dollars an hour. But it was a heck of a lot cheaper than ferrying in and paying for fire crews to scout around in areas where they were not required.

Harry's target area for the next three days was Wawa 43's priority, the fire head—divisions E, F and G. Another helicopter and 510 operator were working the flanks—divisions A, D and part of C.

"Harry, were gonna swing around and do a back pass now." Eric's voice already reflected his state of fatigue. This gave Harry a minute to reflect on just about anything—family, fishing, real retirement, the sky was the limit. He chose scanning equipment.

Although there were other options, Harry's infra-red scanning equipment of choice was the Aga 510. It was light and compact, like a 1990's version of a camcorder. It could be powered by a standard six volt rechargeable battery. You could integrate what it captured with a monitor for second-party viewing or a recorder device for play back. A GPS unit could be hooked up to it to punch in hot spot locations. It could also be integrated with a lap-top computer loaded with Geographic Information Systems data. Consequently, you could log and numerically identify the hot spots on a GIS map.

The optimum time for use was early morning before objects such as rocks, broken glass, pop-cans and other metal debris have a chance to heat up due to the sun. They would show up as bright white spots as well. It would be difficult to differentiate them from sub-surface fire.

The 510 had four ranges to optimize its intensity—automatic, and one to three. With a good operator, it could be used at other times during the day. Scanning could often be successful in rocky areas during the afternoon using range 3. The other big advantage of the 510 was that it was portable enough to be used out of a truck or walked on the ground.

Like all thermal scanners, it did have its limitations. Interference from forest canopy resulted in the need to fly an area from two directions: along the outside of the fire line scanning inward and along the inside of the fire line scanning outward. Deeper, sub-surface fire might show up as a pale white glow—or not at all, unless the heat source was strong enough to penetrate the duff layer above to the surface. Heavy dew or light rain could coat the surface of the forest floor and result in a delay in infra-red operations. Heavy smoke conditions could distort the image received from the ground.

Wind speed above twenty-five kilometres per hour caused helicopter to jockey and it would become difficult for the scanning person to find and hold targets. High winds with low, slow flying also became a safety hazard. Flying at one to three hundred feet above the ground put the helicopter in the "Deadman's Curve" with no time and space to recover if there was a mechanical problem. Slow speed compounded the issue. Wind speed from fifteen to twenty-five kph was marginal at best—all the more reason for early morning flights. Wind speed was usually down in the morning.

Harry woke from his erotic equipment dream and looked into the 510 view-finder. He spoke into his live mic, intentionally now. "Can you pull up here? Time to change the battery."

Without responding, the pilot pulled up on the collective, gained altitude and "parked" the helicopter in a hover.

Harry pulled himself back into the helicopter and began to change the battery. As he hummed an unrecognizable tune, he reflected on his situation. *Gonna be a long day. Who needs this shit?* And he smiled.

Chapter 76

DAYS 20 TO 33
DAY 20: MONDAY,
AUGUST 8TH, 05:30 HOURS

W*E'RE GETTING DOWN TO THE FINE STROKES.* Harry Page was again playing "Michelin Man", garbed in a snowsuit, hanging out the side of a helicopter. This was day four for him, and things were beginning to come together at the head of Wawa 43. He was now down to hunting single hot spots along the perimeter of divisions E, F and G. Each of the division supervisors took their turns up front when their division was being scanned.

For detailed scanning, the helicopter was now flying lower, around two hundred feet above the forest canopy and slower—fifty kph. Harry now had an additional task. He had to mark the hot spot on the ground so the fire crew could find it and put it out. When a hot spot appeared in the 510 viewfinder, he would advise the pilot to hover over the location. Once he was satisfied with the helicopter's position, Harry would then drop a marker, an adding machine tape roll. The technique was simple. Extend the roll low and away from the helicopter, hold on to the starting end of the roll, release the roll, then let go of the end once one to two metres had become unravelled. As the tape dropped to the ground (or tree) it would almost completely unroll, leaving a streamer for a fire crew to locate. To facilitate the search, the division supervisor up front in the helicopter was also punching the hot spot in a

GPS unit. The recorded data was given to the appropriate fire crew leaders, who also carried hand-held GPS units. That would get them close to the hot spot locations and the tape would give them a visual reference. Once the hot spot was found, dug up and extinguished, the crew would tear up the tape into pieces and leave it on the ground. This was a visual reference for Harry and the division supervisor. It was a sign that the hot spot received additional attention. If it showed up hot again on the 510, the crew would be advised to return.

The process would continue each day until "clean" scans (no hot spots) were found. Harry knew, however, that there was still considerable scanning to be done. An eighty thousand hectare burn would not be a clean burn. There would be countless islands of unburned patches within the fire perimeter. They would include poplar and birch stands, fringes of green cover around ponds, rivers, streams and wetlands and areas where fast running fire had run through coniferous stands. All had the potential for sub-surface fire and re-burn.

They would be planned for and handled in two ways. After two or three good drying days, when conditions were right, any forest fuels harbouring fire remotely close to the perimeter would be burned out, either by aerial ignition or hand ignition. Better to deal with it now, with the resources on hand, than weeks later. Others would be scanned. If they were clean, case closed. If they still harboured fire, then the appropriate tactic would be used. It usually depended on the size of the islands and their PIA (pain in the ass) factor. Harry expected to be on this fire for a couple of weeks or until the next torrential rain, whichever came first.

WITH THE HEAD AND BACK OF WAWA 43 IN GOOD SHAPE, it was time to focus on three issues: one; strategy for the divisions on the fire flanks; two, pulling fire equipment from the camps and cottages that had been threatened, and three; repatriating Hornepayne.

Division A's scan, half way down the fire on the west flank was no surprise—concentrations or "strings" of hot spots showed as a well defined fire line. This flank had back-burned into prevailing south-west and west winds. As with any back burn, it moved slower, and forest fuel burning was more complete and deeper. And because it was a west flank, with winds likely to come from the west on good drying days, the likelihood of fire escape was diminished—it would run into the burn. Type 2 fire crews were being moved into division A as rapidly as possible to consolidate control lines and hammer sub-surface fire.

The north half of Division C and all of D on the east flank were another kettle of fish. They contained a complicated series of small fires on a flank where fire would be pushed by west winds on good drying days. Infra-red scanning showed a vast array of hot spots sprayed across sixteen hundred hectares of difficult terrain. The use of Type 1 crews, power pumps and hose and continuous direction from the division supervisor in a helicopter was required. This area was assigned to crews from British Columbia. They were used to slope driven fires that moved fast and had poorly defined perimeters. A CL415 package was on alert at Wawa and would likely be required here more than at any other area on the fire. In addition, initial attack on red alert status was set up at Hornepayne. Two medium helicopters and four fire crews were on standby there to jump on anything that smoked or flamed up that wasn't easily accessed by crews already on the ground.

Both Bill and Justin agreed that they were in no hurry to pull the pumps from the camps and cottages. Wawa 43 was not in the UCO stage yet and since road blocks were still in place to turn back owners and rubber-neckers, there was little concern for theft or vandalism. As Justin had said to Bill, "We know where the pumps are if we need them. They'll be included in our demobilization plan."

The return of residents to Hornepayne was the real flavour of the day. Mayor Touluce was in fine form, attempting to bully anyone who might be able to influence the decision. Much to his obvious displeasure no one would be bullied. The decision to repatriate Hornepayne was that of the incident commander, Bill Gorley, who advised the regional director, who told the Wawa district manager, who advised his emergency response coordinator who told Ted Touluce, "Bill says things are beginning to look good. He'll give us a firm answer in two days." Ted walked away, looking for a plank to walk. His face and body language reflected his need to kill something.

WHERE FIRE CREWS WERE IN PLACE, mop up had begun in earnest. The process was organized and methodical. A crew would fan out and begin the process of cold trailing and with the help of GPS coordinates, looking for adding machine tape. They worked an area out from the fire perimeter like a grid, with the crew leader keeping them on lie with compass and a map. Their objective for the first day might be to work thirty metres in for the length of their fire line. Total length of their fire line would dictate the depth of mop up. The longer their fire line, the narrower a day's work would be. When a hot spot was found, they worked it in pairs, digging it up and drowning it with water. The location would be marked with flagging tape and re-visited the next day. Hot spots closest to the fire line were dug and drowned simultaneously with water pressure from a pump and hose. After ten or fifteen minutes, the target resembled a big bowl of dirty porridge. At the end of the day, the crew would mark their progress with flagging tape. The following day, the process would begin again, revisiting the previous day's targets and eventually moving deeper into the burn. If their line was a priority, they might get an additional scan from the air.

It was difficult to keep people sharp during mop up. The frequent adrenalin rushes associated with fire attack, and the long, hard hours had taken its toll. This was certainly not "sexy" work. Hours of work were shortened to both reduce personnel burn-out and save money (less overtime), so more evening time was spent in line camps. Boredom resulted in bitching and complaining. Aches, pains, rashes, cuts, bruises, insect bites, crotch rot, foot fungus and shitty food became the focus of evening discussions.

Line camp life also invited another problem—unwanted visitors of the two to four hundred pound, black, furry kind—black bears. Once a black bear found a line camp, it was usually around for the long haul. Rattling pots and pans at 2:00 a.m. did little to discourage it. Bear bangers delivered by the division supervisor, replicating the sound of gun-shots worked—for one or two nights.

Shooting them was out of the question. Why destroy an animal if you were only there temporarily. Moving the line camp meant moving the pump and hose and was a costly exercise. It was also only a temporary measure. The bear would just work its way down to the next line camp. One single bear could have a really disruptive effect on a fire organization. If all else failed, a conservation officer was flown in to handle the problem using a tranquilizer gun. Once found and put to sleep the bear would be airlifted by helicopter and cargo net to another location. It wasn't uncommon to watch a helicopter flying overhead, towing a cargo net with a black bundle in it.

To alleviate the fall-out associated with line camp life, crews were rotated back into base camp every seven days or so for an overnighter that included food at a base camp cookery, a hot shower, first aid, access to a telephone and a chance to compare notes with other crews. The next day, clean, refreshed and having made peace at home, the crews were returned to the line. At this stage, fighting a fire became as much a personnel issue as a fire tactical issue.

TWO WEEKS LATER, the dragon was surrounded, and the attack was methodical and relentless. Three hundred and forty fire fighters were supported by twenty-two helicopters and eighty service and administration personnel. Infra-red scans were showing fewer hot spots. Wawa 43 was declared UCO on August 22nd. It was time to put the demobilization plan into effect and then turn the fire over to the Wawa fire management supervisor. At this stage of the fire, thirty-three days later, the total bill was close to four point five million direct operating dollars.

Chapter 77

DAY 34: MONDAY, AUGUST 22ND, 17:00 HOURS, WAWA DISTRICT

"IT'S SIMPLE. THE FIRE IS UNDER CONTROL—NOT OUT. Until we get squeaky clean infra-red scans, it won't be declared out. I don't see that happening until late September." The two men sat across a busy desk from one another. Their meeting was relaxed, not confrontational. Bill Gorley was patiently explaining to the Wawa district manager, Francis DesRoches, why he still required some of the district's staff on Wawa 43. "The job of demobilizing a project fire is just about as big as gearing up for one."

A lanky Francis leaned over his desk slowly, like an inch worm searching for a foot-hold. Cookie monster eyebrows lifted like a two-piece drawbridge. "I understand the concept, Bill, but Northshore has been on my ass about access to the fire to determine salvage requirements. I need my foresters to inventory the damage and you have both of them doing service work at White Lake. You know the window here. Northshore and their contractors have about three months to get at salvageable wood before the "Long-horn" and "Bark" beetles nock the crap out of anything of value."

Bill began to leaf through the forty-page demobilization plan he and his team had put together over three exhausting nights. "What are their names?"

Francis leaned even further in anticipation. "Larry Brooksbank and Gaeten Rainville."

491

Bill dug further into the cavernous document. "Here they are. They're due for release in two weeks."

The inch worm touched down on the desk with his head. The gesture was not lost on Bill. "Look, I'll arrange a couple of replacement retirees for them. You should have them back within two days."

The inch worm rose back up. "Now you're cookin' with gas." *Time to push for more.* "What about the rest of my staff?"

Bill delivered a slow don't push it smile. "Tell you what, Francis. I'll leave you this copy of the plan. Check the section on personnel releases. If there is something that really gives you heart-burn, let me know. Keep in mind, the demob plan hasn't yet been approved by the regional fire people."

"Why wouldn't they?"

Bill chewed on his answer. "Well, there are over four hundred people that have to be returned home. Some are from other provinces, and others are from as far away as New Mexico. U.S Customs and Immigration need a heads up and a plan for clearing their citizens back into their country. Air and bus transport has to be arranged. En route accommodations have to be booked. Every fire fighter has to be debriefed. All equipment has to come out of the bush and be accounted for. All the actors along the way have jobs to do. It's an organizational chain reaction with the East Fire Region in Sudbury, the Aviation and Forest Fire Branch in Sault Ste. Marie, The Canadian Interagency Forest Fire Centre, CIFFC, in Winnipeg, and the National Interagency Fire Centre, NIFC, in Boise, Idaho all in the loop, not to mention the various home bases that receive their staff."

Francis was a district manager and by default, could not be admonished or overwhelmed. He planted his tongue firmly in his cheek. "Seems simple enough to me."

Both men smiled, stood up and shook hands. Their grasps were firm and spoke of mutual respect and understanding. The chance of the two meeting again was likely remote.

HORNEPAYNE WAS BACK TO NORMAL. It had survived a potential disaster. Not everything, however, was 'hunky dory'. The fire chief, Ken Waal had decided, when the time came, to try his hand at local politics. He thought the job of mayor would be right up his ally and an improvement in that position was in order. He had quietly declared to the incumbent, Ted Touluce that he was tired of his tirades and snivelling and that come election time, he would whip his sorry ass into the next century. Ted's indignant "You can't talk to me that way" was cut short by an enthusiastic "Fuck off you little weasel." Ted wrung nervous hands and did just that.

People had already tired of Ethel Abernathy's declaration of sainthood for her Sushi. Her story of how Sushi had single hand-ily saved the town with her early warning barking had grown thin and unwanted like a cheap Mexican blanket. For her part, Sushi never really understood what all the fuss was about. Give her a place to squat, a bowl of kibble and an occasional stale dog cookie to pulverize or a rubber toy to destroy and she was one happy puppy.

The talk now turned to the fire, lost wood and lost jobs and what the Ministry (Natural Resources) was going to do about it. Those residents whose revenue streams were intact talked about trucks and boats and ATV's and the moose coming back due to fire and how good the hunting might be.

One thing, however, was a constant. Hornepayne was a small Northern Ontario town, and like many others, it would struggle to survive in the long haul. Bear statues, black flies and super-tanker sized mosquitoes were not considered attractive enough for most tourists. A tongue-in-cheek motto might read "Come to Hornepayne where you can photograph fake bears and get eaten alive by bugs at the same time!" wasn't actually an endorsement for a swell time. Like typical small town northerners, the people of Hornepayne could be forgiven if they wore cloaks of resignation and dragged invisible chains of desperation. But *no light* at the end of a tunnel wasn't necessarily a bad thing. Their "tunnel" could provide shelter, comfort and anonymity. Group resilience could be an aphrodisiac, and the people of Hornepayne were tough and deeply in love with their town, the land around it and the lifestyle it provided. If anyone could keep this town alive, they could, even if it meant living in a bubble forever.

IT TOOK FIVE DAYS TO DEMOBILIZE down to an equipment and personnel threshold that met the comfort level of the Wawa fire management organization. It would be their fire to monitor and respond to once the incident commander turned it over to them. Within that five day period, the level of activity was epic in scope and complexity.

Under the logistics section, a demobilization specialist was assigned to the equipment manager to coordinate the retrieval of equipment. Demobilization of personnel was according to plan, delivered by their respective supervisors and vetted through personnel staff on the team.

Staging areas had been pre-selected around the fire to receive equipment and personnel from helicopters. Buses, vans and pick-up trucks would be waiting to load crews and personal gear. Cube vans, stake trucks and even tractor trailers would be waiting to take on equipment and unused supplies. Service personnel would be assigned to each staging area for handling equipment, registering staff and providing on site security. Where necessary, haul roads would be graded and repaired to handle transport requirements.

On the fire lines, thousands of lengths of hose would be melon rolled and carried out of the bush. Pumps would be retrieved, camps broken down and sites cleaned up. All garbage came out of the bush. If that meant hauling bags by helicopter, so be it. Lines would be checked and re-checked for misplaced equipment. Hand tools, hose wrenches, stranglers and hose packs did not come cheap. Burned hose had to be inventoried and metal hose couplings retrieved to be used again. If the computerized inventory did not balance out with returned equipment, then detective work was required. Whoa be the fire managers that couldn't find their pumps or hose. Many an incident commander and team lost precious sleep over the rationalization of their equipment. On paper, it was simple: if one hundred and sixty-two pumps and thirty kilometres of hose went in, then one hundred and sixty two pumps and thirty kilometres of hose (or equivalent in couplings) better come out.

At the two base camps associated with Wawa 43, White Lake Provincial Park and the Hornepayne airport, frustration would occur daily over the retrieval of fire crews. Cooks would be overwhelmed when on any given day they planned to feed one hundred people and ended up with one hundred and fifty. Service officers would be frustrated that they couldn't get enough prospector tents to house the crews or juggle the food orders to meet ever-changing requirements. Personnel staff would be considered magicians if they could track, record and report on everyone that filtered through their base camp. Generators quit, washroom trailer privies malfunctioned. Johnny-on-the-Spot honey wagons (poop pumpers) were routinely late, propane showers didn't run well if there wasn't any propane and fire crews brooded as they waited for transport home. Miraculously, everyone found a place to eat, sleep, wash and relieve themselves.

Staff at the Regional Fire Centre in Sudbury had their hands full. Transport arrangements had to be made for crews and staff leaving the province. All crews and staff within the East Fire Region had to be accounted for on a daily basis. The coordination of helicopter releases was a logistics nightmare. The regional aircraft coordinator had to factor in tariff rates, unused hours (most were guaranteed four hours of flying a day), ferry home distance, time and cost, and short term requirements within the East Fire Region since some helicopters had to stay.

The fire service centre just across the tarmac from the fire centre had to prepare to receive, inventory and recycle tractor trailer loads of equipment. Pumps would go to a contract recycler for testing, maintenance and repair. Hose would go to a contract hose facility for washing, testing, repairing, drying and boxing. All other equipment was recycled at the Service Centre. Pumps, hose and other fire and camping equipment were from other locations as well, including other provinces. Once recycled, they would be transported back to their respective owners by cube van, transport, or air.

All of the transactions had to be communicated between partners. If a truck load of pumps was being returned to Manitoba, the East Fire Region in Sudbury would notify the Aviation and Forest Fire Management Branch in Sault Ste. Marie. AFFMB would notify the Operations Division of Manitoba Conservation and CIFFC, the Canadian Interagency Forest Fire Centre, simultaneously.

If a plane load of HotShot crew-members needed to be transported by air back to Boise, Idaho, (Home of the U.S. National Interagency Fire Centre) then EFR in Sudbury would request arrangements through the Aviation and Forest Fire Management Branch in Sault Ste. Marie. AFFMB would then notify NIFC and CIFFC simultaneously. It would literally take months to finally rationalize equipment inventories across North America. Equipment that was damaged beyond repair or couldn't be accounted for would be written off by the end of the fiscal year, March 31st—just in time for the start of a new fire season.

Chapter 78

MONDAY, SEPTEMBER 12TH, 2005, WAWA 43

THREE WEEKS AFTER WAWA 43 WAS DECLARED UCO all appeared quiet on one of the largest forest fires in Ontario's history. Fire base camps had been collapsed but the Wawa district still maintained daily fire line aerial patrols and helitack capabilities out of Hornepayne and White River. Would Wawa 43 get away on them? Not likely. *Could* Wawa 43 get away on them? It was possible. But for now it was a beautiful day across an ugly landscape.

SHE WAS AN ARMORED EATING MACHINE. Her inch long, dark brown body was mottled with soft-white speckles. Her plated wing covers had a white dot on each base. Her signature feature was a pair of long antennae, at least half again as long as her body. She was a white spotted pine sawyer, a member of the longhorn family of beetles. She played no favourites and attacked white pine, red pine, jack pine, balsam fir and white and black spruce indiscriminately. Her skills, hard wired and honed over a million years, were instinctive. They required no rationalization and begged no forgiveness. She bore holes through the bark layer of a tree and ate to survive. She survived to lay eggs. It would be her many larvae that eventually destroyed a tree already weakened by fire.

She was not the first to arrive. The black fire beetle, using a pair of built in receptors, soon detected the infra-red source of radiant heat associated with the big fire. This flat headed, wood-boring beetle was constantly in search of breeding grounds and would mate while the fire was still burning. It would be the first to attack in countless numbers while there was still smoke on the horizon.

Not long after the beetles arrived, black-backed woodpeckers moved in to feast like cruise ship seniors at the buffet. They were a burnt forest species of woodpecker, supreme opportunists who relied on wildfire to attract their prey. These medium sized woodpeckers (9 inches) had black heads, backs, wings and rumps. Their underside was white from throat to belly, and their flanks were white with black bars. The one distinguishing marking was the yellow cap on an adult male. Soon other members of the woodpecker family would arrive. The northern flicker, downy, hairy, large pileated woodpeckers and the yellow-bellied sapsucker would do justice at a feast of fat beetle grubs. Like a percussionist's section of a symphonic orchestra testing their instruments before a show, the forest would echo with the rap and staccato of a thousand heads pounding trees.

IT WASN'T THE PRESENCE OF BEETLES that worried Amos Alfelski, woodland manager for Northshore Logging; it was the wood damage caused by the larvae that lived to eat. The seven thousand hectares of salvageable wood remaining on the eighty thousand hectare fire needed to be harvested now. Rushed aerial inventory, frantic ground truthing and frequent late night meetings with MNR foresters and sub-contractors finally resulted in a plan. As licences were being issued, equipment and manpower was being rallied. It was like the end of the "Big One", the Americans and British under Montgomery racing against the Russians under Zhukov to see who could destroy Germany first. In this case it was Northshore Logging led by Amos, racing against Mother Nature and her legions of beetles to see who could destroy a victim already brought to its knees. Amos was more like General Patton. He had a mission, and it would be a brave (or stupid) soul that got in his way.

Not to be outdone by their woodland manager, Northshore and sustainable forestry licence foresters— intermediaries between MNR and the licensees for a given area, were in heated negotiation with MNR foresters for more wood. Best estimates suggested Northshore had lost ten years of wood supply on Wawa 43 (assuming a hot economy and demand for product remained constant). If MNR didn't assign them more wood from a (phantom) reserve, mills would close, jobs would be lost and towns would fold. Terms like "profit margin" and "shareholders" crawled into the closet. Heaven forbid that anyone would think greed was a motive.

For their part, the MNR foresters would throw their hands up and declare that there wasn't any surplus, shy of shortening rotation ages and cutting trees that hadn't reached full size and volume potential. And that wasn't going to happen (unless the local politicians jumped into the fray).

The next best option was trading marbles, like in "I'll give you three 'cat's eyes' for a 'boulder.'" In this situation, the traders weren't kids, they were competing licensees. Northshore might need jack pine to satisfy a mill. A competitor might need white pine or poplar. While trading went on, MNR stood by like a stressed parent making sure its children didn't get carried away. In the meantime, an army of beetles chomped away at their new found treasure. Politicians finally waded in, and deals were struck that would satisfy short term needs. Everyone breathed a sigh of relief. They could deal with any long-term fall-out down the road. Most of them would be retired by then anyway.

IT WAS NOW TIME TO DEAL with whipping Wawa 43 back into shape. Sure, Mother Nature could do it over time, but patience was not one of humanity's strongest virtues. Reconnaissance results produced a mosaic of opportunities for the eighty thousand plus hectares. The high grounds burned down to bed rock were non-recoverable. They were write-offs—other than providing an opportunity for geologists to search for mineral deposits they might have missed somewhere along the way. Of course there were pockets of poplar and birch that had survived ground surface fire. Fire scarring might be an issue, but the market for strand board (chip board/particle board) was hurting. The poplar could be ignored for now.

Of particular interest, however, were sites with deeper soil. Pine stands were associated with these sites. Fire had done a number on the jack pine sites. The trees grew crowded by nature, so there wasn't much to salvage unless fast moving crown fire left a good first log or two in the tree. Salvage would take place here. Along with those stands that weren't salvageable, bulldozing would result in miles of windrows and the resulting sites, like rough, gigantic football fields, would be re-planted with jack pine. Where stands of white and red pine were hit lightly by fire, there would be a selective salvage cut, leaving some trees as a seed source for natural regeneration. It was the harder hit stands of white and red pine where salvage was a priority. Aerial seeding or hand planting would depend on terrain.

THE PLAN WAS SIMPLE. Wawa 43 would begin its cycle of productivity over a four-year period of regeneration. Of the eighty thousand, one hundred and fifty hectares available, twenty-one thousand hectares were non-treatable. They consisted of lakes, water courses, wetlands and areas burned down to bed rock. Fifteen thousand hectares were classified as areas 'not requiring attention'. These were largely stands of poplar and white birch that survived less intense ground fire. Twenty-four thousand hectares would be left to regenerate naturally (this was considered a form of "attention"). These were pre-fire "jungles" of white spruce, balsam fir and the low-land black spruce. It would be another century before these stands were really given any attention ... in the form of harvesting.

The twenty thousand, one hundred and fifty hectares remaining were lavished with the attention usually reserved for royalty or rock star status. Salvage cutting had already begun. Seed trees would be left on twelve thousand hectares. Where the stands were red pine, the number of trees left to provide seed were limited with distances between trees of thirty to fifty metres. Red pine was intolerant to shade and grew best in open areas, exposed to sunlight. Where the stands were predominantly white pine, more trees were left, some in groups to provide a seed source. White pine was shade tolerant and grew best with protective over-story. In both situations, scarification with heavy equipment would occur to turn over the soil and prepare a seed bed.

Of the remaining eight thousand, one hundred and fifty hectares, five thousand would be aerial seeded with helicopters and three thousand, one hundred and fifty would be hand planted. Once a salvage cut was complete, bulldozers would clear and windrow the debris (slash). Trees would be planted by legions of tree planters at an average of eighteen hundred trees per hectare. Within four years, Wawa 43 would have over five and a half million new planted seedlings standing proudly in wobbly rows that would be ready for the chain saw or feller-buncher or full-tree harvester (or whatever new technology existed for harvesting) in eighty to a hundred and twenty years.

THE OLD WHITE PINE WOULD HAVE BEEN AMAZED at the level of activity over the next four years. Humans scurried like ants that had their hill kicked apart. There would even be a fresh crop of pine seedlings punched into the soil in the valleys below him. If the old guard could feel regret, it would lament that it had not survived to stand watch over the next generation of forest struggling to survive and mature on the eight hundred square miles below. Old pine trees could not be *amazed* or feel *regret* ... could they? Well, of course not. And like God, mankind knows everything.

EPILOGUE

"Sir Knight, I have slain the dragon
We are saved now.
Here is your sword."

"You have done well, young page,
But hold fast—he won't be the last.
You have taken up the sword.
It is now your cross to bear."

EARLY SPRING, 2009—ALMOST FOUR YEARS LATER, WAWA 43

THE FOREST STOOD NUDE AND GROTESQUE like an elderly, obese banker found beaten and robbed, stripped of his tailored suit and undergarments. With all the trappings of wealth and power removed, there was nothing left to admire. All that remained was an overwhelming mantle of disillusion and shame.

It was almost four years since the great fire had passed through. The vista of black, skeletal remains seemed to stretch to infinity. If the panorama was a canvas, it had been painted with bold, angry strokes using cruel, implacable colours, bearing witness to the rage within the artist.

There still remained intrusions of contrast to the army of Satan's spindly soldier-trees. Ridges of barren rock, criss-crossing the landscape in stark, soiled, white contrast, had largely remained unchanged in the four years that had past. Rings and borders of greenery, the last defenders of lakes, ponds and streams, still remained intact. At a distance, it was as if time had stood still. The enormous, black mark on the landscape would remain forever as a testament to the awesome power and cruelty of nature.

THE DESOLATION WAS A RUSE. At a closer look, when one got over the shock of devastation, there were subtle, yet remarkable changes. The macro was disturbing, the micro, intriguing, for it wasn't just humankind that had been busy attempting to repair the damage. Armies of insects had spawned larvae. Both insects and larvae attracted an eclectic array of birds.

504

Flycatchers such as the "Olive-Sided" and "Alder" species were in their element. The Woodpecker family of birds had settled in nicely since the big fire. The small songbirds such as chickadees and nuthatches were now fewer in number, but they were there, confining their activities to any of the forested areas that had survived. As more insect-eating birds moved in, so did the northern corvids—grey jays, often referred to as whiskyjacks, blue jays and ravens specializing in raiding nests for eggs and new-borns.

Most of the small ground mammals, such as voles and mice had survived in their tunnels. They had propagated enthusiastically in their new environment, but without the old ground cover, were easy targets for raptors such as the northern harrier, broad-winged hawk, great horned and barred owl. Nature was working overtime to maintain balance and connectivity. The healthy populations of red squirrels and porcupines had either not survived the fire or had moved out with the loss of forest cover. Gone, too, were their natural predators—the pine martin, fisher and weasel.

There was, however, new growth as a result of fire and man's attempt at regeneration. It attracted a robust population of snow-shoe hares, the small summer-brown, winter-white rabbits with long feet. Not far behind were their predators, the lynx and red fox. In another five years, the ruffed grouse would move in seeking the protection of immature and sapling-sized trees to savour the accessible winter buds of poplar and birch. The lynx and fox would be waiting.

The largest ungulate in Canada, the moose, moved in for the new growth as well—especially poplar, white birch, and striped maple. Wherever there was a healthy moose population, invariably there would be an increase in their predators, timber wolves and hunters. After all, man *was* just another animal but one that required constant regulation, or both the moose and wolf could be exterminated in a decade.

What was really impressive, however, was the explosion of wildflowers, grasses and wetland flora. It was as they had been hidden in captivity then released from a deep, dark dungeon into a sundrenched, nurturing environment. God's paintbrush was busy on Wawa 43. It was a botanical smorgasbord that attracted pollinating insects that attracted more insect-eating birds that attracted more corvids and raptors.

The happiest dinner guest at the Wawa 43 table was the black bear. It would eat just about anything. If insects and grubs were the appetizer, then blue berries were the main course. The post-fire blueberry crop had been bumper two years running.

It was a revolving door of flora and fauna. The geography associated with Wawa 43 was the apartment building and Mother Nature was the landlady. The type of tenants she attracted depended on the shape she kept her building in. Humankind, with no shortage of arrogance, puffed out its chest and saw itself as the groundskeeper. It planned and fretted and regulated and patted itself on the back. Then Mother Nature would smile benignly, wag a recriminating finger, wave her magic wand and set things right. The landscape was forever changed and forever changing. Man would take early credit while nature had a sleeve full of tricks and had just begun to "abracadabra" Wawa 43.

The eighty thousand hectares of burned landscape would be fine, over time—as long as man's efforts, some misguided, did not interfere with, or somehow break the chain of natural consequence. The real, constant threat was to the healthy forest beyond Wawa 43. Ironically, it would be man's own predilection to self-destruct that might save the day.

THE BOARDROOM TALKING HEADS for Northshore Logging, scratching and clawing for more wood four years earlier, had garnered concessions from MNR. The gloating and swagger as a result was short-lived. The U.S. economy had come spiralling down like a damaged parachute. Misery needed company, and the U.S. dragged its trading partners down with it. Greed and avarice accomplished what good, common sense couldn't. It knocked the snot out of the demand for wood products. Mills were closed and wood harvesting ground to a halt. The forest could return to its corner, take a breather and gain some ground until the next round with the monster harvesting machines.

The respite even gave the spin doctors an opportunity to toss around terms like "forest sustainability" and "bio-diversity" as if man's withdrawal from the forest was a product of judicious planning. Short memories and the total absence of a conscience were just a few of tools in the corporate tool box. Once the demand for goods and services picked up, and it would, "sustainability" and "biodiversity" would quietly slip from corporate vocabulary. Terms like "job opportunity" and "production schedules" and "shortened rotation age" would crawl out of the boardroom woodwork, slither across the floor, crawl up CEO pant legs and eventually roll off forked tongues, and with amazingly little effort. But for now, as long as things were bad for humankind, they were good for Mother Nature.

THUNDER BAY, ONTARIO

HE SAT AT THE TABLE shaking hands and signing books. Richard Head was a "mini-me" of his original self. His brush with mortality was a dance with the devil so he had decided to squeeze a life-time of change into a four year window. Yes, he had a book in him. It had been somewhere deep down inside, a treasure, waiting to be discovered. He had possessed the map but initially lacked the strength and courage it would take to go there.

Before he could tell his story, Richard had to mend and mentally prepare himself. The alcohol and cloak of self-loathing had created the caricature that had been Richard Head. The epiphany as a result of his brush with death and even more so, his pitiful reaction to it, was monumentally cathartic. It took two years to wrestle down the demon in the bottle, a demon that was only too willing to come back for a re-match—if he allowed it. At the end of his first year of sobriety, Richard removed the mirrors in his apartment. He swore that the next time he looked at himself he would see someone else—someone who would not make him feel like a gluttonous toad wallowing in pond scum.

It started with walking, short walks at first, but distances increased with time and energy. Then he followed up with workouts in the gym, very early each morning when fewer people were there to pretend not to see him. Turning down a drink was nothing compared to opening the gymnasium door, sneaking furtive looks at all the beautiful people, then walking in to sign up. He began to diet. He cut out the junk food he couldn't afford and focused on frequent, small healthy snacks. As Richard became stronger he rediscovered his childhood love of biking and travelled everywhere by bicycle. And as he morphed, he began to write.

His had intended to focus solely on his experience on the big fire. It lent itself well to dramatization. He could paint himself anyway he wanted, for no one else was there to bear witness. He entertained thoughts about targeting (and if necessary, pre-fabricating) fire program waste, tactical bungling and bureaucratic cover-ups. He could, as he once mused, "sensationalize the shit out of it." But the new and improved Richard realized that the story that needed to be told had to be honest and had to focus on *his* failure, not a phantom failure of an organization that tried its damndest to do a good job.

So he wrote about himself. He realized that it was honesty and self-discovery that would free Richard Head. Every story has a beginning, middle and an end. His previous life and failure as a person was the beginning. His forest experience was the middle. Today, the first signing of a successful novel was the end.

SUDBURY, ONTARIO

THE CAFETERIA DOWNSTAIRS IN THE FALCON RESPONSE CENTRE was crowded. It was Rick Sampson's last day. He had managed three more fire seasons since Wawa 43 and it was really time to retire. Everyone had an Achilles heel, and Rick's was the rush that came with conducting a large fire response organization when wildfire was on the horizon. He was the ultimate dragon slayer, but the effort was relentless and it would take its toll. His wife, Beth, had left him. There would be no reconciliation.

As Rick stood to make a short speech, his tall frame was now leaning forward as if the effort to straighten up might cause him to topple over. His most distinctive feature close to four years ago, his salt and pepper hair, was now mostly salt with very little pepper. If his body belied a certain frailty, his grey eyes still commanded attention. They were sharp and, when necessary, like a welding torch, still had the ability to cut through metal.

Rick cleared his throat, smiled and looked down to his left. Sheila Monahan looked up at him. No one could see that they were holding hands below the table. At that moment, Rick thought to himself that sometimes it took failure to make things right.

MESCALERO APACHE INDIAN RESERVATION SOUTH-CENTRAL NEW MEXICO

NATE RAMIREZ SAT IN THE FRONT PORCH SWING and challenged Sierra Blanca Mountain to do something dramatic. He was growing restless and needed a diversion. Another fire season was on the way. Last year, however, was his last. He had resigned from the Rio HotShot crew and took a permanent job with Mescalero Forest Products. Damp mornings in small tents, blisters and arthritic pain had sealed the deal.

The mottled brown landscape stretching from his front porch towards the ancient mountain was splattered with colour from the spring flowers and blooming cactus. God had dipped His paint brush in every colour arranged on His palette, raised it and flicked His wrist in merriment. A hundred yards out, a lone prairie dog stood ramrod straight on hind legs, perched on a mound of earth. It had its back to Nate, head up, sharing the same spectacular work of art—two amigos, lost in appreciation and wonderment.

Nate's wish for a diversion was soon delivered on two fronts. He sniffed the air around him, and like a snake charmer, his nose coaxed the supper kitchen aroma through the screen porch. Celina's culinary magic stroked his senses. His brain lacked discipline and conjured up a variety of dishes and desserts and he began to salivate. He thought it was time to go inside and offer a compliment or two. That usually guaranteed a second helping. Just when he began to rise, his second diversion appeared out of no where. A fairy princess with a basket of flowers plunked herself down on the porch step. Seven year old Nadey had spent the afternoon picking wild flowers.

"I smell Biscochos, Daddy." She offered him a pixy smile and conspiratorial look. The anis and cinnamon short bread cookies were her favourite.

"And I smell fried chicken and sweet potatoes." And those were Nate's favourites. "We must have done good things today, Nadey." She had told him in no uncertain terms last week that the baby names he often called her were out. He would have a tough time turning the corner.

"I see you've been busy. You've got quite a haul there."

Nadey beamed at him with pride. She reached in and pulled out a prickly stem with pinkish, lilac type flowers. "What's this one, daddy?"

"That's a desert thistle."

"And what would your great-great grandfather Naiche say it was used for?"

"Why, he'd put on his serious face and say that it was good for treating chills and fevers."

Warming up to the game, she pulled out another flower. "And what's this bright, red one?"

"That, my dear lady, is called foothill's paintbrush. And great-great grandfather would say that it could relieve aches and pains."

Now, with much confidence and bravado, she whisked out another then wiped a hand on her shorts. The dense, yellow flower heads were sticky. "Bet you can't tell me what this is."

"Bet I can."

"Bet you can't."

Nate screwed up his face like he had to reach real deep for thought. "Well, you got me there."

Nadey's smile was one of victory.

"Oh, now I remember. It's a curly cup gumweed. And it's good for a toothache."

Nadey stomped a foot in mock anger. Before she could pull out another flower, a two-worded song twirled out of the house. "Supper's on."

Both father and daughter raced for the screen door, pulling and shoving and laughing. The door slammed with a bang. It wasn't long before an orange, bald-pate sun began to drop below Sierra Blanca and the music of happy conversation and laughter slipped through the screen and out into the evening.

IXTAPA, MEXICO

CINDY STRETCHED OUT LONG LEGS in a bleached white, plastic lounge chair perched on a never-ending beach. It was anchored in sand the colour of old copper laced with ribbons of gold. Clear, easy waves slid to the shore, washed past the legs of the chair, rolled, produced a fringe of diamond-laced froth then disappeared. Her hands were resting on a swollen belly, protecting a new life within. She opened reluctant eyes and followed the palette of ocean blues to foothill clouds perched on its chalk-line sea-edge. From just above her toes, light cyan flats ran into royal blue wavelets where the sea bed began to drop off. A slight tilt up of her head gave Cindy a view of deeper, more turbulent waters. Royal blue turned to steel blue separated by rows of aggressive waves. The late afternoon sun facing her, tossed random gold and silver garlands at the distant clouds. They hung, suspended on white to grey cloud-pillows. An occasional snap of lightning, like an old 1930's camera flash, appeared, diffused then faded in the bank of clouds. It was distant. No sound followed.

Cindy's hormones were out of whack, and her emotions just couldn't make up their mind. Right now she was thinking of Wally as *her* loss, and it was close to four years later. She smiled wryly when she realized how self-centred her thinking was. *I could have learned so much from you, you old prick.* She looked above the clouds. *You're up there, somewhere aren't you, Wally? You and your stubborn streak, giving Saint Peter and the angels a hard time.*

Another flash of lightning seemed to confirm her convictions. She thought about the over-turned canoe and wondered why he had forfeited his life for a sow bear and cub. His daughters had suggested 'redemption'. *We'll never really know, Wally. But I bet you had a good reason.*

A shadow passed over Cindy. Rob had waded in with two large cups of something cold and refreshing—a non-whatever for Cindy and industrial strength 'zinger' for him. She moved her legs down to each side of the lounge and Rob sat on the end.

"Here you go Mom. One 'wish-it-was-something-stronger' for you and a 'liquid defibrillator' for me."

Cindy looked at him with a critical eye.

"I know … I know. It's not fair. I just wish it was me who was pregnant. But then, it would be a miracle and we'd have no peace. I'd be doing the talk show circuit and you would be jealous."

"Let's see. My stomach and ass are getting bigger. I can't fit into my clothes and have to wear expando pants. I've been nauseated and exhausted for five months, and in the first two, my favourite companion was an aluminium bowl to vomit in. You get drinks with exotic names and I get Mexican freshy. The all-*you*-can-eat buffet sports two thousand varieties of food and all I seem to crave are pickles, ice cream and dry crackers. I have to wear this stupid sombrero to avoid the sun, and the cover-up you bought me looks like it came out of Dipsy the Clown's wardrobe. The other tourists think I'm part of the Mariachi show here at the resort. And *you* think I would be jealous."

"Well, I see they have whole wheat crackers. What more do you want?"

Cindy replied, a look of desperation clouded her face. "I want to be able to sit up and spring out of this lounge like an athlete instead of rolling over and ending up in the ocean on all fours before I shuffle to my knees and force my bulky frame to stand up and defy gravity."

Rob had no sympathy for what he could never really hope to comprehend. He knew, however, that it was time for a kind work or gesture. He just had difficulty delivering. "Do you want some crackers with your coffee?"

Her look could melt candle wax.

"Awe common, Cin, I'm just kidding." *I need to change the climate.* "Have you thought more about names? What if it's a boy?" They had chosen not to know the gender ahead of time.

Cindy paused, giving the question some care. "I've been thinking about the trapper." With a single, short statement, she had turned the tables.

"Geez! Not 'Wally' or 'Walter' or 'Wallace'!"

Cindy smiled. "Walter Corrigan Cruikshank. Has a nice ring to it."

"Come on, gimme a break. You can do better than that."

"OK. I was thinking more like 'Derek'."

"Where did that come from?"

Cindy's emotions kicked in and her eyes welled up with tears. "That was Wally's middle name. He said I was one of the few people privy to that gem of information."

Rod tested the name. "Derek. 'Deek' for short. Like deeking a goalie in hockey or soccer. I like it. But what if it's a girl?"

"Not likely, not the way this guy kicks."

"But what if it is?"

She looked at Rob, pursed her lips and squinted—her eyes in a mock effort to think. "Then, I'd like to go with one of those cute names. You know, the ones cooked up by 90% of the high school drop outs—the ones that got pregnant first, then married—the ones that barely managed grade nine home ec. We could go for 'Dakota' or 'Kansas' or 'Nevada'. I kind of like 'Colorado'. Yeah, 'Colorado Cruikshank'."

Rob wasn't sure if she was serious. "You gotta be kidding!"

He had taken the bait and now it was time to set the hook. "No good? How about something exotic like 'Trixy' or 'Candy' or 'Cherry'? I've got it! How about 'Destiny'?" She drew the name out in a husky, sensuous voice.

Rob caught on to her game. "I think I like 'Cherry'. Her middle name could be 'Candy'. 'Cherry Candy Cruikshank'. Wouldn't she be popular."

Cindy smiled and thought about Wally. She had poured her heart out to him almost four summers ago in his cabin on Siren Lake, his Lake Jewel. He had offered little advice. He mostly listened. He listened until she sorted herself out. He listened until she understood her relationship with Rob. And he listened until she finally realized what she really wanted, and needed, out of life.

When he finally talked, he talked of his love for his wife and the amazing life they had spent together. He talked about his girls and how proud he was of them. And he talked about his only regret—his last few years and his self imposed isolation. His words had been a gift, a subtle message about family and caring. *You were right, old trapper. We are all mysteriously connected, and life does go on. There's new life in my body, and you still live in my thoughts. Thank you for your words that night on Lake Jewel.*

SIREN LAKE (LAKE JEWEL)

NIGHT WAS SLIPPING IN QUIETLY LIKE AN EMBARRASSED SPECTATOR, leaving in the middle of the first act. The sky just above the ragged tree line to the west changed from bold orange to a pale pink hue that bled into a washed blue. In a matter of seconds the orange streak became intense, desperately clinging to life before sinking beneath a black shroud of burned out forest.

A washed-grey, V-hulled boat droned resolutely towards shore, pushing a dark shadow below its prow and trailing a narrow, broken shadow behind it through a rippled lake canvas of orange, gold, silver and black. Two silhouetted figures hunkered down in the boat, attempting to shrink from the chill. The evening would have wrapped itself in solitude if the boat's occupants had remotely grasped the concept of silence. But their chatter was a litmus test for living. It was simple for Earl and Henry. They knew they weren't dead if they could talk. An arm would raise or finger point occasionally as the two old friends debated world issues, politics, religion and the price of fishing equipment.

"Earl, who the hell would pay twenty dollars for a fishing lure? So what if it was made from real fish skin. You think the fish are smart enough to know the difference. I can just hear one fish talking to another: "For crying out loud, Billy, don't eat that lure, it could be a relative!'"

"Geez, Henry, it was guaranteed to catch fish. How was I to know that I'd lose it to a big pike?"

"Earl, think of it terms of micro-economics. It makes more sense to lose a fifty cent jig. You could lose forty jigs before you touched the price of that lure. Now there's a fish down there somewhere braggin' about the new twenty dollar lure stuck in his lip." Henry paused to raise the pitch in his voice, thinking that fish must talk in a higher range. "Hey fellas! Look what the short, fat guy up there gave me—one of those real expensive crank baits—you know, the ones the pro anglers use, the twenty dollar ones! It tastes—well, it tastes—expensive! Ha, Ha, Ha. Although I do believe I still prefer jigs. I guess I'm just a meat and potatoes pike." Henry laughed enthusiastically at his ability to conjure up creative repartee.

The boat slipped towards a narrow rock-strewn point. Their banter rose and fell with the evening breeze then trailed off with the boat as it disappeared behind the point. The two old fishermen had been oblivious to the barren expanse of burned-out forest around them. They were intent on drawing life from the warmth of their friendship and making every moment counted. Besides, who had time for loss when stretching time was so much fun?

The dark of night began to creep in. It would soon be "night's" turn to become "lake maestro." The lake became still, but by no means, quiet. As if on cue, a creature-orchestra began a rhapsody of life. A string section of mosquitoes accompanied trombone bullfrogs and piccolo spring peepers. A quartet of Canada geese circled and trumpeted, looking for the perfect place to settle for the night. Somewhere deep in the forest on the east side of the lake a barred owl rolled out its saxophone "who-cooks-for-you?" All were there to humbly support the grand dame of the lake, the not-so "common" loon. She spread her cape-like wings, rose above the water line, puffed out a magnificent chest and in quavering soprano, delivered an inspiring, show-stopping finale.

EAST OF WAWA 43

SHE HAD ABANDONED HER MALE CUB at the beginning of its third year. She had done the best she could and it was time. There was no sense of loss or abandonment. It was simply a right of passage. That the juvenile had survived one season, in itself was a miracle. It had never recovered completely from the early effect of malnourishment. Even in early adulthood, it was a runt, a target for other boars, especially during the mating season. Last fall, it had made the single mistake of tracking a female in heat. The pursuit was based more on curiosity than urge. The large boar had appeared out of no where. Its attack was confident and swift. The smaller male was dispatched with a single blow. Nature wasn't cruel, it just *was*.

At this moment, she rested in a hollow, surrounded by a phalanx of jack pine—tall protectors with olive-flecked, dark amour. Her infant twin cubs were nestled in the crook of one foreleg, both snoring and wheezing in blissful slumber. One was curled up, the other flat on its back with legs splayed, oblivious to any threats that might be out there. The old sow was now past her prime. This would be her last litter. She harboured no recollection of the big fire—suffered no memory of her anxiety and flight. She was what she was, one of God's creatures, part of the great connection, blessed with abundant instinct and unencumbered with the twin pariahs of memory and conscience.

THE CAMP

LAUGHTER TWIRLED AND SKIPPED ACROSS THE LAKE —little whirling dervishes of sound bouncing over water. Across the lake, a burnt-orange sun slipped down beneath the ridge, tumbling its final rays, like dice, across a dark, flat table of water. It would be the last toss until a full moon rose later on. Cabin light flickered on from the propane lanterns within. The cabin was Wally's legacy, the people within, his family.

Wally had past on close to four years ago. To his mild surprise, he did so with dignity. The doctors made sure there was no pain. He managed to capture and cling to three months, held it tight to his chest like cradling an infant. It was an eventful three months. He had memorable visits from old friends who resurrected stories of shared follies and triumphs. He had frequent visits from Cindy and Rob who shared their plans for a new life. Their joy became his joy. And he had constant vigil from his daughters and their husbands and his grandchildren. He frequently made them laugh with his stories of growing up and the good times he had with their mother/grandmother. He made them promise that they would keep the camp on Lake Jewel and use it often so that they wouldn't forget him. He told the husbands where to fish and told his two grandsons how to catch frogs and skip rocks. He told his two granddaughters where the best wildflowers grew and where to find grandma's recipes for peanut butter squares.

In the quiet moments, he would apologize to his daughters for his withdrawal and draw their forgiveness in like breaths of spring flower-scented air. They would counter with the good times and guidance he had provided as they were growing up.

He knew his final day had arrived and he welcomed it. Jewel had told him so in a dream. She had appeared to him in living colour, and he could feel his dream-heart ache. Their conversation was hurried, like a happy couple that couldn't wait to exchange their thoughts and feelings.

"Wally, you're coming home!"

He sulked a little. "Well, it's about time." He paused, a little sheepish over his petulance. "You look beautiful, Jewel."

"And you look terrible, my love."

"But won't I look like you when I go to heaven?"

Julie could be playful and liked to yank his chain. "First off, you're making a rather large assumption about going to heaven. And secondly, you won't look like me. You'll look like a younger, healthier you."

Wally began to sweat in his dream. "You're kidding, right, about not going to heaven?"

Julie wore her serious, "I'm not kidding you" look. "You have to do one last thing before you pass on if you want to be any part of this." She waved her hands in display mode from her chest to her waist and paused. Chain yanking never felt so good.

"Jesus, Jewel! I mean, damn it, Jewel! I mean, come on, Jewel." He was getting desperate and now sensitive to any offence he might create.

Tears welled up in her large eyes. She took a deep breath to compose herself. "After you wake up, I want you to see all of our family—one at a time—and tell them you love them. And tell them why."

Wally chewed on that one for a minute. He was desperate and his voice croaked. "Even the sons-in-law?"

Julie smiled and put her hands on her hips. Wally loved that pose and his heart skipped a beat.

"No dear, just say goodbye to them—and make them promise to take care of our girls and grandkids."

"It's a promise, Jewel. I'll see you shortly."

"Yes you will, my love."

And Wally kept his promise.

THE RIDGE

THE "SENTINEL NO MORE", stood like a barren mast of an old ship-wrecked schooner, without garb or purpose. It had suffered the onslaught of beetle and woodpecker attacks with as much dignity as it could muster. As life slowly seeped out of the old guard's armour, its concern was not for itself, for it had lived longer than most and had grown weary. It wept for children in the valley below. Who would watch over them? A white resin tear slipped from a fresh wound and slowly descended to the ground below. The Sentinel could feel it, like a cool bead of perspiration, creating tiny sensations in its journey. Despair led to curiosity, and it watched its life-blood trickle down, settle on a clump of dry pine needles and disappear into the earth. This is how it would pass on, one tear at a time.

In its attempt to look to the sky and cry out for deliverance, the old pine saw something just beyond the path of the last tear. What was it? A tiny, dark green stem stood just above a bed of needles, protected by a circle of stout rocks. It supported fragile, spindly branches with five-clustered needles. It was an infant white pine, sharing the ridge. It was the old guard's offspring.

Even as its resin tears fell to the earth, the old guard could now pass on with dignity and, above all, hope. The circle of life on the ridge was not broken.

The valley would someday have a new Sentinel.

CONCLUSION

THE IMPACTS OF ESCAPED WILDFIRE CAN BE STAGGERING. However, the benefits of wildfire should not be discounted. Many of our forest stands exist today because historically, fire was allowed to run its course.

Ontario's fire fighting machine is large and occasionally a response can be unwieldy. Organizations on project fires grow quickly and sometimes exponentially. The philosophy "better to have too many or too much than not enough" is certainly safer than the results associated with "not enough." But today's fire managers tend to avoid both philosophies. They may be quick to load up, but it's common practice to monitor attack weight as it occurs, apply a measured response and stand down when the time is appropriate.

The business of managing wildfire is a complex one. I hope I've left the reader with a sense of what it takes to plan for and respond to wildfire. Most project wildfires have seen (and will continue to see) their share of glitches. But in the final analysis, the job will always get done.

ABOUT THE AUTHOR

J IM MORAN was a 1967 graduate of the Ontario Forest Technical School in Dorset, Ontario. He worked for the Ontario Ministry of Natural Resources for twenty-nine years and consulted in resource related matters for six years after that.

The benchmarks in Jim's career were his roles as forest operations manager in Algonquin Park, fire management supervisor for the Sudbury Fire Management Area and fire analyst for the East Fire Region.

Within the last ten years of his MNR career, Jim functioned on several project fires as an 'Incident Commander'.

He is now fully retired and resides in Beckwith Township outside of Carleton Place, Ontario with his wife Joan.

This is Jim's first novel but says there may be another one hidden away and lying dormant somewhere inside.

CHRONOLOGY OF KEY PROJECT FIRE EVENTS

2005:   Lightning strikes the white pine on the ridge, the
              Sentinel. A wildfire starts at the base of the pine.

Day 1 -   Wednesday, July 20th, 09:00 hours to 17:00 hours:
              Cindy Corrigan assesses the fire at **10 hectares (25 acres).**
              Her crew are set down neat the fire and prepare to at-
              tack it. The crew begin ground attack. The fire escapes.

Day 2 -   **Thursday, July 21st, 09:00 hours to 19:00 hours**
              The senior fire officer in Wawa, Russ Gervais, assesses
              Wawa 43. He is assigned as incident commander.
              Russ determines that burn-out is required to protect cut
              wood west of the fire. He carries out a combined aerial
              and hand ignition burn-out. The burn-out is successful.
              As anticipated, Wawa 43 continues to grow in a north-
              easterly direction.
              By 18:00 hours, Wawa 43 is **1200 hectares (2965 acres).**

Day 3 –   **Friday, July 22nd, 05:00 hours to 13:00 hours**
              The town of Hornepayne, north-east of Wawa 43, is
              smoked in. An MNR emergency response coordinator,
              Greg Walsh, is sent in to assist the mayor and fire chief.
              Russ Gervais uses helicopters and fixed wing aircraft
              to set up protection on camps ahead of Wawa 43 and
              prepares fire crews for a possible wind switch from the
              north.
              By 09:00 hours, Wawa 43 is **3000 hectares (7413 acres).**

Day 4 –   **Saturday, July 23rd, 15:00 hours to 17:00 hours**
              The wind had now switched, bringing strong winds out
              of the northeast. The cut wood to the southwest is in
              jeopardy and the town of White River to the south could
              be in harm's way. Fire crews are being moved to combat
              a new fire front.
              By 15:00 hours, Wawa 43 is **6500 hectares (16,061 acres).**

Day 5 –   **Sunday, July 24th, 13:00 hours to 16:00 hours**

Wawa 43 is turned over to Bill Gorley, incident management team commander, and his team.
Bill and Justin assess the fire by helicopter.
Cindy Corrigan and crew, as well as other crews, establish their burn-out lines.
Russ Gervais begins aerial burn-out using a helitorch.
The relative humidity drops and the crews are unable to hold the lines. They are evacuated.

Day 6 – **Monday, July 25th, 17:00 hours to 20:00 hours**
Wawa 43 has now become priority #1 in the east fire region.
Much of Canada and the northern U.S. are experiencing significant wildfire issues.
By now, the fire has grown considerably to the south.
The winds switch back and come from the south.
Wawa 43 takes a significant run north-west.
Hornepayne prepares to evacuate.
As of 15:00 hours, Wawa 43 is **56,000 hectares (138,400 acres).**

Day 7 – **Tuesday, July 26th, 06:30 hours to 14:00 hours**
Ranger crews, including the Cindy Corrigan crew are put into the head of the fire near White Owl Lake. They all struggle to contain it.
As anticipated, Wawa 43 is now running north-west.
The fire crews manage to hold their lines.
Hornepayne evacuates.

Day 8 – **Wednesday, July 27th, 10:00 hours to 20:00 hours**
HotShot crews arrive at White Lake Provincial Park, the fire's base camp.
The Bill Gorley incident management team organize the base camp.
As of 12:00 hours, Wawa 43 is **59,000 hectares (145,800 acres).**

Day 9 – **Thursday, July 28th, 05:00 hours to 22:00 hours**

Wawa 43 breaks through the fire lines and crews are evacuated.

The incident management team have been advised that weather will be favourable for another burn-out to protect Hornepayne and plan their course of action.

As of 20:00 hours, Wawa 43 is **62,000 hectares (153,200 acres).**

Day 10 –   Friday, July 29ᵗʰ, 10:00 hours to 11:30 hours
Justin Bailey begins another burn-out just south of Hornepayne.

The ranger crews, supporting the burn-out to the north, hold their fire lines.

As of 18:00 hours, Wawa 43 is **78,500 hectares (194,000 acres).**

Day 11 to 13 – Saturday, July 30ᵗʰ to Monday, August 1ˢᵗ
Moderate precipitation falls on Wawa 43.

The incident management team plan and gear up for major fire attack.

Resources will be deployed both from White Lake Provincial Park and the Hornepayne airport.

Fire attack is aggressive and monumental in scope.

Day 14 to 34 – Tuesday, August 2ⁿᵈ, to Monday, August 22ⁿᵈ
The fire is contained with the help of precipitation.

Tuesday itself is a drying day and the fire attempts to re-burn the following day.

The re-burn is contained.

On Thursday, August 4ᵗʰ, Wawa 43 receives significant rainfall. Mop-up and infra-red scanning begins.

On Monday, August 22ⁿᵈ, demobilization of the fire begins.

Wawa 43 is UCO at **80,150 hectares (198,000 acres).**

CAST OF CHARACTERS:

> **Significant characters ***

Wally McNeil*	Trapper
Sentinel*	Ancient white pine tree
Sow Bear and cub*	
Julie (Jewel) McNeil	Wally's wife
Hailey and Emily	Wally's daughters
Ray McNeil	Wally's father
Cindy Corrigan*	Fire crew leader
Jim Henderson	Crew Boss on Cindy's crew
Tim Hogg	Crew member on Cindy's crew
Sam Mendez	Crew member on Cindy's crew
Rick Sampson*	Regional fire duty officer, Sudbury
Sheila Monahan*	Regional intelligence officer, Sudbury (reports to Rick Sampson)
Beth Sampson	Rick Sampson's wife
Norm Pendleton	Zone duty officer, Sudbury (reports to Rick Sampson)
Zander Cybulski	Project fire duty officer, Sudbury (reports to Rick Sampson)
Jack Grossman	Regional weather technician, Sudbury
Brad Simpson	Response coordinator, Sudbury (Rick Sampson's supervisor)
Doug Rainville	Fire program manager, Sudbury (Brad Simpson's supervisor)
Norm Bennet	Northeast regional director
Mark Delviccio	Southern regional director
Darryl Kurtyn	Fire management supervisor, Wawa
Russell Gervais*	Senior fire officer, Wawa (reports to Darryl Kurtyn)
George Williams	Sector response officer, Wawa (reports to Darryl Kurtyn)
Francis DesRoches	District manager, Wawa (responsible for all resource management)
Randy Urbanski	Conservation officer from Wawa
Trevor Gilmore	Turbo Beaver pilot

Bill Gorley*	Incident management team commander
Justin Bailey*	Incident operations chief (manages fire response)
Tom Gregory	Incident logistics chief (manages service and support)
Ed Buckner	Incident planning chief (manages fire planning and information)
Eric	Division E supervisor on Wawa 43
Tim Feldman	Division F supervisor on Wawa 43
Rob Cruikshank*	CL415 pilot, Tanker 271
Jamie Verstraten	CL415 co-pilot, Tanker 271
Terry Dynel	Birddog officer, Birddog 18*
John Sutter	Aerial detection pilot
Andy Radford	Aerial detection observer
"Short" John Silver	Bell 212 helicopter pilot
Sid	Helitack 21 pilot
Mel	Helitack 13 pilot
Chester Wilkes	U.S. HotShot superintendent, New Mexico
Naiche (Nat) Ramirez	U.S. HotShot captain (reports to Chester Wilkes)
Nick Rankin	MNR liaison officer for HotShot crews
Ted Touluce	Mayor, Hornepayne Ontario
Ken Waal	Municipal fire chief, Hornepayne
Greg Walsh	MNR emergency response coordinator, Hornepayne
Ethel Abernathy	Hornepayne resident, owner of 'Sushi'
Sushi	Boston terrier that first noticed smoke in Hornepayne
Richard Head	Newspaper reporter
Earl and Henry	Fishermen on Siren Lake (Lake Jewel)
Amos Alfelski	Woodlands manager, Northshore Logging
Louise	Radio operator, Chapleau
Rennie Fullton	Reeve of White River
Harry Page	Aga 510 (infrared) operator